# "That's not possible, Connor," Isabelle murmured.

Their eyes met, and Connor's were full of questions. "My family isn't in my life at the moment," she admitted. The enormity of the situation came crashing over her. Despite being at an event crowded with people, Isabelle was achingly alone.

"Oh, Ella. Please don't cry. It's going to be all right." Connor quickly swallowed up the distance between them and put his arms around her. She let out a muffled sob against his chest. She felt his hand moving on her back as he murmured soothing words. It was comforting to be held by him.

Isabelle breathed in his woodsy, masculine scent. Although she knew it wasn't possible, she didn't want this moment to end. It had been a long time since someone had made her feel safe and protected. For so long now she had been trying to protect her family members from harm as well as herself. It was nice to take shelter, if only for a little while, in Connor's arms…

**Belle Calhoune** grew up in a small town in Massachusetts. Married to her college sweetheart, she is raising two lovely daughters in Connecticut. A dog lover, she has one mini poodle and a black Lab. Writing for the Love Inspired line is a dream come true. Working at home in her pajamas is one of the best perks of the job. Belle enjoys summers in Cape Cod, traveling and reading.

## Books by Belle Calhoune

### Love Inspired

#### Home to Owl Creek

*Her Secret Alaskan Family*
*Alaskan Christmas Redemption*
*An Alaskan Twin Surprise*
*Hiding in Alaska*

#### Alaskan Grooms

*An Alaskan Wedding*
*Alaskan Reunion*
*A Match Made in Alaska*
*Reunited at Christmas*
*His Secret Alaskan Heiress*
*An Alaskan Christmas*
*Her Alaskan Cowboy*

*Reunited with the Sheriff*
*Forever Her Hero*
*Heart of a Soldier*

Visit the Author Profile page at Harlequin.com.

# Hiding in Alaska

## Belle Calhoune

**LOVE INSPIRED**
INSPIRATIONAL ROMANCE

**LOVE INSPIRED®**
INSPIRATIONAL ROMANCE

Recycling programs
for this product may
not exist in your area.

ISBN-13: 978-1-335-48874-9

Hiding in Alaska

Copyright © 2021 by Sandra Calhoune

This edition published by arrangement with Harlequin Books S.A.

For questions and comments about the quality of this book, please contact us at CustomerService@Harlequin.com.

Love Inspired
22 Adelaide St. West, 40th Floor
Toronto, Ontario M5H 4E3, Canada
www.Harlequin.com

**Printed in U.S.A.**

He healeth the broken in heart,
and bindeth up their wounds.
He telleth the number of the stars;
he calleth them all by their names.
—*Psalms* 147:3–4

To my beloved neighbor, Rosalie "Rose" Healey
(1926–2019).
One of the kindest, loveliest people
I've ever known. A wonderful friend. Missing you.

## Chapter One

Isabelle Sanchez shivered as the cold Arctic wind whipped against her cheeks. This type of weather would certainly take some getting used to, she thought as she wrapped her arms around her middle. She didn't feel at all like herself in the navy blue parka with the fur-trimmed hood. A wool hat was perched on her head, covering her ears from the frigid temperatures. It was the first time in her life she'd ever owned a thick winter coat and it felt cumbersome and unnatural. She was far more used to wearing shorts, shades and sundresses. Bathing suits rather than boots. There was no point in dwelling on it. She had agreed to come live in this Alaskan hamlet, and there was no going back.

A sigh slipped past her lips. Her entire life had changed in an instant, and it still felt surreal. The sign by the side of the road said it best: *Welcome to Owl Creek, Alaska.* The harsh reality of her situation caused her to suck in a steadying breath. She would need to call on every ounce of strength she had in order to rebuild her life. There was no doubt in her mind it would be the hardest thing she'd ever do.

She wasn't Isabelle Sanchez from Miami, Florida, anymore. Now, as part of the Witness Protection Program, she was Ella Perez from Flagstaff, Arizona. She felt a sudden chill pass over her that had nothing to do with the frigid weather. WITSEC—the United States Federal Witness Protection Program—had provided her with a new identity and placed her in Owl Creek, a remote Alaskan town she'd never heard of until a few weeks ago. It appeared to be a charming and picturesque village, unlike anything she'd ever known. She was a Floridian, born and bred. Sandy beaches, sunny skies, and the hustle and bustle of city life were the norm for her. The sight of white-capped mountains looming in the distance served as a breathtaking reminder that she wasn't in the Sunshine State any longer. She no longer had a home, and it made her heartsick just thinking about it.

Her life had been forever altered by the events of a few months ago. Even though she was trying to be strong, Isabelle was afraid. She'd never wanted to be so far away from her loved ones. She had left everything she held dear back in Miami—family, friends and a job she enjoyed. It was the first time in her life she'd ever felt all alone. She didn't know the slightest thing about life in a small Alaskan town. But she didn't have a choice in the matter. Isabelle had to make it work here in Owl Creek. Her very life hung in the balance.

"The truck is over there in the lot. It's time we headed over to your new home." The deep voice interrupted her thoughts, and she swung her gaze in the direction of the tall, ginger-haired man who had accompanied her all the way from Miami. Despite his gruff demeanor, U.S. Marshal Jonah Kramer had a streak of kindness that meant the world to Isabelle. It's what she needed most at this moment as she faced an uncertain future. Over the past few weeks he'd tried to reassure Isabelle at every step in the process. She felt a tad guilty about taking him away from his wife and family in Homer, but she knew it was simply part of his job to help her relocate.

Once they were sitting in the hunter green truck with Jonah in the driver's seat, he turned toward her. "You'll be safe here, Ella. Just try to blend in with the townsfolk. I know it's hard to wrap your head around it, but you can't contact anyone from your former life under any circumstances. We've drilled that into your head, but it bears repeating. It's crucial to make a clean break from everything and everyone. If you slip up, it could be catastrophic."

Isabelle nodded. She knew the drill. It was the most heartbreaking aspect of her joining WITSEC. Just the thought of never seeing her family again caused tears to well up in her eyes.

*Ella.* She would have to get adjusted to her new name. Although she'd been allowed to assume a first name that wasn't too far off from her own, it would still take some getting used to, since no one had ever called her Ella. Her nickname had always been Izzy. Her head was spinning with all the things she had to get acclimated to in her new surroundings.

The situation she found herself in was far from ideal, but after witnessing the brutal slaying of her boss, Saul Martino, in a turf war, her world had spiraled out of control. By God's grace she had been spared. Because the killer, Vincent Burke, had locked eyes with her before she fled the club, he had known her identity when she'd reported him to the police. Threats and attempts to silence her had ensued, turning her mundane life into a chaos-filled existence. And even after she'd provided testimony in his trial that had put him in prison, she had still been in jeopardy from his criminal enterprise. There had been numerous attempts on her life that left her feeling terrorized and vulnerable. She would never again be safe in her former life. Those extreme circumstances had led her straight to the quaint town of Owl Creek.

The wintry Alaskan scenery passed by in a blur as Jonah drove them to her new residence. When they pulled up to 10 Kodiak Lane, a sigh escaped Isabelle's lips. She was instantly charmed by the log cabin–style house. It radiated a cozy vibe. Snow-covered bushes surrounded a wraparound porch. Two sturdy Adirondack chairs sat on the front porch. Although she had never fantasized about living in Alaska, this picture-perfect house was the stuff of dreams.

Once the car was in Park, Isabelle got out of the vehicle and walked up to the porch, bags in hand. Isabelle knew she would have to make a few trips back and forth to collect all of her things from the truck, but she felt an urgent need to go inside and get settled. Jonah walked behind her, juggling a few bags before placing them on the landing and handing her a key to the house. Her hands were shaking as she reached for it. Jonah gave her an encouraging nod. When she turned the key in the lock and pushed the door open, the smell of freshly baked cookies rose to her nostrils. She stepped inside and looked around, feeling grateful for the warm atmosphere and all the beautiful little touches. A vase of baby's breath mixed with dried berries sat on the kitchen counter. A plate of chocolate chip cookies had been placed on the table with a welcome note from Beulah North, her new employer. When she pulled open the fridge, it was fully stocked with all of her favorite food and drinks. She wandered from room to room, soaking in all the details. Jonah didn't follow after her but remained in the kitchen, presumably to give her some space.

Was she really going to make a new life for herself in this small Alaskan hamlet? Isabelle still felt as if she might be dreaming as she began the process of unpacking all her bags and sorting through her belongings.

Jonah stayed until late evening to help her get settled, then he left to stay the night at a bed-and-breakfast in town called Miss Trudy's. He reminded her that he was scheduled to fly back to Homer the next morning. Fear seized her by the throat as she settled in for the night. Although she knew Jonah wouldn't be too far away in the event of an emergency, it still felt as if she was on her own.

Sometimes when she was all alone and things were quiet, Isabelle's mind flashed back to that terrible night at Club Oasis. Isabelle had worked nights at the popular dance club as its manager. When the shots rang out in the club on that particular evening, Isabelle had just locked up her office for the night. Seeing Saul's body riddled with bullets had been terrifying and surreal. Witnessing Burke standing over Saul's body with a gun in his hand had been traumatic. He was one of the most powerful men in Miami, one who'd always been tied to organized crime. Although she'd been frozen with fear, Isabelle's survival instincts had kicked in. She'd fled out the back entrance and evaded Burke's deadly aim. In the aftermath, Isabelle hadn't even had time to deal with Saul's death or her own trauma. Her entire life had imploded once she had told the police about what she'd witnessed.

"You're safe in Owl Creek now," she whispered to herself as her eyelids grew heavier and she drifted into slumber.

The next morning Isabelle drove with Jonah to the airstrip so he could catch his flight back home. On the ride over, Isabelle had the opportunity to ask him a few last-minute questions, hoping with each answer she would gain strength.

"This is where I leave you," Jonah said as he pulled up in front of the hangar and parked the truck. "If you need anything, don't hesitate to reach out. You'll be fine."

Before she could even say an adequate goodbye, Jonah had grabbed his bag from the back seat and was walking toward the seaplane. She swallowed an instinct to call out to him and beg the U.S. Marshal to stay a little bit longer. But she knew it wasn't possible. For all intents and purposes, she was on her own. Isabelle was like a newborn baby trying to get acclimated to life outside the womb. Everything would be brand-new to her.

This entire situation was unfair. She hadn't been involved in any criminal enterprises. Isabelle had always been a law-abiding citizen. She'd simply been caught in the wrong place at the wrong time. No matter how many times she went over it in her head, it still seemed surreal. How could her life be turned upside down in an instant? Although her testimony had placed a criminal in prison, he still had the ability to get to her from the inside. And because he'd appealed his sentence, she might be forced to testify again. Would her life always be in limbo?

Isabelle scooted over and settled herself behind the driver's seat as she watched Marshal Kramer walk toward the seaplane. A heavy feeling settled on her chest. "Lord, please give me the strength to go through with this," she uttered in the stillness of the vehicle. Ever since the shooting, Isabelle had been leaning on faith to sustain her.

How would she ever get used to the quiet in this town? She was accustomed to the loud voices of her family members, the hustle and bustle of a pulsing city and the rhythms of salsa music emanating from her mother's dance studio. Owl Creek, Alaska, seemed so tame in comparison to the world she inhabited. But wasn't that the whole point? To get away from the dangers she would be facing by continuing to live in

Miami. She'd had enough drama and excitement to last her a lifetime.

It was breaking her heart to come to terms with the finality of it all. Never seeing her loved ones again would hurt worse than any pain she'd ever endured in her twenty-seven years on this earth. But she would have to suffer the agony and push through it.

"Just put one foot in front of the other," she told herself, breathing in deeply through her nose as she listened to the GPS instructions to Kodiak Lane and slowly maneuvered the truck along snow-packed roads. As she drove through the downtown area, she smiled at the sight of numerous Christmas decorations still on full display. Although the holiday season had been over for several weeks, the town had clearly decided to keep the celebration going. Isabelle felt a smile twitching at both sides of her lips. There was something so endearing about the sentimentality of prolonging the celebratory season. She loved Christmas. She had chosen to postpone her relocation so she could have one last holiday with her family. It had been beautiful and heartwarming and achingly sad at the same time. But she wouldn't trade it for anything in the world. She would hold on to those memories for the rest of her life.

She slowed down as a gold and cream sign caught her attention. *North Star Chocolate Shop.* It was her new place of employment. The company, North Star Chocolate, was a well-known chocolatier and famous for creating exceptional chocolates. Although she couldn't see inside the place, the exterior was inviting. In the storefront window sat a display of confections that tempted her sweet tooth. Brightly colored teapots accompanied them. She was really going to have to resist the temptation to sample every morsel of chocolate in the shop. As she continued driving down Main Street, a fantastic aroma began to filter into the truck. Suddenly a pink neon sign came into view that explained the smell. The Snowy Owl Diner.

The establishment looked so pretty set against the white snow and the mountains. She couldn't remember the last time she'd eaten at an old-fashioned diner. It had to be over a decade ago, at the one back home in Miami. Her family had frequented the place when she was little. Eating there had always been an adventure.

On impulse, Isabelle drove into the lot and made her way to the entrance. Her stomach was grumbling fiercely. The nervousness she'd felt all morning had made eating breakfast impossible. Now she was starving. Nothing less would have prompted her to stop in at the establishment way before she considered herself ready to be in any social setting. Determined not to change her mind, she pushed open the door with extra force, her head held high. She heard a loud thump followed by a cry and a crashing sound. Within seconds she realized the door had hit someone.

She stood in the doorway, horror-struck at the sight that greeted her. A man was on the floor surrounded by a sticky substance that looked an awful lot like syrup amid broken pieces of ceramic. All eyes in the diner were focused on her and the unfortunate man.

Isabelle's heart sank. Her instructions had been to blend into the fabric of Owl Creek without attracting any attention to herself. Yet her first foray into the heart of town had resulted in garnering way more attention than she wanted or needed. Although her very first instinct was to turn tail and run as far away from the Snowy Owl Diner as her legs would carry her, it was far too late to do so.

Connor North had frantically tried to save himself from falling, but once the syrup spilled, his heel slid on the sticky parquet floor and he'd landed with a thud on his backside. Pain sliced through him, and he let out a loud groan.

"Oh, no! I'm so sorry! Are you all right?"

He looked up at the sound of the soft, melodic voice inquiring about his well-being. The woman he was staring up at was definitely not a resident of Owl Creek. He would have noticed a woman this beautiful before now. Jet-black hair fell around her shoulders in soft waves. Her sweet brown eyes radiated compassion. Thick, soot-colored lashes framed them.

He wondered what she was doing in town. Perhaps another tourist eager to experience North Star Chocolates and a quaint village in Alaska.

Connor sprang to his feet, wincing at the sticky sensation on his hands. He brushed them against his sweater to clean them off.

"No need to worry. I'm fine. I'm Connor North. And you are?" he asked, holding out his hand so she could shake it.

She gazed at him with wide eyes. Her mouth opened, but no words came out. She looked down at his hand with a blank stare. "I… I'm Ella. Ella Perez. I'm so very sorry for making such a mess." He withdrew his hand when she didn't shake it.

"You're forgiven, Ella. Accidents happen," Connor said with a nod, trying to put the stranger at ease. She was gazing at him with a look of trepidation. Had he done something to alarm her? Maybe she thought he was upset about the fall.

"Is everything all right over here?"

Connor swung his gaze toward Piper Miller, the owner of the Snowy Owl Diner. Piper was the town's resident sweetheart, as well as his younger brother Braden's fiancée.

"It's fine, Piper," Connor said, making a face and looking down at his soggy pants. "I just had a clumsy moment. Sorry about the mess." He pointed toward the syrup and broken dish on the parquet floor.

"No worries," Piper said. "We're used to spills around here. I'll have it cleaned up right away."

"He's being kind," Ella interjected. "I swung the door too hard when I came inside and it crashed into him. I'm so sorry for the trouble." Regret rang out in her voice. "It was entirely my fault."

"You must be new in town if you think that's trouble," Piper responded. "I'm the owner of this place by the way. Piper Miller."

"Ella Perez. I… I've just moved to Owl Creek," she explained, running a shaky hand through her long dark tresses. Connor was trying not to stare, but he couldn't seem to help himself. Ella Perez was without a doubt the prettiest woman who'd ever stepped foot in Owl Creek.

"Let me show you to a table." Piper looked back and forth between them. "Unless the two of you are sitting together?"

"No! We're not together," Ella said in an emphatic tone that brooked no argument. "I just need a table for one."

"That can be arranged," Piper said. "Follow me and I'll get you situated. Connor, why don't you go over to the counter and grab some more syrup?"

"Nice to meet you," Connor said with a nod as Piper led Ella to a table by the window. He grabbed another container of syrup from the counter and headed back to eat his breakfast.

His two best friends, Gabriel Lawson and Hank Crawford, were seated at their regular table waiting for him to bring the syrup back. When he reached the table he could see the two of them trying to stifle their laughter.

Connor placed the syrup down on the table with a bang. "As you saw, I took one for the team by going to get this."

"And we're mighty appreciative of your service," Hank said with a smirk. He reached over and picked up the container, pouring the syrup liberally over his flapjacks.

Hank handed the syrup to Gabriel, who did the same. "Looks like you made a new friend." Gabriel wiggled his eyebrows. Connor pretended not to notice. Anytime he was within a ten-mile radius of a single woman, his best friends couldn't resist teasing him about his prolific dating history. Lately it had been bugging him.

Although Connor's stomach was growling and he had a full breakfast plate sitting before him, something was bothering him. He knew he'd never met Ella before, but her name pricked at him. Why did it sound so familiar?

He stroked his jaw. "I can't put my finger on it, but I feel like I know her name for some reason. Ella Perez. Does it sound familiar to either one of you?" he asked, trying to recall why the woman's name lurked in the back of his mind.

Gabriel and Hank exchanged a pointed glance. Both of them began to chuckle as if they were sharing an inside joke.

Connor let out a sigh. "What are you guys laughing at now?"

"It's just that you make it a point to know every pretty woman in Owl Creek, even the tourists," Gabriel explained.

"Neither her name nor her face ring a bell with me," Hank added, still chuckling. "But then again, I'm a happily married man."

The laughter erupting from their mouths threatened to drown out all of his thoughts. Couldn't he even talk to a woman without people assuming he was interested in her? Sure, Ella was stunning, but it didn't mean he wanted to date her.

Normally, Connor didn't mind being teased about his love life, but lately it had rankled him every time

Hank and Gabriel joked about his status as Owl Creek's most popular bachelor. He didn't know why it bothered him so much as of late, but it was beginning to get old. He wasn't the same man he'd been a year ago. Connor had grown and matured.

So much had changed in the last year with the return of his long-lost sister, Sage. She had been kidnapped as a baby from their family home in Owl Creek, only to return to the fold twenty-five years later. The reunion had also brought his brother, Braden, back to town, making the family unit complete. Although he should have been on solid ground, he'd been feeling unsettled. His best friends were both newlyweds—Hank had married Sage, while Gabriel had reunited with his first love, Rachel. Even Braden had fallen in love with Piper, his best friend since childhood.

Everyone seemed to be moving forward in their lives, except him.

"Hey! We're just having a little fun," Hank said, clapping him on the shoulder. "What's troubling you?"

Connor stabbed his fork on the plate and picked up several pieces of pancake. He shrugged as he stuffed the forkful in his mouth, then swallowed. "I don't know, guys. I'm just feeling a bit out of sorts these days. Things have been pretty intense lately. I think it's all beginning to catch up with me."

"They really have been," Gabriel agreed. "Personally speaking, the past few months have been a whirlwind. Rachel and I are married now and raising twin toddlers." He grinned. "God blessed me when I least expected it."

"You deserve every ounce of happiness," Connor said, raising his glass of orange juice in Gabe's direction.

"We're here for you, Connor. You know that. The Three Amigos for life." Hank held up his hand and bumped fists with him.

Connor grinned. Having his two closest friends in his corner always made him feel as if he could conquer the world. And since Braden had recently decided to forgo working at the family business, the North Star Chocolate Company, he would need all that confidence and determination to ensure the company's success. Not that he held it against his younger brother. He admired Braden's desire to live life on his own terms. He had the type of courage Connor wasn't sure he himself had.

For the next half hour Connor and his friends ate and talked, focusing on local matters in Owl Creek. As town sheriff, Hank always had his ear to the ground. A few times Connor found himself looking across the diner at Ella as she ate her meal. He was curious as to what she was doing here in town.

She'd casually mentioned being a new resident in their small village, but he wondered if she had family or friends here. Had she relocated for a romantic connection? In these parts it was entirely possible. Or perhaps she'd come here for an employment opportunity.

A job! His family's chocolate emporium. That's why her name sounded so familiar. Ella Perez was the new manager at the North Star Chocolate Shop right down the street. He'd seen her résumé and offer letter just the other day on his grandmother Beulah's desk.

When he glanced back over in Ella's direction, she was sailing out the front door.

He reached into his pocket, pulled out some bills, then plunked them down on the table. "Spending time with you guys was a pleasure, but I have to settle some work-related business," he said, standing up and pulling on his parka. "Breakfast is on me."

Before Gabe or Hank could say a word, Connor hustled toward the exit. If he moved really quickly, perhaps he could catch up to Ella and introduce himself as a member of the North family and welcome her to town.

He immediately spotted her heading toward the parking lot. "Ella!" he called out in a raised voice. When she didn't turn around, Connor called her name in an even louder voice. When she didn't respond, he picked up the pace, closing the distance between them in a few quick strides. Although he continued to call out her name, she didn't turn around.

In a last ditch effort to get her attention, he tapped her on the shoulder. Ella whipped around to face him, a look of pure terror etched on her face. Her entire body had stiffened up.

"Hey. I didn't mean to scare you," he said, immediately regretting touching her. He didn't think he'd crossed a boundary, but perhaps he had unknowingly done so.

"You didn't," she said, her voice trembling. "You just caught me off guard."

"Sorry about that, but I had to catch up to you before you left. When we met I couldn't help but think you seemed familiar to me. And I know exactly who you are, Ella Perez."

# Chapter Two

Isabelle felt frozen in place. Her hands began to break out in a sweat. A wild rhythm began to beat in her chest. A huge lump sat in her throat, making speaking impossible. How on earth had Connor figured out her identity? She'd barely been in town for twenty-four hours. Jonah had assured her that her identity would be secure in Owl Creek as long as she abided by the rules. To her knowledge, she hadn't broken a single one. How could things have fallen apart so fast? Now she would have to leave this Alaskan village and plant roots somewhere else.

"You know who I am?" she asked, her voice sounding raspy.

Connor nodded as a grin slowly stretched across his face, making him appear even more handsome than she'd initially thought. "You're the new hire for my family's chocolate shop. If I remember correctly, you're starting this week."

She felt her entire body sag in relief. *Phew.* Due to

her nerves, she'd completely misread the situation. Her status in WITSEC wasn't in jeopardy after all.

"I guess I should have picked up on your last name," Isabelle said. She'd been so nervous after she'd caused him to fall that she hadn't made the connection between him and the North Star Chocolate Company. "My start date is tomorrow actually. I'm really grateful for the opportunity."

"Welcome to Owl Creek, Ella. I think you're going to love our little part of Alaska. I know I'm biased, but it's a fantastic place to live."

"Well, it's unlike anything I've ever known. Florida never sees snow. There's a whole lot I'm going to have to get accustomed to, particularly the climate." A feeling of dread washed over her. She'd just said Florida out of habit. How had she slipped up so early on? "I meant to say Flagstaff not Florida. Though I've spent many summers in the Sunshine State," she quickly added, praying Connor hadn't noticed anything strange about her statement. Even though she'd practiced reciting her backstory with Jonah a hundred times or more, clearly it hadn't stuck.

"What made you apply for a job so far from home?" he asked, his brows knitted together.

Her heart began to hammer in her chest. Was he suspicious of her or simply asking normal questions? It was hard not to feel paranoid under the circumstances.

What would Connor North think if she told him the truth? That she'd chosen to rebuild her life in Alaska because it was far away from the danger she faced in Miami. Planting herself in a remote Alaskan town had been about survival. She'd made the hardest decision in her life by leaving everything she held dear in her rearview mirror. As a result, her heart had been completely shattered.

She shifted from one foot to the other. "I needed a change of pace," she said instead. "Owl Creek seemed like it would do the trick."

"That was mighty brave of you. Alaska isn't for the faint of heart, especially when you're used to a warmer climate."

Isabelle nodded. "I also happen to really love chocolate, so I'm excited about working for North Star Chocolate. So far I've been communicating with Beulah. She's been incredible. And very kind."

Connor grinned. "That's my grandmother. She's can be quite a character, but she always leads with her heart."

*His grandmother.* Her heart ached for her own sweet-faced *avo.* Carmen Sanchez was the most loving woman in the world. She'd helped to raise Isabelle. It was near impossible to imagine not being in her grandmother's presence. Due to her grandmother's serious medical condition, Isabelle had no expectation of ever seeing her again. Her eyes felt moist, and she knew she needed to get in the car before she started crying in front of Connor. That would certainly raise a red flag.

"Well, thanks for the warm welcome. I should head back to the house. I'm still getting settled in." She tried to inject positivity into her tone, even though the reality of her situation had just crashed over her with full force. Nothing would ever be the same.

"Enjoy the rest of your day. Before you know it, you'll be able to navigate Owl Creek like a pro."

With a lame wave, Isabelle turned toward her new vehicle and slid into the driver's seat. She turned the car on and let the engine warm up a little before she headed away from Main Street and toward the northern part of town. Although she felt the urge to turn back and get one last look at Connor, she knew it wouldn't be wise to take her gaze away from the snow-packed road. She wasn't used to driving in these conditions, and she needed to focus all of her attention on the road.

With his dark hair, blue eyes and rugged frame, Connor North was gorgeous. He radiated an air of confidence. At the moment she could use a dose of it to bolster her frame of mind. Even in syrup-stained pants, he'd walked around the diner as if he owned it. There was no harm in looking at an attractive man, she reminded herself. Though anything more was out of the question. How could she ever start a relationship knowing her entire life was a lie? The rules of WIT-SEC forbade her from ever telling a romantic partner the truth about her existence.

She refused to go down that road. It was hard enough making everyone in Owl Creek think she was someone she wasn't. Adding in romance would be disastrous.

Connor watched as Ella headed off in the direction of her new digs. A strange feeling had settled over him during his conversation with North Star Chocolate's newest hire. He couldn't fathom why he felt it so intensely, but Connor knew instinctively she wasn't as she appeared to be. This beautiful newcomer to town was running from something. He had no idea what it was—a divorce, a bad relationship, a fractured family? Perhaps she was a criminal. The possibilities were endless. As they'd spoken, there had been something radiating from her that didn't ring true. Just now she'd mentioned Florida, then corrected herself to say Flagstaff. And she hadn't responded when he'd called out her name. He didn't think he was imagining things either. Connor knew he was more jaded than most people, but he trusted his instincts. He'd grown up in a household that had never recovered from the trauma of his baby sister's abduction at three months old. As a result, Connor had been mistrustful of people, particularly tourists and newcomers to Owl Creek.

Ella Perez was raising all of his hackles. Her stunning looks hadn't rendered him incapable of picking up on certain cues she'd emitted. She'd acted nervous, as if she was on edge about something. What if she was up to no good here in town? He let himself into his vehicle, chiding himself for not asking more probing questions.

The newcomer seemed out of place in a town like Owl Creek. Why had a woman like Ella come all the way to Alaska for a job at his family's company? Alaska was at times a harsh and unforgiving land. For a man who considered himself to be pragmatic, it didn't make a lot of sense.

Connor let out a sigh and rested his head against the steering wheel. His paranoia was rising to the surface and threatening to choke him. He tended to believe the worst of people based on his family's past trauma. Although he tried to control his suspicious nature, Connor didn't trust strangers. He always felt as if he was waiting for them to peel back the mask and reveal their true selves.

In all likelihood, Ella was a sweet young woman who was merely nervous about starting a brand-new job in a world completely unfamiliar to her. Guilt sliced through him. He wasn't being fair to her or himself. He needed to let go of the past and accept people at face value. Being so cynical wasn't a good quality. As a man of faith, he knew it wasn't right to judge others so harshly. But he still couldn't quiet the voice inside him warning him against accepting Ella at face value.

By the time he reached the chocolate factory, Connor was ready to focus on something other than the mysterious new resident of Owl Creek. He enjoyed working at his family's company. As an executive in charge of distribution and product development, he had helped the company grow and expand its reach in key markets over the last five years. He also oversaw the operation of the Owl Creek factory and served as the CEO's right-hand man. Thankfully, Beulah was the CEO, and he adored collaborating with her.

The aroma of chocolate permeated the air as he walked inside. Every morning before he made his way to his office Connor enjoyed strolling through the factory where the chocolate was being made. He liked talking with the employees and even helping out on the conveyer belt. When they were kids, he and Braden had gotten a thrill out of plucking chocolate confections from the assembly line and popping them into their mouths. More times than not it had resulted in a competition between them. Trying to consume chocolate the fastest had always led to bellyaches and admonishments from Beulah.

"Chocolate is to be savored, not devoured." Just the thought of his grandmother uttering those words to the pint-size version of himself made him chuckle out loud. Beulah had always been a fountain of wisdom. Nothing much had changed in that regard. His grandmother was still a unique woman who continued to fascinate him.

The factory had been his and Braden's stomping grounds—they'd learned the business as they played and explored in the chocolate factory. Despite the tragedy involving the abduction of their sister, there had been an abundance of joy in their lives. Of course there had been sorrow as well. None of them had ever fully recovered from the loss until Sage's recent return to the fold. Now he should be completely over it, but he wasn't. He still harbored a lot of anger. The woman who'd abducted his sister had been visiting town as one of the leaders of a youth group. No one had ever suspected her of wrongdoing or been suspicious of her actions. Over the years, people had sought to take advantage of his family by pretending to have information about his sister's whereabouts. A few women had even presented themselves as the missing North family member, which had only added to their pain.

It showed him that people couldn't always be trusted. A person always had to be on guard.

"Good morning, my dear. How was your breakfast with the boys?" Beulah's voice rang out as he walked toward the executive offices. When he turned around, his grandmother was walking toward him with the vigor of someone half her age. As always, Beulah North was dressed in a suit jacket and matching skirt, with her signature pearls draped around her neck. She believed in dressing to impress as the CEO of the North Star Chocolate Company.

Connor pressed a kiss on her cheek after she caught up to him. "Morning. It was delicious. And I just met our new hire at the diner."

"Which one? We've hired several in the past few weeks."

"Ella Perez," he said.

"Oh, yes. She starts tomorrow at the chocolate shop. I'm going to be there to greet her in the morning. What was your impression? Her résumé and telephone interview were impressive."

Connor hesitated a moment before speaking. He didn't want Beulah to think he was being hard on their new hire. "Are you sure she's right for the job? There was something about her that didn't really gel with Owl Creek or the manager position."

Beulah frowned at him. "Whatever do you mean?"

Connor shrugged. "I don't know. She fumbled a bit when we were talking. I'm not sure how to explain it without sounding paranoid, but I just got the feeling she wasn't being fully transparent. It was like she was hiding something."

Beulah stared at him without speaking. Her eyes began to blink like an owl, which served as a sure sign that his grandmother was gathering her words. "You've just met her, Connor. Why don't you extend her a measure of grace rather than being suspicious?" She reached out and touched his cheek. "You have to stop focusing on the worst parts of humanity, especially since there are so many good people in the world. What happened to our family all those years ago was horrific, but God brought our sweet girl home so we could heal. I'm worried you're still stuck in the past, Connor."

His grandmother's words served as a punch to his gut. He hated the notion that he was stuck in the past, especially since everyone else seemed to be doing fine. Connor had tried to find closure with Sage's return to Owl Creek, but he still harbored feelings of resentment for all the years that had been stolen from them.

"I'll try to do better," he vowed, wishing the words resonated more within him. He felt a sense of powerlessness. Connor knew he hadn't been able to conquer this issue no matter how hard he'd tried. But he couldn't admit that to his grandmother. She was counting on him to be the future of the chocolate company.

"That's all I'll ever ask of you," Beulah said, tears pooling in her eyes. "I count on you more than you realize. You're my North Star. No pun intended," she said, letting out a cackle. The corners of her eyes crinkled up.

Leave it to Beulah to make him laugh when two seconds ago he'd been feeling badly about himself. She was an incredible woman. He wished that he could be as resilient as Beulah. She was the strongest member of their family.

Connor looked at his watch. "I'm going to get prepped for our meeting with the distributors."

"Good idea. I'll see you in the conference room. I can't wait to taste the new white chocolate hot cocoa." Beulah rubbed her hands together and grinned. As the driving force behind the company, she still felt enthusiastic about her work. It was one of the main reasons for the success of North Star Chocolates. Passion combined with heartfelt dedication.

"I think we might have another hit on our hands," Connor drawled, feeling proud of the collaboration between himself, Sage and Braden. Creating new products was one of the best aspects of his job. Working with his siblings on this special project had been so much fun, particularly since it rarely happened. It had almost made up for the fact that Braden wouldn't be working alongside him at the company. It was reassuring to know their bond was still tight.

Connor made his way to his office. Just looking around the room made him grin. He'd decorated it with a fun vibe in mind. Since he spent so much time at work, he'd wanted it to be comfortable yet functional. The bubble gum machine served as a colorful reminder that he was still a kid at heart.

Connor sat down at his desk and logged on to his computer. Even though he was trying to focus on the upcoming meeting, thoughts of the mysterious new-comer refused to completely fade away. There was something about her that caused curiosity to well up inside him. Although he knew his grandmother had given him sound advice, he couldn't stop wondering about Ella Perez.

He imagined she knew very little about Alaskan living. He had only been to Arizona a few times on business, but it was clear to him how vastly different it was from Owl Creek. He couldn't imagine it would be easy for Ella to get her bearings while navigating a new job. She didn't know a soul here in town and she'd probably left family and friends behind in Arizona. As a hometown boy, Connor had only left Owl Creek in order to attend college in Anchorage. Unlike Ella, he'd only been a short flight away from home and his loved ones.

A feeling of shame seized him. Instead of harboring suspicions about Ella, he should be wholeheartedly welcoming her to the North Star Chocolate fold. He should be trying to help her get acclimated. In a perfect world he would be more like his grandmother. He let out a ragged sigh. The truth nagged at him. He hadn't healed from his family's trauma, and he wasn't sure he ever would.

Isabelle let out a huge sigh of relief as she turned off Route 65. She had driven by the turnoff several times without realizing she should have taken the right turn rather than continuing straight ahead. Seeing a Moose Crossing sign a few miles back had caused her adrenaline to race. She had immediately slowed down to five miles an hour out of an abundance of caution. Thankfully her new home wasn't too far from town. If she hadn't gotten confused with the GPS directions, it would have only been a ten-minute ride. At least she didn't have to travel too far to reach her place of employment.

When she pulled up to 10 Kodiak Lane, she felt a huge sense of relief at being safely home.

*Home.* She felt a little hitch in her heart at the notion that this quaint little abode now belonged to her. Once she made her way inside the house, Isabelle sank down onto the sofa and pressed her eyes shut. Her temple was pounding with a tension headache. Everything was beginning to weigh her down. Tomorrow was her niece's second birthday, and she'd be missing the special celebration. It was breaking Isabelle's heart knowing she would miss all of Celia's birthdays and special occasions from this point forward. Celia would grow up without knowing Isabelle. Her sister, Denise, was her best friend and closest confidante. Who would she go to the movies with? Who would wish her a happy birthday? Or cheer for her when she experienced a triumph?

Tears slid down her face as a feeling of hopelessness swept over her. In the morning she would have to report to work at the North Star Chocolate Shop and put on a brave face. It would be a huge step in the development of her new identity. But she didn't feel courageous or strong in the slightest bit. Isabelle felt as if she might crack into a million little pieces at any given moment. And sadly, if she did, there wouldn't be anyone who cared enough about her to pick up the pieces.

## Chapter Three

Morning came well before Isabelle was ready to leave the coziness of her down comforter and heated blanket. She let out a groan as her alarm blared, putting an end to her peaceful slumber. She'd been a little chilly last night and she'd rummaged around in the hall closet looking for bedding since she couldn't locate the thermostat in the furnished rental. Her footed pajamas, along with the comfy blankets, made her feel as if she was snuggled in a cocoon and she was reluctant to get up.

After dragging herself out of bed, Isabelle fixed herself some oatmeal and coffee before heading back upstairs to wash up and get dressed. She looked at herself in the bathroom mirror. She'd pulled her long black hair back into a ponytail. She was only wearing a light dusting of concealer and mascara. In her black sweater and matching slacks, she looked competent and professional. Isabelle took a deep breath and began to recite her daily mantra.

"You cannot go home. You cannot contact anyone from your former life. Don't do anything to raise suspicions. If you follow the rules, you'll be safe."

Just saying the words out loud felt surreal. She felt like one of those hapless women from a TV movie. How on earth had her life spiraled out of control so quickly? The last few months had been a living nightmare with each day bleaker than the last. It had been bad enough to witness a brutal crime, but things had taken a turn for the worse once the authorities asked her to provide testimony against Burke, who'd put a hit out on her. Several harrowing attempts had been made on her life. Although each one had been unsuccessful, the fear escalated with each attempt.

She shook her head, willing herself not to go down this road. Today was her first workday in Owl Creek. A rush of adrenaline raced through her. It reminded her of the way she'd felt on the first day of school—nervous mixed with excited. In order to maintain her sanity, she needed to embrace everything Owl Creek had to offer. Moping around wouldn't serve any purpose other than to dampen her spirits even further. She needed to stay hopeful and grounded in her new reality. Her life wasn't over, even though it sometimes felt like it. Maybe she would fall in love with her managerial position at the chocolate shop. Perhaps Owl Creek would be an answer to all of her most fervent prayers. She yearned to feel safe, despite the fact that she'd had to move so far away from home and sever all ties with her former life in order to make it happen. Suddenly, she was second-guessing herself. Had she made the right choice in entering WITSEC? Maybe she'd allowed fear to guide her decision.

*Lord, please help me to have a positive outlook as I take these first few steps in Owl Creek. I'm so frightened, and I feel so alone. I've never been without my family. Help me navigate my way through the darkness.*

As she drove toward town, Isabelle made sure she traversed the roads carefully. Driving over snow-packed roads wasn't for the faint of heart as she was beginning to realize from firsthand experience. She gripped the steering wheel tightly as the tires slid over an icy patch. Her nerves were on edge.

*You can do this.* Her mother's voice buzzed in her ear, enveloping her like a warm embrace. Isabelle missed her more than she could ever express in words. Though the Sanchez family had never had much in the way of material things, Mama had always given her children wings and allowed them to soar. The thought of never seeing Mama again or hearing the lilting tone of her voice gutted her. Hot tears pooled in her eyes.

*Do not cry!* she urged herself. Today was not the day to break down. She needed to establish herself in this town and get her bearings in her place of employment. Despite her stomach being tied up in knots, Isabelle had to project an air of composure. It was going to be way harder than she had ever imagined. This was where her faith would be more important to her than ever.

"'I can do all things through Christ which strengtheneth me,'" Isabelle said, reciting the verse from Philippians as a calming mechanism. She often drew from

Bible passages in troubled times. This one was no different.

By the time the shops on Main Street came into view, she had managed to collect herself. The white chalet-style shop looked even more charming this morning. She pulled into the back lot as she'd been instructed and parked. Walking inside the North Star Chocolate Shop felt like stepping into a whole new world. The interior was done in shades of gold and cream with splashes of brown and pink. A small chandelier hung above a display case that was a chocolate lover's dream. The aroma filled her nostrils, and she felt a heady sensation to be surrounded by so much chocolate.

"Good morning. You must be Ella!" A very distinguished-looking woman greeted her from behind the counter. With her jet-black hair streaked with silver and a widow's peak, the woman had a striking appearance. "I'm Beulah North," she said, sticking out her hand in greeting as she moved toward Isabelle.

Isabelle reached out and shook hands with her new boss. "Yes, I'm Ella Perez. It's great to meet you in person, Mrs. North, after all of our phone conversations."

"It's a pleasure to meet you face-to-face. You're lovely," Beulah crowed. "We're mighty pleased to have you here in Owl Creek. Welcome to the North Star Chocolate family. And I'll be offended if you don't call me Beulah."

Something about this dazzling woman made her smile. She couldn't put her finger on it, but she just knew they were going to be fast friends. "I'm happy to be here, Beulah."

"This is my granddaughter, Sage Crawford," Beulah said, turning toward the younger woman by her side.

Sage was beautiful in a girl-next-door kind of way. She radiated happiness. Sage smiled at Isabelle, and said, "Hi, Ella. We're so happy you'll be working with us. I just know you're going to love being here."

Isabelle waved her hand around the area. "What's not to love? This place is fantastic. Every chocolate lover's dream. If the chocolate is even half as good as it smells, I'll be delighted."

"Oh, our chocolate is divine," Beulah crowed. "I'll make sure to give you plenty of samples to take home with you tonight. Then you can tell us your favorites."

"That sounds like a great homework assignment," Isabelle said, garnering laughter from Sage and Beulah.

"Why don't we give you the grand tour?" Sage suggested. Isabelle nodded, then followed behind the women as they led her around. Although she had worked in retail spaces before such as coffeehouses, clothing shops and bookstores, Isabelle had never been employed by a company the caliber of North Star Chocolate. Everywhere she looked were examples of excellence. Awards of distinction were framed on the wall. The display cases were filled with so many assortments of chocolates—Belgian chocolates, pecan clusters, chocolate-covered raisins, truffles, nonpareils and so many more, many of which she'd never heard of before.

Although her head was spinning with all the details, she was beginning to feel enthused about working at the chocolate shop. She knew she had a lot to learn about the company, and as manager, she would be in charge of the store as well as its employees. Once Sage and Beulah finished showing her around and introduced her to the employees, they sat down in the café portion of the shop and enjoyed cups of North Star's signature hot chocolate.

"You weren't exaggerating when you raved about the hot cocoa," Isabelle said after taking several sips of the delicious treat.

"Thank you. I'd tell you the secret ingredient but it's a North family secret," Beulah said, winking at her. Her eyes twinkled with delight. Isabelle had the feeling Beulah North was a unique individual with many different facets to her.

Isabelle chuckled. "I don't blame you one bit. The recipe is pure gold."

"Speaking of family, what does yours think about this move to Alaska?" Sage asked, a hint of curiosity in her tone.

Isabelle's mind went blank. What could she say? That her family was devastated by her decision to enter WITSEC? Should she explain that the minimal risks to her family members' lives hadn't justified their participation in the program?

"I don't have much family to speak of," she answered. She felt awful for denying the existence of her large, bustling family, but it would be better in the long run so it wouldn't look strange not to mention them.

Cutting her family out of her past, present and future was her new reality.

Beulah made a tutting sound. "I'm sorry to hear that, but in a town like Owl Creek, it won't be long before you'll be considered as one of our own."

Sage flashed a wide grin. "I can attest to that!"

"Well, I hate to drink and run, but I need to head over to the factory for a meeting. Sage will stay with you and show you the ropes," Beulah explained. "We'll have to get you over there one day this week. I'd love for you to meet the team and see how the chocolate is created and assembled. Even after all these years I find it fascinating."

Isabelle didn't dare tell Beulah that she'd already met her grandson. She still felt mortified about being responsible for Connor's fall. The very last thing she wanted to do was cause Beulah to think badly of her. Maybe in the future she would look back on the incident and find it hysterically funny, but at the moment it was humiliating.

Way to make a wonderful first impression on her boss's family, she scolded herself. She wouldn't blame Connor if he was questioning why Beulah had hired her in the first place. Although he'd treated her with an abundance of kindness yesterday, Isabelle knew he had just been doing his job as the company's ambassador.

A man like Connor North had the world in the palm of his hand. He was good-looking, charming and one of the heirs to a chocolate empire. She imagined he had his fair share of admirers. He was what her mother called a catch. If the situation was different, Isabelle wouldn't mind getting to know him better. But it simply wasn't possible. Any type of relationship—whether a casual flirtation or something more meaningful—was off the table. It wouldn't be fair to get close to someone and have to lie to them about the most important parts of herself.

According to the rules of WITSEC, she could never divulge her former identity to anyone, not even her future spouse. As a result, Isabelle knew she would never settle down or have children. It was hard enough having to live a life filled with so many fabrications, but she refused to drag anyone else into the mess. She'd grown up watching her parents enjoy a marriage based on mutual trust and admiration. They were best friends and partners who finished each other's sentences. And she couldn't imagine either one harboring secrets from the other. To this day they were completely in love with each other. They even had weekly date nights that they never missed. Ana and Rio Sanchez were her romantic ideals.

If she couldn't aspire to that type of partnership— where truth reigned supreme—then she didn't intend to have one at all. Not ever.

Connor had a million things to do at work, but somehow he'd ended up on Main Street standing in front of the North Star Chocolate Shop. It was only one block away from the chocolate factory where he worked, so it had been a simple walk to get over here. The shop was a great draw for both the townsfolk and tourists, while the factory was where all the confections were made and packaged.

Just the sight of the store made him grin. His first job had been working the register after school. It had taught him about discipline, hard work and his family's legacy. And even though he'd loved chocolate since he came out of the womb, he had fallen in love with it all over again. Seeing the joy it brought to customers had been a life-changing experience. He'd known at that moment that he didn't want to do anything other than work for the North Star Chocolate Company for the rest of his life.

Curiosity about Beulah's new hire had been nipping at his mind all morning long. Was Ella enjoying working at the chocolate shop? Was she feeling at all overwhelmed about settling down in a small Alaskan town? He couldn't help but wonder if she would stay in Owl Creek. Occasionally, newcomers who weren't used to the harsh weather and the Alaskan way of life had packed up and left without giving Owl Creek a fair chance.

He pushed the shop door open and inhaled the sweet scent that was as familiar to him as his own name. Being here felt like going back to his roots. The sights, smells and sounds were awakening all of his senses. It made him smile to see so many townsfolk milling about the shop, excited about picking out their favorite chocolates. He immediately spotted Ella standing behind the counter with his sister. The two women were chatting amiably as if they'd known each other for years.

"Good afternoon, ladies," Connor said as he walked toward them.

Although he tried not to stare, he couldn't seem to look away from Ella. With her hair swept away from her face, her stunning features were on full display. Her attire was professional and stylish. She looked right at home in the shop.

"Hey, Connor. What brings you over here?" Sage asked. "Are you checking up on me?"

Before he could answer, she continued speaking. "Ella, this is my brother, Connor North. Connor, this is Ella Perez, our new store manager."

"We've already met," Connor said, the corners of his mouth twitching in amusement at the memory of their first meeting at the Snowy Owl.

"At the diner," Ella said as she shot him a pointed look. Clearly, she didn't want Sage to know about the incident with the syrup. He sent her a slight nod, letting her know her secret was safe with him. He didn't want to do anything to make her uncomfortable. As it was, he felt pretty guilty about telling his grandmother she might be concealing something. He knew he had to make it up to Ella in some way for doubting her authenticity.

"I'm glad you stumbled upon the Snowy Owl," Sage said. "My sister-in-law, Piper, is the owner, and she makes the best flapjacks in the state of Alaska."

"I'll remember that for next time," Ella said, grinning.

"So, how are things going?" he asked. "I hope your first day has been enjoyable."

"It's going very well," she answered, looking at Sage for confirmation. "Your sister and grandmother really rolled out the welcome mat for me. I couldn't have asked for more on my first day."

"We're so glad you're here," Sage said, placing her arm around Ella. "Can you just excuse me for a moment? The mother of one of my students just walked in. I'd like to say hello."

"Students?" Ella asked, furrowing her brow as Sage hustled away.

"Sage is a part-time teacher. Her teaching schedule allows her to help out here and at the factory a few days a week," Connor explained.

Ella nodded. "I imagine she's a wonderful teacher. She's been so patient with me today."

Connor had no way of knowing if Ella knew his sister's backstory. It had been front-page news when it had been revealed that the long-lost chocolate heiress had returned to Owl Creek. There was nothing in Ella's expression or voice that hinted at anything other than pure admiration for Sage. As far as he was concerned, his little sister was the most resilient, loving person he'd ever known.

"So, did Beulah pick out some chocolates for you to take home?" he asked, knowing it was his grandmother's signature gesture she extended to new employees. Chocolate was Beulah's love language, and she didn't hesitate to shower people with it.

"She did. She asked me what my favorites were, and I told her that I love it all. I'm not sure how a person can have an absolute favorite."

Connor felt his eyes widening. He let out a sharp laugh.

"Did I say something funny?" Ella asked with a slight frown.

"I'm sorry," Connor said, his tone apologetic. "I didn't mean to be rude. Let me show you something." Connor walked behind the counter and opened the display case. He scanned the rows of chocolates, homing in on several before he picked them up and placed them on a napkin. He turned toward Ella and pointed toward the chocolates. "These three chocolates are my all-time favorites. This one here is the purest milk chocolate. I fell in love with it when I was eight years old." He broke the confection in half and handed it to Ella, who gingerly bit into it. "Now this one here is a chocolate truffle. When I was eighteen, you couldn't tell me there was a finer chocolate." Once again he split the chocolate in half. He watched as Ella eagerly popped it into her mouth.

"Oh, this is delicious," she said, letting out a contented sigh. "So when did you fall in love with the third one?"

Connor held up the piece of white chocolate. "This one has only been a recent discovery. I spent most of my life thinking white chocolate just wasn't on the same level as regular chocolate. At the advanced age of twenty-seven I fell head over heels in love with white chocolate." Connor dramatically snapped the piece of white chocolate in half and handed Ella one as he bit into his own portion.

"Sounds like a serious relationship," she said with a

chuckle. The sound of Ella's tinkling laughter warmed his insides. She seemed more relaxed today. He was beginning to see glimpses of her personality shining through her reserve.

They were standing so close to one another their arms were brushing against each other. A slight awareness flared between them seconds before Ella moved a few steps away from him. A shuttered expression came over her face and he had the distinct impression his close proximity had made her uncomfortable. At the moment, Ella was giving off signs he rarely encountered.

Connor was used to being playful and friendly with the women in Owl Creek. In fact, he had gained a reputation of being a ladies' man. Just because he'd always had a healthy dating life didn't mean he was a player. And even if he had been at one point, wasn't he allowed to evolve?

Suddenly, a bang emanated from outside, echoing in the shop.

Ella let out a scream as her features creased with fear. For a moment Connor was struck by the sheer terror on her face.

"There's nothing to be afraid of," Connor said, instinctively moving toward her and placing his arm around her. All of his protective instincts had gone into high gear.

"W-what was that sound?" she asked, her eyes wide, lips trembling.

Connor strode toward the window and peered outside. In a matter of seconds, he turned back toward her. "It was just a truck backfiring."

"Otis's truck? Not again! He really needs to get that thing fixed," Sage called out from across the store. She shook her head and made a face.

"I'm so embarrassed," Ella said, ducking her head. Her body was still shaking.

"Hey. It's nothing to feel badly about. You should see me during a thunderstorm," Connor said, trying to ease the tension.

Ella sent him a smile that didn't make it all the way to her eyes. One moment everything had been fine, and the next she'd been falling apart. It didn't make any sense. Was she the high-strung type?

"Is everything okay over here?" Sage asked as she walked back over to the counter.

"Everything's fine," Ella said. "Let's get back to it." She rubbed her hands together.

"You'll have to excuse us, Connor. I'm still training Ella, and there's lots more to go over," Sage said, gently pushing her brother toward the direction of the door.

He held up his hands. "I can take a hint. I'll see you ladies later."

Connor took one last look in Ella's direction. Although she appeared a bit steadier, there was still an unsettled expression on her face. She seemed wary, as if she was waiting for something bad to happen.

As he made his way back to the chocolate factory, Connor replayed the incident with Ella in his mind. Her reaction to Otis's vehicle backfiring had been over-the-top. He hadn't imagined her terrified response to the loud boom. It had been dramatic. What had she been so afraid of? So many possibilities flashed before him.

None of the scenarios was pleasant. Maybe Ella had been hurt in the past by someone. And perhaps she'd come all the way to Owl Creek to get away from a turbulent situation with an ex. It chilled him to the bone to imagine Ella as the victim of domestic violence.

Warning bells were clanging in his head. He needed to avoid conflict-filled situations, especially since he was still grappling with the emotional fallout from his sister's recent return. He had no idea what Ella had been through, but he felt certain it had been intense. It radiated from her every time he was in her presence. Even though Ella Perez was the loveliest woman he'd ever laid eyes on, it was clear to him she'd come to town with burdens weighing her down. His family's painful history had taught him that he wasn't the sort of man who dealt well with secrets. Or lies.

There was something about Ella that tugged at him, but he couldn't allow himself to get pulled into her world. Not now or ever.

# Chapter Four

$\smallsmile$

At the end of the day, Isabelle locked up the front door of the chocolate shop. Back in Miami she would have turned on a security system, but as Sage had explained to her, the chocolate shop didn't have one. She turned the knob just to make certain the establishment was secured. It would be terrible if someone broke in on her first day as manager. Although Sage hadn't said it in so many words, Isabelle had the feeling that Owl Creek didn't have a lot of crime. It had been silly of her, then, to get so frightened earlier at the sound of the vehicle backfiring, but to her ears it had sounded like gunshots. Although Connor had been very comforting, she still felt terribly embarrassed. She worried that she'd made a misstep by overreacting.

It was hard to move forward, she realized, when she hadn't fully healed from the past. The shock of what she'd been through still affected her. Fear still cropped up at the most unexpected times. She knew it might be post-traumatic stress from having been victimized.

Witnessing Saul's death and surviving the attempts on her own life had been devastating experiences. Isabelle prayed being in a safe haven like Owl Creek would help her heal. She didn't want to feel this way for the rest of her life.

Once she'd finished locking up, Isabelle took a quick look at her watch. It was just past five o'clock despite the darkened sky. She hadn't quite adjusted to the increased hours of darkness in Alaska. Her body was having a hard time acclimating to the lack of sunlight. Back in Florida it wouldn't get dark until after dinnertime.

Main Street was a charming area. It really did resemble something from a postcard. For such a small town there was an abundance of shops. There was a particular one that called out to her. Tea Time. From the moment she'd spotted the quaint tea shop, Isabelle had been intrigued by it. She'd always wanted to visit a tea emporium but had never had the opportunity back home. The townsfolk here led a quieter life.

She peered through the window, letting out a wistful sigh at the eye-catching decor. A soft light emanated from inside, providing a warm glow to the place. The place wasn't full of customers but there were a few people scattered around the dining room. In her direct line of sight were two women who were sitting at a table sipping tea and chatting. They seemed so happy simply spending time in each other's company. Suddenly, Isabelle's throat thickened as tears blurred her vision. Although she'd wanted to visit the tea shop, it hurt to realize she didn't have a single person with whom to share the experience. What she wouldn't give to sit down for tea with her sister or her best friend, Kara. She wondered if this ache would ever go away. Would she spend the rest of her life missing people and pretending to be somebody she wasn't?

Honestly, she wasn't sure what kind of existence that would be.

Isabelle turned away from the shop and made her way to the parking lot. It felt as if a huge weight was sitting on her chest. Her first day at the chocolate shop had been a success, but the very thought of going back to a quiet house made her want to sob. Although the marshals had done everything in their power to prepare her for a brand-new life in Alaska, she didn't feel very solid at the moment. She felt as if she was falling apart. Sitting by herself at a table at Tea Time would have only served to heighten her loneliness.

She started up the truck and began driving back to the house. Earlier she had overheard one of the customers saying that the roads were snow packed and a bit slippery due to the dipping temperature. She tried to cast off the feelings of doubt about driving on unfamiliar roads in less than desirable conditions.

Isabelle let out a groan as the GPS suddenly lost its connection. Talk about bad timing! She bit her lip as she reached a fork in the road. She was fairly certain she was supposed to bear to the right, but since she'd never traveled down this road in the dark it was a bit of guesswork.

As Isabelle made the turn, the truck's wheels skidded on the ice and she desperately tried to remember what to do in this particular situation. But before she could act, the vehicle swerved off the road, sideswiping a spruce tree and landing in a snowy ravine.

Isabelle sat still for a few moments, her hands tightly gripping the wheel. Her breathing was shallow. She'd been too frightened to let out a scream. And now she had no idea how to get help or even alert the local authorities as to her destination. Because of the darkened roads she was now thoroughly confused as to which road she was on.

She needed to call 911. Isabelle reached for her phone, frustration building inside her as she realized there was no cell signal. Isabelle let out a brittle-sounding laugh. Somehow she had managed to evade numerous attempts on her life by a hardened criminal, yet she was unable to find a way to help herself after a car wreck. She closed her eyes and began breathing deeply in and out.

*Dear Lord. Please help me to not give in to this feeling of fear. I am stronger than I realize. With You by my side, I can do anything.*

"Well, sitting here isn't going to solve this problem," Isabelle said, unfastening her seat belt as she prepared to exit the truck. Perhaps if she walked down the road a bit she might get a signal or come upon another driver or a nearby house. She looked down at her feet. She was thankful she'd switched from her work shoes to a pair of sturdy winter boots. Just as she reached for the door handle, bright headlights illuminated the truck. For a moment Isabelle waffled between gratitude and nervousness. Who had ridden up and stopped on the shoulder of the road? What if it was someone who meant to do her harm? Her heart began to beat at a rapid pace while her hands suddenly felt clammy.

*Relax.* She knew it was unlikely that Burke or his associates had located her in Owl Creek. That being said, it didn't stop her pulse from racing or the dark thoughts from materializing. Sweat broke out on her brow as she watched a tall figure exit the vehicle and slide down the incline toward her truck. With shaking fingers, she lowered the window just as the masculine voice washed over her. "Hey there. Are you all right? Are you hurt?"

Isabelle looked up and locked eyes with Connor. She let out a little sound of surprise at the sight of him. Gratitude rose up inside her at seeing a familiar face. Although she was thankful to be rescued, there was something about Connor North that made her feel as if he could see straight through all of her lies. And it made her incredibly nervous about being able to successfully reinvent herself in Owl Creek.

"Ella? What happened?" Connor asked as he peered into the truck window, needing to reassure himself that she wasn't injured. He'd spent a large portion of his day thinking about North Star Chocolate's newest employee, so it was a little jarring to come upon her on the side of the road with a smashed-up vehicle.

"I'm not hurt. The truck slid off the road. I didn't know what to do when I hit an icy patch. It felt like the truck had a mind of its own," she explained. Although she was trying to keep a stiff upper lip, Connor had the distinct impression she was unsettled. Her voice was trembling slightly and her big brown eyes were wide with alarm. A feeling of protectiveness swept over him. Crashing your truck on your first day of work in a new town had to be nerve-racking.

"Let's get you out of here," he said, extending his hand to pull her from her seat to a standing position. Isabelle reached for her oversize bag, murmuring a thank-you before slipping her hand into his. He walked her up toward level ground, holding on to her hand until she was standing by his vehicle. He only let go so he could hold open the passenger door for her. Once she was inside, Connor quickly made his way to the driver's side. He revved the engine, eager to make sure Ella was warm. She'd been shivering a few moments ago.

"I'll have the truck towed into town for repair," Connor said. "We're in a tricky area for cell service, so I might have to drive down the road in order to make the call."

"Oh, no. I need the truck to get to work."

"You live on Kodiak, right?" Connor asked. He remembered his grandmother telling him she'd moved into the Barkers' former residence. He could easily picture her living in the charming home.

Ella nodded. "Yes, 10 Kodiak Lane. The sweet log cabin–style house with the bright blue chairs on the porch."

Connor smiled at her. "Good thing I live a few minutes away. We can figure something out. In the meantime, let me take you home. I'm sure you've had a long day."

She nodded. "It has been. I never imagined it would end with a car wreck." She made a face. "I've always been such a careful driver."

"Hang in there. Alaska roads can be tough to navigate."

"I'm not used to driving in snow."

Connor frowned. "I thought it snowed in parts of Arizona."

Silence stretched out between them before Ella answered. "Y-yes, it does, but not a lot," she explained in a shaky voice. She didn't sound very sure of herself, which once again raised a red flag with him. His friend Walt had lived in Flagstaff for two years and he'd told Connor they always experienced loads of snowy weather. Was it possible she really wasn't from that area? If that was the case, why would she fabricate something like that?

As his mind whirled with questions, he began driving in the direction of Ella's home. Connor knew these roads like the back of his hand. He'd been navigating them since he was seventeen years old. There wasn't anything quite like the freedom involved in getting behind the wheel and hitting the wide-open road.

"So, how was your first day at work?" Connor asked, trying to fill up the silence. A quick look in Ella's direction showed she was feeling more relaxed. Her lips were curved upward in a grin that made her even more attractive. If that was even possible.

"It was good. Really good, in fact. Sage and Beulah were amazing. Your sister walked me through everything and made me feel so comfortable."

Pride swelled inside him. Sage was such a giving person and a tremendous asset to the family business. "I imagine it's tough acclimating to a new town and a job all at once."

He heard a little sigh slip past her lips. "I'm not good with change. My life has been fairly predictable up till now," she admitted. "I'm not complaining, though. Owl Creek is a lovely place to start over."

*Start over.* There was something about her comment that made him curious. He wondered what exactly she'd left behind in Arizona and why she was eager to start over. The possibilities were endless. And even though he knew Ella wasn't obligated to disclose such personal information, a part of him still felt suspicious. What if she was running from something really awful that might compromise his family's business? He really needed to relax. He was becoming paranoid.

"My advice is to dive right in to the town. It has a lot to offer, from being a part of our choral group to dog mushing." He let out a throaty chuckle. "And if you're into bird watching, this town has some of the rarest species of birds in the country."

"Dog mushing? That sounds fascinating. I'm not sure I'm dog musher material, but I'd definitely love to watch sometime."

"That can be arranged. Owl Creek is hosting our fifth annual dog mushing race. It's a fun event. You shouldn't miss it."

"It sounds fun. Who can resist dogs?" Connor could hear the smile in her voice. He turned to give her a quick look, needing to see her face lit up with joy.

Now at least he knew a little something about her. She was a dog lover. That was a start. He wasn't sure what it was about Ella that made him so curious about her backstory, but each and every time he was in her presence he found himself questioning if she was being truthful. The combination of his jaded nature plus Ella's evasiveness kicked his suspicions into high gear. Every time he felt tempted to scrutinize her résumé, he had to remind himself that she'd already been fully vetted before being offered the position.

In all likelihood he wasn't being fair to the beautiful newcomer, but some instinct warned him to keep a healthy distance. Easier said than done, he reminded himself. If she wasn't on the up-and-up, Connor needed to make sure his family wasn't exposed to anything that might hurt them. They'd already been through enough pain to last them several lifetimes. He wouldn't allow anyone to trick them again.

As he pulled up in front of Ella's home, he couldn't help but notice the huge spotlight lighting up the exterior of the house. It covered the entire perimeter of the front of the property. It struck him as the type of lighting someone might use to protect themselves against a home invasion. He stifled the urge to tell Ella that Owl Creek's crime rate was incredibly low. Break-ins were unheard of. Perhaps in Arizona things were different. Or maybe she just needed reassurance as a single woman living on her own.

"Thanks for the lift," Ella said, jerking open the door and jumping down to the snow-covered ground.

He stepped out of the truck and walked around to the front of it, holding his phone up in the air. Connor frowned as he studied his cell phone. "I'm still not getting a signal."

Halfway down the walkway, Ella turned around and looked at him as if she was sizing him up. She raised her hand and motioned him over.

"No need to stand outside, Connor. Come on in and make the phone call from the house. You're doing me a favor after all by contacting the auto body shop."

"Thanks for the offer. I'll probably get a better signal from inside," he said.

By the time he caught up with her, she'd unlocked the door and stepped across the threshold. Connor walked in the house behind Ella, still feeling a bit surprised at her invitation. So far she had been very reserved, although she'd lightened up a bit during the ride to her house. Perhaps he should cut her a break. There wasn't anything wrong with being a private person, especially when she was a newcomer to town. After all, it wasn't as if he'd told her his own life story. It wasn't fair to hold her to a higher standard.

Ella took off her boots and placed them on a nearby mat. Connor followed suit, not wanting to track snow on her gleaming hardwood floors.

The place was roomier than he remembered. The large living room had a comfy gray sofa with a matching love seat and a brightly colored rug on the floor. A few pieces of artwork were scattered on the walls. He didn't recognize any of the artists, but they were all vibrant works with splashes of color. The scent of pine cones lingered in the air. Although the place wasn't fully decorated, Ella had done a fine job of making it look homey and comfortable. It suited her.

Having been at the house before, Connor knew there was a stunning view of the mountains from the back deck. He enjoyed a similar view from his own place. Each and every morning he looked at the majestic peaks and thanked God for creating all of His beautiful masterpieces. Perhaps Ella would also find comfort in the breathtaking Alaskan vista. Although he was biased, Owl Creek was a magnificent place to call home.

Within minutes he'd made the call to Rusty's Auto Body Shop and made arrangements for Ella's car to be towed into town this evening.

Once he ended the call, he turned around to face her. "Rusty is going to take care of your truck for you. He's a really dependable mechanic. He's going to reach out to you once he takes a look at the damage."

"That's great. I appreciate it, Connor." She bit her lip. "I just hope the damage isn't too extensive."

"I'm no expert, but I don't think it's a total loss. Rusty won't charge you an arm and a leg either. His prices are reasonable. He's as solid as they come."

He watched as relief washed over her. Connor felt badly about the accident placing any kind of economic strain on her. Maybe he could arrange something with Rusty so the bill would be reduced. He shook off the thought. It wasn't his place to ride to the rescue, even if there was something about this woman that made him feel things he wasn't used to feeling.

"Why don't I swing by in the morning at eight?" he suggested. "I can drop you off at the shop, then head over to the factory."

Ella crossed her hands. "I'm so grateful, Connor. I'd hate to mess things up my first week on the job."

"No need to worry about that. Judging by the way my grandmother was singing your praises earlier today, you don't have anything to worry about." Beulah had talked nonstop about Ella and how she'd hired the perfect person for the position. His grandmother was a tough customer, so praise from her was rare.

"Would you like a cup of tea or some water?" she asked.

He held up his hand. "No, thanks. I need to head home so I can feed my pup."

"You have a puppy?" she asked. A look of surprise was etched on her face.

"Well, he's not actually a puppy. Bear is three and he's a Siberian husky." He let out a throaty chuckle. "He really enjoys dinnertime."

"I'm sure he does. Those are fairly large dogs." Ella giggled. The tinkling sound of it surprised him. It was light and airy. Laughter looked good on her. Her eyes lit up and there were little crinkles around her mouth. He couldn't take his eyes off her.

"Well, good night. I'll see you bright and early," Connor said, beating a fast path to the door. He felt as if he needed to get some air so he could think straight. More and more, Ella was growing on him, and he didn't know what to do to stop it. He felt helpless. Attraction was humming and pulsing in the air around them. He wondered if she felt it, too.

Connor resisted the impulse to turn around to see her one last time as she stood in the doorway. Only when he heard the door shut was he able to let out a sigh of relief.

On the way home Connor couldn't stop his thoughts from veering toward Ella. There was a reason he didn't want to feel anything romantic for her. Something about her just wasn't sitting right with him. Although her house was decorated stylishly and it exuded a cozy vibe, there were no pictures of family or friends. Not a single one. Where were the family photos? Mom and dad? A sibling or two? A group of friends? Connor couldn't figure it out. Surely Ella had people in her life she was close to. Loved ones. Moments she wanted to highlight in her new home. The absence of those personal touches confounded him. Something was missing.

Who was Ella Perez? Other than being a transplant in Owl Creek and a newly hired manager for North Star Chocolates, she was an empty slate. He knew the weight of the past hung around his neck, but he was convinced Ella was hiding something. The fact that she was easy on the eyes wasn't going to distract him from the warning signs he was observing.

One way or the other, Connor was going to keep a watchful eye on Ella. Perhaps he was imagining things, but if he wasn't, he needed to be on alert. In the past his family had been victimized by a kidnapper and preyed on by people who sought to exploit their pain for profit.

He wasn't going to allow anyone else to hurt his family ever again.

## Chapter Five

Isabelle woke up bright and early, determined not to make Connor wait for her. He'd been picking her up every morning for the past three days and dropping her off at the chocolate shop.

It was very sweet of him to do her a favor and she didn't want to push it by not being ready on time. Normally, Isabelle wasn't a morning person, but waking up at this hour allowed her to glimpse a glorious Alaskan sunrise—vibrant shades of orange and yellow bursting into view over the horizon.

Connor was proving to be a very kind person, even though she'd caught him staring at her on several occasions as if she was a puzzle he wanted to solve. She'd slipped up a few times in his presence regarding her backstory. She wasn't sure if he'd picked up on it, but most likely she was being paranoid. He seemed like a very direct person, who would ask her if he thought her résumé wasn't on the up-and-up. Sometimes it felt as if she was walking around with a huge neon sign around her neck that declared her status as a WITSEC participant. It was hard not to wonder if she'd messed up big-time and inadvertently blown her cover. Up until her relocation to Owl Creek, Isabelle had no secrets to speak of. Now she was hiding almost everything about herself.

It wasn't smart of her to be around someone like Connor. His easy manner and charm tempted her to put down her guard and let him into her world. There was something about him that drew her in. As a result, it was a struggle to maintain an emotional distance from him. But there weren't many other people she knew here in town. Even though it would be tricky, she needed to forge friendships. She had to make a life for herself in Owl Creek, and without connections, she would be miserable.

Isabelle felt a burst of hope rising up inside of her. Beulah had invited her for a tour of the chocolate factory this morning. Ever since she was a kid, *Willy Wonka & the Chocolate Factory* had been her favorite movie. The prospect of getting a behind-the-scenes view of the North Star Chocolate Company's factory was thrilling.

She took a long sip of her cappuccino and let out a sigh of appreciation. What she loved most about her new house was her ability to enjoy breakfast and a wonderful view of the mountains while sitting at her kitchen table. Despite the intense feelings of homesickness she was battling, her new life was beginning to take shape. Her job at the chocolate shop kept her busy and focused. She hoped she could establish some sort of social life. Those connections would be vital if she was going to make things work here in Owl Creek.

Just as she finished washing and drying her breakfast dishes, she heard the sound of tires crunching over snow. After shrugging into her parka and stepping into her boots, Isabelle sailed out the door with her purse slung over her shoulder. She didn't want to examine too closely why the sight of Connor standing by the passenger-side door made butterflies flutter in the pit of her stomach.

"Good morning," he said with a smile as he opened the door for her. He was dressed in a dark wool coat and charcoal-gray slacks. An oatmeal-colored sweater peeked out from under his jacket. He always looked nice, but for some reason he appeared more handsome than ever today.

"Morning," she answered, shivering at the frigid temperatures. Would she ever get used to the weather in Alaska? Was it possible that this quaint village would someday feel like home? It seemed a million miles away from reality.

Once Connor was in the driver's seat, Isabelle turned toward him, and said, "You don't have to open the door for me every morning. It's pretty cold outside."

Surprise flared in his eyes. "What's the problem? I'm not complaining."

Suddenly, she felt foolish. "I don't mean to sound ungrateful." She shrugged. "I suppose I'm just not used to gestures like that."

"I'm sorry about that, but my folks raised my younger

brother, Braden, and me to be gentlemen." He smiled at her. "If you see me around town, you might even catch me walking little old ladies across the street."

Isabelle chuckled. Connor's comment managed to defuse any awkwardness she'd been experiencing. "Sounds like you might be wearing a cape under that coat," she teased.

He raised a finger to his lips. "Shh. That's a well-kept secret here in town."

They continued the ride in companionable silence, with Isabelle soaking in the wintry scenery. Snow-covered trees—spruce, pine and birch—dotted the landscape. Once she'd found out she would be relocating to Owl Creek, Isabelle had done a bit of research on Alaska. She was now able to recognize several types of trees. She was hoping to spot some rare species of birds she'd read about. It still felt surreal that she'd come all the way to the last frontier to evade a killer's wrath.

As they drove, Isabelle wanted to ask Connor a million questions about the chocolate factory, but she refrained. Some things were just better to experience yourself. When Connor pulled into the parking lot minutes later, Isabelle could barely contain her excitement. As soon as Connor put his truck into Park, she practically vaulted from the vehicle, making it unnecessary for him to hold the door open for her.

She stopped walking and simply gazed up at the building. The factory was a large brick edifice with steam rising from the top of a stack. There was a grand set of granite steps leading to the entrance. A gold-and-brown sign with swirly writing hung by the entrance, welcoming visitors to the North Star Chocolate Company.

"Are you coming?" Connor asked, turning around to address her.

"O-of course," she said, trailing after him. "I wouldn't miss this for the world. I've been waiting my whole life for a Willy Wonka moment." Once the words escaped her lips, she felt a little bit goofy for expressing those sentiments. Perhaps she should just try to be composed. She was visiting the factory in a professional capacity after all.

Connor's laughter rang out in the silence. "It's pretty special, but don't expect chocolate fountains or edible wallpaper. And there aren't any gardens full of lollipops," he teased. His reaction put her at ease. Clearly, as the heir to the chocolate empire, he understood her giddy feelings. She probably wasn't the first person to be so enthusiastic about visiting.

He beat her to the top of the stairs, then held the door open with a flourish, bowing at the waist as he said, "After you." She had the feeling he was making a teasing reference to her earlier comment about not needing doors held open for her. It showed her he was willing to make fun of himself.

Once she stepped through the doors, Isabelle sucked in a steadying breath. The sights, sounds and smells all competed with each other for her attention. She wasn't even sure where to look first. She let out a sigh of contentment as Connor steered her down a hallway with windows that overlooked conveyor belts and vats of chocolate. Isabelle felt like a little kid as she pressed her face against the glass. All the employees were dressed in baby blue uniforms with matching gloves and hairnets.

"Wow!" she said as employees plucked confections off the line and placed them in boxes, while others carried the boxes to another area. It looked like a finely honed operation. "This is quite the setup. Everyone is working in unison without skipping a beat."

"It's pretty spectacular, isn't it?" Connor asked. "We have the best employees in the world, if I do say so myself." Even though she hadn't done anything so far to earn praise, Isabelle felt buoyed by his words. It was nice to know he valued the employees.

She simply nodded, feeling overwhelmed by everything around her. The aroma of chocolate permeated the air. Isabelle felt certain she'd never smelled anything so delectable in her entire life. She couldn't put her finger on the specific type of chocolate floating in the air but it was probably an assortment of flavors. The smell was making her mouth water.

"It smells like my mama's chocolate-and-almond cake. It's a family favorite." A groundswell of nostalgia caused the words to burst from her mouth. She'd planned to avoid any mention of her family, but it wasn't as easy as she had imagined. Baking this particular delicacy was a tradition in their family going back generations. It was a huge part of her history. She would give anything to be seated at her family's large dining room table digging into a slice of the sweet baked good.

Connor nodded his head approvingly. "I've never

had the pleasure, but I've heard of it. If you decide to make it, don't forget to bring me a slice."

Although a part of her enjoyed the lighthearted banter between them, Isabelle continually had to remind herself to maintain a distance from Connor. From the first day they'd met, Isabelle had felt an attraction between them. If things weren't so messed up in her world, she wouldn't hesitate to flirt with Connor, perhaps even go out on a date with him if he asked. But her conscience wouldn't allow her to develop anything more than a friendship with him. It would be wrong to lead him on when she couldn't tell him the truth about being in the Witness Protection Program.

Honestly, she might be getting way ahead of herself. For all she knew, Connor had a long-term girlfriend in town, although she'd seen no signs of it. She'd overheard her staff talking about Connor being a sought-after bachelor in Owl Creek. Perhaps she was misreading things between them. Maybe she was the only one who felt something simmering in the air between them.

"You can enjoy the full tour later on, but I think we should head to my grandmother's office. I know she's eager to see you," Connor said, leading her toward a bank of elevators. When they reached the second floor, he led her down a hall of executive offices. They passed by one with Connor's name engraved on a brass plaque, but Isabelle didn't get an opportunity to get much of a glimpse of the interior. All she spotted was a tall bubble gum machine situated next to a sleek-looking desk. Connor slowed down when they reached a grand office a few doors down from his own.

Located at the end of the corridor, Beulah's office was bright and welcoming, much like the woman herself.

"Ella! It's great to see you here," Beulah said as she rose from her chair. She quickly made her way around her desk and reached for Isabelle's hands, joining them together with her own.

For a second Isabelle felt startled by the greeting. She hadn't yet gotten used to being called Ella. It was still a bit jarring. Seeing Beulah felt wonderful, though. The older woman had been so kind and supportive on her first day. With her oversize personality and stately air, she reminded Isabelle of her own mother. They both exuded an air of confidence mixed with benevolence.

"Thank you for the invitation, Beulah. From what I've seen so far, this place is amazing," Isabelle gushed.

Beulah beamed at her praise. "I won't disagree with you. Not even a little bit. One of my smartest decisions was marrying my husband, Jennings. Not only did I get a cherished life partner, but it brought the North Star Chocolate Company into my life. His family created it, but I couldn't love it any more if I was born into it."

Connor put his arm around his grandmother. "You were destined to be a part of it."

Beulah beamed up at Connor. The interaction between them was heartwarming. She could feel the love flowing in the air.

"I would like to show you something, my dear." She strode over to her desk and pointed at a framed picture hanging on the wall. "This photo was taken over one hundred years ago when the factory first opened."

Isabelle's eyes widened as she studied the black-and-white photograph. At the time the image was taken, the factory was a simple brick building no more than a few thousand square feet. "I can't believe it's the same place. What a difference a century makes," Ella said.

"It might surprise you, but I wasn't born yet," Beulah said with a wink.

Connor and Isabelle joined in on the laughter. It was impressive to see such a distinguished businesswoman have the ability to laugh at herself. Connor was blessed to have her as his grandmother. Isabelle felt a burst of gratitude that she'd secured a position at Beulah's company.

"I'd like to show you some behind-the-scenes areas of the factory. It's a rite of passage for new employees," Beulah said, gleefully rubbing her hands together. "I might even share some trade secrets."

Connor leaned in toward Isabelle, speaking in a loud whisper as he said, "But then she'd have to make you disappear."

Connor's close proximity caused her pulse to quicken. A rich, woodsy scent hovered around him. Although Isabelle had met men like Connor before, she'd never met anyone who appeared to be the whole package. His dark hair and blue eyes combined with chiseled features and a rugged build made him one of the most attractive men she'd ever seen. He was smart and confident, with a loving family by his side. And judging by the lack of a wedding ring and local chatter, he was still single.

Beulah swatted her grandson. "I'd do no such thing.

Follow me, Ella. There's plenty of intriguing aspects of this operation."

Isabelle nodded and walked over to Beulah. The CEO was a font of information and she couldn't wait to hear more from the older woman about the craft of making chocolate. She would be the perfect tour guide.

"I'm going to head back to my office and make a few phone calls," Connor said, glancing at his watch. "I'll see both of you in a little bit."

Isabelle felt a stab of disappointment. She loved Connor's whimsical side and the factory seemed to bring it out in him. She couldn't deny that Connor was quickly becoming a distraction. He tempted her to think of quiet nights by the fire and snowy walks on the town green.

What was it about Connor that brought out this side of her? She'd already decided to steer clear of any romantic entanglements in Owl Creek, knowing it would only serve to complicate her life if she became involved with anyone. But time after time her thoughts kept veering toward Connor.

For the next hour, Beulah walked Isabelle around the factory. There was so much to see behind the scenes. Isabelle was fascinated by the process of making such delicious chocolate from a simple cocoa bean. After seeing her keen interest, Beulah invited her to put on a uniform and take a turn on the assembly line. She was intrigued by the entire operation and the history of North Star Chocolates. Beulah rattled off so many details as they continued the tour, providing her with so much information that Isabelle's head was spinning.

Along the way Isabelle was introduced to numerous employees, all of whom appeared to hold Beulah in high esteem. Even though she was the CEO, Beulah was down-to-earth and likable. She treated everyone in the factory as if they were as important to the company as she was.

At the end of the tour Isabelle was treated to a new product that was being rolled out in the factory. It was the most delicious white hot chocolate cocoa created by Connor and his siblings. Beulah even tucked a few packets in a little pouch for Isabelle to take along with her.

As Beulah accompanied Isabelle back to the corridor where they'd started, she stopped in front of the office that Isabelle now knew belonged to Connor.

"I'm going to leave you here with my grandson. I hope you enjoyed the tour."

"It was truly wonderful," Isabelle said. "Thanks for making time for my visit. It means the world to me."

Beulah reached out and squeezed her hand. "It's impressive that you came all the way from Flagstaff to work for our company. I have a really good feeling about you, Ella. And I don't say that often."

Isabelle's heart sank. Guilt pricked at her. Beulah believed in her. The CEO of the North Star Chocolate Company had no idea that she'd hired a person who didn't actually exist. Ella Perez was a creation of WITSEC. Beulah's kindness made her feel like a complete and utter fraud. All she could do was stuff down the feelings of worthlessness and plaster a placid smile on her face.

"I appreciate the vote of confidence," Isabelle murmured.

"Thanks for coming, my dear. Don't be a stranger. I hope to see you at some of our town events, starting with this weekend's festivities," Beulah said as she strode down the corridor. Isabelle knew she was referring to the dog mushing event that Connor had briefly mentioned. Signs promoting the event had been plastered all over Main Street and the town green. She didn't plan to miss it. It would provide her with a bona fide Alaskan experience.

Isabelle called out a feeble goodbye. Guilt threatened to swallow her up. She wished there weren't so many things about herself that she was hiding. Spending time with Beulah would be so much more rewarding if she could truly be Isabelle Sanchez. Beulah North was such a genuine person. She liked to think they had that in common, but at the moment, Isabelle couldn't credit herself with that attribute.

"Are you all right?" Connor asked, concern threaded in his voice as he came to his office door.

"I… I'm fine," she murmured. But she really wasn't. Isabelle didn't enjoy feeling as if she was earning praise under false pretenses. The North family had treated her warmly ever since she'd arrived in their small Alaskan town. Beulah felt like an old friend, and she didn't want to ever let her down.

"You look a little shaken up," he said as he ushered her inside. "Can I get you anything? Perhaps some ice water?"

"No, I'm okay. Just a little headache," she said,

pressing her fingers against her temple. She swung her gaze around Connor's office. It was a bright and airy space with colorful decorative touches. The tall bubble gum machine told her a lot about the man. It was a fun and imaginative touch. Maybe he was a kid at heart.

Connor followed her gaze. "That's my own homage to Willie Wonka. As a kid I always wanted a machine like this one in my bedroom." He flashed her a smile. "Clearly, my parents knew that it wasn't a good idea back then. I would have eaten them nonstop."

Isabelle grinned at the idea of a pint-size Connor yearning for a bubble gum machine. She could easily imagine a mini version of him. "Well, you finally made it happen. Good for you."

"Hey! Before I forget, I need to take your picture. HR usually does it for new employees, but I'm filling in for them this week. Let me grab my camera," he said. Connor turned toward his desk and began rifling through one of his drawers. After a few moments of fumbling around he located it.

*Her picture?* Her heart began beating a wild rhythm in her chest as her mind buzzed with questions.

"Why do you need to take my picture?" she asked. Isabelle could hear the panic in her own voice.

"You need an employee ID with your picture on it," Connor explained. A frown marred his brow. "It's standard procedure for new employees. And we might use the same photo for our company newsletter down the road. We always like to give a nice introduction to our new employees."

Fear gripped her. All of a sudden it felt as if she couldn't breathe. She hadn't anticipated this happening and she had no idea how to shut it down. What if having her picture taken placed her in a compromising position? Connor's casual mention of a newsletter was alarming. There were always so many what-ifs running around in her brain. It was nearly impossible to turn off the worry. What if someone recognized her from the company's newsletter? Just the idea of having her photo in the company's database made her feel uneasy. How many times had Marshal Kramer reminded her to keep a low profile? Although the idea of Vincent Burke and his cohorts tracking her down in Owl Creek seemed far-fetched, it still didn't stop the panic from rising up inside her. With Burke's request for a new trial pending, there was even more reason for him to want her out of the way. She was still in real danger.

"No!" she said in a heated voice. "I'm sorry! I really don't want to have my picture taken."

The vehemence in Ella's tone floored Connor. At first, he thought she was joking, but one look at the way her mouth was set in a thin, hard line convinced him otherwise. She was bristling with emotion. It radiated off her in waves. Some instinct warned him to tread lightly.

"Is there some reason you don't want your picture taken?" he asked. He shouldn't assume, but most women who looked like Ella were photogenic. He didn't understand what the big deal was at all. Was he missing something?

She shook her head, and said, "I… I probably look a wreck. I don't feel camera ready." He watched as she smoothed her hair back. She had a light sheen of perspiration on her forehead.

"You look great, Ella. Trust me, you have absolutely nothing to worry about." He was trying to put her at ease, but her body language didn't relax. She still looked as if she wanted to be anywhere else but here. Although he felt bad for her discomfort, he still felt stumped as to why she was making a big deal out of it. In the scheme of things, it shouldn't matter at all. Unless there was some reason why it mattered more than she was saying.

He prodded her. "Can I get a little smile? You're going to need this ID for the foreseeable future. You don't want to be frowning in the photo."

The corners of her mouth lifted, but the emotion didn't make it all the way to her eyes. It didn't feel genuine. He snapped a few photos, then lowered the camera and studied the images. Just as he'd suspected, the camera had captured Ella's beauty as well as her discomfort. "I'm sure one of these can work for your ID."

She knit her brows together. "That's good. So, you're just using the photo for my ID? Nothing else?"

"I promise you, we're not going to put it on the front page of the *Owl Creek Gazette*. And our newsletter is a mail out that is only sent out to people who work for us, so you're not going to become famous." His tone was teasing, but he wasn't sure the situation was funny. Ella was clearly ruffled. Why was she acting so camera shy? All morning he'd been able to put aside his niggling doubts about Ella. Until now. Suddenly his mind was drifting to all the strange things he'd observed about her ever since they'd met. He continued to have so many questions about her.

Ella's shoulders noticeably sagged with relief. "I should probably head back to the shop. Being here was a nice treat, but I don't want to overstay my visit."

"You're welcome here anytime," Connor said. And despite his doubts, he meant it. Ella was a breath of fresh air in Owl Creek and at the chocolate company. When a person grew up in a small Alaskan town they were part of a tight-knit community. Connor had always loved that aspect of his hometown. On the downside, you knew everyone, and in return, they knew everything about you. There weren't too many opportunities to peel back the layers. Maybe that was what was really bothering him about the beautiful newcomer. She seemed to have a wall up, despite the sweet air she exuded.

"Let me walk you back to the entrance," Connor said. "These hallways can be a bit tricky."

Ella nodded and walked alongside him. Along the way, employees gave them hearty greetings and a few times she threw out questions about the factory. She appeared to be genuinely interested in the workings of his family's company.

Connor couldn't help but notice the curious looks in Ella's direction. As a newbie to the small town, Ella stood out from everyone else who'd been born and bred in Owl Creek. Folks were bound to be curious about her. He wasn't sure what exact feelings he was battling against when a few male employees smiled extra long in her direction. Was he being overly protective or slightly annoyed at their interest in her?

"Thanks for everything. I talked to Rusty and it's going to be a little bit longer to make the repairs." Ella winced. "It seems I really did some damage in the accident. He had to order some special parts from Anchorage."

"It's not a problem. We're neighbors. I'm available for as long as you need me." Ella seemed beholden to him for the daily rides to town and back, but in reality she was doing him a favor. She was keeping him company and brightening up his day. He enjoyed hearing about her daily adventures at the chocolate shop and finding out about the new trends in customer purchases. It felt as if he was seeing things through a brand-new pair of eyes. He planned to be a creative force at North Star Chocolates for the remainder of his working life. One day he would take over the reins from Beulah, since his parents had already decided they didn't wish to be at the helm. He planned to inject his own special brand of creativity and passion into the company. Until that time he was going to be a sponge and soak up all he could regarding the business.

"As long as it's not an imposition. As soon as I get the truck back I plan to practice driving on the roads near my house just to get some experience." Ella's expression was sheepish. He sensed she was still beating herself up about the accident.

"Don't stress yourself about it. You'll get the hang of these Alaska roads in no time."

"I sure hope so," she said with a shake of her head. "I'm eager to explore Owl Creek during my off time. I've heard about the wonderful birds that inhabit this town and I'd love to see some of them."

"This place has a lot to offer. It's not flashy or grand in any way, but it has a lot of charm. Before you know it, Owl Creek will feel like home."

A look of sadness crept over her face. As quickly as he'd noticed her expression it was gone, replaced by a serene look. "Thanks for the pep talk. See you later," she said as she headed outside into the blustery morning.

He stood inside and watched as Ella walked down the steps and headed in the direction of Main Street. Even though he had back-to-back meetings scheduled and countless emails to catch up on, he felt an urge to push past the doors and take a walk with Ella to the chocolate shop. Along the way he could point out interesting landmarks, specialty shops and tell her a little bit about the town's history. Maybe he could get her to laugh by telling her about the prank he, Hank and Gabriel had played on the townsfolk one Christmas. It had involved a Nativity scene, six roosters and a Cabbage Patch doll. Even though they'd gotten in trouble for it, the Three Amigos still chuckled about it to this day.

There was something about Ella that made him feel the need to be carefree and seize the moment. She had the type of beauty that wasn't just on the surface. It seemed to come from deep inside of her. His grandmother certainly seemed drawn to her, judging by the expression stamped on Beulah's face. That had to mean something about Ella's character, he told himself. His grandmother didn't suffer fools gladly, and she had a knack for sniffing out insincerity. So was Ella the real deal after all?

Connor shook off the notion of leaving the factory and catching up to Ella. Regardless of how she made him feel, he knew there was way more to her than met the eye. Every instinct was warning him to tread lightly. He wasn't a man who took chances. And something told him that Ella Perez was a risk he couldn't afford to take.

## Chapter Six

Once Isabelle made it back to Main Street, she found herself slowing down as she passed by Tea Time. The elegant shop beckoned her to go in and treat herself to oolong tea and a plate of cucumber sandwiches and scones. It would be such an amazing indulgence. If she hadn't already spent hours at the factory, she would have gone inside and basked in the lovely surroundings of the tea emporium. As it was, she really needed to scoot.

"If you're wondering if you should go in, I would highly encourage it."

Isabelle spun around at the sound of the familiar voice. Sage was standing behind her with a wide grin etched on her face. She radiated a pure joy that caused Isabelle to yearn to find such serenity in her own life. What would it feel like, she wondered, to experience life in this amazing town with nothing to hide? She envied Sage's seemingly blissful life while at the same time acknowledging it couldn't have been granted to a kinder person.

"Hi, Sage. You caught me in the act. It isn't the first time I've looked longingly through this particular window," she admitted with a chuckle. "This place looks so appealing, although I've never had a chance to go in."

"Well, now you do. Come on inside with me. I have business with the owner, Iris Lawson. I'd love for you to meet her."

Sage bit her lip. "I really should head back to the chocolate shop. I've been at the factory all morning." She took a quick look at her watch. "This morning has just flown by."

"Just for a few minutes. I promise," Sage said, taking her by the hand and leading her through the doorway. Isabelle didn't put up much of a fight. Her curiosity to see the interior of Tea Time had been pricking at her for days now. She would check out the establishment, but she wouldn't linger for long.

As she trailed after Sage, Isabelle soaked in all the details of the tea emporium. The first thing that drew her attention was the vintage chandelier shimmering from the ceiling. Intimate tables were adorned with beautiful tablecloths and lace doilies. Flowers sat in a small bouquet on each table. Beautiful gold curtains and lush velvet chairs added an air of refinement. Peering in from the front window didn't do this place justice.

"Isn't it magnificent?" Sage asked.

Isabelle nodded. A sweet smell hovered in the air. She inhaled deeply as she tried to pin down the scent. It wasn't a single aroma, she realized. It was a myriad of tea scents all floating in the air. This, she thought, was paradise. If only she had time to partake in the experience.

"It feels like we've stepped into another era. Those drapes remind me of something from the Jazz Age," Isabelle remarked. She loved reading historical novels set in the 1920s. Tea Time would fit right into the setting of one of her favorite books.

Suddenly, a tall woman with brown skin began making a beeline in their direction. With her animated features and an almost regal bearing, she exuded pure elegance. "Sage. It's great to see you. I've been wondering when you would stop by."

"Hey, Iris. I'm sorry it took me so long to circle back. Things have been crazy lately. I wanted to check in with you regarding the wedding shower Rachel and I are throwing for Piper."

Iris clapped her hands together. "Rachel has been finalizing some of the details, so I think we're really in good shape." Iris turned toward Isabelle, shooting her a curious look.

"Oops. Where are my manners? Iris, I'd like to introduce you to Ella Perez. She just relocated here from Arizona." Sage grinned. "She's working at the chocolate shop. Ella, this is Iris Lawson, the owner and creative genius behind Tea Time."

Iris beamed at the compliment. "Ella, it's such a pleasure to meet you. It's wonderful to see a young person like yourself planting roots here."

"Your place is lovely, Iris. Every time I walk by it

just pulls me in," Isabelle said. "Your interior decorating aesthetic is fantastic."

Iris beamed. "Thank you. In my youth I wanted to go to design school, which wasn't possible, so I was able to fulfill all of my decorating dreams right here at my shop."

"Iris's son, Gabriel, is one of my husband Hank's closest friends," Sage explained. "And he recently got married to Rachel, who is a dear friend and an amazingly skilled nurse. She's helping me plan Piper's bash."

"And along with Rachel came two beautiful little girls, Faith and Lizzie. We're all so blessed," Iris said. "Our family has blossomed in the last few months."

"It sounds like it," Isabelle said. Family was everything. Watching it grow and expand through marriage and children had always been so gratifying for Isabelle's own mother. She felt a pang at the thought of missing out on motherhood.

"Well, why don't the two of you take a seat?" Iris asked. "I just made the most enticing batch of lemon bars."

Isabelle wished she could take Iris up on her offer. "Any other time I would love to, but I really have to get back to work. I've been away all morning."

"That's a shame." She wagged her finger at Isabelle. "I'm going to give you a rain check. Come back anytime and there'll be a table waiting for you. In the meantime, I'm going to wrap up some lemon bars for you to take with you. On the house. It's my welcome to Owl Creek gift."

As Iris quickly made her way back to the kitchen,

Isabelle turned toward Sage. "The owner is just as lovely as the establishment."

"She must like you," Sage said. "Iris has a bit of a sharp edge at times. She's a little like my grandmother in that regard," she confessed.

"Something tells me they're both strong women." Isabelle wished she could be a little bit more like the two older women. These days she always felt as if she was coming apart at the seams. She needed to dig down deep and draw strength from God. Ever since this ordeal began, He had been with her. Back when she was working at the club in Miami, Isabelle hadn't lived a faith-filled existence. That had all changed after witnessing a murder.

*Lord, please grant me strength. I have miles to go on this journey. If I'm going to stay in Owl Creek, I need fortitude. I need to be as strong as an oak tree.*

"Hey!" Sage said in a raised voice that drew Isabelle out of her thoughts. "I just had a great idea. Why don't you come to Piper's bridal shower?"

"I know who Piper is. She's a sweetheart. I met her at the Snowy Owl. She's the owner, right?"

"Yes. That place is her pride and joy. Piper is my husband Hank's sister. She's marrying my brother, Braden."

Isabelle shook her head, feeling confused. "So, wait. Does that mean she'll be your sister-in-law twice over?"

Sage chuckled. "Yes, it does. It's a little confusing, but I couldn't ask for a better friend than Piper. She already feels like my sister."

Isabelle experienced a twisting sensation in the region of her heart. She knew all too well about the powerful bonds of sisterhood. Not being able to talk to her own sister made her feel as if she was missing her right arm. She fought past the lump in her throat. "That's wonderful. A sister is a lifelong treasure."

"I agree," Sage said with a smile. "She would be thrilled to have you there. Please join us."

"Oh, no," she exclaimed. "I wouldn't want to intrude on such an intimate gathering of friends and family."

"You'll be an invited guest, Ella. In Owl Creek we don't stand on ceremony." She crossed her hands in prayerlike fashion. "Please come. It will give you an opportunity to meet some very special people. I know firsthand what it feels like to be a stranger in a new town. It's not easy."

Isabelle heard the sincerity in Sage's voice. It sounded like she had been in Isabelle's shoes at one point in her life. That knowledge made her feel even closer to Sage, even though they had only recently met. And although she didn't want to admit it to herself, she yearned to find friends in Owl Creek. The idea of attending a party at the tea shop and meeting the residents in a festive setting was extremely appealing to her.

Just then Iris returned with a little white box tied up with black ribbons. "Here are the lemon bars. Enjoy them," she said, handing them over to Isabelle.

"Thank you, Iris," Isabelle said. "What a thoughtful gesture." With every kind act performed by one of the residents of Owl Creek, her heart began to open up a little more to the idea of becoming a member of this community. Their generosity filled up her soul.

"I hope to see you at the town festivities this weekend. Dog mushing. Crepes. Ice cream. Arts and crafts." She clapped her hands together. "You'll have a ball!" With a smile, Iris turned back toward the dining room and began stopping at tables and checking in on her customers.

Isabelle looked over at Sage. "If you're sure it's okay, I'd love to come to the party," Isabelle said. Joy fluttered in her chest. It was so nice to feel included. She couldn't remember the last time she'd attended a social event. Her entire life had collapsed in an instant back in Miami, and her world had gotten very small.

"Great!" Sage said, clapping her hands together. "The party is a week from this Saturday at noon. Don't worry about bringing a present. Only your presence is required. And don't forget it's a surprise."

"Perfect. I really need to get to the shop before the staff thinks I've gone missing." With a wave of her hand, Isabelle strode toward the exit. As she made her way down the street, Isabelle's heart felt lighter than it had been in months. So far, today was shaping up to be a banner day. Even though her transition from her old life in Miami felt a bit shaky at times, she had to concede that certain things were moving her in a good direction. Perhaps happiness was in her future. If she could just manage to keep looking forward and not dwell on the past, maybe it would be within reach.

When the sign for the chocolate shop came into

view, Isabelle's thoughts turned to Connor. It was becoming increasingly difficult not to think about him. Seeing him every day surely wasn't helping matters. She let out a groan of frustration. If she had a checklist for a love interest, Connor would score a perfect ten. But she couldn't imagine delving into a relationship with him, all while hiding her truths under the surface. The North family had been so good to her by employing her and encouraging her to become an integral part of Owl Creek. Pretending to be someone she wasn't still felt wrong on so many levels, even though it had been borne out of necessity.

Even though she was safe in her new Alaskan life, Isabelle still had vivid nightmares about Saul's death and the attempts on her life. In some of the dreams Isabelle hadn't managed to flee the nightclub. Instead, she'd met the same end as Saul at the hands of Burke. She still felt broken about all she'd gone through. It was hard not to question whether she had done the right thing by testifying and agreeing to participate in the Witness Protection Program. It had turned her entire life upside down, as well as the lives of those near and dear to her. It still felt surreal to her to be living as Ella Perez.

She was still grieving the loss of Isabelle Sanchez. There was no way of knowing if she would ever get used to being this new version of herself.

Connor bit into his crab cakes and let out a groan. As usual, the menu at the Snowy Owl did not disappoint. Although he was no slouch in the kitchen, Connor couldn't compete with the diner's offerings.

Piper stood by the table, grinning at his reaction. "They're good, huh?"

"If my brother wasn't already marrying you, I might just propose so you could make me these for the rest of my life," Connor said.

"That's about as likely as a heat wave in December." Braden North stepped up and wrapped his arms around Piper's waist, then leaned down to place a kiss on her cheek. "She's taken."

"I am indeed," Piper said, grinning at her fiancé.

"Settle down, little brother." Connor made a face at Braden. "I'm trying to eat my dinner. Take that kissy-face stuff to another booth."

Piper rolled her eyes. "Let me know if you guys need anything else." She walked off toward the kitchen with Braden by her side. Connor's gaze trailed after them. He still couldn't believe the lifelong best friends had fallen in love. Connor hadn't seen it coming at all, but he knew they were as perfect for one another as a couple could be. Contentment shimmered off them in waves.

What would it feel like to know his destiny was tied up in another human being? He imagined it would be epic. When he looked at Braden, it seemed as if his brother's heart had grown by leaps and bounds. Loving Piper had brought out the very best in him. Hank had said the same about his sister.

Knowing he needed to focus on why he'd met up with his best friends for dinner, Connor turned back to

Hank and Gabriel sitting across from him at the table. "Okay, now that they're gone we can keep planning the bachelor party."

"I'm not sure about your idea. It doesn't sound fun to me. Maybe we can stage an elaborate game night," Hank suggested.

Connor groaned. "Come on, guys. Have a little creativity. This is supposed to be my little brother's prewedding send-off. Who wants to sit around playing checkers?"

Gabe let out a snort. "No one said anything about checkers. We just don't think Piper would appreciate placing her husband-to-be in any jeopardy."

Connor scoffed. "Braden has done every extreme sport you can imagine. I don't think that a little night skiing would be a problem."

Hank shook his head. "Connor, you need to start brainstorming again. Considering how Jack died, I think it could come across as insensitive."

Connor let out a groan and slapped his forehead. "I have no idea where my head is at. That would really be problematic. Not to mention downright inconsiderate. Maybe we can do a bowling night and rent out the place just for the party. With food and music, it could be just right. Thanks for the save, guys."

Piper's father and Hank's stepfather, Jack Miller, had passed away after a snowmobile accident on one of the mountain trails. It had caused a huge rift between Piper and Braden when it was revealed that Braden had been arguing with her father shortly before the tragic accident. Thankfully, they had sorted things out and reconciled. Their spring wedding was mere weeks away.

"No problem. We're all excited that Braden and Piper are making it official." Gabriel grinned as he put a forkful of rosemary potatoes in his mouth.

Hank frowned. "He better treat my little sister right or he's going to answer to me." The menacing expression stamped on his face gave way to a smirk when he couldn't keep a straight face. Gabe and Connor began chuckling along with him.

"I've always wanted to say that. You know I think the world of Braden," Hank admitted.

Connor grinned. "The feeling is mutual. He's looked up to the three of us ever since he was in diapers," Connor said, struggling to keep his emotions in check. Growing up in the shadow of a tragic event such as his sister's kidnapping had forged a strong bond between the two brothers. Although they were now traveling on different paths since Braden was opening a business specializing in Alaskan adventures, the love between them couldn't be any stronger. Watching him fall head over heels in love with his best friend had been awe-inspiring. The happy couple was also working together with Piper's pie business, Pie in the Sky.

"So, how are things going with the new girl in town? Ellen? I heard she's working at the chocolate shop," Gabe said.

"Ella," he said, quickly correcting his friend. "She seems to be acclimating well to our little town. She had an accident with her truck so I've been giving her a lift to work until Rusty makes the repairs," Connor explained.

"That's too bad she had a wreck," Gabe said. "I hope she's all right."

"She didn't have so much as a scratch, but the truck wasn't as fortunate," Connor answered. "I'm just praying she doesn't get jittery about driving on these icy roads. I remember when I had that accident back in high school. It took me a long time to work up the courage to get back behind the wheel."

Hank nodded. "Sage is raving about her and how well she's doing at the chocolate shop. I think my wife has found a new friend."

"That's great. Sage is the perfect person for Ella to bond with." Just the thought of the two women becoming friends made him smile. His sister was compassionate and understanding. "It must be challenging being new to Owl Creek. Most of the townsfolk have been in each other's pockets for all of our lives."

Hank took a big swig of his hot chai. "Something tells me you're doing some bonding of your own with Ella, judging by that look on your face."

"We're just friends," Connor said, not wanting Hank or Gabe to get the wrong idea. He knew all too well how fast rumors spread here in town. "Even a blind man can see she's beautiful," he conceded, "so there's a definite attraction. I feel this pull in her direction that makes me want to be around her."

Gabe leaned forward across the table. "I can hear a 'but' coming."

Connor let out a sigh. "At the risk of being considered paranoid, I'm pretty certain she's running from something in her past." He looked back and forth between his friends, waiting for skeptical expressions to appear on their faces. When it didn't happen, he continued to speak. "I can't say for certain what it is, but something doesn't feel right about her backstory."

"Maybe she had a bad breakup," Gabe said. "People relocate all the time due to their personal lives."

"True." Connor sighed. "Trouble is, the only woman who makes me feel anything romantic at all these days is Ella."

"And why is that a problem?" Hank asked.

"Because all of my instincts are telling me she's sitting on a mountain of secrets. I can't put my finger on it, but our new employee isn't as she appears to be. And it's putting up a wall between us."

"What do you think she's hiding?" Gabriel prodded.

Connor shrugged. "I have no idea. Something just doesn't feel right. Her reason for coming all this way to Alaska is a bit shaky."

Hank scratched his jaw. "People move all the time. Maybe her old life wasn't working, and she wanted a fresh start. It's not far-fetched at all. We have several residents who transplanted here from other places."

Connor let out a frustrated sound. "Okay. It's possible I'm just putting up roadblocks, but my instincts are telling me something is off with her. And I have to admit, it has crossed my mind that she could be involved in something illegal."

"As a member of law enforcement, I have to caution

you against going down that trail without evidence. It's a huge leap," Hank said.

"What your family has been through would make anyone a bit jaded," Gabe added. "I know when Sage revealed herself as your long-lost sister, you were the last family member to believe it was true. You're a pragmatic person, Connor, but sometimes you tend to see cracks when there really aren't any. Just keep that in mind."

"He's right," Hank chimed in. "And the problem is, you could be blocking your greatest blessing in the process."

*His greatest blessing.* Lately, Connor had been thinking about his future and dreaming of a life different from the one he was leading. He loved his job, adored his family and his hometown, yet there was a void in his life that nothing had been able to fill. Although he would never admit it to his best friends, he was lonely. He'd never yearned for love before, but he knew it was the missing ingredient in an otherwise charmed life. Keeping women at a distance was his strong suit, but it hadn't helped him move forward on his journey.

Could Ella become someone special in his life? Perhaps he was foolish to even think it, since they barely knew one another. Another part of him couldn't help but wonder. He felt a strong, inexplicable pull in her direction. If he gave it a chance, would something develop between them? He had no idea. Keeping her at arm's length seemed practical to him, but he couldn't discount Gabriel's and Hank's comments. If he continued to do as he'd always done, the path he was taking would lead him to a lifetime of loneliness.

## Chapter Seven

It was a beautiful January evening in Alaska and Chinook Woods was one of the loveliest places she'd ever seen. Isabelle had decided to attend the dog mushing event that featured a well-known dog musher, Ace Reynolds, who had ties to Owl Creek. Despite the frigid temperature, no snow was falling from the pewter-colored sky. Although Isabelle thought the fluffy white stuff was pretty, she still hadn't gotten used to being surrounded by it. She inhaled the pristine air, then exhaled. It was true, she realized, what folks said about the Last Frontier. The air felt purer than any other place she'd ever been.

Day by day she was learning how to dress for the Alaskan climate. Tonight she had taken great care with her attire. She had decided on a black turtleneck sweater, a pair of black thermal leggings and a cranberry-colored parka. A pair of genuine Alaskan Lovely boots completed the outfit. The boots had been delivered to her house courtesy of Beulah. The gesture had been so thoughtful and kind. She felt very grateful that she'd landed in a town filled with sweet-natured people who never stopped going out of their way for her. Just this morning Rusty the mechanic had reached out to her, telling her that his repairs on her truck would be completed by tomorrow. He'd even offered to take her out on the icy roads for a few driving lessons. It had been such a heartwarming gesture, especially when Rusty told her he'd taught all of his four daughters how to drive on snow-slickened Alaskan roads.

Each act of kindness made her feel one step closer to becoming part of the Owl Creek community. It would make all the difference in the world to her if she was embraced by the residents. And she would try her best to reciprocate, even though she was having a bit of trouble opening up. She was so afraid of making another misstep and arousing suspicion.

Isabelle had graciously accepted a ride to town from one of her staff members, Lissa Montgomery. She hadn't bothered to ask Connor, since she already felt so indebted to him for all of his transportation assistance. She didn't want to make him feel as if he was her permanent chauffeur. And what if he'd brought a date tonight? She would have felt like an awkward third wheel. The idea of it made her shudder.

She could see him across the way, talking with two men she recognized from her first visit to the Snowy Owl Diner. The three men were all extremely animated. If she had to guess, Isabelle would say they were close friends of his. They seemed so comfortable in each other's presence. That's what she hoped to find here in town. A friend she could laugh with and share special moments with.

"Ella! I'm so thrilled you could make it!" Sage, accompanied by Piper and a striking woman with warm brown skin and a lovely smile, strode over to her. Sage leaned in to envelop her in a tight hug.

Isabelle grinned. "I'm happy to be here. I was just contemplating whether to grab some hot apple cider or a hot cocoa."

"I'd go for the hot cocoa," Piper said. "It's straight from the chocolate factory."

"And indescribably yummy," the other woman added.

Sage introduced the woman. "This is Rachel Lawson. Rachel, this is Ella Perez."

"Nice to meet you," Rachel said, extending her mittened hand.

"You as well," Isabelle said, recognizing the woman's name as that of Iris's daughter-in-law.

"Why don't we get some of the hot chocolate?" Piper suggested. "I've been on my feet all day at the diner. I need a little pick-me-up."

Rachel looped her arm through Piper's in a show of support. "Aww. You deserve it."

As they walked toward the concession stand, Isabelle fielded questions about how she was acclimating to life in Owl Creek.

"Every day gets a little easier. The weather and the lack of sunlight are the two hardest challenges. I love working at the chocolate shop. And I'm not just saying that because your family owns it, Sage," she teased, drawing laughter from the three women.

Sage nodded. "I'm glad you're settling in so nicely."

"Everyone has been very welcoming," Isabelle answered. It still astounded her how the townsfolk were being so warm and helpful.

"Are you single?" Rachel asked. Although the question was a bit abrupt, Rachel exuded an air of kindness that made the inquiry palatable.

"Very much so," Isabelle said. "I haven't had a boyfriend in years," she admitted. For so long Isabelle had thrown herself into her work at the club, never stopping to acknowledge how her hectic work schedule and unorthodox hours had made a relationship impossible.

"Something tells me you might not be single for long," Rachel said with a knowing look etched on her face.

Isabelle quickly spoke up. The last thing she needed or wanted was prodding about her romantic life. "I'm not really looking for a relationship."

Piper let out a loud chuckle. "That's what I said right before I fell in love with my best friend. Now we're getting married in a few weeks."

"Life and love has a way of changing all of our plans," Sage said. "None of us were looking for love, but it sure found us."

Piper and Rachel both nodded their heads in agreement.

"We could put our heads together and make you a match!" Rachel said in a voice brimming with exuberance.

"That would be so much fun!" Piper said with a squeal.

"And since we know everyone in town, we could really home in on the best prospects," Sage added. Excitement hung in the air as the women hatched a plan for Isabelle's love life.

Isabelle shook her head. "I hate to rain on your parade, but I can't think of anything that I'd dislike more than a fix-up. I've been on some blind dates that were the stuff of nightmares. I promised myself I'd never go down that road again."

Isabelle didn't miss the look of disappointment stamped on all three faces. They sounded so well-meaning. She knew they were trying to do something nice for her. Shame threatened to swallow her up. But none of them had any idea that she wasn't like them. Her whole foundation in Owl Creek had been built on lies. Who would want to be in a relationship with a woman who couldn't even tell the truth about her own name?

"I'm sorry," she apologized. "Right now, I just want to focus on my job and getting acclimated to Alaskan living."

"Don't fret on our account," Rachel said. "You're a beautiful woman, Ella. You radiate pure positivity." She winked at her. "You'll be just fine."

As they stood in line and ordered their cocoa, Isabelle thought about what her new friends had suggested. Though a part of her would love to be coupled up, it just wouldn't be fair for her to become involved with someone when she couldn't be honest with him about being in the Witness Protection Program. It was hard to imagine living happily-ever-after without complete truth and transparency.

*And ye shall know the truth, and the truth shall make you free.* It was one of Isabelle's favorite Bible passages. Lately, she had been reciting it several times a week and drawing strength from it. She still harbored a little kernel of hope that her situation might change one day. Every night she prayed to get her life back.

Isabelle let out a ragged sigh. Her life here in town would be so different if she wasn't in Alaska under the guise of being a completely different person. What would it be like, she wondered, to be as carefree as Sage, Rachel and Piper? They all seemed to lead such happy and contented lives, free of problems or worries. A feeling of envy rose up inside her. She missed the days when her biggest concern was whether she was going to get a raise at work. It was hard not to wish for simpler days when she didn't have to struggle to keep her story straight or look over her shoulder in fear.

And it was even more difficult to imagine being drawn toward someone in Owl Creek other than Connor. Even though she knew better than to try to pursue anything romantic with him, she couldn't deny his massive appeal or her own excitement whenever they were together. She wasn't sure there was a man in Owl Creek who could compare to him.

Connor stood back and surveyed all of the revelry taking place in front of him. He was grinning so widely the sides of his mouth were beginning to feel the strain.

There were so many people who'd come out tonight to support the dog mushing event. It's what he loved most about Owl Creek. The townsfolk truly loved gatherings where they could socialize and support one another. All the proceeds from this evening were going to support rescue dogs through the outreach of Best Friends, a local veterinary clinic in town owned by Maya Roberts.

Maya had recently returned to Owl Creek in order to take over the practice from her dad, Vance Roberts, who had made the decision to retire. So far, she was impressing everyone in town with her skill and generous heart. Her advocacy on behalf of rescue dogs had almost convinced him to adopt a four-legged companion. He wasn't sure Bear was ready for another dog in the house, but Connor still had his eye on adopting. Once his Siberian husky was better trained, Connor was going to reach out to Maya.

Try as he might, Connor couldn't manage to look away for long from Ella, who was standing with Sage, Rachel and Piper. His gaze kept veering back to her. Seeing the foursome amiably chatting made him happy. Ella needed connections in town in order to properly settle in to her new life. She couldn't befriend three more fabulous women than the ones she was with at the moment.

"So, why are you standing over here when Ella is over there? Clearly she's on your mind judging by the way you keep staring at her." Gabe jutted his chin in Ella's direction. Connor swung his gaze her way for what felt like the hundredth time. In her cranberry-colored parka, matching hat, boots and black leggings, she looked ready for the Alaskan elements. Fashionable and functional. Always stunning.

"I'm not staring. Can't a person just look around at the scenery?" Connor asked through gritted teeth.

"Did you bring her here tonight? I thought maybe she was your date," Braden inquired in a loud voice.

Connor glared at his brother. "We are not on a date. Can you keep your voice down? The last thing I need is to have everyone in town spreading that rumor around. You know how it goes."

Hank, Braden and Gabriel had identical grins on their faces. He could tell they didn't believe a word he was saying about not being paired up with Ella.

"Come on! It's not funny. We're not an item!" Connor protested.

"Not yet," Hank said. "But with your smooth moves, it's only a matter of time." He wiggled his eyebrows, garnering more laughter from the group.

"You guys don't know what you're talking about," he snapped. There were way too many reasons why a relationship between them was an impossibility. Above all else, he didn't trust her. There were too many red flags popping up. Her nervousness about having her ID picture taken had been bizarre.

"It's obvious you like her. You've had the same tell since we were in elementary school," Gabe said with a smirk.

Connor frowned at him. "What are you talking about?"

Braden pointed at his feet. "The way you rock back

and forth on your heels. It's a dead giveaway that you're into Ella. You've been doing it ever since she got here."

Gabe and Hank nodded in agreement.

Gabe placed his hand on Connor's shoulder. "I hate to break it to you, but two of the Three Amigos have settled down. And Braden will be married in no time at all. You might be next. You've got to be open to it, though," Gabe said. "Don't stick your head in the sand."

Connor let out a groan. It wasn't as if he hadn't already thought about the fact that Gabriel, Hank and Braden had all found the loves of their lives, while he'd been sitting on the sidelines. How could he forget when his mother kept hinting about his single status? It was beginning to grate on him. "I'm not in any rush to settle down. That's not my goal." He'd been using this stock excuse for years, but for some reason it no longer felt one hundred percent true. Seeing everyone else in his inner circle pair off had caused a shift inside him. He no longer wanted to walk through life alone.

"And that's fine," Hank conceded, "but it isn't like you not to pursue someone you're clearly interested in. You did tell us you wanted something more substantial in a relationship."

He couldn't deny the validity of Hank's words. Hank, Braden and Gabriel knew him so well. They were always able to see straight through him and all the way down to the parts of him he didn't always like to share with the world. He had no doubt they knew he'd been feeling alone lately.

There wouldn't be any harm in approaching Ella

this evening. They were friends after all. He'd been a bit surprised when she had turned down his offer for a ride into town tonight. He had been looking forward to spending more time in her company. He let out a sigh. It was silly for him to be disappointed about something so trivial, yet he couldn't deny how he felt. The car ride would have provided another opportunity to get to know her. Despite his doubts about Ella, he wanted to find out more about her life in Flagstaff and all the small details about her likes and dislikes. Was red her favorite color? Did she envision living out the rest of her days here in Owl Creek? What type of music did she enjoy?

Even though all of his instincts were warning him to steer clear of Ella, he couldn't deny he felt a strong pull in her direction. He vacillated between believing she was hiding something terrible in her past and thinking she was some kind of wonderful. One way or the other, he intended to find out which one was the truth.

"They say the moon is bigger here in Alaska."

Isabelle turned around at the sound of Connor's voice. Although she had glimpsed him from across the way, nothing compared to seeing him up close. Dressed in a pair of dark colored jeans and a navy blue parka that almost matched his eyes, Connor looked casual yet rugged. For the millionth time since she'd arrived in Owl Creek, Isabelle wondered how he had managed to stay single. No doubt it was by choice. She didn't think many women could resist him.

He grinned down at her. "And brighter."

Isabelle felt a smile tugging at the corners of her mouth. "I won't argue with you on that, although I've always heard that the moon is the same size regardless of where you are in the world."

"Rule number one. As a new resident of Owl Creek, you shouldn't question town folklore."

Isabelle laughed. "I see." She held up her mittened hands. "I promise not to ever question Alaskan lore again."

"So, are you having a good time?"

"So far it's been a really fun night. I've never been part of a small-town community before, so it's quite interesting to see how everyone comes together for an event."

"Owl Creekians are friendly, if a bit nosy. Don't be surprised if you're asked about your great-grandmother's little sister's second husband."

She burst out laughing. "Owl Creekians? Is that really a thing? You're kidding, right?"

Connor folded his arms across his chest. "O ye of little faith. I'll have you know that one of my ancestors, Barnabus North, came up with that particular name for the townsfolk."

"B-Barnabus?" Isabelle sputtered, devolving into a fit of the giggles. Unable to stop herself, she ducked her head and continued laughing. "I'm so sorry for laughing at your ancestor, but that name sounds a million years old."

"Thanks a lot. That's my middle name," Connor said, his expression shuttered.

"Woops!" Isabelle raised a hand to cover her mouth.

"I'm really putting my foot in my mouth tonight, aren't I?"

A sly smile began to spread across his face. "Gotcha. I'm just teasing you. I was named after my father. Connor Nathaniel North."

"I like it," she said. "It's a bit more distinguished than Barnabus."

"Hey! Leave Barnabus alone. He was a very distinguished town founder. Just ask Beulah. She happens to be coming this way."

When she turned in the direction of Connor's gaze, Isabelle instantly spotted Beulah, resplendent in a peony pink ensemble. She was walking alongside an older man, who Isabelle assumed was her husband. Another couple was with them, holding hands and making a beeline toward Connor.

Beulah's voice rang out as she greeted her. "Ella! You came! I'm so glad you decided to join us."

"Good to see you as well, Beulah. That color looks lovely on you," Isabelle said.

"That's what I told her," the older gentleman said as he reached out to take Beulah's hand. "I'm Jennings North, Beulah's husband. I've heard a lot about you, Ella. All good things of course." He stuck his hand out and shook hers with vigor. "Welcome to Owl Creek, my dear."

"Thank you," she murmured, surprised to discover he knew who she was. It made her happy to know Beulah had spoken about her in a positive light. She thought Beulah and Jennings just might be the most adorable couple in town.

"These are my parents, Willa and Nate," Connor said, nodding in the other couple's direction. "This is Ella Perez. She came to Owl Creek by way of Arizona to work for us."

Connor's parents looked like they had just stepped out of a healthy Alaskan living ad. Willa bore a striking resemblance to Sage, although her eyes were a bright blue while Sage's were brown. They shared similar features and nearly identical noses. Willa was a petite woman who was dwarfed next to her tall husband. Nate North was just as handsome as his son. With his full head of dark hair and an athletic physique, he appeared quite youthful. Both were smiling in her direction, which immediately calmed her unease at meeting so many people all at once.

"Thank you for coming to work for North Star Chocolates," Nate said, his eyes full of warmth. "We're always grateful for fresh ideas and innovations."

"You're a lovely addition to Owl Creek," Willa gushed. She sent Connor a pointed look, which caused Isabelle to squirm a little bit. It was clear Connor's mother also appeared to have her matchmaker hat on. What was it with small Alaskan towns and people feeling the need to pair people up?

After exchanging pleasantries, they heard an announcement through the loudspeaker that the dog mushing event would be starting soon. Isabelle found herself swept up in the crowd as everyone moved toward another area of the woods. For a moment it was a bit disorienting, until she felt Connor reach for her hand. Although she sensed he was simply ensuring

# FREE BOOKS GIVEAWAY

2 FREE ROMANCE BOOKS!

2 FREE SUSPENSE BOOKS!

# GET UP TO FOUR FREE BOOKS & TWO FREE GIFTS WORTH OVER $20!

We pay for everything!

## Complete the survey below and return it today to receive up to 4 FREE BOOKS and FREE GIFTS guaranteed!

# FREE BOOKS GIVEAWAY
## Reader Survey

**1**

**Do you prefer books which reflect Christian values?**

○ YES    ○ NO

**2**

**Do you share your favorite books with friends?**

○ YES    ○ NO

**3**

**Do you often choose to read instead of watching TV?**

○ YES    ○ NO

**YES!** Please send me my Free Rewards, consisting of **2 Free Books from each series I select** and **Free Mystery Gifts**. I understand that I am under no obligation to buy anything, as explained on the back of this card.

❏ **Love Inspired® Romance Larger-Print** (122/322 IDL GQ36)
❏ **Love Inspired® Suspense Larger-Print** (107/307 IDL GQ36)
❏ **Try Both** (122/322 & 107/307 IDL GQ4J)

| | |
|---|---|
| FIRST NAME | LAST NAME |

ADDRESS

| | |
|---|---|
| APT.# | CITY |

| | |
|---|---|
| STATE/PROV. | ZIP/POSTAL CODE |

EMAIL ❏ Please check this box if you would like to receive newsletters and promotional emails from Harlequin Enterprises ULC and its affiliates. You can unsubscribe anytime.

LI/LIS-520-FBG21

she wasn't left behind, it was hard to deny how good it felt to have his hand around hers. It gave her a feeling of safety, as if Connor was protecting her from harm. She knew it wasn't romantic, but for a moment Isabelle imagined what it might be like to hold hands with Connor for real.

*Stop dreaming about things that won't ever come to pass. It's a complete waste of time.* She needed to be firmly rooted in reality.

By the time they reached the area where the mushers were located with their sled dogs, a large crowd had assembled. There was a buzz of excitement in the air.

"What exactly are we going to see?" Isabelle asked. It was slightly embarrassing, but what she knew about dog mushing would easily fit on a postage stamp.

"This is just a demonstration of how dog mushers and their teams perform. They're all going to race along the trail and back to give us an idea of what the longer races look like and how the dogs work as a team to get the job done," Connor explained. "We're raising money tonight to go toward shelter dogs."

"That's a wonderful cause. My family had a Great Dane for twelve years. She was a shelter dog. Her name was Daisy, and she was amazing."

"Great Danes are a handful, much like huskies. Bear keeps me on my toes."

"Yes, they are, but Daisy was a sweetheart. We lost her a few years ago. I still miss her."

"Sounds like you might be in the market for a shelter dog. The vet clinic is doing adoptions all month, just in case you're interested."

Adopting a dog! The idea of doing so hadn't even crossed her mind, although she knew it would do wonders for her loneliness. But what if she had to abruptly leave Owl Creek and move to another location? There was no telling how many different towns she might relocate to. Would it be difficult for a pet to be moved around so much if the need arose?

Isabelle shrugged. "It's something to think about," she said, not wanting to give up on the idea so soon. She would love to have a stable life where owning a dog was possible. Maybe she really could put roots down in Owl Creek without having to look over her shoulder all the time. Perhaps it was possible to live a normal life.

Connor pointed toward one of the mushers. "See the guy in the front wearing the red parka? That's Ace Reynolds. He's an exceptional dog musher," Connor said. "One of the best."

"I heard he grew up here in Owl Creek."

"He sure did. Folks here in town are awfully proud of him. He's going to compete in the Iditarod this March."

Isabelle wrinkled her nose. "The Iditarod? It sounds familiar, but I have to confess that I don't know anything about it."

He winked at her. "As a born and bred Alaskan, I've grown up on it." He let out a chuckle. "The Iditarod is a yearly sled dog race that stretches from Anchorage to Nome. It takes place over the course of eight days or so. It's pretty intense and only for those who are dedicated to the craft. When I was a kid, I wanted so badly to be a dog musher and compete in the Iditarod. Ace was born into it. Both his father and his grandfather competed, so I guess one could say it's in his blood. He's spent so much of his life training and raising the pups. I can't really imagine him doing anything else."

"Are the dogs safe?" she asked. "It's hard to imagine them racing in such a cold climate. Or for such long stretches of time."

"You'll never meet anyone as passionate about dogs as Ace. He treats all of them very well. They're his family."

"That's good to know," Isabelle said, her heart warming at his words.

"These guys are the best of the best," Connor said. "It's a pretty tight-knit group. Some are them are retired, but a few, like Ace, are still competing. It can be very lucrative, but mushers like Ace aren't in it for the paycheck."

Isabelle nodded. Connor was giving her quite an education. It was an interesting sport with a rich history in Alaska.

"I think they're getting ready to begin," Connor said, pointing toward the starting line. "The teams are going to go two at a time."

Isabelle turned back toward the action as a horn began to blow and a voice announced that the event was about to begin. Since Connor had given her the background on Ace, her eyes were trained on him and his team. When it was his turn to race, the crowd noisily cheered him on, distinguishing him as the clear favorite in the lineup.

As Ace and his team came flying down the path, the noise from the crowd was deafening. A feeling of exhilaration gripped her. The speed and finesse of the mushers and their dogs were spectacular. With the wind blowing in her hair and a fierce chill in the air, Isabelle almost felt as if she was riding on the sled herself. It was no small wonder why this sport was so popular and drew such large crowds. It was an invigorating event, one she never could have experienced back home.

As all the dog mushers crossed the finish line, loud applause broke out among the crowd. Isabelle joined in, clapping enthusiastically.

"That was really incredible," she said.

"There's nothing quite like the first time you see it." Connor flashed her a smile. "It's the official sport of Alaska. Cool, huh?"

"I had no idea," she admitted. "But it makes sense. I can't think of a more thrilling event to watch."

"It's pretty cool seeing it through your eyes." Connor's own eyes twinkled as he looked down at her. His voice injected a feeling of coziness into their conversation. For a moment she almost forgot that they were at a public place and surrounded by an entire community. Everything else faded away.

Was Connor flirting with her or simply being nice? Did it even matter, considering the albatross hanging around her neck? For all intents and purposes she wasn't a free woman. Her past in Miami shadowed her every single day. It never let her forget her limitations.

"I'm really happy to be here," she said lamely, wishing she could simply let loose and go with the flow. But she couldn't, and anger rose up inside of her. She had witnessed a brutal murder that had put her own life in jeopardy. And now, because of it, she had to steer clear of the one man in all of Alaska who made her feel as if good things might be coming her way.

Connor stayed where he was, mere inches away. "If you're hungry we can check out the food truck. They serve a mean gumbo if you want to ward off the chill in the air. There's also a melt-in-your-mouth chocolate bread to satisfy even the biggest sweet tooth." His smile served as an invitation. "What do you say?"

She should make an excuse and get as far away from Connor as possible. Perhaps she could tell him she needed to check in with Lissa about what time she wanted to leave the event. But she was hungry and the fare sounded scrumptious. A myriad of thoughts raced through her mind. Before she could rein herself in, Isabelle blurted out, "I'd love to check out the food truck. I haven't eaten since this morning and my stomach has been grumbling so loudly it sounds like a grizzly bear."

"Well, that sounds serious. We better do something about that right away," Connor replied. He held out his arm, and she looped hers through it as they headed off in the direction of the food truck. Although Isabelle knew she was heading into dangerous territory by spending time alone with Connor, she couldn't seem to help herself. He drew her in with the force of a magnet. Just for tonight she was going to enjoy herself with him, secure in the knowledge that it was only a moment in time. When tomorrow morning rolled around, Isabelle would revert back to her plan to stay away from him.

Getting close to a man like Connor would only make her life in the Witness Protection Program way more complicated. As it was, Isabelle felt as if she was trying to keep her head above water with one arm tied behind her back.

## Chapter Eight

Connor tried to avoid the curious stares and whispers of the townsfolk. He could feel dozens of eyes focused on him and Ella as they dug into their food. His love life had always been the subject of much speculation in Owl Creek. Since Ella was a newcomer to town, it added a whole new dynamic to their gossip. While a part of him wanted to shoot them dirty looks, he knew taking the high road was more practical. All of his life Connor had been aware of his position in Owl Creek as a member of the North family. As the future CEO of the town's main industry, it was his responsibility to act in a dignified manner.

"Do I have something on my face?" Ella asked him. A frown line marred her brow.

Connor studied Ella for a moment. She looked pretty perfect as far as he could tell. "Not that I can see. Why do you ask?"

She darted a look around them. "Quite a few people are gawking at me. I thought maybe I had chocolate on my nose or something." She took another bite of the sweet treat, emitting a satisfied sound as she munched on it.

Connor stifled a chuckle. She really had tucked into the chocolate bread, and he relished watching her enjoy it so enthusiastically. Ella seemed to have no idea that the two of them were the object of the town's curiosity. "They're not staring at you. It's the fact that we're together that interests them," he acknowledged with a grimace. "It's kind of a town hobby."

Ella's eyes widened. "Oh. I see," she said in a surprised voice.

"I'm sorry. I know it must be a little awkward, but certain folks in a small town love to speculate if they see two people hanging out." He tamped down his irritation. Connor didn't want Ella to feel uncomfortable or to think that the townsfolk were small-minded gossips.

"I get it," she said. "I grew up with a Brazilian grandmother." She ducked her head and giggled. "She and my great-aunts put me under the microscope my whole life. If I was even spotted with a boy, he was automatically my boyfriend. I understand how this all works, even though it can be frustrating."

"I know they don't mean any harm," Connor said. "Much like your grandmother and aunts, I imagine. Because you're new in town, they want to know more about you. And—" he paused dramatically "—the whole town wants to marry me off."

Ella let out a surprised sound. "Wow. So they're trying to march you down the aisle, huh?" The corners of her mouth were twitching with amusement. He liked seeing this lighthearted side of her. Perhaps he'd simply been picking up on her nervousness about relocating to Alaska up to this point. Tonight she seemed as if she was coming out of her shell.

"Yes. It's an open secret here in town. It doesn't help that my brother, Braden, is getting hitched soon. You know how that is. People have started to look at me cross-eyed because both my younger siblings have settled down."

"That's a bit of pressure, isn't it?"

Connor shrugged. He didn't want to admit that lately it hadn't been as easy to shrug it off. He spotted Sage, Hank and his niece, Addie, standing across the way. Whenever he was in their presence, Connor wondered what it would be like to fall so deeply in love with someone that you wanted nothing more than to devote your life to that person. He'd never felt anything remotely like that.

"It is, but I suppose it's a bit of a compliment. Everyone in town has known me since the day I was born. They really want me to be happy."

"Aren't you happy now?" Ella asked. She was gazing at him intently, as if she really cared about his welfare.

"I'm very content with my life, but when I see my sister and her family, I wonder how much better things could be," he admitted, jerking his chin in Sage's direction. His sister was holding Addie in her arms while Hank was making her giggle by tickling her. Anyone could see that they were a picture-perfect family.

He'd surprised himself by being so honest with Ella. Maybe it was easier to admit something of that nature to someone he didn't know very well. Somehow it took the pressure off.

"They do look blissful," Ella said. "Their little girl is precious. She's the spitting image of her daddy."

"That's my niece, Addie. When Sage met Hank, he was a single father, so my sister became a mother when they got married. She fell in love with Hank and got Addie as a beautiful bonus."

"They're such a sweet family. Sage looks like she's a great mom to Addie. She's so loving and attentive. And a schoolteacher to boot. She's like the Mary Poppins of mothers."

The image of his sister swinging down from the sky with an umbrella brought a smile to his face. Connor shifted his gaze in Sage's direction. "She really is incredible, isn't she? It's been amazing getting to know her."

Isabelle furrowed her brow. "What do you mean? Shouldn't you already know her? She's your sister."

Connor let out a ragged sigh. "I didn't grow up with her. This is going to sound pretty wild, but she was kidnapped from our home when she was only three months old. She was missing for twenty-five years. We were only reunited with her a short while ago. Thankfully, we've all bonded, but it's been a tough journey."

Isabelle gasped. Clearly she hadn't known about his family's tragedy. Sometimes it seemed to him as if the entire world knew about what had transpired. When Sage had returned to Owl Creek last year it had coincided with the twenty-fifth anniversary of her abduction. As a result, there had been an abundance of media attention. The headlines had broadcast the story of Sage's return all over the country.

"I do recall hearing the news story, but I didn't pay much attention to it at the time. I can't believe that was Sage."

"The woman who stole her from us actually ended up raising Sage," Connor explained. Although he didn't mind telling Ella about his family's tragic past, it still hurt to discuss it. Jane Duncan, the kidnapper, had passed away last year, but he still harbored anger toward the woman who had perpetrated such a heinous act.

"I imagine something like that would devastate your whole family," Isabelle said. "For the life of me I can't imagine how my own family would have weathered such a storm. A stolen baby must've led to such unimaginable loss and uncertainty."

"It did. The tragedy was never far from us," he acknowledged. "We could be enjoying a wonderful Christmas celebration when it would rear up and bring us all crashing down to reality. Even as a small child I felt it. There was a void in our family that could never be filled until Lily returned."

Isabelle frowned. "Lily?"

"That's what my parents named Sage at birth. By the time she came back to us, she wasn't Lily anymore. The woman who stole her ended up raising her as Sage."

Isabelle made a tutting sound. "The name change

must have been a painful reminder of the abduction, although Sage's return is an incredible blessing."

Connor nodded, then bowed his head. "We all prayed for years for her return. I don't think my folks ever gave up hope. God brought her back to Owl Creek so we could make our family complete. Now we can't imagine how we made it through all those years without her being with us. It just feels so natural."

"I'm feeling a bit ashamed of myself," Ella admitted.

"For what?" he asked. He froze for a moment, wondering if she was about to confess something about her past.

"Ever since I met your sister, I've been viewing her as this perfect woman living a storybook existence." She let out a hollow laugh. "In reality she was an abducted child who was separated from her real family for decades. I can't begin to wrap my head around what that knowledge did to her."

"Sage has been through a lot," he acknowledged. "There's no way you could have known about the burdens she's carried. She walks through life radiating positivity. We like to think that God was with her for every step of her journey. He gave her the strength to seek out her family." He shook his head. It still stunned him to reflect on Sage's courage and tenacity.

"She's way more incredible than I realized. And your family is, too. To endure such a devastating loss, then come together the way you've all done is awe-inspiring."

"I'm fortunate to have a really strong family. It took a little convincing to make me accept Sage as being

Lily, but she won me over. I think a big part of me didn't want to be crushed if it turned out she wasn't my sister." He let out a brittle laugh. "Every Christmas when I was a kid I used to insist on hanging up a stocking for my baby sister. At first I think it made my parents uncomfortable, but over time it became something special we did to hold her close to our hearts during the holiday season. Not that she was ever far from us. My family always believed she would come home to us."

"Faith," she murmured. "They believed in something they couldn't see or touch."

"Yes," he answered with a nod. "My folks never gave up on the notion that they would be with their Lily again. It taught me so much about holding fast to one's beliefs."

"Your family sounds incredible. I'd give anything to be with mine right now. Don't get me wrong," she quickly added, "I really value the opportunity to stretch my wings by working for your family's company. I suppose I'm just a bit homesick."

Connor heard the catch in Ella's voice, and it threatened to knock him off his feet. There was so much yearning in her voice. It made him ache for her. She sounded vulnerable and a little bit lost.

He needed to take a step back from this woman, because with every moment they spent together she reeled him in more. And Connor wasn't sure he had the wherewithal to put a stop to it. She'd gotten under his skin. All he could think about was getting closer to her when he knew he should be putting distance between them.

\* \* \*

The words had slipped past her lips before she could stop herself. Talking about her family was off-limits. She was really talking up a storm tonight and letting things slip that she shouldn't. She prayed Connor didn't ask her any questions. She really didn't want to have to fabricate a story. It was becoming increasingly difficult to justify her lies. It wasn't making her feel any better by telling herself that the WITSEC program and the danger she was in mandated it.

"Invite them to visit. This town will roll out the red carpet for them. Visiting Alaska makes for a nice family getaway." Connor sounded so excited about the possibility of her family visiting.

"That's not possible," she murmured. Their eyes met and Connor's were full of questions. "They're not in my life at the moment," she admitted. The enormity of the situation came crashing over her. Despite being at an event crowded with people, Isabelle was achingly alone. There was no one who would wish her a happy birthday or bring her chicken noodle soup when she was sick.

Tears pooled in her eyes. *Don't cry*, she told herself. Becoming emotional would only draw more questions from Connor. How could she ever explain herself? Isabelle felt moisture on her cheeks. Despite her best efforts, the tears were flowing. Before she knew it, he was whisking her away from the main area and toward a copse of trees, where they were almost hidden from the festivities.

"Oh, Ella. Please don't cry. It's going to be all right."

Connor quickly swallowed up the distance between them and placed his arms around her. She let out a muffled sob against his chest. She felt his hand moving in a circular motion on her back as he murmured soothing words. It was so comforting to be held by him. Isabelle breathed in the woodsy, masculine scent of him. Although she knew it wasn't possible, she didn't want this moment to end. It had been a long time since someone had made her feel safe and protected. For so long now she had been keeping a stiff upper lip and trying to protect herself and her family members from harm. It was nice to take shelter, if only for a little while, in Connor's arms.

After a few moments, Isabelle pulled away from him. Embarrassment made her cheeks feel flushed. She'd been clinging to him as if he was a life preserver.

"I'm so sorry," she said, dabbing at her eyes with the hem of her sleeve.

Compassion flared in the depths of his blue eyes. "There's no need to apologize. Clearly you love your family. Don't ever give up on making things right with the ones you care about."

She shook her head. "It's not likely to happen. We might never be a part of each other's lives ever again."

He narrowed his gaze as he looked at her. "You're talking to someone who was reunited with his missing sister after twenty-five years. Don't stop believing that you'll reconcile with them. With God nothing's impossible."

Even though Connor didn't understand her specific circumstances, his words were still powerful. Deep down in her heart, Isabelle believed she would see her family again, despite what she'd been told by law enforcement. At moments like this one, it was hard to keep believing. She prayed on it each and every day.

Connor was a man of faith, which was refreshing.

He reached out and smoothed his gloved hand across her cheek. "You can talk to me if you need someone to lean on. I've been told on occasion that I'm a good listener."

How Isabelle wished she could confide in Connor. Would he understand what she'd been through after being a witness to a violent murder? Or would he be horrified by her involvement in WITSEC? Either way, she was forbidden from disclosing it to him.

He represented everything solid and upstanding. Connor made her want things she knew were out of her reach. But even though Isabelle understood that Connor didn't factor into her plans, it didn't make her yearning any less.

Perhaps it was wishful thinking, but the way he was looking at her made her believe he was seconds away from kissing her.

Their eyes locked and held. He felt something humming and pulsing in the air between them. Connor knew if he dipped his head down a few inches his lips would be on Ella's. He was tempted to kiss her. He imagined her lips would be soft and inviting. They might just taste like the hot cocoa she'd been drinking. Instead of doing so, he sucked in a deep breath. It was too soon to kiss Ella, despite how badly he wanted to do it. He was still trying to decide if she was hiding something or if he was jumping to conclusions about her.

She was pretty amazing with her compassionate insight into his family's devastation and trauma. And she was opening up more and more. She didn't feel like such a stranger anymore. She'd told him about her family dog even though it had clearly been a painful topic. Maybe he just needed to be more patient.

He didn't know if kissing her would give him clarity, but he was willing to give it a try. *Just go for it*, he told himself. He inched closer and leaned down toward her.

"Connor!"

The sound of his name being called had him instinctively moving away from Ella. He wanted to protect her privacy as well as his own. He didn't have a single doubt in his mind about the town gossip that would ensue if he was spotted kissing Ella. The abrupt interruption made him feel as if someone had poured a bucket of cold water over him. The mood had been ruined.

Much to his surprise, his grandparents were standing a few feet away in the clearing.

"Beg our pardons for the interruption." Beulah sent a pointed look in her husband's direction. "I daresay we have bad timing."

"I'll say," Connor mumbled under his breath. Disappointment washed over him now that the moment had slipped through his fingers.

He darted a glance at Ella. Her cheeks were flushed.

Instinct told him it had nothing to do with the frosty temperature. The almost kiss hung in the air between them. He was trying to pay attention to the conversation with his grandparents, but his thoughts kept veering to Ella's kissable pink lips. "We wanted to pass along a message to Ella," Jennings said sheepishly. "Sorry about the intrusion."

"No worries," Connor said, placing his hand on his grandfather's shoulder. He couldn't quite put his finger on it, but Jennings looked so much more vital these days. He had been a virtual shut-in after the kidnapping of his grandchild. Only recently had he begun to venture out into the world. Connor felt gratified that he had rebounded so well.

"Ella, the young lady who drove you over here tonight had a medical emergency," Beulah explained. "She was covered in hives."

"Oh, no," Ella said, her face crumpling. "What happened?"

"It seems Lissa had an allergic reaction to something she ate," Jennings explained. "She had to leave so she could get an EpiPen shot at the clinic."

Ella raised a hand to her throat. "That's so scary. She brings one in to work with her every day. Is she going to be all right?"

Beulah patted her on the shoulder. "She's in good hands. One of the town's most eligible bachelors stepped in and drove her to the clinic after Rachel Lawson looked her over. I'm wondering if God is trying to push those two together." Beulah's wide grin threatened to take over her entire face. Connor arched an eyebrow in her direction. Sometimes his grandmother's matchmaking goals were a bit over-the-top.

"Grandmother, let's focus on Lissa's health rather than her social life," Connor said.

Beulah sent him a surprised look. "I apologize if I sounded insensitive, but I have a very good feeling about those two."

Jennings reached out and clasped his wife's hands in his own. "You always do, my dear. You always do."

Beulah had a habit of matchmaking, but her attempts at bringing couples together had a dismal success rate. Not a single one of her matches had even come close to being a successful couple. And yet she persisted.

"Your heart is in the right place, Beulah," Ella said. Connor could tell Ella's comment pleased his grandmother. She was practically beaming from the praise.

"Let me take you home, Ella," Connor offered. "I think the event is winding down."

Ella finally glanced over at him. She'd been studiously avoiding his gaze ever since his grandparents had shown up. "Thanks. I'd appreciate it. I'm going to call Lissa later to make sure she's all right," Ella added.

"How kind of you," Beulah said. "Please keep us posted."

"I will," Ella said. "She's a real sweetheart."

As they walked as a foursome out into the main area of the town green, Connor noted that the crowd had thinned considerably. Although he'd wanted to catch up with his old friend Ace, a general scan of the area indicated he may have already departed.

Connor, along with Ella, said good-night to his grandparents and swiftly made his way over to his truck. He'd parked it on the street right by the Sheriff's office. Once they were both inside the vehicle, Connor turned on the radio in the hopes of erasing the tension that hung in the air.

Ella hadn't said two words to him in the last ten minutes. He wondered whether she was simply worried about Lissa or pondering the fact that he'd almost kissed her. If it was the latter, Connor had no way of knowing whether his kiss would have been well received. For all he knew she might not have been receptive to it. Maybe his grandparents had rescued him from embarrassment.

Perhaps not kissing Ella had been for the best, considering his reservations about her. It wouldn't be wise to go down a romantic road with all these questions about her that continued to crop up. He kept telling himself that he wanted something steady in his personal life. It wouldn't be wise to go down that road with someone whom he wasn't sure he could trust.

Secrets had a way of coming out from the shadows into the light. His own life had taught him that valuable lesson, and it wasn't likely he would forget it anytime soon.

# Chapter Nine

Isabelle gazed out of the window as the Alaskan scenery flitted by her car window. A brilliant moon still hung in the sky, surrounded by dozens of twinkling stars. A graceful snowy owl swooped over the branches of a tree, causing Isabelle to let out a gasp of wonder. She had never seen one in person before, and it was a majestic sight. There were so many things she was experiencing in Alaska that she hadn't been exposed to before now. With each passing day, Isabelle was falling more and more in love with the little town of Owl Creek. Although she had never imagined ever calling it home, it now felt like one. It was a bittersweet realization, since she still yearned for Miami and the people she had left behind.

For the most part, the car ride home with Connor had been filled with awkward silences. Was Connor thinking about the fact that they'd almost shared a kiss? Probably not. Most likely it had been an impulsive act on his part, soon to be forgotten. Men didn't tend to analyze things the way women did.

A smile twitched at her lips at the memory of Beulah and Jennings when they'd interrupted them. Both had appeared sheepish, stunned and incredibly embarrassed. If she hadn't felt so awkward in the moment, Isabelle might have laughed out loud.

As Connor pulled into her driveway, Isabelle took a moment to drink in the coziness of her new abode. A single light shone from inside, lending the house an inviting warmth. There was another light by her front porch that served as a welcoming beacon. It gave her an added sense of security.

She turned toward Connor. "Thank you for bringing me home. Rusty is dropping off my truck in the morning, so I won't need a ride to work anymore." She looked up at him, suddenly feeling a bit bashful. More than ever, she now had an awareness of him as a man. A ruggedly handsome one at that. "I appreciate your kindness. It made things a lot easier for me."

"You're welcome," Connor said. "But I should be thanking you. Driving you made my days more interesting by far. I enjoyed all of our chats." The way he grinned at her made her limbs tremble. She took a slow, steadying breath. The more time she spent in his presence, the more she was tempted to toss her vow of staying away from him out of the window. Who wouldn't want to spend time with him? What woman wouldn't want to be kissed by Connor North?

"That's sweet of you to say, but I'm still grateful. Good night, Connor," she said, quickly opening the door and stepping down before he could come around and open it for her. She heard Connor's voice bidding her good-night, and she turned around to wave before making her way across her snowy walkway to the front door. Once she was inside, she peeked out the window to see Connor slowly driving away. Clearly he'd waited until she was safely in her home before taking off. A true gentleman.

She let out a sigh. Being around him was like sneaking a chocolate from a candy box that she knew she wasn't supposed to eat. In the world of confections, Connor was a truffle—unique, bold and memorable. If only things were different. If only she could be Isabelle rather than Ella.

Tonight they had almost shared a kiss. If Beulah and Jennings hadn't interrupted them, she was certain it would have happened, even if it would have been too soon.

A part of her had been relieved that they hadn't kissed, while another piece of her yearned to share a tender moment with him. Although she had never had a shortage of boyfriends, Isabelle couldn't ever remember feeling this way before. Excited. Nervous. She cared about him way more than she ever wanted to admit. Sharing even brief snatches of time in his presence lifted her up.

But there would be no more rides to and from work with Connor now that her truck had been fixed. Not sharing that special time with him would be a huge loss for her.

Connor was in a league of his own. He was funny

and easy to talk to. He was charming, but not in a cheesy way. He'd made her laugh so hard her stomach hurt, telling her stories about Beulah and growing up in the North family. It hurt to know how badly they must have all suffered due to Sage's abduction. Although Connor didn't know it, they'd each gone through trauma that resulted in lasting scars. Connor and his family had already endured the worst kind of pain imaginable as a result of lies and deception.

It had been heartwarming to see Sage, Hank and their child bonded as a loving family. Although it reminded her of everything she'd left behind and all the dreams she would have to forgo for her own future, it hadn't made her want to curl up in a ball and cry. It had given Isabelle hope. Maybe one day she could move past all the trauma from having witnessed a murder. Perhaps being in the Witness Protection Program wasn't the end for her.

*Please, Lord, help me stay positive so I can have the future I've always dreamed of having. I need to have faith in You and the promise of a new day. I need to keep believing even when others tell me my dreams are not going to come to fruition.*

Earlier today she had resisted the strong urge to reach out to her family by phone. She'd ached to hear the sound of their voices and to let them know that she was doing all right. Isabelle worried about her parents and the toll the entire situation had taken on them. Her family had no idea that WITSEC had relocated her to Alaska. Disclosing such information would have risked her status in the program and potentially brought dan-

ger into her life. It would have erased all the efforts of
Marshal Kramer and his team to create a new identity
for her in Owl Creek.

Her loved ones were safer not knowing anything
about her location, even though it hurt to feel so dis-
connected from them. She drew strength from her family and the Lord. God was still beside her even though
she was all alone. It didn't stop her heart from aching,
but He sustained her as nothing else could.

It had taken all the courage in the world not to give
in and make the call to her family. All of her life she'd
played by the rules. Working at the night club had been
her first act of rebellion, one she'd lived to dearly regret.
Her parents hadn't approved of Club Oasis or its drinking and party atmosphere. Now she had to live with the
consequences of her decision. It wouldn't be fair to get
involved with anyone and have him bear her burdens.

Connor's handsome face flashed before her eyes.
Just remembering the way their eyes had locked earlier caused her pulse to skitter. She liked Connor North
way more than she wanted to. He was growing on her
and she was powerless to stop it. He represented all of
the things she had once dreamed of in a romantic partner. But he was off-limits. Connor had already been
put through enough turmoil in his life. By becoming
involved with him, Isabelle would only be dragging
him into another terrible situation filled with half-
truths and lies.

The next morning, Connor drove to the factory all
by himself. It felt strange not to have Ella beside him

in the passenger seat, even though he'd been doing the ride solo for many years before she'd arrived in Owl Creek. Suddenly, it felt like something was missing. It didn't take a rocket scientist to figure out it was Ella's sweet presence. The knowledge hit him squarely in the face. His feelings for Ella were growing incrementally each day.

Connor hit the brakes as a caribou loped across the road roughly fifty feet ahead of him. He took a moment to admire the graceful creature. He hoped Ella didn't run into any animals on her way into work. The last thing she needed was to have another wreck or be frightened at the sight of an animal.

*It's not your problem*, he reminded himself. Ever since Ella arrived in town, Connor had made it his business to look out for her. As a result, he'd veered way over the line with regards to keeping a distance from her. Despite his gut instincts warning him about the newcomer to town, he'd continued to befriend her. Last night he'd almost kissed her!

Who was he kidding? he asked himself. Kissing Ella would have been amazing, even if he still harbored doubts about her past. It would have been a moment of discovery between them. Maybe then he could have figured out if his interest in her was reciprocated. As it was, he'd just been left with more doubts.

He felt a funny sensation in his chest at the thought of merely being friends with Ella. It wasn't what he wanted, but he couldn't be anything more than her friend with so many doubts still swirling around regarding the secrets she was keeping.

He didn't feel like his usual self as he made his way through the building. Although many employees called out to him as he walked by, Connor could only nod his head. Things couldn't go on this way. He needed to completely forget about growing their friendship into anything more meaningful.

Connor closed his office door behind him and settled behind his desk. For the next few hours he focused on work without talking to any of his colleagues. When something was bothering him, Connor tended to go inward. He'd always been this way, going back to childhood. Not even Gabe or Hank could penetrate his mood.

When a knock sounded on his door, Connor couldn't stifle his annoyance.

"Come in," he said gruffly. He didn't really care who was on the other side of the door. At the moment he was feeling grumpy and completely out of sorts.

"Well, good morning to you, too." At the sound of his grandmother's voice, Connor lifted his head. She was standing in the doorway dressed in a bright blue pantsuit that only Beulah could get away with. And for the life of him, he couldn't be aggravated when she was nearby.

"Morning, Grandmother." He glanced at the clock on his desk. "It's almost afternoon, though. I don't know where the time is going."

She was gazing at him with a look of compassion in her eyes. "I can tell you have a lot on your mind, but I won't pry," Beulah said.

"I'm just having an off day," he said. There was no

way he was going to talk to Beulah about Ella. The last thing he needed was to have his grandmother meddling in his personal life.

"All right," she said. "I'll take what you're saying at face value."

"What's up? You look like you're about to burst. Has something happened?" Connor asked. He knew this woman well. She was overjoyed about something and it showed.

"We've picked our latest employee of the week," she announced. "We printed up a certificate of distinction, and we're giving her a gift card and flowers."

"Who got it? I'm sure it'll brighten their day."

"It's Ella. I was wondering if you wanted to stop by the chocolate shop and tell her in person. She'll be thrilled to hear the news, I imagine, and get the recognition."

Hearing that Ella was being hailed by the company uplifted Connor's dark mood. It gave him a kick just thinking about her reaction to the news. But he didn't want to be near her right now. It was still confusing trying to figure out how he was going to stay solely in the friend zone with Ella. Steering clear of her might make it easier.

"Uh, I actually have a call later on. I can't do it, although I know the award will make her really happy."

Beulah appeared crestfallen. Her smile vanished and her brows knitted together. "I thought you and Ella were getting along like a house on fire, judging by last night." She fluttered her eyes.

He should have known his grandmother wouldn't let

what she'd witnessed last night go by without a comment. It wasn't in her nature. She had a tendency to meddle in the lives of her family members. He knew it came from a place of love, but at the moment it only added to his frustration. "I'm not even going to respond to that. There's nothing romantic between us. We're just friends."

Beulah arched an eyebrow. "That's even more reason to be the one to tell her the good news. It won't be the same if I send one of my employees over there who doesn't know Ella. It won't be as meaningful."

"It can't be helped," he said tersely. With every word Beulah uttered, Connor felt his willpower faltering. He would love to head over to the chocolate shop and surprise Ella with something encouraging like employee of the week. Was he being selfish by only considering his own feelings? Truthfully, he was protecting himself. He was getting in way too deep with his feelings for Ella.

"It might be a nice pick-me-up," Beulah said. "Not just for Ella, but for you as well. Get outside, take a nice walk in the fresh air. Give someone some good news. It might cheer you up."

Connor let out a sigh. He knew when Beulah sounded like this she wasn't going to give up until she got her way. He might as well save himself a colossal headache and agree to do as she'd requested. No matter how he tried to stay away from Ella, forces kept pushing him in her direction. He just had to stay strong. Connor would present the news to Ella as a friend. Nothing more.

"All right. I'll swing by the shop. Happy now?"

"I'm always happy when people do the right thing," she answered in a singsong voice. "Let me go back to my office and bring you the certificate and the goodies." Beulah sailed out the door with a spring to her step. She returned a few minutes later with a canvas bag. The bouquet of flowers was poking out of the top.

Before he changed his mind, Connor put his coat and boots on in preparation for the walk to Main Street. As he strode along, he had to admit that getting a dose of the crisp Alaskan air was good for him.

When he entered the store, Connor immediately noticed a commotion going on inside the normally orderly place of business. Kids were scattered everywhere. Connor's gaze immediately settled on Ella. She was bent over at the waist talking to a little girl whose lip was stuck out in a dramatic pout. Ella was speaking in a low voice, and although he couldn't hear what she was saying, he knew it was soothing. The little girl leaned in for a hug and wrapped her arms around Ella before darting off to join some pals. When Ella stood up, their eyes met across the shop. A hint of a smile played around her lips at the sight of him. That simple act buoyed him. Connor made his way to her side.

"Connor! What brings you here?" Ella asked. "As you can see, this place is jumping today with first-graders. Sage arranged a tour for her students." Ella's eyes twinkled. "Giving chocolate samples to six-year-olds is a bona fide way to make them happy."

Connor looked around the shop at all the happy little

faces. He let out a chuckle. "Sage might regret giving them candy before they head back to class."

Sage and another teacher were doing their best to quiet the kids down to a dull roar. His sister looked over and sent an apologetic look in Ella's direction. In return, Ella simply smiled.

"Only one piece of chocolate per child," Ella said. "That's the rule."

"A wise decision," he said. "I'm a big fan of the stuff, but too much of it can make children bounce off the walls."

Ella grinned. "That's what my sister always says." Once the words were out of her mouth, Ella's expression changed. All the light faded from her eyes, replaced by a somber expression.

Connor could see the sadness emanating from her eyes. He knew the source of it was homesickness. Braden had left Owl Creek for three years as a self-imposed penance for the accident that had killed Piper's father. He'd later confided in Connor about the deep sense of isolation he'd experienced due to missing his family members and friends. Connor imagined Ella felt the same way. He didn't want to ply her with questions about her sister or do anything to accentuate her sorrow.

"I came to ask you if you wanted to grab lunch." Connor blurted out the invitation. The words had poured out of his mouth like water from a faucet. Lunch? Where had that idea come from? All he'd been planning to do was to deliver the good news to Ella and then head back to the factory. It wasn't like him to veer so wildly off course. Evidently, this woman brought it out in him.

"I'd love to go to lunch," Ella said, smiling at him as she answered. "If you can wait fifteen minutes or so until Sage's class leaves."

"I can wait," he said with a nod. "I'll get out of your hair until the kids clear out." Connor beat a fast path to the door, stepping outside into the frosty air. As a cold breeze whipped across his face, Connor let it wash over him. All of a sudden he had no actual clue as to what he was doing. He wasn't used to acting so spontaneously. He'd always thought things out and acted in a deliberate manner.

*What am I doing?* Sharing a meal with Ella wasn't taking a step back as he'd vowed to do. He was getting in deeper and deeper without an exit strategy.

Sitting across from Connor at the Snowy Owl Diner was an unexpected development in Isabelle's day. To say she'd been surprised by his unannounced appearance at the chocolate shop would be a major understatement. Try as she might, Isabelle couldn't convince herself that she should have turned his invitation down. Being around him made her feel good. And it was flattering that someone like Connor would ask her out to lunch when most of the women in town would jump at the chance. Working at the shop gave her an opportunity to listen to the chatter of the customers and her staff members. Connor North was a hot commodity in Owl Creek. From the sounds of it, he had dated prolifically, yet he hadn't ever had a steady love interest.

Frankly, his romantic history in town was none of her business. He was free to date half the town if he so desired. This wasn't a date! It was merely a simple lunch between friends.

Isabelle focused on the menu, even though she knew exactly what she was ordering. The salmon cakes with a cup of crab stew would make for a divine lunch. Looking at Connor across the table was akin to falling into the void. Why did he have the most piercing blue eyes? And the steadiest gaze. It always made her feel as if he could see straight through her. She shivered at the idea that he knew she was a woman harboring secrets.

By the time the waitress had arrived at their table and taken their orders, she and Connor had started up a conversation about the best places to spot rare species of birds in Owl Creek. Isabelle was really intrigued by the idea of bird-watching in Alaska. If anyone had told her a year ago she would be contemplating such an activity, she would have laughed herself silly.

Isabelle took a long sip of her hot cocoa. It felt nice to be inside and away from the cold. She still hadn't gotten used to being bundled up all the time and the frequent snowstorms. Perhaps years from now she would be acclimated to Alaska.

"So, I actually brought you out to lunch to celebrate."

"Celebrate what?" she asked. He'd completely piqued her curiosity. It was flattering to think he'd chosen her as a companion to revel in good news.

He reached into his bag and pulled out a folder. Connor handed it to her with a flourish.

"Congratulations," he said. "You've been chosen as employee of the week by Beulah. That's your certificate. I've also got flowers and some goodies you can take with you." He handed her the bag he'd carried in. "She's really proud of the hard work and extra hours you've put in."

"Me?" she asked, feeling incredulous. "But I haven't worked for the company for very long."

"Well, what can I say? Beulah makes those distinctions and she really sang your praises. It isn't easy working for the North Star Chocolate Company when you don't have a background in chocolate. You've made a tremendous effort to learn your craft. It hasn't gone unnoticed."

Warmth flooded her cheeks. It was an exhilarating feeling to know that she'd made a difference. She had always been a hard worker, but she hadn't always been proud of her work environment at Club Oasis. This was different from any other job she'd ever held. Isabelle felt a deep sense of pride in working for such a prestigious chocolatier.

"I… I don't know what to say." Her eyes moistened with emotion. This time the tears stemmed from a joyful place. It was a wonderful feeling to finally be happy about something after a long period of being fearful and uncertain. Perhaps this was a milestone. Maybe she was finally stepping out into the light.

Connor reached over and placed his hand over hers. "Savor the moment. You've earned it."

Isabelle nodded. It was hard for her to toot her own horn, but she knew that the recognition from Beulah was a game changer. Ever since she'd arrived in Owl Creek, she had been afraid to be herself. It was almost as if she'd been walking around with a costume on this entire time. The employee of the week distinction was an acknowledgment of her strong work ethic. Even though she'd been raised to be humble, Isabelle wanted to bask in Beulah's kudos for a few moments. It made her feel as if she was on top of the world. Something told her it might not last, since her life under the Witness Protection Program was stressful and unpredictable.

She was feeling a bit emotional after Connor's news about her employee of the week award. All of the employees she worked with at the store were hardworking and diligent. Compared to the late nights she'd spent working at Club Oasis in Miami, her position at North Star Chocolates was delightful. She was now working normal hours as opposed to heading into work at night and not getting off until the wee hours of the morning. And she always felt safe.

When the waitress returned with their food, Isabelle found her appetite had lessened due to her excitement. She took a few bites of her salmon cakes while Connor voraciously tucked in to his pollack, french fries and coleslaw.

"You better pinch me because it feels like I'm dreaming," Ella said.

Connor reached out and gently plucked the skin

by her wrist. "There. I did it. And it doesn't change the fact that you earned this distinction. Kudos, Ella."

She raised a hand to her cheeks. Warmth flooded her face. She wasn't sure if it was because of his compliments or his close proximity. It was getting harder and harder to ignore that Connor North was dangerous to her equilibrium.

"So, do they hang up a photo of me in the chocolate shop? I can't wait to be queen for a day," she teased.

"Yeah, we like to make a big deal out of it. We're going to shout it from the rooftops. We'll put your picture up in the store and at the factory. Then we'll place it on the company website and add it to our monthly newsletter. You'll be famous by the time this month is done." He let out a low chuckle.

"It's going on the internet?" Ella asked, swallowing past the lump in her throat. All of a sudden her heart began beating a fast rhythm within her chest. *No!* she wanted to scream. She couldn't run the risk of her face being plastered on the internet. Although it was unlikely the people who wanted to harm her would ever see it, she wasn't willing to take a chance. If Burke and his cohorts got a lead on her whereabouts, they wouldn't hesitate to track her down in Owl Creek. The very thought of it made her shudder.

"Maybe. I'm not really sure," Connor answered. "Hey. What's wrong? Aren't you happy about this?"

"O-of course I am. I just don't like all the attention that comes with it." She bit her lip as her mind raced with how to explain her sudden wariness about the distinction. She had been over the moon about being employee of the week until discovering there might be online fanfare.

Connor frowned. "You're confusing me. I hope you understand this is a good thing. You aren't trying to hide your light under a bushel, are you?"

She shook her head. "In what way?"

"It's something my grandfather used to say. Basically it means don't hide your talents or abilities. Let them shine. The Bible verse comes to mind. 'Let your light so shine before men, that they may see your good works.'"

She was familiar with the Bible verse, but Isabelle didn't see herself reflected in it. She wasn't hiding her light. Isabelle was trying to preserve her status in WITSEC by not being exposed.

Isabelle nodded and continued to nibble her meal. At this point it tasted like sawdust. All she felt was a growing sense of dread. She didn't know how she could do this for the long haul. Would she ever be able to sit back and relax without feeling as if a dark cloud was hanging over her head? Would she ever not wake up terrified in the middle of the night? And now, just when things had started to solidify for her in Owl Creek, she was being plunged back into fear, doubt and second-guessing herself.

If her picture was plastered all over the internet, would she need to leave town? She felt a pang in her heart at the idea of packing up and leaving. Where would she go? And how could she leave everything behind?

"I hate to eat and run, but I have a conference call

this afternoon." Connor's comment drew her out of her thoughts. She hoped he hadn't noticed her inattention. She'd deliberately stuffed down her feelings regarding her commendation going online. She couldn't afford to make a scene about it or betray her deep concerns. There were already too many instances where she'd acted strangely in his presence. Connor was a smart guy. He'd probably picked up on her odd behavior. It was only a matter of time before he began to question what was going on with her.

She looked at her watch. "Oops. Where did the time go? I need to head back to the shop. Thanks for the lunch invitation. And for giving me such great news."

"Well, thanks for joining me. And again, congratulations. It says a lot about you that you earned this praise." Connor seemed genuinely happy for her.

"It means a lot to me. Please tell Beulah how thrilled I am." Isabelle warmed at the compliment. She did feel proud, and she hoped Connor had been able to see her happiness despite her shattered nerves.

Connor pulled out some bills and plunked them down on the table. He walked with Ella to the exit. As they stood outside, Ella tilted her face upward. Snowflakes were falling gracefully from the sky. If only she could just enjoy this beautiful moment instead of worrying about her status in the Witness Protection Program. She longed to cast all her troubles aside and simply live the way other people did. Without fear or regrets.

"It was very thoughtful of you to come deliver the news in person," she said. "I appreciate it." She had been telling herself all this time she couldn't afford to feel anything for Connor, but at moments like this one her will was being tested. Being with him always made her feel good.

He handed her the bag he'd brought with him. "I like seeing you smile, Ella. It was my pleasure. I hope to see you soon." As Connor strode off in the direction of the factory, Isabelle paused for a moment to admire him. She liked the proud tilt of his head and the way he carried himself. Once he turned the corner and disappeared from view, her mind began to whirl with worry.

She needed to call Jonah immediately. This was definitely an emergency situation that called for her to contact the U.S. Marshal. Her entire cover could be blown if her picture was circulated online. Isabelle dug in the side pocket of her purse and pulled out her cell phone. Jonah had programmed his number into her phone when they'd parted ways. Isabelle walked to the parking lot behind the chocolate shop and made her way to her truck. Once she was inside, she placed the call.

As soon as she heard the familiar voice on the other end, Isabelle spoke into the phone. "Jonah, it's me, Isabelle Sanchez. I don't know what to do! My employer might be uploading my picture online. I might have to leave Owl Creek."

# Chapter Ten

Connor looked around the crowded tea emporium and pondered sneaking out the back entrance. He felt a bit out of place with all the frilly lace and velvet cushions. He thought Tea Time was a wonderful business for Owl Creek, but he'd never really been tempted to sit down and indulge in an afternoon tea party. Connor had to admit that Iris and the bridal party had created a lovely ambience.

"How did I get dragged into a bridal shower?" Connor asked. He turned to question his brother, who was standing next to him.

"Because you were invited. Just like I was," Braden answered. "And you didn't want to let Piper down. She's the only sister-in-law you're ever going to have."

"I didn't realize these things were now coed." There were a decent number of men who'd showed up for the event. Way more than he'd envisioned. Gabe and Hank were across the room having a disagreement over tea flavors. Since Gabe's mother owned Tea Time, he was an expert on the subject. Hank, on the other hand, adored tea and considered himself a connoisseur.

"Me neither, but I'm making the best of it. Piper deserves a nice surprise."

"Speaking of the blushing bride-to-be, what time is she expected to arrive?" Connor asked, studiously trying to avoid the flirty looks he was receiving from across the room. Lana Travers had been trying to get him to take her out for the last few months. Although she was attractive and sweet, he simply wasn't interested. Now that Ella had arrived in town, he'd lost interest in dating around.

Braden glanced at his watch. "In ten minutes or so. She thinks we're meeting for a romantic high tea."

Connor snickered. "That in itself should make her suspicious. You're not the tea emporium type of guy."

"That's not true!" Braden protested. "Just because I'm into outdoor adventures doesn't mean I can't appreciate the finer things. I'm a Renaissance man."

Just as Connor opened up his mouth to dispute his brother's comment, he spotted Ella walking into the tea shop. She was carrying a gaily wrapped present in her arms. Trudy Miller, Piper's mother, greeted her at the door and whisked her toward the coatroom. Connor stood up straight and smoothed his hair back.

"Has something gotten your attention? You haven't heard a word I said."

He turned back toward Braden. "I'm sorry. What were you saying?"

Braden was shaking his head and chuckling. "She's very pretty. Ella, right?"

"Yes. She really is," he answered, not bothering to pretend as if he hadn't been distracted by Ella's arrival. "I haven't known her very long, but she's different from any woman I've ever met." He felt sheepish admitting it. "I probably sound ridiculous. Most people view me as this perpetual bachelor, don't they? I'm not supposed to have feelings."

"I'm not most people, Connor. I'm your brother. I happen to like this side of you. And I wish more people could see that your greatest asset is that big old heart of yours."

"It's my own fault for always playing it cool. That gets old after a while," he admitted. He couldn't blame others for viewing him in a certain way when he'd earned the title. Now he was hoping to go a different route. Lately, he'd prayed a lot about it, asking God to shoulder him through his journey.

*Trust in the Lord with all thine heart; and lean not unto thine own understanding. In all ways acknowledge him, and he shall direct thy paths.*

The passage from Proverbs 3:5–6 had been his cornerstone as of late. He'd been reciting it every day without fail.

"Just remember, it's never too late to change," Braden said. "Follow your heart. That's what I did with Piper."

*Follow your heart.* That's what it boiled down to. His head over his heart. All the doubts he had about Ella had prevented him from pursuing her romantically. But in doing so, wasn't he coming from a place of fear and suspicion? It felt as if he was allowing his own family's tragic past to shape his actions. Just because one person had done a horrible thing didn't mean he should be suspicious of all strangers. Was he biased against Ella because of Sage's kidnapper, a single woman who'd come to town and stolen his baby sister? Was he allowing a twenty-five-year-old tragedy to cloud his judgment?

"You'll figure it out," Braden said, clapping him on the shoulder. "I'm going to check in with Piper just to make sure she's running on schedule." He held up his cell phone as he walked toward a private area.

Just then, Ella walked into the main tearoom wearing a cornflower blue dress and a pair of black heels. She radiated a bright and festive air. She looked over at him and waved, right before heading in his direction.

"Hey, Connor. I'm surprised to see you here."

"Not as surprised as I am to be here," he said with a laugh.

"I've never been to a coed shower, but I like the idea of it. Why shouldn't your brother share in the revelry?" She looked around. "Should we be getting in position to hide? Sage said this is a surprise party."

"Braden is checking in with Piper. She's supposed to arrive anytime now."

"It was nice of your sister to invite me. I'm afraid I don't know Piper very well. I think Sage felt sorry for me since I'm new in town."

"No, that's not it at all. She was a newbie in town once, so she knows how it feels to be out of the loop. Plus, I saw you hanging out at the dog mushing event with Piper, so you're not strangers. What you might not have realized yet is that you're really not an outsider for very long in Owl Creek. You're part of the fabric of this community now."

A grin broke out on her face. "That's good to hear. It makes me feel better that I decided to come today. I almost chickened out."

"I'm awfully glad you didn't. Seeing you was a nice surprise for me." As soon as the words tumbled off his lips, he wondered if his comment sounded sappy. Or too flirty? Just as Ella opened her mouth to say something, Piper's mother raised the alarm.

"Piper is right around the corner. Everybody hunker down," Trudy shouted.

Everyone began shuffling around and ducking out of sight. Connor found himself crouching down beside Ella behind a table. They were so close together he could smell a sweet aroma emanating from her dark tresses. He could hear the light sound of her breathing. Their faces were so close to one another that Connor could see the light flecks in her brown eyes. From where they were hiding, he could see Braden walking toward the entrance to greet Piper. The room was eerily quiet as Piper walked in and Braden welcomed her with a tender kiss. As soon as Braden led her toward the dining room and uttered the words, "You look lovely," all of the guests popped up and shouted, "Surprise." Piper looked around the room with an expression of utter shock stamped on her face. She then burst into tears. Braden lovingly placed his arm around her as she thanked everyone for gathering in her honor.

Connor looked over at Ella. A look of pure radiance emanated from her. Seeing her so happy and at ease caused a groundswell of emotion to rise up inside him. It was evident she was starting to feel a sense of belonging, despite second-guessing her invitation.

If he hadn't fully realized it before, it was now stunningly obvious. Ella Perez had a hold on him. And for the life of him, he wasn't sure what to do about it.

With the bridal shower tea party in full swing, Ella couldn't think of a time when she'd had more fun celebrating an upcoming wedding. Her cheeks hurt from smiling so much, but she couldn't rein herself in. Being at Piper and Braden's celebration made her feel included. Seeing the couple being celebrated by the whole town was heartwarming.

Connor was one of the good guys, and he deserved far better than a woman who might spend the rest of her life hiding her true identity. Connor came from a strong, loving family who lived their lives out in the open. He wasn't a man who abided secrets. He'd told her as much when he had spoken about Sage's abduction. A man like Connor North wouldn't want to have anything to do with her if he knew she was living a lie.

The other day had been a nerve-racking experience until Connor had later informed her that her picture wasn't going to be placed online on the company website. He'd agreed to only list her name and her award. She couldn't help but feel that he'd sensed her extreme discomfort and made an adjustment. Isabelle had quickly contacted Jonah to update him on the news. Although the U.S. Marshal had clearly been relieved by the update, he'd been very firm in telling her to keep her guard up and to continue to stay alert to any potential situations that might compromise her identity. Getting reassurance from Jonah that she was safe made all the difference in her state of mind. It had allowed her to attend the bridal shower and cast her fears aside, at least temporarily.

At the moment she was trying to enjoy the festivities and bask in the happy vibe in the air. She took a sip of her tea, marveling at the unique taste and the elegant gold-and-pink teacup and saucer. There were so many lovely details here on display. The refreshment table was filled with finger sandwiches, scones, croissants and tarts. A two-tiered cake had been placed in the center of the table. A plentiful assortment of teas sat on another table. Everything was lavishly displayed in soft and inviting colors.

"It's so great to see you here." Ella turned toward Rachel, who was standing alongside her with her mother-in-law in tow. Iris reached out and enveloped Isabelle in a tight hug.

"I'm so glad to see you're making yourself at home," Iris gushed. "There will always be a table for you at Tea Time."

"That's so kind of you to say, Iris. Everything is so beautiful here. I love this lavender tea. I've never had anything quite like it." Isabelle took another sip of the fragrant tea.

"It's also a favorite of mine. We actually have favors with tea packets inside, so you can take some samples home with you," Iris said.

"That's a perfect party favor," Isabelle answered. She looked over at the refreshment table, where Connor was standing with his parents.

"He's a good-looking man, isn't he?" Iris asked, jerking her chin in Connor's direction. She turned her gaze to Isabelle, shooting her a questioning look.

"Umm, yes. He's all right, I suppose," Isabelle said, trying to keep her voice neutral.

She knew how small towns worked. If she raved about Connor's dark good looks, the townsfolk would soon be talking about her and how the new girl in town was crushing on the heir to the North Star Chocolate Company. Her face felt flushed just thinking about how embarrassing it would be if Connor got wind of any chatter. She was supposed to be keeping her head down and maintaining a low profile. Being the subject of matchmaking schemes or gossips wouldn't aid her objective.

"Just all right?" Iris asked in a voice full of outrage. "Ella, I think you might need glasses. Connor North is Alaskan eye candy."

Rachel playfully swatted at her mother-in-law. "Iris! Stop it. You're incorrigible."

Iris stood up straighter and puffed her chest out. "I might be a woman of a certain age, but there's nothing wrong with my eyesight. He's as single as a dollar bill, Ella. And from the looks of it, he's always ready to mingle. Beulah is hoping he'll settle down and focus on one woman instead of hopping from woman to woman as he's always done."

Isabelle did her best to hide her discomfort. Although Iris clearly adored Connor, she wasn't putting him in the best light. Clearly, Isabelle's impression of Connor had been far from reality.

"He sounds like a player," Isabelle murmured. She shouldn't be surprised. Men who looked like Connor often had their pick of women. It didn't hurt that he hailed from a prominent family and held an executive position at North Star Chocolates.

Rachel none too subtly jabbed Iris in the side. "We don't want Ella to get the wrong idea about Connor. He's a good man."

"Of course he is. It's not his fault he's cut a huge swath through all the women in town. Ever since he was young, he's been the object of every girl in town's affection."

"Umm, hello. Not mine," Rachel interjected. "I always had my eye on a certain pilot."

Iris leaned in and pressed a kiss on Rachel's cheek. "Bless your heart. You sure did. My son is blessed to have you. I should scoot and replenish the refreshments. I'll catch up with you later."

Isabelle felt thankful for Iris and her chatty ways. Iris's intel on Connor made her feel grateful that she hadn't locked lips with Connor the other night. Clearly, he viewed women as conquests. She felt embarrassed that she'd thought Connor was interested in her. According to Iris, he played the field like a champion. She stuffed down the feelings of disappointment. It would have been an impossible situation between them anyway, but it rankled a little bit to realize she wasn't special in his eyes.

"I wouldn't quite describe Connor the way Iris did," Rachel said, interrupting her thoughts. "My mother-in-law is very opinionated, so I wouldn't take her words to heart. Everyone in Owl Creek adores Connor."

Clearly, Rachel felt an allegiance to Connor, and she didn't want Isabelle to think poorly of him. She appeared to be doing a bit of damage control.

Isabelle shrugged. "It's not my place to judge him. I honestly don't know him that well."

"He's a really good person. I've known him my entire life," Rachel added. An earnest expression was stamped on her face.

She nodded her head but didn't comment any further. She didn't want to talk about Connor anymore. Iris had dropped a little bombshell on her. It served as a wake-up call and she was still trying to process what she'd learned. His past really wasn't her business, although it did give her perspective.

For the remainder of the party Isabelle did her best to mingle and enjoy the festivities. She participated in a variety of games, even managing to win a round of bridal song trivia. Her prize was a large surprise packet that she couldn't wait to dig into once she got home. It was thrilling, since she never won anything.

Piper made a point to seek her out during the party. Isabelle wasn't expecting to receive a bear hug from the guest of honor, but it reinforced her feelings about the lively bride-to-be. She was just as sweet and kind-hearted as Isabelle had imagined. Slowly but surely Isabelle was becoming a part of things here in Owl Creek. She didn't feel quite so lonely anymore. Now, when she walked down Main Street, there were friendly faces who called out to her by name. Customers in the shop asked for her when they came through the doors. Although she still looked over her shoulder from time to time, Isabelle felt safe in her small Alaskan haven. She prayed that her identity was never compromised. She didn't want to be forced to leave town as she'd feared a few days ago.

Fear was still a living, breathing thing inside of her. Would she ever have an aura of peace surrounding her? Or would the past always hang over her head? Isabelle needed to have faith in Jonah and his assurances.

*Lord, please give me a spirit of grace and not fear. I'm so tired of looking over my shoulder and wondering if I'm still in danger. Please lift me up so I can see beyond my anxieties. Bless my future and help me banish the past.*

As the party began to wind down, Ella left the main tearoom to gather up her belongings in the coatroom. She'd already said her goodbyes to Piper, Iris, Sage and Rachel. Just as she was putting on her coat, Isabelle felt a slight tap on her shoulder. When she turned around, Connor was standing there.

"Hey. Are you heading out?" he asked.

"Yes," she answered, zipping up her coat before adjusting her hat. "It was a great party, but I'm tired."

"I barely got to talk to you at all," he said.

She shifted from one foot to the other. It wasn't as if she'd been avoiding him, but she hadn't sought him out either. Truthfully, she felt a little self-conscious around him now, based on the information Iris had shared with her. It was ridiculous on her part, considering Connor could never be anything more than a friend.

"Well, the place was packed. All these people must really love Piper and Braden."

Connor nodded. "Everyone enjoys a good love story. They were childhood best friends throughout their lives, so it's all the sweeter that they fell in love."

It was utterly charming. No wonder they were the town's sweethearts. It's what everyone wanted. Marrying your best friend and making a beautiful life together would be a dream come true for most people. A heaviness settled on her chest. Something so wonderful wasn't destined for her. And it was beginning to weigh on her. Isabelle had always been the little girl dreaming of a big wedding filled with family and friends. Most importantly, she had fantasized about marrying a man who brought her joy.

"I'm so happy for them," she said, though her voice sounded wooden to her own ears. She hated feeling this way and wondered when she'd return to her usual upbeat and positive vibe.

"I have to get going," she said, before quickly striding toward the door. She imagined Connor thought her actions were abrupt, but she didn't stop walking at a fast clip until she reached her truck, which was parked down the street. Along the way she breathed in big gulps of the cold air, all the while reminding herself that this too would pass. Surely better days were coming. Every step on her journey would carry her through the darkness. Isabelle prayed she would be strong enough to see it through.

* * *

Connor had felt a slight chill in the air as he said his goodbyes to Ella—and it had nothing to do with the actual temperature. He wasn't sure what he'd done, but instinct told him she was annoyed with him. Perhaps he should have made more of an effort to seek her out at the party, but he'd been worried about smothering her. It was fantastic that she'd been welcomed, but now he was scratching his head about what he'd done wrong. It mattered to him what Ella thought about him. He wasn't the type of man who had ever been overly concerned about the opinion of others, but with this woman everything had been turned upside down.

A half an hour later Connor was helping with the cleanup and still racking his brain to figure out Ella's frosty demeanor. Earlier, she'd been fine. Perhaps he'd stepped over the line with her in some way that made her uncomfortable.

Sage made a beeline in his direction. "Hey. Have you seen Ella anywhere? I can't seem to find her."

"She left a few minutes ago. You just missed her."

Sage let out a groan. "She left behind her goody bag and the prize package she won. I guess that I could swing by her place tomorrow after Addie's Gymboree class and give it to her."

"I can take it to her if you want. She lives a few minutes down the road from me, so it's not a big deal."

Sage's eyes lit up. "Seriously? That would be fantastic. You're the best, Connor."

"Of course I am," he teased. "I'm still waiting for that favorite brother T-shirt."

Sage put a finger up to her lips. "Shh. We don't want Braden to hear." They both laughed as Connor once again marveled at how wonderful it was to have his sister back. He tried not to dwell too much on all the lost years. If he thought about it for too long it always took him to a place of resentment and anger.

As everyone joined in to help clean up, Connor began to second-guess his offer to drop off Ella's items at her house. Clearly he'd jumped at the opportunity just so he could spend more time with her, even if it was only a few moments. But he wanted to figure out why she'd been acting so cold.

Connor looked at his watch. He wanted to get over to Ella's house before it got too late. He'd already agreed to help Braden bring some of the gifts over to the new house he'd just built as a wedding surprise for Piper. Once he had done that, he didn't hesitate to get back on the road.

Connor cranked up the volume on the radio. Somebody was singing a poignant country song about losing the love of his life. He drummed his fingers on the steering wheel to the fast tempo. Maybe he should just turn the truck around and go home. Ella seemed to be a private person who might not embrace the idea of him just showing up at her door. His mind kept flitting back to her shuttered expression and closed off body language. Why had he thought that this was a good idea?

He was failing miserably in staying away from Ella. This was a prime example. Connor was going out of his way to be in her presence when he could have left well enough alone. Despite his conflicted feelings about whether Ella was someone he could trust, he liked her. A lot.

Maybe his suspicions about her were nothing more than his own wild imagination. Perhaps he was just used to knowing everything about everyone in his hometown. It wasn't right to judge her for not being an open book and for appearing frightened. If he made a list of pros versus cons, he was certain the pros would far outweigh the cons.

Or maybe he was simply trying to stuff down his grave reservations. She was beautiful and sweet natured, and he didn't want to run the risk of letting something wonderful slip through his fingers.

Yet nothing had changed to allow him to feel confident that Ella wasn't still harboring secrets that might blow up in his face.

## Chapter Eleven

Isabelle let out a sigh as she put on a pair of sweats and a comfy top, then settled in with a book of devotionals. It was the perfect way to unwind after a long day. Earlier she had fixed herself a simple meal of pasta and salad for an easy dinner. The bridal shower had been lovely. It had felt good to meet new people and to celebrate Piper and Braden's upcoming wedding. That's what life was all about, and once she'd stopped feeling mopey about her situation, she'd been able to truly appreciate the scope of what she'd experienced. Back home her family always celebrated birthdays, weddings, anniversaries and graduations in grand style with Brazilian music and amazing food. She missed those moments so much it left an ache in her soul.

Other than the things she'd learned about Connor, it had been a great day. Despite her best intentions, thoughts of the handsome chocolate heir kept creeping into her thoughts. For a variety of reasons, she didn't want to like him. But she did.

"Focus on something else," she said as she turned a page in her book. She began highlighting passages and reciting words out loud.

A whistling sound began to resonate from outside her bedroom window. She sucked in a sharp breath. Perhaps it was just the wind. The strange noises continued, shattering her sense of peace and security. Every creak and groan made her almost jump out of her skin. Was someone out there in the darkness? Her pulse began to race. She raised a hand to her throat. Isabelle felt paralyzed with fear. Her mind began to whirl with all the possibilities.

Marshal Kramer had assured her that she would be safe here in Owl Creek. At the moment she wondered if he'd been mistaken. Had danger followed her to Alaska?

She needed to stay calm. *When thou passest through the waters, I will be with thee.* The passage from Isaiah came to mind, encouraging her not to allow anxiety to outweigh reason. In all likelihood there was some reasonable explanation for the creepy sounds.

*Just breathe*, she told herself. *You're letting your imagination run wild.*

Another loud sound echoed in the house, a boom from the rear. Then she heard a shuffling noise that almost sounded like someone was walking up the steps. Isabelle's first instinct was to hide. If only her brain could convince her body to move. Her mind flashed back to the terrifying night a man had broken into her apartment and tried to harm her so she couldn't testify in Burke's trial. That very moment had determined her future in the Witness Protection Program. She had been fortunate to make it out of the situation alive. And now, all these months later she was still in the grip of unrelenting terror.

Even though she'd closed the door on her former life and assumed a new identity to protect herself, Isabelle was still in jeopardy.

As Connor drove up to Ella's dimly lit house, he immediately spotted a few lights glowing from inside the home. He wasn't sure if he should ring the bell or not.

"Just go home," he muttered. "Maybe she's made an early night of it."

He was annoyed at himself because he was acting like an uncertain teenager on his first date. Normally, Connor was pretty composed, and he didn't waste time second-guessing himself. He was simply doing a favor for a friend. *Humph!* Who was he kidding? There was absolutely nothing platonic about the way Ella made him feel. She left him breathless.

He couldn't sit in front of her house all night. Connor let out a frustrated sigh before taking off his seat belt and grabbing the items Sage had given him before exiting his truck.

As he strode to the door he wondered if he could just leave it at her doorstep. With snow expected to fall in a few hours, it probably wouldn't be wise. Just as he raised his hand to rap on the door a scream rang out from inside Ella's house. For a moment he wondered if he'd imagined it. Then he heard it again. A loud, panicked scream.

He pounded on the door, calling out to Ella. Connor pushed his shoulder against the doorjamb, hoping he would be able to gain entry. All of a sudden the door gave way and Ella was standing before him. A look of pure terror was etched on her face.

"Connor! I'm so relieved to see you. I heard noises outside. I think someone was outside trying to break into the house."

Connor could clearly see Ella's discomfort. He didn't want to minimize her concerns, but he knew it would be highly unusual for a break-in to happen in Owl Creek. Because his best friend was town sheriff, Connor knew the statistics. It would be as likely as a heat wave in February.

He gently placed his hands on her shoulders. Connor needed her to stay calm and listen to him. "Ella, try not to panic. Stay right here while I look around the perimeter of the house." She clung to his jacket, slowly nodding her head as she let go of him. Connor headed outside and walked over to his car, fumbling around in the glove compartment for a flashlight. As soon as he located it, he made his way around the outside.

It didn't take him long to spot the large branches that had fallen on a portion of the roof. They were pretty massive. No doubt the sound of them had been terrifying. He made his way back to the front of the house and went inside. Ella was sitting on the living room couch with wide eyes. He sat down next to her.

"It was two large tree branches that fell on the house. The noises you heard were probably the limbs groaning before it happened. Nothing to worry about.

And I didn't see any damage to the roof, but you'll be able to get a better look in the morning."

Ella simply stared at him with her arms wrapped around her middle. Her whole body was trembling.

"I… I thought I was—"

In that moment, Connor saw it all in her eyes. Terror. Someone had wounded this woman. And she was still living in a place of fear. The scars were visible in her actions, even though she tried to hide them. He'd gotten it all wrong. Ella hadn't done anything wrong in the past. She had been terrorized, to the point where she thought someone was coming after her. In Ella's mind the sound of tree limbs had transformed into her worst nightmare. And although he didn't know exactly who or what was scaring her, he knew it was a very real threat in her eyes.

Connor put his arm around her and pulled her against his chest.

"No one is going to hurt you. Not ever. I won't let them. You're safe, Ella." His voice rang out with intensity. A few weeks ago he hadn't even known this woman, but he knew he would do everything in his power to protect her from harm. From this point forward, he considered it his sacred mission.

She let out a sob, then raised her fisted hand to cover her mouth. He could tell she was trying to rein in her emotions. The sight of her tears threatened to do him in.

He reached out and wiped away her tears with his fingers. "You're safe with me."

"Thank you. But it isn't your job to dry my tears. I'm beginning to feel like a wet blanket."

Connor shook his head and chuckled. "Okay. No more corny jokes for you."

"Well, at least I can laugh at myself," she said, chuckling along with him. "I'm so sorry for being such a mess over a few tree limbs. I can't imagine Beulah freaking out over something like this."

"My grandmother is a tough bird, but so are you. There are all kinds of strength in this world. I admire your willingness to pick up stakes and make a new life for yourself in Alaska."

"Thank you, but Beulah's in a league of her own. She's an incredible woman. It's safe to say I want to be like her when I grow up." Ella's voice sounded wistful, and Connor knew she was feeling badly about her re-action to the noises she'd heard. Maybe even a touch embarrassed.

"I think you're pretty amazing, Ella Perez. Not to mention absolutely beautiful. You don't need to be any-one other than yourself."

Ella bowed her head. Her cheeks looked flushed. "You're being really kind."

Connor reached out and lifted her chin up so he could look her in the eyes. "I'm being honest. You're the most stunning woman I've ever laid eyes on. And you have a lot of strengths." He ran his fingers over her lips, tracing the shape of them. "I hope I'm not out of line, but I'd like to kiss you. I've been wanting to since the first time I saw you."

Even though Connor still wanted to know Ella's

truths, he couldn't deny the deep yearning to kiss her and give her comfort. Hopefully, over time, she would confide in him. At the moment, he felt reassured enough to move forward.

As he moved closer, their gazes locked. Ella's eyes widened imperceptibly. The flecks in her brown eyes resembled embers. He leaned over and placed his lips on hers. A sweet floral scent filled his nostrils, instantly bringing to mind Alaska's state flower, forget-me-nots. Her lips were soft and inviting. They tasted like cinnamon and sweetness. She kissed him back with equal measure, her lips moving against his with a tenderness that blew him away. He placed his hand on the back of her neck, anchoring her to him as the kiss intensified. In response, Ella placed her hand on his chest. He wondered if she could tell his heart was beating extra fast.

This was the moment he'd been hoping for over the past few weeks. It gave him confirmation that the attraction wasn't one-sided. Ella felt something for him! In all of his life Connor had never experienced a kiss like this one. It was so natural and tender. It felt like coming home, as if they'd known each other all of their lives. Was this the elusive feeling he'd been missing out on all this time?

For a few moments they were lost in the kiss. Time seemed to stand still. For the life of him Connor didn't want it to end. He didn't want to go back to a place where he still had unanswered questions about Ella. This moment felt so perfect since it came from a place of feeling and not reason. All that mattered was this connection between them.

As the kiss ended and they drew apart, Connor swept his palm against her cheek. She looked up at him, her sooty lashes framing her beautiful eyes. He could stay here for hours just looking at her.

"I should head home. You need to get some sleep, Ella."

"I am feeling pretty tuckered out," she admitted. "Now I can sleep soundly and not worry about strange noises from the darkness."

"I've lived here my whole life. I can't remember a single instance when folks had to worry about break-ins. You're safe here."

He watched as her shoulders sagged in relief. Whatever was troubling her, he was happy he'd been able to allay her fears, even though he was still struggling to figure her out. Connor still felt curious about her situation and who was responsible for frightening her, but he sensed that she wasn't going to open up to him. He had a sinking feeling in his gut. No matter how deeply he wished she would confide in him, only Ella could make that decision. And so far she was choosing not to do so.

As they said good-night by the door, Ella reached up and placed a swift kiss on his cheek. "Thank you, Connor. I don't know what I would have done if you hadn't stopped by."

"I'm glad I did. I actually stopped by to bring you the goody bags from the party. I put them on the table in the foyer."

"Thank you," Ella murmured. "That was very sweet of you."

"I'm here for you, Ella. I'm a good listener and I don't judge. I can be a strong shoulder to lean on if you need one."

His gaze didn't waver as he looked at her. One word from Ella and he would head right back into the house and listen to anything and everything she wanted to tell him. All this time Ella had been an enigma, a puzzle he'd been trying to figure out. Even though they had just shared a tender moment, there were still many pieces missing.

Connor felt a stab of disappointment when she bade him good-night without taking him up on his offer. As he walked to his truck and settled in behind the driver's seat, he couldn't deny the confused feelings warring inside of him. The kiss he'd shared with Ella had been exhilarating. But her secrets still stood between them.

He was impatient to finally get some answers about the things she'd been hiding. Until that time, Connor knew he couldn't offer her anything more than friendship.

Isabelle woke up the following morning from a very unsettled slumber. She knew her sense of unease had everything to do with Connor's visit and the kiss they'd shared. It had felt nice in the moment, but her conscience wouldn't allow her to proceed any further. A man like Connor North deserved truth and transparency, neither of which she could give him.

She had every intention of spending a leisurely Sunday doing a few things around the house after she returned from church. In order to subdue her grumbling stomach, Isabelle headed down to the kitchen and made herself a bowl of oatmeal and two pieces of wheat toast with genuine Alaskan blueberry jam. Despite her state of mind, every bite tasted delectable.

Just as she was about to head upstairs for a shower, a knock sounded on her front door. She looked down at her leisure wear—a pair of sweatpants and a matching top, along with a pair of fuzzy socks. She looked somewhat presentable, she guessed. But what if it was Connor? She really didn't want him to see her looking so frumpy.

Oh, well. If it was Connor, he might as well see her in an unfiltered way since they were stuck in the friend zone. With a sigh, she got up from her chair and headed toward the door. Right before she pulled it open, Isabelle let her hair free from a ponytail holder and shook it loose, running her fingers though the strands to tame it. She yanked open the door as her greeting froze on her lips.

"Jonah! What are you doing here?" The question flew out of her mouth. The U.S. Marshal was standing at her doorstep dressed in a pair of dark jeans, a black puffer jacket and a pair of Ray-Ban sunglasses.

"You sounded pretty frantic during our phone call. My boss agreed it was time for me to make a house call."

"I can't believe you came. Come inside," she said, ushering him into the house.

"Thanks. Homer is just a short flight away," Jonah

said as he crossed the threshold and entered her house. "It gave me an opportunity to ride in a seaplane. That doesn't happen every day."

"Why don't we go into the kitchen and I'll make us some hot cocoa," she offered. She had dozens of packets, courtesy of North Star Chocolates.

"Sounds good," Jonah said as he trailed after her and settled himself at her farmhouse-style table while she prepared the cups of hot chocolate. "How are you getting acclimated to Owl Creek?"

"I'm getting there," she said. "It's been difficult at times, especially missing my family." Her throat tightened. "But the people here have been pretty wonderful," she added as Connor's face flashed before her eyes.

"And the company you're working for?" Jonah asked as she placed a cup down in front of him and sat down across from him with her own mug of cocoa.

"So far, it's been incredible. I have nothing to say but positive things." She smiled at Jonah. "What's not to love? I'm able to be around chocolate all day and I get lots of samples to take home. I wish I had more self-control," she admitted with a laugh.

Jonah nodded. "Everything sounds like it's falling into place. I thought you might have packed up your suitcases and given your employer a resignation letter." He took a sip of his cocoa and let out a satisfied sound. "You sounded pretty frantic the other day when we spoke. Even after you found out your photo wasn't going online, I got the impression you were still jittery."

"I was," she answered, shuddering as she remembered her anxiety from a few days ago. She had been in such turmoil that she'd honestly considered leaving Owl Creek and asking to be reassigned to another locale. "Thankfully, the CEO decided my picture was only going to be hung up at the factory and the chocolate shop with only a brief mention in the employee newsletter. I have the feeling her grandson might have told her it made me uncomfortable." She let out a ragged sigh. "I may have overreacted. I'm sorry if you wasted a trip."

"It's not a waste, especially if you've decided to stay put here in town. It gets a bit messy when things fall apart so quickly. As you know, relocating isn't easy. Of course it would be your decision, but you would have to start the whole process all over again. That would be very stressful for you."

Isabelle didn't want to go anywhere. She couldn't imagine finding a better relocation spot than where she'd landed. Now that the panic had dissipated, she could see her situation clearly. Staying put was the best move.

"I like it here. It's miles apart from anything I've ever known, but it's growing on me." It was gratifying being able to give Jonah a good report after the anxiety she'd experienced the other day. It served as a reminder that sometimes she needed to breathe before allowing her mind to take her to dark places. She wanted to be in a place where she was living in a state of grace and not fear.

"That's what we like to hear. Keeping you safe is

our number one priority, but we also want you to live the best life possible. A life without fear."

That was her goal as well. It made her soul soar to know she was more than just a case number to the marshals assigned to her protection.

"I have a question for you. Has anything changed with the case? I know it's a long shot, but are there any updates?"

Jonah quirked his mouth. "I hate being the bearer of bad news, but it's part of the job description. One of Burke's cronies who was serving as a witness was killed yesterday."

Isabelle let out a gasp and raised her hand to her throat. "Oh, no! That's awful."

Jonah's expression was somber. "We have no doubt Burke was behind it. His reach extends beyond prison. The witness wasn't under the protection of WITSEC however, since he refused to participate. Burke has appealed the case, which means it would benefit him if you can't testify in any future trial. You're still in jeopardy, Ella. Don't ever forget it."

Isabelle wrapped her hands around her heated mug. Despite the warmth, she felt a shiver run through her. Jonah didn't pull any punches. Her life was still in danger. Another witness had been killed by Burke. She had no doubt he would enjoy tracking down her whereabouts in Owl Creek and doing the same to her.

After Connor's assurances last night, she was beginning to feel secure in this quaint Alaskan town. As if it was her haven from the ugliness of bullets and violence. For the first time since her arrival, Isabelle

could envision living out the rest of her days in Owl
Creek. She knew instinctively it had a lot to do with
her friendship with Connor.

In the cold light of day, she regretted having kissed
him, but her feelings were a bit all over the place. Iris
had made it clear to her that Connor was an expert at
playing the field. Was she just another conquest? On
the other hand, the kiss had given her comfort and a
sense of security at a time when she'd badly needed it.
And it had offered her hope. Maybe she didn't have to
be alone for the rest of her days. But Jonah's announcement brought her squarely back to earth.

After an hour or so of chatting, Jonah announced
that he needed to get going. Isabelle no longer felt surprised by the covert actions of Marshal Kramer. Although his visit had been short, she deeply appreciated
the face-to-face drop-in to tell her about the witness's
murder. Isabelle stood by the door and waved as Jonah
drove away in a dark sedan. He was gone just as mys-
teriously as he'd arrived. She couldn't explain it, but
she had the feeling this was the last time she would
ever see the U.S. Marshal. Today she felt stronger than
she had a few days ago. It was a God moment. All this
time she'd been praying for strength, and she finally
was feeling empowered.

Even though Jonah had delivered some alarming
news it hadn't shattered her. She was still standing.
She was committed to living her life without constantly
looking over her shoulder. Although it was a sober-
ing reality that her life would always be in danger, she
was finally coming to terms with it. She now knew she

could face fear head-on and come out the other side. She could make a life for herself in Alaska. It might not be like the one she'd left behind, but it could be a good existence nevertheless.

Hope. In order to make this work, didn't she need to have faith in rebuilding her life?

After she closed the door and came inside from the cold, Isabelle went upstairs to get ready for the late morning service. She had so much to be thankful for, and she wanted to worship with the townsfolk in God's house. Would Connor be in attendance? She was a bit nervous to see him again after the tender kiss they'd shared last night. Isabelle prayed things wouldn't be awkward between them. After all, they were both adults, right? Surely they could both see that the kiss had been ill-advised and a result of the nerve-racking situation she'd found herself in.

Nothing had changed between them, despite the kiss. It didn't matter how deeply she yearned to push past friendship with Connor. It simply wasn't possible.

## Chapter Twelve

On Sunday, Connor didn't have much time to dwell on the situation with Ella. Running into Ella after church service had put things into perspective about his relationship with her. Just because he wasn't able to pursue a romance with Ella didn't mean he couldn't be a good friend and ally. She was a stranger in an unfamiliar town that was full of interesting places to explore. He'd invited Ella to go sightseeing with him, offering himself as her Owl Creek tour guide.

A few hours later he was with Ella, staring up at a sky full of stars set against a velvety backdrop. He knew she'd been wanting to get a glimpse of the town's legendary owls, so here they were at their final destination after hours of exploring various locations in town.

He was sitting on a snowbank, shoulder to shoulder with Ella. "See that right there?" he asked, pointing up at the inky sky.

Ella let out a gasp. "What is it? I've never spotted anything like it before."

Connor dragged his eyes away from Ella and looked up at the crimson-colored moon. "They call it a super blood wolf moon. It doesn't come around very often, but when it does, it's spectacular."

"It's stunning. I never even knew it existed."

Connor turned toward her. "Stick around, kid. Alaska has a lot of hidden treasures. You just have to be open to it."

Ella nodded her head vigorously. Her enthusiasm was effusive. She almost resembled a wide-eyed kid with her excitement. Her brown eyes shone with wonder.

"It's funny how the things that are truly wonderful always seem to come out of the blue. Like a double rainbow or a shooting star. Or in this case, a super blood wolf moon." Her tinkling laughter filled the air. He wanted to hear more of it. The smiles. The joy. The happiness. It only served to enhance her natural beauty.

"Wait till you see the northern lights. Every time I witness them, it makes me feel like a kid on Christmas morning," Connor said.

"Well then, I hope to catch a glimpse one of these days."

"Oh, you'll need more than a peek. Hopefully it won't just be a flash. The best sightings are the ones that stick around for a while."

They sat for a few moments in companionable silence. It was nice that neither one of them needed to fill up the silence. He could sit like this for hours just gazing up at the heavens. Even the frigid temperatures weren't a problem right now. All was right in his world.

"Look. It's a snowy owl!" she cried out, pointing at the bird gracefully flying through the air. "It's so beautiful."

"Alaska is really showing off for you tonight. A blood moon and a snowy owl. You're really getting a show."

She shook her head, her long strands of hair whirling around her shoulders. "I'm glad you brought me here tonight. It's perfect."

As their eyes met, something shimmered and pulsed in the air between them. He reached out and clasped her hand in his, pulling her closer. What he saw glistening in her eyes reflected his own sentiments.

"Ella," he murmured, dipping his head down toward her. Her eyes fluttered closed, and he knew she anticipated the kiss as he made his move. He pressed his lips against Ella's. He thought he heard her let out a little sigh of appreciation. He took her face in his hands and tenderly moved his lips over hers. She wrapped her arms around his neck and pulled him closer.

He'd never been one to talk about romantic moments, but this tender interlude was everything. Their first kiss had been a sweet exploration, whereas this one was filled with more emotion. He could feel her heart fluttering inside her chest. It matched the beats of his own. He thought it might burst straight out of his chest. Feeling these emotions was confusing, since he was determined to avoid any romantic entanglements with Ella. At the moment he knew he was playing with fire.

If it was at all possible, Connor would stay here

with Ella until the diamond-like stars were erased from the sky. He cared about this woman way more than he wanted to. She'd managed to burrow her way into his heart when he wasn't looking. And now all he wanted in this world was to be with her. Every second they shared was sacred to him because, as much as he wished a future with her was possible, it wasn't when he still couldn't be sure of what she was hiding.

Connor still wondered what she was running from. What could possibly be so awful that she was determined to keep it under wraps? He winced as his mind began whirling with awful possibilities. Try as he might, Connor couldn't stop thinking about the terrible price his own family had paid at the hands of a woman who'd harbored devastating secrets. Jane Duncan had stolen his sister due to the fact that she'd been unable to have her own child. It was only on her deathbed that she'd confessed her sins to Sage. His family had never received a word of apology from her for her heinous act. Her actions had wounded all of them in the worst possible way.

There was no way in this world he could allow it to happen to his family again.

Over the next few weeks, Ella became more entrenched in the vital community of Owl Creek. Joining the choir, making new friends at North Star Chocolates and spending time with Connor helped make her feel as if the small Alaskan town was becoming a home. While it had once been a hideaway, a safe place to live while she was rebuilding her life, now it was so much more. It was a place where she could imagine herself growing old. She was sure of that this morning when she had received an invitation to Piper and Braden's wedding. She couldn't stop gazing at the beautiful stationery and thinking how fortunate she was to be invited to the nuptials. Getting the special piece of mail made her grin from ear to ear.

When she gazed at the invitation for the hundredth time she found herself tracing the gold script that spelled out Ella Perez. Tears sprang to her eyes. Would she ever get used to this? Being someone other than her truest self? Sometimes she wanted to scream out that she was Isabelle Sanchez from Miami, Florida. But she couldn't. Not if she wanted to stay out of Vincent Burke's reach.

Ella Perez wasn't real. Her story was a fabrication. Her own life had been erased. She needed to accept it.

Isabelle couldn't get any closer to Connor with all these secrets lurking under the surface. What if one of Burke's men did come looking for her in Alaska? Connor might be placed in jeopardy simply by his connection to her. She couldn't let that happen.

She still had nightmares from time to time, but they were less frequent than they had been when she'd first arrived in town. Isabelle had taken some steps forward over the last few weeks—she no longer jumped at sudden noises or had flashbacks of the shooting. For the first time in a long time she didn't have a tight sensation across her chest. She could breathe now.

The biggest thing weighing her down was the knowledge that she couldn't tell Connor a single thing about her past. Sometimes she had the impression he suspected something. He would look at her strangely at random moments or ask probing questions. Perhaps she was just feeling funny about living a life that really wasn't her own. Maybe she was projecting her worries onto him. Even if they could never be a couple, he'd proven himself to be a solid friend.

"You're Ella Perez now," she said out loud as she gazed into the mirror. Although she looked the same as she always had, Isabelle knew she was changing every single day. Pretty soon, Isabelle would be nothing more than a memory.

And it broke her heart into a million little pieces.

Connor parked his truck a block away from the Snowy Owl Diner and began walking down Main Street. He was in the mood for a little walk down the main thoroughfare. He forced himself to smile at the townsfolk he crossed paths with, engaging in light conversation before going on his way. It was a gorgeous February morning with freshly fallen snow glistening on the tree branches. Everyone seemed to be out and about, frequenting the shops, running errands or indulging in an aromatic cup of tea at Tea Time. Normally, he would feel upbeat on a day like this, but Connor's mood was contemplative. He'd arisen this morning with more questions than answers. He didn't enjoy feeling so unsettled. Was he making too much of an issue about Ella's mysterious past? It was still weighing on him.

He didn't have to know everything about Ella's history in order to know he was falling in love with the beautiful newcomer. Maybe that's what he should focus on. The hope that one day they could turn their friendship into something more.

"Morning, Trudy," he said as he spotted the lovable innkeeper.

Trudy Miller greeted him warmly. "Hey there, Connor. Nice to see you. I think your two sidekicks are waiting for you at the diner."

"I'm on my way," he said, pausing to plant a kiss on her cheek as he breezed by.

Trudy grinned and waved him down the street.

A few steps later he almost collided with Maya Roberts, the town's veterinarian.

"Woops. Sorry, Maya. I wasn't paying attention," he apologized.

Maya smiled. "No worries. I just sent you a postcard. It's time Bear came in for his shots."

"Thanks for the reminder. I'll bring him in ASAP," he said before continuing on toward the diner. Things had been so hectic lately. He'd completely forgotten about Bear's annual shots.

Connor bounded up the diner stairs and held the door open as his friend, Otis Cummings, exited the establishment with his lady friend, Birdie McCuller. Otis frequented the diner for breakfast several times a week. The older man was dipping his toe into the relationship pool after losing his wife a year ago. It was nice to see Otis so happy with Birdie.

"Hey there, Connor," Otis said, tipping his hat at him.

"You're such a sweetheart," Birdie crowed as she sailed through the door. "And a true blue gentleman."

"Have a great day, you two," Connor said as he stepped inside. The smell of pancakes and eggs hovered in the air, causing his stomach to grumble in appreciation. He'd woken up to a hearty appetite and he was eager to dig in to one of the diner's breakfast specials.

He spotted Gabe and Hank at their usual table at the back of the restaurant. As soon as he sat down in the booth, his friends greeted him.

"Well, look who's gracing us with his presence," Hank drawled. "A sight for sore eyes."

"I barely recognize him," Gabe said, giving Connor the once-over.

"Give it a rest, guys. It hasn't been that long." Connor forced himself to smile. The last thing he needed was for his two best friends to pounce on him. They were both pretty intuitive about Connor's state of mind. He knew it was only a matter of time before one of them brought up Ella.

Rosie, one of the new waitresses, brought over a carafe of orange juice and began filling their glasses before taking their orders.

"So where've you been?" Hank inquired once Rosie left. "Rumor has it you've been seen around town with a certain dark-haired beauty."

"Yeah. We've been spending time together. Just as friends, though. It's not exactly front-page news," Connor said. He wasn't at all surprised that his name had been linked with Ella's. Connor felt a stab of disappointment that the townsfolk had gotten it all wrong. His relationship with Ella had never developed into a romantic one. He was partly to blame for it, due to his overly suspicious nature.

Gabe chuckled. "You clearly don't know the people in this town. They live for this kind of stuff. Next thing you know they'll be marrying the two of you off."

Connor rolled his eyes. He loved how people went from zero to a hundred in the span of a few weeks. He hoped Ella didn't catch wind of any of the rumors. Connor knew Ella didn't want a romantic relationship. He would hate for her to feel any awkwardness about being the focus of town gossip.

Connor needed to make sure his best friends understood. "She's pretty amazing, although we're just friends."

"Are you sure? That look on your face suggests otherwise," Gabe remarked.

He shook his head. "Yeah, I am. We were getting close, but honestly, I have so many doubts about her past. So we're just buddies."

Hank leaned across the table. "Are you saying you'd like to be more than friends in the future?"

Connor quirked his mouth. "I'd like to, but it's not possible. She's not interested in me that way."

"It's nice she had a visitor," Gabe said, taking a huge sip of his juice. "It's never easy starting over in a new town."

Connor frowned. "A visitor? No, you've got it wrong. I don't think any of her family or friends have come to see her. She's been talking a lot about being homesick."

Gabe scoffed. "Well, someone did. A man chartered a flight a few weeks ago. Lawson Charters had to communicate with his plane to make sure we weren't in the same airspace. The plane landed at my hangar."

His throat felt dry. Owl Creek was only accessible via plane and water. Coming to town wasn't an easy process. Surely Gabe wouldn't have gotten it wrong. Suddenly, Connor's stomach was tied up in knots. This felt off. Why hadn't Ella mentioned having a visitor, especially since she'd confided in him about yearning for her loved ones?

Rosie returned with their orders, but all of a sudden he wasn't hungry. He knew that he wouldn't even be able to swallow. Connor couldn't shake off the feeling that once again Ella was hiding something.

"How do you know he was here to see Ella?" he asked Gabe.

Gabe locked gazes with him. "You know how small towns are. Nothing's invisible. One of my mechanics spotted him coming and going from Ella's house. And he said this wasn't his first visit."

Town gossips! He clenched his jaw as heat spread through his chest. Didn't people in Owl Creek have anything better to do than flap their jaws? Resentment flooded him. He didn't even know why he was getting so wound up over it, but he felt aggravated.

"I wish people would mind their business." Connor angrily spit out the words.

"What are you getting so upset about?" Hank asked. His face was creased with a frown.

"I'm not upset," Connor said, denying the raw emotions he was battling.

"I shouldn't have said anything," Gabe muttered. "Next time I'm going to mind my business."

"You don't have to treat me with kid gloves, Gabe," he snapped.

"If that's the case, I'm just going to ask… What's bugging you?" Gabe asked. "From what you've said, you and Ella are just friends."

"We are, but I can't pretend I don't wish something deeper has been brewing between us," Connor said.

"Don't be that guy, okay? Just because she had a man visit her, you can't assume it was romantic," Gabe said. "Don't let a misunderstanding get in the way of something terrific."

Although he was experiencing a little spurt of jealousy, that wasn't the main issue. The bigger question was why hadn't Ella told him a friend was flying into Owl Creek. Why were there so many things about her past she seemed to be hiding? Just who was Ella Perez? Gabe's mention of the mysterious visitor to Owl Creek was the final straw. He'd allowed his feelings for Ella to cloud his judgment. He had suspected something was off with her since the very beginning.

"It's not just that," he said, letting out a deep sigh. "There's a dozen reasons why I couldn't allow myself to get involved with Ella. I would've had to push past every single doubt I had and allowed my heart to rule my head. And trust me, there have been times when I wanted to do just that."

"We thought you'd put those issues to rest," Hank said. "I guess we assumed since the two of you were spending a lot of time together that you trusted her. Even in a friendship that's important."

"To be honest, the doubts never went away. Maybe I was just fooling myself, thinking it wasn't necessary to have full disclosure in a friendship. I can't explain how overwhelming it is. It feels like a tidal wave is crashing over me." He ran a shaky hand over his face.

"Talk to her," Gabe said. "Tell her how you feel. Straighten things out before it festers, Connor."

"I second that," Hank added. "If you want to squash these reservations, put it all out there. Don't leave anything unsaid. If she's as special as you believe, she'll have answers for you."

Connor nodded. "Thanks. That's exactly what I intend to do. And there's no time like the present." He gritted his teeth. "I need answers. And I need them now."

## Chapter Thirteen

Despite Gabe's and Hank's attempts to settle his nerves, Connor hadn't been able to calm down. He hadn't been able to eat his breakfast and he'd bolted from the diner as soon as the tab was paid. He didn't even bother calling Ella before showing up at her house. They'd talked last night, and she'd told him she was going to be running some errands, but Connor was just going to take a chance she'd be there. When he pulled up, he spotted her truck outside the house, serving as confirmation that she was inside.

Finding out about her mysterious guest had caused something inside of him to crack wide-open. For the entire time Ella had been in Owl Creek, Connor had questioned her truthfulness. Now it felt like she'd smacked him straight in the face with her evasions.

Was he blowing things out of proportion? He didn't want to barge into her house spewing accusations. His fervent hope was that she would have a simple answer to his question that would quell all of his uncertainties.

*Lord, please give me clarity. I'm so confused right now, and I don't want to let anger cloud my objective. I need answers from Ella. I want the truth. Please grant me the strength to deal with whatever she might tell me.*

When he knocked on the door, Ella answered it with a look of surprise mixed with joy etched on her face. "Connor! I wasn't expecting you. Come on in," she said. Ella was treating him like a treasured guest, and it gutted him.

This wasn't a friendly visit. He'd come here seeking answers, and he wasn't going to allow her to deflect or steer him away from his purpose.

"Can I get you anything? I made some biscuits earlier and—"

"No," he said quickly, cutting her off. He needed to talk to her before he lost his nerve. There was something about Ella that always made him feel badly about questioning her. "I've already had breakfast at the diner. I need to talk to you about something."

"All right," she said. "Why don't we go to the living room and sit down?"

Connor trailed after her, all the while thinking of what he wanted to say. When Ella sat down on the couch, he resisted the urge to sit next to her. Instead he sat in a high-backed chair across from her.

"Is everything okay? You seem upset."

He inhaled a calming breath. "I heard something earlier from Gabe. He said you had a visitor fly in from out of town. Is that true?" He was watching her reaction carefully, eager to see her response.

Ella looked like a deer caught in the headlights.

She was staring at him with big eyes and picking idly at her long-sleeved shirt. "Yes, it's true," she said in a halting voice.

"Who is he?"

"H-he's a friend."

His jaw clenched. So why hadn't she told him? Why had it been such a secret?

He knitted his brows together. "From where? What's his name?"

"Connor, what's going on? Why are you grilling me like this?" She wiped her hand across her forehead. She appeared to be nervous. In his heart he'd wanted her to be calm, cool and collected with nothing kept secret.

His heart sank. She was getting defensive and not giving him any of the answers he so desperately needed. Perhaps he was springing this on her, but if she wasn't keeping him in the dark it shouldn't be a problem. And it wasn't just this omission. There had been so many piling up for weeks now. He cared so very deeply about her. Getting to the truth was the only way they might ever have a chance at a future together. And if he was being honest with himself, that's what he wanted more than anything.

"Has he been here before?" he asked, his suspicions intensifying with every passing second.

Ella bit her lip. She nodded. "Yes. Once before. When I first came to Owl Creek he helped me get settled."

A feeling of disbelief swept through him. Clearly this man was important to her. He wasn't a member of her family, and yet she wasn't doing much explaining about his presence in her life. If he didn't suspect she was sitting on a world of secrets, maybe this development wouldn't bother him so much. In many ways it was the final straw of weeks spent wondering about the skeletons in Ella's closet. He'd had enough!

"His name is Jonah. Like I said, he's a friend."

"He flew all the way here, but you didn't want to introduce him to anyone? Show him around town?" If Ella had toured a stranger around town, Connor would have heard about it. The town gossips would have had a field day over it. But at least it would have been done out in the open. It would make sense.

She looked down instead of meeting his gaze. "H-he wasn't here long. There really wasn't time for sight-seeing."

Connor shook his head. It made no sense. Ella was playing him for a fool and pretending as if her actions weren't suspicious. It felt like she was gaslighting him.

"You said you're not used to snow, but Flagstaff gets tons of it," he blurted out. "You didn't know how to drive in the snow. You were completely unnerved when I wanted to take your ID picture. You didn't want your picture put online. And the very first day we met you didn't answer me when I called out your name. How do you explain these inconsistencies?"

"I… I can't explain those things, Connor." Her tone was flat and unemotional.

"Can't or won't?" he asked. Frustration had gotten the better of him. Although he felt badly about blind-siding her with his questions, he'd been driven to the brink. He was trying to bridge this chasm between them, but she wasn't giving him anything to hold on to. She wasn't giving him any answers. Nothing made sense. At this point he wasn't even sure he could justify a friendship with her based on all of her evasions. After what his family had experienced in the past, Connor knew better than to ignore warning signs.

Ella wasn't even trying to make eye contact with him now. She was shutting down on him, and he had no idea of how to get through to her. Perhaps he was being too insensitive. Maybe she needed a sympathetic approach.

He softened his voice. "Ella, I know you might be scared. I think you've been through something that frightened you. I think there are things you haven't been able to express."

Ella's expression was shuttered. How could she be this calm? She wasn't reacting as if any of this was a big deal at all. Didn't she care about how he felt?

"Ella, I grew up with secrets. My whole childhood was affected by lies and deception. I can't go through that again. It hurt too much the first time. And that pain only recently began to heal with Sage's return. I care about you, but I can't be involved with someone who won't be honest with me. The truth is too important to hide."

"I understand," she said calmly.

"Is there anything you'd like to tell me?" he asked, offering her a final chance to open up to him. "I'm here, Ella. Here beside you, willing to listen."

For a moment he thought he'd gotten through to her. She met his gaze and he saw a spark of something in her eyes that made him believe she cared about him enough to unveil herself.

"No, Connor. There isn't," she answered.

Her response almost brought him to his knees. He'd been holding on to hope until this very moment and praying for her to come to her senses. Instead, she'd flatly rejected his plea. And judging by the reserved look on her face, it didn't bother her at all.

He let out a ragged sigh, then stood up from his seat. "Thanks, Ella. You've made everything perfectly clear. I'll see myself out."

Just as he reached the door, Ella called out to him. "Connor. Wait!"

Hope rocketed inside of him. *Please, God. Answer my prayer.*

"I'm so sorry," she said.

"I am, too," Connor said before stepping out the door. He didn't bother looking back. Ella had made it clear that she wasn't willing to bend in order to be with him.

After he got in his truck, Connor roared down the road, trying his best to leave all thoughts of Ella Perez in his rearview mirror.

As she covertly peered through the window and watched Connor drive away, Isabelle's heart cracked into a million pieces. She knew she should feel relieved that her friendship with Connor was over. At least now she wouldn't have to feel guilty any longer about the secrets she was withholding from him. She wouldn't have to agonize about every slip of the tongue or the answers she could never provide to his questions. Shouldn't she feel free right now? Free from having to tell the man she loved more lies. Somewhere along the way she'd fallen in love with Connor, which totally explained the knifelike sensation twisting in her gut. He would no longer be involved in her life. She'd seen it written all over his face right before he left.

When she was a little girl, she'd had a habit of curling up into a little ball and shutting out the world anytime she had been in pain. Although she'd outgrown the habit, this fresh hurt made her long to revert back to old patterns. Maybe she could forget about Connor and her feelings for him. Perhaps it wouldn't hurt so badly if she stuffed them all down into a vast black hole and pretended as if nothing had happened between them at all.

*When thou walkest through the fire, thou shalt not be burned; neither shall the flame kindle upon thee.*

Yet she did feel terribly burned. She had gotten way too close to Connor, mistakenly believing that friendship would suffice even though her feelings had blossomed over time. Isabelle had hurt him. She'd seen the raw pain emanating from his eyes. He was a proud man who always tried to shield himself from emotional upheaval. It was a defense mechanism he'd constructed as a child due to the trauma of Sage's abduction. And now, thanks to her, Connor was dealing with more anguish. She'd wounded him. And that knowledge caused a twisting sensation in the pit of her stomach. Tears swept down her face. She'd lost Connor's goodwill and friendship. Their relationship had been littered with half-truths. The foundation had been weak at its core.

He didn't even know her real name. She'd never had the pleasure of hearing him call her Isabelle. And now she never would. Everything felt bleak now. Suddenly her life in Owl Creek felt smaller and less substantial. Connor's absence would leave a hole the size of Kachemak Bay.

*Lord, please help me heal this broken heart. I love this man with all of my soul and I can't erase what he means to me. The emotions run too deep. He's too firmly embedded in my heart. And I fear he will always be there.*

A knock on her door startled her from her prayers. Was it Connor? Had he come back to try to straighten things out? She raced to the door and flung it open, wanting nothing more than to see Connor's handsome face greeting her. Her body sagged as she saw Sage standing at her doorstep.

"Sage," she said. Isabelle could hear the disappointment lacing her own voice.

"Ella! Did you forget I was swinging by to pick you up?" Sage asked.

"Yes. No. I guess so," she said. She'd made plans with Sage to check out the vintage store on Main Street. They were meeting up with Piper and Rachel so they could shop and have lunch together at the diner.

"What's wrong? You look shattered. Did something happen?"

"Oh, no. I'm fine," she said. Her voice was trembling and she could feel the hot sting of tears in her eyes. Before she knew it, tears were streaming down her face.

Sage reached out and pulled her into her arms. Something broke inside her as Sage began whispering soothing words of encouragement. Isabelle began to sob, huge heart-wrenching cries spilling out of her. She had been trying to hold it together for so long now. In the process she had stuffed down all of her feelings of distress, anxiety and pain. In order to make a successful transition to the Witness Protection Program, Isabelle had been forced to maintain a good-natured facade so as not to arouse suspicion. It had all taken a tremendous toll on her.

She wasn't fine. Not by a long shot.

Connor wasn't all right. The weight of pretending as if everything was fine was beginning to weigh on him. He'd managed to sit through a special dinner at his parents' house without choking on his food. Thankfully, the dinner was in Piper and Braden's honor. All attention was focused on their wedding tomorrow. Just watching the joyous couple made him think about Ella and all that she meant to him. It hurt so much to come to terms with the fact that she didn't trust him enough to come clean. Why did this cause him so much angst? Why did she have such an effect on him?

Needing a breath of fresh air, Connor walked toward the front door, shrugging into his jacket before heading outside. The moon hung up in the velvety darkness like a beacon guiding travelers home. He thought back to the night he'd watched the blood moon with Ella and they'd shared tender kisses. That evening had been full of so much promise. Until the bottom had fallen out of his world.

How could he heal this awful ache inside of him when he couldn't even look at an Alaskan sky without thinking about her? Missing her. Wanting to hold her in his arms. Wanting way more than he'd ever been able to claim.

A slight sound caused him to turn around. His grandfather was behind him, bundled up in his winter coat.

"What're you doing out here? It's pretty cold this evening."

"I just needed to be alone with my thoughts," Connor said. "No offense."

"None taken. You've been awfully quiet lately. That's not like you," the older man observed.

"I'm just tired. I've been working too hard, I suppose." He winked at his grandfather. "You need to tell that wife of yours to go easy on me."

Jennings chuckled. "As if she'd listen."

"I need to get some sleep before the wedding tomorrow. It's going to be a big day for our family." What he wasn't saying was that sleep had been elusive lately. More times than not, he tossed and turned until the wee hours of the morning. All was not right within his soul.

"A joyful event. It's just what we need after so many years of sorrow."

For a moment they both settled into the silence. After all they had endured during the years when Sage was missing, a wedding truly was a blessed event.

*Weeping may endure for a day, but joy cometh in the morning.* The passage from Psalms resonated with him. It always reminded him of his family and what they'd been through. It was finally their time to experience unbridled joy.

"So, if you don't mind my asking, what's going on with you and Ella? I thought the two of you were on track to become Owl Creek's next sweethearts."

Connor made a face. "It never got off the ground. We were just too different, I suppose." He didn't want to tell his grandfather the nitty-gritty details that had prevented him from getting romantically involved with her.

"That's a shame. She's a fascinating woman."

Connor turned toward his grandfather. "What do you mean? You barely know her."

His grandfather chuckled. "I'm not just a birdwatcher, son. I'm a people watcher, too. I've only been in Ella's presence a few times, but I came to the conclusion that she's not as she appears to be."

Connor let out a brittle laugh. "You're way smarter than I am. It took me months to confirm it."

Jennings narrowed his gaze as he looked at him. "And what exactly did you deduce about Ella?"

"That she's not a truthful person. I have no use for people I can't trust." He hated speaking badly about Ella, but he needed to be honest with his grandfather.

"Hmm. That's not what I observed."

"Don't leave me hanging. I'd love to know your thoughts," Connor said, folding his arms across his chest.

"I saw the pain beneath her beautiful exterior, along with a trace of fear. She tried to hide those things, but I recognized them. When I first met your grandmother, she radiated those same emotions. But, with time and patience, I broke through her tough exterior and found a sparkling diamond underneath."

Connor couldn't imagine two people being more different. His grandmother was as tough as an Alaskan winter on the tundra, while Ella reminded him of forget-me-nots—beautiful yet delicate. He didn't quite see the resemblance.

"Why was grandmother in pain?" he asked.

"People come to us as they are. Beulah's childhood was miserable. It's one of the reasons she was so happy to join the North fold. She didn't just emerge from the womb as the magnificent woman she is today. She grew and evolved over time. Imagine if I'd written her off back then?" Jennings had a contemplative expression on his face. "I would have missed out on so many wonderful moments."

"You wouldn't have lived out your amazing love story," Connor said. "And I wouldn't be here right now."

Jennings nodded his head. "Amen. Connor, I'd like to ask you a question. Do you love her?"

The question was thrown at him like a curveball. All this time he'd been Ella's friend. They'd never really moved past that stage. Did he love her? He'd never been in love before. Hadn't even come close. He froze for a moment, overwhelmed by the reality of his situation. All of these emotions roiling around inside him added up to one thing. The realization hit him squarely in the chest. He was head over heels in love with Ella.

"Yes, I do. I love her more than I ever imagined I could love someone," he confessed. Something told him that his grandfather already knew what he'd just admitted. He didn't look at all surprised by Connor's declaration.

"So what are you going to do about it?"

"What can I do? Loving her doesn't negate the fact that she won't open up to me about her past. How can I move forward without complete honesty? Not to mention I have no idea if she loves me."

"You have to ask yourself what's worse. Living a life with unanswered questions or living a life without the woman that you love. And if you truly love her, you need to start putting the pieces together. Why would she have come to a remote Alaskan town? Why is she so skittish? Add up everything you know about her. Fill in the blanks. Do some digging on your own."

The words crashed over him with the force of a tsunami. They were powerful and heart-wrenching and moving. And it caused his brain to go into overdrive.

His grandfather put his arm around him. "Let's go inside. Get some rest. You have a lot of thinking to do."

He did. And even though he needed to get plenty of rest in preparation for Braden's wedding festivities, something told him he wasn't going to sleep a wink tonight. He was going to do a deep dive on the internet, checking in places like Arizona and Florida to see if he could unearth anything about any criminal cases. Perhaps she'd been a victim of an assault or a stalk-

ing. If there was even a shred of information, Connor
was determined to find it.

Isabelle sat in her truck and looked out her window
at the festively decorated church. Flowers had been
artfully placed by the entrance along with pink ribbons and an elaborate wedding banner. She watched
as guests streamed into the church. Most of them she
recognized from around town.

Isabelle had thought about not attending the wedding, but after realizing it wouldn't be right not to
show up, she'd decided to honor her commitment. She
looked in the rearview mirror, checking to make sure
her hair and lipstick were in order. She knew there was
a chance she might run into Connor. Her stomach was
full of butterflies about how she should react to seeing him, especially now that she knew she was in love
with him. Should she casually say hello or avoid him at
all costs? It would be for the best if their paths didn't
cross. It would be easier for both of them.

A quick glance at her watch served as a warning to
go inside the church before Piper made her grand entrance. Once inside, she made a point to sit toward the
rear. She didn't want to draw any attention to herself.
She'd already had a few townsfolk question her about
the rumors about her and Connor over the past week.
It had been very awkward and uncomfortable. Somehow she'd managed to answer them tactfully.

From her vantage point she was able to see Connor
standing right next to Braden at the altar. Even at this
distance he caused a riot of emotions within her. Most

of all, a yearning to be with him tugged at her. If only the situation was different.

When the wedding march played, three adorable toddlers teetered down the aisle—a pair of brown-skinned twins, Faith and Lizzie, who she knew belonged to Rachel and Gabe, along with Addie, Hank and Sage's little girl. The little ones practically stole the show until Piper appeared with Hank at her side. Connor had told her that Piper's dad, Jack, had died four years ago in a snowmobile accident. Isabelle imagined having her brother standing in as a substitute was an emotional moment. Tears pooled in Ella's eyes as she watched Piper, resplendent in a white lace and tulle long-sleeved dress, glide by. There was nothing but pure joy etched on her lovely face. She looked like a fairy-tale princess.

Isabelle dabbed at her eyes throughout the awe-inspiring ceremony. Their vows were achingly romantic. When Piper and Braden were declared man and wife, they joined hands and walked back down the aisle followed by their bridal party. As Isabelle spotted Connor approaching, she braced herself for him to look away from her, but as he passed by, their eyes met. The way he stared at her caused her pulse to quicken. Instead of anger, Isabelle saw tenderness.

*Stop being fanciful*, she urged herself. If nothing else, Connor had made his feelings quite clear to her. He didn't think she was a good person. That realization still hurt.

Isabelle waited till the church was almost empty before she exited. Given the circumstances, she didn't think she would go to the reception at the North estate. It wouldn't feel right since she and Connor were at odds. He should be able to enjoy his brother's special day without any distractions. That's what she was at this point.

When she pushed open the door and walked into the vestibule area, Isabelle sucked in a shocked breath. Connor was standing a few feet away with an earnest expression on his face. It was just the two of them in the corridor. Her first instinct was to retreat, but if the last few months had taught her anything at all, it was to tap into her inner strength. *Fear thou not; for I am with thee.* She wasn't standing alone. He was always with her.

"Ella. It's good to see you." His deep, soothing voice was music to her ears.

Her stomach lurched. Why did he have to look so handsome in his dark suit and tie? Had his eyes always been so blue? It was true what they said. Absence made the heart grow fonder. Isabelle knew down to the days and hours how long it had been since they'd spoken to each other. She ached from missing him.

"Hey, Connor. How are you?" Isabelle forced the words out of her mouth. She was desperate to appear as if her heart hadn't been crushed.

"I'd like to talk to you, if it's all right?" he asked.

"Don't you need to go to the reception?" Isabelle knew the bridal party and the family usually departed together. No doubt they would be looking for Connor outside.

"It can wait. I told them to go on without me."

Isabelle nodded. "Okay," she said, her mind whirling with questions. What could he possibly want to talk to her about? Hadn't they already said it all? Her heart began to thunder wildly inside her chest. Was she being fired from North Star Chocolates? That would be a devastating blow.

She raised a hand to her throat. "Are you letting me go from the chocolate shop?" she asked. What would she do for work now in Owl Creek? Did this mean she would be forced to relocate?

"Of course not," he said. "Why would you ever think that?"

She let out a sigh of relief. "I… I really love working there and I just thought—"

"I'm sorry, Ella," he said, cutting her off. "I've been doing a lot of thinking. About you. About the things I know you're keeping under wraps. The fear. Your inability to open up to me. The sketchy details about your life. I kept going back to that day in the chocolate shop when the car backfired. You were terrified. Now that I think about it, you were exhibiting signs of post-traumatic stress." He took a deep breath. "I think you witnessed an act of violence. I think you're here because you're a witness. A few years ago Hank told Gabe and me about a program where witnesses to violent crimes are placed under protection and given a new identity." His voice suddenly sounded hoarse. "I think that's you, Ella."

She let out a sob, then covered her mouth with her hand. Shock roared through her. Connor continued talking.

"I did some fishing around on the internet last night. At first I was searching Arizona cases, but then I looked in Florida since you mentioned spending time there. That's when I found it. You provided testimony after witnessing your boss's murder. Because of you, he was put away for a long time. But it didn't stop his criminal enterprise from coming after you. Which, I suspect, is why you might have entered WITSEC. To save your life." He pulled a piece of paper from his pocket and unfolded it before holding it out to her. "This is you, isn't it? Isabelle Sanchez from Miami, Florida."

Isabelle looked at the printout of the newspaper article. It was all there in black and white. She wiped away tears with the back of her hand. The rules of the WITSEC program didn't stipulate what to do if the person you were madly in love with came to you with decisive proof about your former identity. He was holding the evidence in his hands. She'd done her very best to protect herself and to uphold the standards of the program. But this was an extraordinary development in her story.

Her heart began to thunder in her chest. Because Connor had stumbled upon the truth, her status in WITSEC could be compromised. She might be relocated from Owl Creek to another location. She might have to say goodbye to Connor. The very thought of it caused a twisting sensation in her gut. Words were stuck in her throat.

"I'm sorry for not being gentler with you. I let my pride and my past get the better of me. I'm ashamed of how I acted. I'm asking you to forgive me, but I understand if you can't." He reached out and took her hand. "I want to move forward with you. I know your life is complicated and fraught with danger, but I'm prepared to never divulge a word of this to a single person."

"What are you saying, Connor?" She was practically holding her breath waiting for him to spell it out. Hope was within her grasp and she wanted so badly to grab ahold of it. If there was any chance that they could work through her being in WITSEC, she wouldn't hesitate to do whatever she could to make it happen. She believed in Connor. He would be worth it.

"I thought that I needed to know everything about you in order to forge a relationship with you, but I already know all the things that matter or will ever matter. I know how it makes me feel when you smile at me. I know you would never hurt anyone. You radiate kindness and empathy. I know someone hurt you and made you fearful. And that makes me angrier than I can ever express in words, but I also know it's made you strong and resilient." He took a deep, steadying breath. "I don't want to spend another day apart from you. My life is richer with you in it. I've been so consumed with your past I forgot to focus on the present and the future. Our future. For so long there was a big hole inside me that needed to be filled up. You've done that, Ella. And I don't want to live a life without you in it."

Tears were streaming down her face. She let out a sob. "Are you sure? My life is a bit complicated, and there are lots of dos and don'ts involved. And there's no guarantee that danger might not present itself, not only for myself, but to you as well. And the Marshals might decide to relocate me to another town. That's a distinct possibility now."

"Ella, I'm more certain about us than I've been of anything in my life." Connor reached out and ran his thumb against her cheek. "I love you."

"I love you, too, Connor. So very much," she whispered.

She stood on her tippy-toes and placed a kiss on his lips. In this one moment she was happier than she'd ever imagined. Connor loved her! He'd put the pieces together, and she didn't have to worry about hiding the truth from him because he already knew it. She'd have to convince Jonah that she be allowed to stay now that Connor knew about her past. There were still obstacles to face. But for now she wanted to revel in this moment.

"There's one thing I'd like you to do," she said as their embrace ended.

"Anything."

"Now that you know my real name, please call me Isabelle just this once." She grinned up at him, buoyed by the love she saw radiating from his eyes. Her emotions threatened to burst out of her chest. She was deliriously happy.

"Isabelle," he murmured. "I like the sound of that."

Hearing her real name rolling off his lips was such a simple thing, yet it filled her with unimaginable bliss.

# *Epilogue*

A light snow gently fell from the sky as Isabelle and Connor burst through the wooden doors of the church followed by a crowd of well-wishers. Happiness hung in the air as the newly married couple was bombarded with forget-me-not flower petals and shouts of congratulations.

Connor reached for his wife's hand and pressed it to his lips. "I love you, Mrs. North."

She was no longer keeping any secrets from her husband. Jonah had met with her and Connor. He'd given her the green light to discuss her participation in WITSEC with Connor since he'd already uncovered the truth online. Connor had reassured Jonah that he would never divulge Isabelle's secrets or put her in harm's way. Thankfully, the marshal hadn't found it necessary to relocate her from Owl Creek. Everything had come full circle for them. Truths had been brought out into the light. Joy shone brightly in the aftermath.

"And I love you, my husband." Tears of contentment pooled in her eyes. She'd never dared to dream of such a wonderful happy ending for herself and Connor. It had seemed so out of reach until Connor put his faith in their relationship before his doubts. His belief in her and their love had been a powerful force. Thankfully, Connor had deduced her involvement in WIT-SEC, then proposed to her a few weeks later. It had taken all of the pressure off Isabelle, who no longer had to hide things from Connor. As her husband, he was privy to all of her truths.

"Husband. I like the ring of that," Connor said as he dipped his head down and placed a tender kiss on her lips. Isabelle kissed him back with equal measure, all the while rejoicing in the blessings they'd received. She was so very thankful.

"I couldn't be happier," she gushed as the embrace ended. "God has been so good to us."

"I won't argue with you on that. He brought you all the way to Owl Creek…and to me. I'll always be thankful for it, even though I know you came to Alaska out of necessity, not choice."

"I can't imagine being anywhere but here. Right by your side. Every step along the way led me right to you." She smiled up at him, joy shimmering in her eyes. Connor was her happy ending. Her rainbow after the storm. "You and me and a lifetime of happiness."

"That's all I want, baby. For us to walk through life together. You've been through so much, and you've shown nothing but bravery and pluck."

"You were with me, Connor, and because you believed in me…in us, we're standing here right now as man and wife. You stepped out on a limb of faith, even though I gave you every reason to doubt me. You did the work to bring us together."

"You were worth fighting for, Isabelle. You're the strongest woman I've ever known. What you went through back in Miami would have destroyed most people, yet you tapped into your inner strength and persevered."

"There were times I didn't think I would make it through, but I'm so glad I did. Because of you, Connor. And what the future holds for us."

"What we have is everything I've ever wanted in this world." He took her hand and pressed a kiss on her knuckles.

Isabelle smiled as Connor's family members joined the throng of well-wishers. Her new Owl Creek family. Beulah. Jennings. Willa and Nate. Sage. Hank. Rachel. Gabe. Piper and Braden. She was now a part of this amazing tribe of people. Although her parents, grandmother and sister couldn't be present at the ceremony due to WITSEC rules, Jonah had worked out something special to reunite them for a brief visit in another locale in a few weeks. It was way more than Isabelle had ever imagined being possible.

It was bigger than she'd dared to dream for herself. She and Connor had emerged from their struggles, stronger and more faithful. And she no longer had to look over her shoulder because she knew she was sheltered in her new Owl Creek haven. She would never be completely free from danger, but she wasn't going to be living in fear. For now and always, she would be safe in Connor's loving embrace.

* * * * *

*If you enjoyed this book,
look for these other books set in Owl Creek:*

Her Secret Alaskan Family
Alaskan Twin Surprise
Alaskan Christmas Redemption

Dear Reader,

Thank you for joining me on this trip to Owl Creek. Isabelle and Connor's love story was fun to write. I hope you enjoyed it. This book challenged me in so many ways. I tried to put myself in Isabelle's shoes and found it daunting. It would take courage to rebuild your life and say goodbye to your loved ones.

Connor is a charming and caring man, whose life was shaped by the abduction of his sister. This traumatic incident left him with lingering feelings of mistrust, which complicates his relationship with Ella. I have a lot of compassion for Connor because his childhood was affected by the hole in his family, which was the result of one person's act of evil.

Ultimately, the thing that brings Isabelle and Connor together is their yearning for love. Both are suffering from loneliness and a desire to establish something meaningful with a romantic partner. Hope is a thread that runs throughout the story.

I love writing inspirational romance for the Love Inspired line. I'm blessed to do what I love. You can find me on my Author Belle Calhoune Facebook page, as well as on my website bellecalhoune.com.

Blessings,
*Belle*

# Get 4 FREE REWARDS!

### We'll send you 2 FREE Books plus 2 FREE Mystery Gifts.

**Love Inspired** books feature uplifting stories where faith helps guide you through life's challenges and discover the promise of a new beginning.

FREE
Value Over
$20

---

**YES!** Please send me 2 FREE Love Inspired Romance novels and my 2 FREE mystery gifts (gifts are worth about $10 retail). After receiving them, if I don't wish to receive any more books, I can return the shipping statement marked "cancel." If I don't cancel, I will receive 6 brand-new novels every month and be billed just $5.24 each for the regular-print edition or $5.99 each for the larger-print edition in the U.S., or $5.74 each for the regular-print edition or $6.24 each for the larger-print edition in Canada. That's a savings of at least 13% off the cover price. It's quite a bargain! Shipping and handling is just 50¢ per book in the U.S. and $1.25 per book in Canada.* I understand that accepting the 2 free books and gifts places me under no obligation to buy anything. I can always return a shipment and cancel at any time. The free books and gifts are mine to keep no matter what I decide.

Choose one:  ☐ **Love Inspired Romance**
 **Regular-Print**
 (105/305 IDN GNWC)

☐ **Love Inspired Romance**
 **Larger-Print**
 (122/322 IDN GNWC)

Name (please print)

Address                                                                                       Apt. #

City                                      State/Province                          Zip/Postal Code

**Email:** Please check this box ☐ if you would like to receive newsletters and promotional emails from Harlequin Enterprises ULC and its affiliates. You can unsubscribe anytime.

### Mail to the **Harlequin Reader Service:**
**IN U.S.A.:** P.O. Box 1341, Buffalo, NY 14240-8531
**IN CANADA:** P.O. Box 603, Fort Erie, Ontario L2A 5X3

Want to try 2 free books from another series? Call 1-800-873-8635 or visit www.ReaderService.com.

---

## SPECIAL EXCERPT FROM

### LOVE INSPIRED
INSPIRATIONAL ROMANCE

*When a young Amish woman returns home
with a baby in tow, will sparks fly with her
handsome—and unusual—neighbor?*

*Read on for a sneak preview of*
The Baby Next Door
*by Vannetta Chapman.*

Grace found Nicole had pulled herself up to the front door and was high-fiving none other than Adrian Schrock. He'd squatted down to her level. Nicole was having a fine old time.

Grace picked up her *doschder* and pushed open the door, causing Adrian to jump up, then step back toward the porch steps. It was, indeed, a fine spring day. The sun shone brightly across the Indiana fields. Flowers colored yellow, red, lavender and orange had begun popping through the soil that surrounded the porch. Birds were even chirping merrily.

Somehow, all those things did little to elevate Grace's mood. Neither did the sight of her neighbor.

Adrian resettled his straw hat on his head and smiled. *"Gudemariye."*

"Your llama has escaped again."

"Kendrick? *Ya.* I've come to fetch him. He seems to like your place more than mine."

"I don't want that animal over here, Adrian. He spits. And your peacock was here at daybreak, crying like a child."

Adrian laughed. "When you moved back home, I guess you didn't expect to live next to a Plain & Simple Exotic Animal Farm."

Adrian wiggled his eyebrows at Nicole when he seemed to realize that Grace wasn't amused.

"I think of your place as Adrian's Zoo."

"Not a bad name, but it doesn't highlight our Amish heritage enough."

"The point is that I feel like we're living next door to a menagerie of animals."

"Up, Aden. Up."

Adrian scooped Nicole from Grace's hold, held her high above his head, then nuzzled her neck. Adrian was comfortable with everyone and everything.

"Do you think she'll ever learn to say my name right?"

"Possibly. Can you please catch Kendrick and take him back to your place?"

"Of course. That's why I came over. I guess I must have left the gate open again." He kissed Nicole's cheek, then popped her back into Grace's arms. "You should bring her over to see the turtles."

As he walked away, Grace wondered for the hundredth time why he wasn't married. It was true that he'd picked a strange profession. What other Amish man raised exotic animals? No, Adrian wouldn't be considered excellent marrying material by most young Amish women.

*Don't miss*
The Baby Next Door *by Vannetta Chapman,*
*available April 2021 wherever*
*Love Inspired books and ebooks are sold.*

LoveInspired.com

# LOVE INSPIRED

INSPIRATIONAL ROMANCE

## UPLIFTING STORIES OF FAITH, FORGIVENESS AND HOPE.

---

Join our social communities to connect with other readers who share your love!

Sign up for the Love Inspired newsletter at **LoveInspired.com** to be the first to find out about upcoming titles, special promotions and exclusive content.

---

### CONNECT WITH US AT:

Facebook.com/LoveInspiredBooks

Twitter.com/LoveInspiredBks

Facebook.com/groups/HarlequinConnection

# Praise for *WILD TALES*

"Over the decades, his songbook has struck a rare and brilliant balance between the personal and the political, each lending more gravity to the other. . . . His life has been filled with a dazzling cast of lovers, collaborators, friends, and rivals. . . . *Wild Tales* posits Nash's nearly unbreakable optimism as the epoxy that held an infinitely complicated cluster of individuals together."

—*Washington Post*

"There are indeed wild tales to tell. . . . Nash wasn't pulling back on the lurid details."

—*Pittsburgh Post-Gazette*

"Shockingly candid."

—*Daily Express* (UK)

"Though Crosby, Stills & Nash and Crosby, Stills, Nash & Young made more than their share of beautiful music together and lived in a kind of hippie heaven replete with mansions, money, and free love, Nash doesn't hesitate to share the dark side of stardom, too, particularly the drug-fueled ego trips and meltdowns that so often derailed the group. . . . [But] the reader is inclined to believe that the drugs, the women, the accolades, and the money were never the point. 'It always comes down to the music,' Nash says. And that's what makes this trip worth taking."

—*USA Today*

"A no-holds-barred, fiercely honest chronicle of the glories, excesses, disappointments, and joys of the rock-and-roll life. . . . Nash's tour-de-force tale reveals a soul who is 'a complete slave to the muse of music.'"

—*Publishers Weekly*

"The story of a man's life and his unshakable passion to express himself through his art. Fans might say the book is long overdue, but it was definitely worth the wait."

—*Booklist*

"[A] highly compelling and marvelously detailed memoir."

—*Music Radar*

# Wild Tales

## A ROCK & ROLL LIFE

## Graham Nash

THREE RIVERS PRESS

NEW YORK

Originally published in hardcover in the United States by Crown Archetype,
an imprint of the Crown Publishing Group, a division of Random House LLC,
New York, in 2013.

Library of Congress Cataloging-in-Publication Data
Nash, Graham
     Wild tales/Graham Nash.—First edition.
     pages cm
     1. Nash, Graham, 1942–  2. Singers—Biography.
     3. Crosby, Stills & Nash.  4. Crosby, Stills, Nash & Young.  I. Title.
     ML420.N353A3 2013
     782.42166092—dc23
     [B]          2013012077

ISBN 978-0-385-34756-3
eBook ISBN 978-0-385-34755-6

Printed in the United States of America

Book design by Lauren Dong
Photography: © Graham Nash, pp. ii–iii; © Joel Bernstein, pp. vi–vii
Cover design by Michael Nagin
Cover photographs: © Graham Nash

10  9  8  7  6  5  4  3  2

First Paperback Edition

*I dedicate this book to my mother and father. I owe them my life—in every sense of the word; to my sisters, Elaine and Sharon, whose belief in me was never ending; to my dear wife, Susan, without whom I may never have lasted this long; and to my dear children, whom I love with all my heart: Jackson and his partner, Melissa, Will and his wife, Shannon, and my lovely daughter, Nile. When I became a father, my life was changed dramatically for the better and was deeply enriched.*

*I am so grateful to have been married to Susan for the last thirty-six years. She is the love of my life and has kept my feet on the ground ever since the day I met her; a truly extraordinary woman. I thank you all for allowing me to be myself—I am so proud of you. I wrote this book for all of you, especially for Jackson and Melissa's daughter and our new granddaughter, Stellar Joy. The world had better look out for this incredible young woman.*

*In between the release of the hardbound and paperback version of this book, my son Will and his wife, Shannon, had identical twin boys so . . . "Welcome to this wild and wonderful planet Dylan and James" . . . and so it goes . . .*

# chapter 1

*August 1968*

**I**T ALWAYS COMES DOWN TO THE MUSIC.

I had a tune running through my head as my flight touched down a few minutes late at LAX. All my life I've had music in my head, but that night the tune (the theme from the TV series *77 Sunset Strip*) was doing battle on my behalf, helping me fend off the other shit that was rattling around in there. For the past few months, my well-ordered world had been turned upside down, and throughout the long flight from London everything seemed to gang up on me. There was no escaping it in that crowded cabin. With few distractions, I'd taken stock of the difficult choices on my holy mess of a plate.

How's this for starters: I was contemplating leaving my country, my marriage, my bank account, and my band—all at once! Any one of those would have been enough to put a grown man in the hole, but I was close to running the table.

My band, the Hollies, and I had come to an impasse. We had grown up together, spent many years making music, writing songs, drinking and larking about; we'd had a fantastic string of hits, incredible success—but from where I stood we were growing apart. I'd moved on, I was headed in an exciting new direction, and my heart and soul weren't in the Hollies anymore.

The same with my marriage. My wife, Rosie, and I had been drifting for some time. We both knew things were coming to an end. In fact, during the last six months, we'd been seeing other people. Now she was off in Spain chasing another man, and I was on my way to Los Angeles to visit a woman who had captured my heart.

I was also in love with LA and the States. I'd known it from the moment I first set foot on American soil. It was the Promised Land, and I was drenched in the Hollywood scene—the music, the sun, the palm trees, the attitude, the looseness. The way people there asked me, "What do you think?" In England, nobody ever asked your opinion of anything. You learned to keep your business to yourself, to mind your p's and q's. In America it seemed like there were no rules, everything was up for grabs, and I loved the freedom of it. I wanted all of it for myself.

No doubt about it, my life had gotten complicated. I was at a hell of a crossroads. There were plenty of unanswered questions. My plight became more apparent as I got off the plane and headed to the taxi stand. There was no point stopping for baggage. I had my guitar. That was it; that was all I had come with. Nothing else mattered. I was in America. I was going to see my new girlfriend, to be with Joni.

THE SUN HAD just left the western sky as the cab crawled up Laurel Canyon, bathing the Hollywood Hills in the golden flush of summer. I got a great vibe every time I came up here. Only a few minutes from the madness of the Strip, but a world apart. There was a shabby hippie chicness to it, with crazy little houses on stilts teetering along each side of the twisty-turny road. It was a place where there were free-spirited people just like me doing the things that I wanted to do, being creative and making music. I felt the pull of Laurel Canyon, its community spirit. Man, it looked like home to me.

We stopped in front of a small wooden house on Lookout Mountain Avenue. It wasn't a posh affair, just a one-bedroom bungalow, a little jewel box, with a sloping shingled roof and a lovely garden out back on a lick of land. A tiny tree had taken root near the porch. A green VW van was parked by a mailbox at the curb. Inside, lights glowed brightly and I could hear the jingle-jangle of voices rising in unison. I knew she had company; I'd called her from the airport. And I knew who was with her. Still, I hesitated, fearing to intrude. I leaned on my guitar case and considered again where I was and what I was doing. Deep down, I was still a kid from the north of England, a place that continued to leave its mark on me. Sure, I know, I was an English rock star, I had it made. But my past made me feel that I wasn't cool, that maybe, even now, I was out of my element. Ahhh—what the hell? I'd been in all kinds of situations the past ten years. No point in getting hung up on that now.

Suddenly, Joni was at the door and nothing else mattered. It had been a few months since we'd last seen each other—and that was, in fact, the first time we'd met—but our connection was instant. Joni Mitchell was the whole package: a lovely, sylphlike woman with a natural blush, like windburn, and an elusive quality that seemed lit from within. Her beauty was almost as big a gift as her talent, and I'd been pulled into her orbit, captivated from the get-go.

Behind her, sitting at the dining room table, the two men I'd expected to see were finishing dinner. I grinned the moment I laid eyes on them.

"Hey, Willy!" David Crosby called from across the room, using a nickname reserved for my closest friends. He was one of those incredible guys it was impossible not to like, a gregarious character, irreverent as hell, with a gorgeous voice and a great sense of humor. I'd met him almost two years earlier, when he was still a member of the Byrds, and we'd become fast friends. There was something that just clicked when we were together. We were on the same wavelength. We loved the same music and the same kind of women, including Joni, who'd been a lover of his some months back. Croz was a no-bullshit kind of guy who called things as he saw them. Besides, he always had the best dope in LA—maybe the best dope anywhere.

The guy next to him was Stephen Stills, an amazing guitar player who had just left Buffalo Springfield, one of the primo LA bands. We'd gotten to know each other a little the last time I'd been in the States. He was already something of an underground legend, a guy who played and held his own with Clapton and Hendrix, totally unique, with a slew of incredible songs. Together, Stills and Crosby were a powerful combination. They had great chops, and I could tell from things they said that they had something cooking.

Seeing them put me totally at ease. Plus Joni really loved them. Stephen had played on her first album, which David had produced. They were all great friends, really comfortable in each other's company, and were eager to roll me into their circle.

Crosby had been smokin' it before I got there and was reasonably high, so I had some catching up to do. They must have been making some music, too, because guitars were lying all over the place, which I'd come to learn was par for the course. In that Laurel Canyon scene, people always brought their guitars to dinner. They took their guitars everywhere; it was part of who they were. And at some point, someone would always say, "Get a load of this new song I'm working on." You could set your watch by it, never failed.

I hadn't been there a half hour when David whacked Stephen on the arm and said, "Hey, play Willy that song we were just doing." Stephen, who was sunk into an armchair next to a giant antique pig from a carousel, uncurled and grabbed his guitar. He fingerpicked a few bars of a beautiful intro while David walked over next to him and joined him in the verse. *"In the morning, when you rise / do you think of me and how you left me crying . . ."* Their harmonies were gorgeous, airtight, two-part—Stephen on the melody with David underneath—that rivaled the Everly Brothers. *"Are you thinking of telephones / and managers and where you got to be at noon?"* I was blown away. The song, "You Don't Have to Cry," was a killer, and their voices double-killed it. You hear something like that, you know it's special right away. The words and tune were perfectly pitched.

They got to the end and I said, "Fuck, that's a fabulous song! Man, Stephen, you wrote a beauty." I glanced at Joan, who was sitting by the piano, and flashed her a smile before asking them: "Would you mind doing it again?"

They looked at each other, shrugged, and said, "Okay."

The next time around I really concentrated on the lyric and the way their voices intertwined and shadowed each other. Hearing them individually, you'd think they'd sideswipe each other. David's tenor was polished to a high gloss, while Stephen's voice was husky and less disciplined, influenced by bluesy southern roots rock. Somehow they didn't compete so much as complement. And they had a natural vibrato, which cast a haunting shade. Those guys could *sing*.

But so could I.

"Okay, bear with me here," I said when they finished. "Do it *one* more time."

Three times, the same song. They must have thought I was stoned out of my gourd. But I was English and a guest, so they figured, let's amuse this guy. Now, I'm a quick study, so I already knew the words and had the harmony down. I'd been listening to it internally and thinking: I know what to do, I know where to go, I got it—*I got it.* As Stephen launched into the intro again, I casually made my way over, standing to his left, and when they hit the opening line—*I'm there.* I had my breath down, the phrasing, the tuning. I put my harmony above Stephen, and off we sailed. *You are livvvv-ing a reality / I left years ago and it quite nearly killed me. In the lonnnng run . . .* What a sound! We were locked in, tight as a drum. Flawless three-part harmony. It sounded so soft and beautiful, so incredible that a minute or so into the song we collapsed in laughter. Especially when we hit that chorus. It was *insane*!

"Wow! Wait a second. What the fuck was that?"

The three of us were harmony freaks and came from groups that had refined two-part as an art: the Hollies, the Springfield, and the Byrds. But the sound we'd just made was different, so fresh. We had never heard anything like it before. It was the Everly Brothers *plus.* And yet so simple: just one acoustic guitar and three people singing as *one.*

It shocked David and Stephen. I'm not sure they'd ever thought about the song in three parts. But I'd heard it right away.

Crosby was beaming ear to ear. "That's the best thing I ever heard!" he said.

I asked Joni: "Did that sound as incredible to you as it did to me?"

"Yeah, it sounded pretty incredible."

Something magical had happened, and we all knew it. When you sing with two or three people and you get it right—when the whole becomes greater than the sum of its parts—everything kind of lifts a couple feet off the ground. The three of us were levitating, all right. The vibe was so high, it was hard to touch down. There was an intense joy that we had found something new, an original sound different from anything that was out there. It was there, complete, a minute into our relationship. We all felt it, knew it. We *wanted* it for ourselves. But we were reluctant to discuss how to pull it off. It was almost as if we were afraid to talk about it, to let the secret out in case it wasn't there tomorrow morning.

Besides, there were so many roadblocks in our paths. To sing with these guys I would have to sever my ties with the Hollies—not such an easy thing to do. For one thing, they were my mates; I loved those guys. Allan Clarke and I had been joined at the hip since we were six years old, and I was an integral part of the group. I'd have to get out of my record contract, get my publishing rights back. It was a mess, but it could be done.

"We have to make this work," Stephen said.

I nodded. "We have no fucking choice but to make this work." There was no doubt in my mind. The moment I heard that sound I knew the rest of my life was headed in another direction. No two ways about it. I had no choice.

EVENTUALLY THE GUYS left and, frankly, I was happy to see them go. I only had three days to spend with Joan, to get to know her intimately, and there are some things that even music doesn't trump. Nor did I see them the rest of the weekend. I was just with Joan; let's get real. But I couldn't get that sound out of my mind. I was haunted by those voices, the way they'd blended so naturally. And those guys. And their songs.

On the flight back to London, I was more fidgety than ever. Not confused: I knew now what was in my heart. I had fallen deeply in love with Joni Mitchell. I was a goner in that department. And those two rascals, Stills and Crosby, were messing with my head. Maybe I had fallen for them, as well.

Everything in my world was spinning, colliding, but I knew what I had to do. There was no doubt in my entire body. And by the time the plane touched down I had it all figured out. I was going home to untangle the first twenty-six years of my life, and to tie up loose ends for the next however many decades. I had heard the future in the power of those voices. And I knew my life would never be the same.

Me at Carnegie Deli, New York City (© *Joel Bernstein*)

I N 1996, I FOUND MYSELF IN BLACKPOOL OF ALL PLACES, a kind of run-down seaside resort where workers from northern England ventured for relaxation, and where I happened to be spending some precious downtime. My two sons, Jackson and Will, were with me, and one hazy afternoon as we strolled down New South Promenade, I detoured into a joint called the Kimberley Hotel, whose two-and-a-half-star Trip Advisor rating kind of says it all. At the front desk, the porter on duty looked up from a magazine he was reading as we hovered into sight.

"Listen, I have a really strange question," I said.

He waved a hand to cut me off. "It's around the corner. You go down two stairs and turn left."

"I'm sorry," I said, with something less than tact, "but how do you know what I'm about to say?"

"You think you're the only one to start a question that way?" he said. "Every one of you who comes back asks for it the same way."

We followed his directions and there it was: the maternity ward, where I took my first breath, at 1:50 A.M. on February 2, 1942. It was pretty much as I'd imagined it—a dark, dank-smelling thirty-foot-square bunker lined with red flocked wallpaper probably put up during Queen Victoria's reign. That windowless room was a pretty grim affair, but hell, I'd been lucky to even have a roof over my head.

I should have been born in Salford, near Manchester, where I eventually grew up, but in 1942 Manchester, an important industrial

center, was busy being bombed to oblivion. So its squadron of pregnant ladies, of which my mom was a star member, was evacuated
to a safer locale, like Blackpool, where they could have their kids in
relative peace. Which is how I wound up making my debut at the
Kimberley Hotel.

By the time I got back to Manchester, the war was halfway over,
but its scars were visible on every street. Salford, our neighborhood, was a pile of rubble. At least ten houses had been destroyed
by enemy payloads, which peppered the city on a nightly basis.
Streets blown apart, huge craters in the landscape. It was a very
dicey scene. My cousin Ray, whose place nearby had been bombed,
was blown under the fireplace, where he lay trapped until workers
rescued him four days later. Everywhere you looked, there was total
devastation. Then again, maybe it would have been better had the
Germans leveled the neighborhood, considering the dreadful living
conditions. Salford was a ghetto, a warren of unseemly row houses
built around the late 1890s, and, by my count, that was the last time
anyone had made improvements.

Salford wasn't at all representative of Manchester. It had a laid-
back character all its own. I found out later it was one of the worst
slums in the north, maybe in all of England, but when I was growing up it was a poor but honest community. Everyone just trying
to get by best they could. There was no crime to speak of, no one
locked their doors. Horses and carts paraded along the streets. A
bunch of characters, rag-and-bone men, made regular rounds collecting old clothes in exchange for what we called brownstones, a soap-
like block that you would rub against the wet pavement outside your
door to dress it up, give the place a shine. Families celebrated events
together in the streets, like Guy Fawkes Night or when Elizabeth
became Queen in 1952. Kids, future boomers, running all over the
place. Kind of made you forget you were living on top of each other.

The houses—hundreds of identical brick two-up-two-downs,
wedged shoulder to shoulder, block after block—had been built
for Irish and Scottish workmen who had thronged to the north of

England by the thousands and were indentured in the mills and mines. On my street there were maybe thirty houses separated by what we called an entry in the back, and then another thirty behind them—and many more blocks of them stacked right on top of each other. Sure, go ahead, call it the projects, but in those days we knew them more respectably as council houses.

We lived at 1 Skinner Street, a house by the corner. Nothing posh, in fact nothing even middle-class. It was a pretty humble existence. Two bedrooms for the five of us—my parents, me, and my two younger sisters, Elaine and Sharon. One main window downstairs. An exit out the back to a tiny alleyway, where the outdoor toilet beckoned. Not having an indoor bathroom was a pain in the ass, especially in the winter, when you needed to pee and the chamber pot was full. No hot water, either, until years later when we finally got a heater. In those days, Salford was as far as our little world extended. My dad was born and grew up four houses down at 9 Skinner Street. My Auntie Olive and Uncle Ben lived around the corner on Ada Street, my Auntie Peg and Uncle Jimmy a short walk away. It was one big extended family that stretched back generations and probably on into the future. All of us stuck in that vast northern gulag. I used to think there was no escape, but I'm getting ahead of my story. More on that later.

My parents did everything in their power to make our lives bearable. My dad, William, was a big lad—he must have weighed 260, 270 pounds—and he was tall, taller than I am now. But he was a gentle giant, a dedicated workingman, with twinkly eyes and an incredible sense of humor. Like most men in the north of England, he went to great lengths not to stick out. He didn't have a booming voice, he wasn't flashy in any respect. He wasn't opinionated or political. I found my father to be dignified in his simple way, but tough when the situation required it. In any case, you didn't want to fuck with my dad. Once, when he came to see me perform at a local pub, and Allan and I were wearing makeup for the show, some jackass made a remark about us being poofters, and my dad picked the guy up as if he were tissue and threw him right through the door. It was the first and only time I ever saw that side of him.

But much as I loved my dad, we never really got into any deep conversations. Truth be told, we rarely talked, at least not about stuff that mattered. Nothing weird about it, it's just the way things were in our house. And probably in a lot of houses around us. Not a lot of emotional shit. You pretty much kept that stuff to yourself. That's how it was in the north. Besides, my dad left for work at seven in the morning and didn't come home until well after six at night. He'd be exhausted, have his tea, maybe hit the King's Arms, the local pub, and get some sleep before cycling back into the routine the next morning. So I don't know a lot of personal stuff about him.

My mom, Mary Gallagher, grew up around Moss Side, which is a neighborhood right by the old Manchester City football ground. Like my dad, she worked beastly hard all her life, originally at a dairy in the accounts department and later for a betting shop, which is legal in England. She had dreams and ambitions of her own, great fantasies of a more glamorous life, that I didn't learn about until later, when I was an adult, but our circumstances made those dreams impossible to pursue. It was after the war, she got married, had a family to raise, other dreams got sidetracked. My parents struggled all their lives—and they just about scraped by. My dad was an engineer at David Brown Jackson's—David Brown, of course, being DB, who designed the Aston Martins. His firm was an awesome place to a six-year-old kid—a fortress manned by enormous doors, beyond which lay a huge urn of molten iron. My dad would tip that urn and a stream of sizzling volcano lava would make its way down a trough into a mold that later solidified. You'd think that'd be worth something—that he could have made a decent living considering the effort he put in—but he never earned more than twenty quid or so a week.

Were my parents happy? Hard to say. It was difficult for people in the north of England to actually be happy. There was a lot of laughing in our house, but much of it was a device to mask the underlying hardship, a smoke screen to overcome destitution. England had been attacked *twice* in eighty years, lots of family and friends had been lost in the havoc, so everyone was more or less content to just be alive. The way I saw it, northerners were tolerant, thankful, hoping to get through the next day. Happiness was a luxury they couldn't afford.

Money was extremely tight in our family. We didn't have much, but nobody else did either, so it wasn't a big deal. Luxuries were few and far between. I don't ever remember going without eating, but I remember being hungry a lot. I was a skinny little kid, not too much padding on the chassis, pretty much the way I was throughout my life, with wandering eyes and lots of thick hair, even then. I was hungry all the time, thanks in no small part to one of my father's favorite dishes: a cow's heart. He'd buy one of those fucking things from the butcher and boil it up. Man, it was awful! The food in general wasn't anything to get excited about. And wartime rationing was still in effect. Long after the war was over, it was still difficult to get butter, sugar, or milk in the north. Staying warm was also up there on my priority list. One of my earliest chores was taking all the stuff out of my sister's pram, pushing it to the local coal yard, and filling it up so we'd have heat in our house.

When you're poor, like we were, and living in a grim place like Salford, dreams were often the only way out. The first time I ever hallucinated—this was years before I discovered acid—it was sunset after a storm. I was staring out my parents' bedroom window. I can still smell the dust, see the window half open. And I thought I saw a golden city in the clouds. Now, obviously it was deviant sun rays on a cloud formation, but to me, a six-year-old kid with a ripe imagination, it was a golden city on an endless horizon. I heard a sound: the sound of a small town operating. There were few cars in those days, just the horses and carts, rag-and-bone men, a mother shouting for her kids—just life. But to me it was music. And it was the first time my mind opened up to the possibilities of what lay in store.

Growing up in Salford, you had to be pretty creative. There wasn't much for kids to do, except play soccer and explore the skeletons of bombed-out houses, our favorite playgrounds. My mates and I always went around looking in those places, scavenging for any old shit that was left over in the wreckage: pots and pans, chamber pots, broken fireplaces, you name it. A particular treasure was finding bonfire wood for Guy Fawkes Night. Fawkes was one of the leaders of a Catholic rebellion that attempted to overthrow the Protestant monarch. We all wanted to believe the rumor that those rebels had built a tunnel underneath the houses of Parliament so Fawkes could blow them sky-high. In hindsight, our exploits were pretty dangerous; nothing was shored up in those rickety houses, so they could have collapsed at any time. You can be sure I'd have gotten good and spanked if my parents found out I was rooting around there.

When we got bored combing through those houses, we'd take on scaling the coal-slag heap, being careful not to get buried under the mountain of black coal, or we'd climb over the fence at St. Ignatius Church and have a look around the basement. It was pretty harmless, just kids being kids. But if we got caught—and we inevitably got caught—the priest would offer us a choice: either go to the police or take your pants down so he could spank you. There was an obvious outcome that pleased all parties concerned. No way we wanted to go to the police. We were kids, we weren't stealing anything, and going to the police was fucking scary, not an option. And, anyway, the priest was angling for a glimpse of our bare bums. Take my word for it, there was no abuse going on, but he was getting his jollies in that basement, no doubt about that.

Other than that, I enjoyed going to church. I went three times on Sundays, any chance I got. Not that I was religious, nor was anyone in my family. But I was happy to get out of the house and I loved singing in the choir, with that organ swelling like a heavenly score. It was the first time I ever got to sing with people, hearing voices lift, combining in harmony. Man, what a thrill. I had this bell-like voice—and *high*, I could sing high. Even at that age I learned how to put my voice above the melody, something that would serve me well for the rest of my life.

I guess music was my religion, although we had little of either in the house. There wasn't much singing and certainly no records to speak of—we couldn't afford 'em. My cousin Ray had a record player with a big horn on the front, and we would crank up the overture to *Samson and Delilah*. Otherwise there was only the radio in our house, one of those brown plastic jobs with one knob for on-off volume and three push buttons for the BBC stations: one for Light Programme (popular music), one for the Home Service (comedy and feature stories), and the third for the cleverly named Third Programme (cultural, highbrow stuff). Light Programme played lots of northern dance orchestras, plus crooners like Frankie Laine and Rosemary Clooney. Later on there was Johnnie Ray. I don't know how we eventually got Radio Luxembourg on that big old box. It was the third button, and when the weather permitted, its signal came in like magic. But Radio Lux fired up all of my dreams. When I was a teenager, everything they played made an impression on me: the Platters, Fats Domino, Gene Vincent, Jerry Lee Lewis, Buddy Holly, Elvis, the whole pantheon of early rock gods. Otherwise, the only music in the family came when I went for a walk with my dad. He would whistle and I'd whistle back in harmony. Or when we went to the Borough, the cinema on the other side of Ordsall Park where I first saw *The Girl Can't Help It*, a movie that changed my life in so many ways. It went from a grainy black-and-white opening with Tom Ewell explaining the scenario to full-blown Technicolor. Mind-blowing! All of my favorite rock 'n' rollers were in the movie. And the scene where Jayne Mansfield first appears was unbelievable to a fifteen-year-old kid. She looked like an angel—and more. My dad would sing as we cut through the park, and I'd chime in—"Shrimp Boats Are a-Coming," "This Old House," "Ghost Riders in the Sky," silly stuff like that.

My musical life changed forever one day in school. On another mundane morning, while I was daydreaming in Mr. Burke's class at Ordsall Board Primary School, there was a knock on the door and an old lady wrapped in a long dark shawl brought a boy my age, who was clearly nervous, into the room. After a private discussion, Mr. Burke quieted the class. "All right, everybody," he said, "this is Harold Clarke, who just moved from Broughton, and he's going to join us. So, let's see—where is he going to sit?" We all looked around the room and there was only one space, next to me.

"He can sit right here," I piped up.

One of the best moves I ever made. Harold Clarke, who later called himself Allan, became my instant best friend. Right away I recognized that he was me, the same. I'd start to say something and he'd know what it was before I got halfway through the sentence. We liked the same football teams, the same girls. We'd grease our hair the same way, with Brylcreem, so we looked like Tony Curtis. And music—that really joined us at the hip.

In the mornings, before school started, Clarkie and I were part of a group that sang the Lord's Prayer at assembly. The other kids droned on with the familiar melody, but Clarkie and I broke off and hit two fabulous harmonies, totally naturally. We just fell into it and played off each other. Allan had a great set of pipes and a tone in his voice that was undeniable; even then it was rich and powerful, with great control and an arcing falsetto.

Singing harmony became a passion of ours. I have no idea where we picked it up. No one ever taught us how to do it or put it into words. It was just a gift we had, and it gave us so much pleasure. We sang everywhere—in school and in each other's houses, but especially in front of mirrors, where we would pantomime being our favorite artists. I imagined how Elvis would do it. So I made myself a guitar out of an old piece of plywood, painted it red, and shook my bony ass in that mirror, pretending to be the King. Later, when the Everly Brothers came along, we tried to be them, as well. And the Louvin Brothers, Ira and Charlie. We were soaking it all up and churning it out our way.

On Saturdays, we'd walk up to Trafford Road and stare into the window of the local music store. There'd be maracas and harmonicas and ocarinas, as well as an array of classical guitars. Eventually, an electric cutaway appeared in their midst, with a spotlight on it, which would hypnotize me for hours. I'd just stand there, staring, hoping one day, by some miracle, I could afford one of those babies. But I knew that day was a long way off.

Guitars intrigued me much more than school. It seems odd, when I think about it now, because as an adult I consume all the information I can get my hands on. And my friends are some of the most brilliant minds of the day. Nothing stimulates me more than a discussion with a scholar, or a book that lays out some illuminating aspect of life. But when I was in school, nothing seemed to spark my interest. I was an indifferent student at best—never studied, never read. Who knows why? Maybe I can lay some blame on apathetic teachers or my circumstances at home. But really I was off in a world of my own.

Even from a very young age, I've always been a bit of a loner. People are great, they fascinate me no end, but sometimes all that chatter is difficult to bear. I've always looked for places where I could shut out the world and just groove on the solitude that fueled my dreams. At the Ordsall Board school, my options were few. There was no cafeteria there, so we had to use a building in the adjoining park to get lunch. My friend Fred Moore and I would take off running to get there first, ahead of the crowd. But after lunch, instead of socializing, I always ducked out of that scene. I used to sit in the branches of a small tree in the park. It was safe there, no one to bother me. I can still feel the movement of the swaying branches. Just me and a tree. Away from it all. Perfect.

Back at home, I kept busy with another solitary passion, photography. My dad was something of an amateur photographer, and from the time I was little he would set up his darkroom in my bedroom. He'd whip the blanket off my bed, tack it up against the window to block out the light, and lay out trays of chemicals to develop and print pictures. So from the beginning, I was hooked on the magic of photography. Imagine the fascination for a kid my age watching, bug-eyed, as a blank sheet of paper was run through those baths and an image slowly materialized on the page. Fabulous! My dad turned me on to the whole process. And it wasn't long before he put a camera in my hands, where it remains to this day. I was shocked that he could afford it. It seemed an impossibility. But the thrill of owning and using it pushed any questions right out of my head.

From the time I was ten, I've been obsessed with taking pictures, and not just any old snapshots but pictures that captured something significant, something insightful about the subject. Much of it stemmed from my curiosity about people. And a lot of it had to do with not wanting to stick out, trying to remain invisible, like when I was up in that tree, so that the subject would appear natural, not aware that I was there. In the majority of cases, you come up empty-handed, but every once in a while you land a gem. My favorite image from those days is a picture I took of my mother. I remember realizing, *Wow! That's not your normal snapshot.* We had gone on family holiday to the Middleton Towers Holiday Camp, a getaway for working-class people about thirty miles north of Manchester. A young woman who had jumped into the swimming pool must have hit her head because she was floating kind of funny, obviously in distress. Instinctively, my dad dove in and rescued her, and in the process her top came off. Man, it was the first pair of tits I ever saw! I was eleven years old. Are you kidding! This was fantastic! But my mother was sitting in a deck chair at the other end of the pool. It was a broken cloudy day, and she had a plaid coat draped around her shoulders, sunglasses on, a cigarette in her hand. For some reason, I turned away from the woman to watch my mother. She didn't know that I was looking at her, seeing her not only as a mother but wondering, Who really is this person? I caught her in a very quiet, almost distracted moment. And that's when I realized I saw things differently.

Photography really captivated me full-time. I saved every penny I could to buy film for my camera. Luckily, I had a job that brought me a couple shillings. My Uncle Ben was a union rep, and every Saturday morning he sent me out on rounds to collect union subscriptions. I'd go knock on doors—*bam! bam! bam!*—"Union subs!" Sometimes people would peek through a curtain and not answer the door, but mostly they'd pay up. I had a book with names and the amount they owed and a column where I would tick off their name if they made a payment. In any case, I contributed most of what I earned to the family coffers; whatever was left over would go for film. My friend Fred Moore and I set up a makeshift darkroom in his backyard where we developed roll after roll of the images we'd taken.

The camera gave me a new perspective on my young life. But all of that changed by the end of 1953. One evening, after kicking a ball around outside with some friends, I came home to find my mother in an unusual state. "Your dad's in trouble," she said, unable to conceal her anguish.

While I'd been out, the police had come to the door. "Is William Nash in?" they'd demanded.

My mother told them he was having his tea, but they wouldn't be put off. They wanted to know about a certain camera in his possession. Mine, the one he had given me.

"I didn't steal it," he insisted. "I bought it from a friend at work." It was a cheap camera, he said, which cost him about ten pounds.

They wanted a name, which my father refused to provide, because as everyone knows, you don't grass on friends. Unfortunately, the cops weren't buying his story, and they arrested him for possession of stolen goods.

This was really earth-shattering to me. My dad was a good man, an honest man, law-abiding, and proud. He'd never been in trouble. The police never had reason to darken our door before—it was unheard of. Now everything was changed and our privacy was shattered. All of the neighbors knew. When the police come to your door, everybody knows. The jungle drums beat along the Salford grapevine all night long. It was a crushing blow to a man who'd kept to himself all these years.

In the long run, we didn't think it was serious. My dad wasn't any kind of thief, and even if they thought he was, you don't go to jail for stealing a lousy Agfa camera.

One night, soon afterward, I'd been fast asleep for hours when I heard my dad creep into my pitch-dark bedroom. I could tell something was up right away.

"Son, I need to talk to you," he said, and from his tone I knew things had gotten serious. He laid the whole thing out for me, assured me he was innocent, but how none of that mattered in the tangled legal process. "I'm going up on trial, and there is a chance I'll have to go away for a while. If that happens, I'm counting on you to be the man of the family."

I didn't quite grasp what he meant; it didn't make sense to me. But I nodded and gave him a powerful hug. It was the most emotional conversation we'd ever had.

The trial came up quickly. None of the judicial red tape like you have now, where someone lingers for months or even years while the system grinds on. Only a week or two later I was bumping around the house when my mother burst through the front door into the kitchen. She slumped back against the wall and said, "He got a year!" Then she burst into tears. I was shocked, just blown away. It didn't make any fucking sense. Even if they thought he was guilty, he was nothing more than an accessory. A year seemed excessive for such a penny-ante charge. I didn't even have a chance to see him afterward. They took him directly to jail. He never came home until a year later.

My mother told me our situation was going to be different from now on. We'd have to fend for ourselves and all stick together. She tried to put a brave face on things. "We'll make it through," she assured us, but I wasn't so sure. It was obvious the family had been barely scraping by. Without my father's salary, we'd have to sacrifice what little we had.

Sure enough, everything soon turned to shit. They carted my dad off to Strangeways, a brutal high-security prison, with an execution shed and a permanent gallows. You'd see it as you walked through downtown Manchester, dark and ominous, a scary fucking place right out of a Dickens novel. I couldn't imagine my dad being in there with hardened criminals. And neither could my mom—she just came undone, which was so unlike her.

Things got really tough at home. I had to become the man of the house—make sure the front and back doors were locked at night, the oven was off. Kept the outside looking respectable so the neighbors wouldn't talk. My sister Elaine became my responsibility. I'd be going to meet my friends, and as soon as I put my hand on the door, my mother would yell: "Take your sister with you." Awww, fuck! "Okay, c'mon, Elaine." If you think there were no luxuries before this fiasco, now we had to cut back on necessities to pull through. Food was in extremely short supply. Most of my clothes came from the Salvation Army, clothes that neither fit nor matched. I was wearing tops that seemed like Grandpa's nightshirt, coats that hung off me like a tent. One time, after wearing out the soles of my shoes, I was forced to wear a pair of my mother's flat brogues, which was fucking humiliating for a twelve-year-old kid. This came at a time when I was supposed to be cool, trying to attract girls and friends in general. Here I was in these shitty clothes, looking stupid, anything but cool. Man, it's affected me to this day. Even after all the great things in my life, I still have trouble with my coolness quotient.

Before all this had happened, I'd kept my grades up in school and passed the Eleven plus exam, which separated those of us who'd go on to grammar school from those who wouldn't. This took a great and unexpected toll on my friendship with Allan. We'd been best friends since we were six, but around this time we began to drift apart because of the exam. Clarkie's not passing drove a bit of a wedge between us. I'm not sure exactly why. Maybe he didn't feel as bright as I was, although that wasn't the case.

That year was complicated for so many reasons. My dad had

finally been released from prison. He'd been at Strangeways for the first five months of his sentence, then got transferred to a minimum security facility called Bela River.

But the man who came back to Salford, to our home and family, was completely broken. He'd lost his self-esteem and self-respect as a result of the incarceration, and soon afterward he lost his job as well. David Brown Jackson's firm fired my dad for no good reason other than the fact that he'd been in jail; no consideration was given to his years on the job or to his personal character, which was otherwise beyond reproach. Seeing what my dad had gone through had a huge effect on me.

Still, passing the school exam was a pretty big accomplishment, especially in our family, and as a reward my mother bought me a Philips record player. Talk about sacrifices! I have no idea how she managed to scratch up enough to pay for it, because we had absolutely no money to speak of. What a fantastic gift. The first thing like that I ever owned. Man, I *loved* that machine, even if we had no records.

The guy who had the records was named Ralph Etherington, who lived a few doors away, at the bottom of our street. One day, in early 1956, he called out, "Hey, come over here and listen to this." He had an *electric* record player, you didn't even have to crank it. He just flicked it on and dropped the needle on . . . "Heartbreak Hotel."

*Wham!*—it was as though someone had slugged me. My mouth fell open as Elvis powered through that ferocious thriller. No matter how many times I hear it, it still affects me the same way. Oh, man—*are you kidding me?* That smoldering voice just grabs you and refuses to let go. All that anguish, heartache, loneliness, and soul delivered by that *voice.* He just spilled his guts, he put it all out there. It's a piece of musical theater that has very few equals.

From that point on, the heavens opened. I started to hear American rock 'n' roll everywhere I turned, all those great records that people's brothers and cousins were bringing back from having gone to America with the Merchant Navy. "The Great Pretender," "Butterfly,"

"That'll Be the Day," "Hound Dog," "Long Tall Sally" . . . Skiffle, Lonnie Donegan—man, I was *gone*. Lonnie did a number on all us British teenagers. He's the guy who gave us the ticket in—he made it possible for even poor kids like me to assemble a band using things you already had around the house, like a washboard and a tea chest for percussion and bass. It was a brilliant intro to playing music. So many bands in the north started as skiffle groups, including the Beatles, which made Lonnie Donegan a very important cat. But skiffle couldn't compete with the magic of rock 'n' roll. I remember a foggy afternoon in Salford, walking to the local record store. They had little speakers outside that played the latest American hits. Through the fog I heard "Blue Moon" by Elvis and it was . . . perfect.

That did it! Once rock 'n' roll got under my skin, it was all over for me. Instead of listening to my lessons at school, I began doodling, drawing Fender Stratocasters and stage setups. I started practicing my autograph. Daydreams took over, and I pulled myself toward those dreams. No matter what they tried to teach me, I knew where I was headed. Nothing was going to derail my dreams.

Meanwhile, people continued to feed them, left and right. A friend of mine at Salford Grammar, Arthur Marsden, would bring his records to school in a little portable thing that you could plug in and play almost anywhere. One day he pulled out a 78-RPM copy of "Be-Bop-a-Lula," which he agreed to swap for my lunch. Bless you, Arthur. First record I ever actually owned—and what a record! It fired my imagination in so many ways. Gene Vincent's snarly, brooding voice oozed sex and danger, and he wrapped it around an unforgettable lyric. The way he spit it out—man, it just *killed* me. I'd seen a picture of him in a black motorcycle jacket, with his hair slicked back, looking like he was ready to kick some ass. He was the whole package. Rock 'n' roll incarnate.

Clarkie and I were completely besotted. And a couple years later, my friend Fred—he got a two-wheel bicycle for his birthday and rode all the way to Bad Nauheim in Germany, where he met Elvis. So, of course, from that moment I wanted a bike. But music was all we talked about. We craved it like a couple of junkies. Sang together almost every day. We'd meet up after school at the Salford Lads Club, a little social center for kids who didn't have anything to do, where we'd play chess, snooker, and Ping-Pong. Allan and I were in a minstrel show there. Slapped on some blackface, today an incredibly un-PC thing to do, but who knew back then, in the fifties.

Back in 1955, just before I turned thirteen, my mother asked, "What do you want for your birthday?" So of course I said I wanted a bicycle, my own set of wheels, but you know how it is—we were too poor. Can you imagine growing up and not owning a bike? It kept me from going anywhere, from exploring with my friends. But now I had a choice between a bike—and a guitar. That was like one of those Mensa puzzles, and I debated it for days. Bike . . . guitar? Guitar . . . bike? I knew my mother couldn't afford a decent two-wheeler, so I went for a secondhand pawnshop acoustic guitar. It was called a Levin, a sunburst cheapie, with action so high you had to hitchhike to the frets. Man, it was so hard to press the strings down. My fucking fingers would bleed. But I could keep it in tune; I have a damn good ear.

Clarkie got a guitar at the same time and we taught ourselves how to play chords using Burt Weedon's *Play in a Day* books, which is probably the same way Eric Clapton, George Harrison, Dave Davies, and Jimmy Page learned. We'd pass those books around among friends, so we already knew three chords when skiffle came along. I remember learning my first minor chord: A minor. It was from a Crickets record called "Baby My Heart." *Oh my God!* A minor chord! Fantastic! When you learned how to make a new sound, your brain went off in a dozen different directions. It opened up a whole new world for me far from Salford.

Those guitars were never out of our hands. Allan and I practiced all the time, playing at each other's houses. The skiffle hits made up our trusty set list: "Don't You Rock Me, Daddy-O," "Rock Island Line," "Bring a Little Water, Sylvie," "Wimoweh." With two or three chords, you could crank out a couple dozen songs, no sweat. "John

Henry," "Midnight Special," "Cumberland Gap," "Pick a Bale of Cotton," "Worried Man Blues" . . . the two of us got to be very good, not only playing these tunes, but with two-part harmony.

One afternoon, while I was visiting at Clarkie's, his older brother Frank walked in while we were rehearsing. After listening to a few songs, he said, "I really like the way you guys sound. Do you mind if I suggest that you entertain at a club I belong to?" He was a member at a workingman's association called the Devonshire Sporting Club, owned by a famous wrestler called Bill Benny. After Frank put in a word, Benny told him to bring us up. Every kind of performer worked this place—accordion players squeezing off "Lady of Spain," jugglers spinning plates, dogs that barked in a certain sequence, just madness. Two fourteen-year-old skiffle players would fit right in.

Chisel it in stone: It was the very first performance we ever did. Someone asked if I was scared going in. Scared? I didn't even know what they meant. Why would I be scared? This was *exactly* what I wanted to be doing. I was fourteen years old and ready for anything. Besides, we were a couple of fresh-faced kids who thought we were indestructible. And, man, we *killed* 'em that night. We rocked the place, and afterward, I remember Bill Benny taking this huge roll of pound notes out of his pocket and, folding them back to where the smaller denominations were, handing over two ten-shilling notes. *Wow!* I took that home to my family. My first paying gig.

At another show, we got paid even more—something like twenty bucks, a fucking *fortune*! It started to sink in that we could earn some serious bread doing this kind of thing. Especially at pubs on Sunday afternoons, where they had small stages and craved entertainment. We'd hit places like the Yew Tree, where they told us, "You can go on at four thirty, but only two songs." It was less a performance than an audition. There would be booking agents in the audience who would come up to us afterward and, if they liked what they heard, slip us their card. "I'm from St. Ann's Club, and we have an opening Monday night. Do you want to come by? What's your price?" Some of our early contracts were for £2.10s, which was about seven bucks, and were we glad to get it. "Listen, do you want to play in Altrincham next Saturday night for ten quid?" *Ten quid!* Are you kidding me!

Kids our age could play the pubs as long as we weren't drinking, and my mother would occasionally chaperone Allan and me to make sure that was the case. The funny thing is, in a couple of the workingman's clubs we shared the dressing room with strippers. That was the second pair of tits I ever saw. Clarkie and I were in heaven. First of all, we were singing; second of all, we were getting paid; and then the bonus: Occasionally we'd see beautiful women in all their glory. Heaven indeed.

Skiffle was keeping us pretty well entertained, but you could tell music was heading in another direction. I sensed it the day I took the bus into Manchester and paid my shilling at the Theatre Royal to see *Blackboard Jungle*. Man, oh, man, did that movie stir up the kids. Ineffective teachers in an inner-city school, teenagers engaged in antisocial behavior—what *wasn't* there to stir up the kids? There was an undercurrent of energy in those young audiences, a mix of growing up, getting your balls, teenage lust, and rejecting the status quo. Just a cluster bomb of teenage rebellion. And when "Rock Around the Clock" played over the opening and final credits, the Teddy Boys would go absolutely apeshit. They'd tear up the seats, turn on the fire extinguishers, releasing all that energy they'd been storing up inside. I saw that movie *twice.* Every kid saw it. It was utterly fabulous and ignited our fantasies. And when we heard Bill Haley was coming to town—well, that sealed it.

Bill Haley coming to Manchester was a very big deal. Every kid wanted to attend, and there was no way that Clarkie and I were going to miss it. We knew it was going to be special. We *had* to go, no two ways about it.

But—how? Tickets were going on sale on a Monday in early September, at ten in the morning, and we'd both be in school. The concert would be sold out by the time we got to the box office. Another factor was that Allan and I were now at different schools. As

I mentioned, I had passed the Eleven plus, but Clarkie hadn't, so while I had moved on to Salford Grammar, he was still at Ordsall Board Secondary Modern, and this threw a monkey wrench into our plans. One of us had to skip school that day, and one guess who got the nod.

Monday morning, I set out for school. I had my book bag with me, I took my younger sister in her pram to nursery school—kept everything nice and routine. But instead of getting on the number 58 bus to go to school, I hopped on the number 2 bound for Manchester. It was another gray day in the dreary north, chilly and overcast; winter was approaching. The queue wasn't that bad when I got into the city, around 10:30, and made my way to the Odeon on Oxford Road. There were maybe fifty guys my age in line ahead of me, very few girls, all of us bullshitting about how great this was going to be. "I wonder if Rudy Pompilli is still one of the Comets?" "Is Franny Beecher gonna be playing his black Les Paul? We've never seen one of them before."

Finally, it was my turn to buy tickets and I went for a pair in the front row of the balcony, where Clarkie and I could overlook it all. Those tickets were like gold to me. I kept running them through my fingers all the way back to Salford.

The next day at school, after morning announcements, I got called to the principal's office. Something was up, and I knew I was fucked. You never got called to the principal's office for praise. E. G. Simms was a tough son of a bitch and students did everything to stay out of his way. While I was standing there, waiting to see him, one of my teachers, Mr. Lewis, came in, and he wasn't looking happy to see me. Turns out Lewis had ratted me out to Mr. Simms.

"Mr. Nash, you weren't out *sick* yesterday, were you?" Simms growled.

It dawned on me right away: *They knew.* Better not lie. "No," I mumbled.

"You were in the queue, waiting for concert tickets."

"Uh-huh."

As it happened, Mr. Lewis had also been in Manchester on some personal business and saw me outside the Odeon. And of course that prick just had to report me.

Mr. Simms fixed me with one of his most ferocious stares. "You know what happens now, don't you?"

So I got slippered, which was a plimsoll on your ass while you were bent over the desk. That fucker hit me ten times. I'd been slippered before, it was no big deal, but this time I got madder than hell. The so-called crime didn't deserve this kind of punishment, and each hit made me angrier and angrier. I hadn't talked back or disrupted class or cheated on an exam. *I didn't murder anybody,* for fuck's sake. All I did was follow a passion I had. Why didn't they recognize that? Why were they making such an example of me?

Afterward I staggered back to class, where everyone knew I'd been slippered by Simms. Kids were whispering, giggling. I was embarrassed, sure, but sitting there I started to seethe with resentment. The injustice of it all! They had dismissed my passion as if it were something offensive. And I was enraged by their intolerance, a word I might not have known at the time, but the discontent I felt was real enough.

I couldn't stop thinking about how I got punished so mightily. Just like my dad, who went to prison for what I thought was a relatively minor offense. I came to the conclusion there was no such thing as true justice. Justice was malleable and subjective. There was too much politics involved, too many personalities. And I began thinking that if this was the way things worked, then fuck justice— and fuck school. I didn't need any of their rules and regulations.

I'd been on fire before, but, man, after the beating I was really raging. They didn't understand how much music meant to me, how their disdain for it made me rebel. From that moment on, I turned against school and especially against my teachers. Little did they know, this was one fire they couldn't put out.

## chapter 3

*Wednesday, February 13, 1957*

I'LL NEVER FORGET THE DAY AS LONG AS I LIVE, JUST eleven days after my fifteenth birthday. Clarkie and I hung over the brass balcony railing of the Odeon Theatre, watching the crush of teenagers swarming in the aisles. It was intermission, and that old movie house was throbbing at the seams. We were so wired, we could barely stay in our seats. The Kalin Twins had opened the show and soldiered through an otherwise forgettable set, and now the electricity in the place surged to peak—and beyond.

Things spun out of control when the lights began to fade. It's that magic moment when you've been sitting there, waiting . . . waiting . . . and then suddenly the lights go down and you *know*—this is *it*. I love that moment, always have, and as the crowd scrambled back to their seats a charge went up that rippled along the length of my spine.

The light got sucked right out of that theater, and just when you thought you couldn't see your hand in front of your face, a small white spotlight hit the center of the red velvet curtain. A hand pulled it back a few inches, and a face with a spit curl plastered on its forehead stuck through the seam and shouted: "See you later, alligator!"

*"Well, I saw my baby walkin' / with another man today . . ."*

The curtain swung open, and the sight left an indelible mark on my soul.

There he was: Bill Haley, in the flesh. He wasn't pretty to look at, he wasn't Elvis, wasn't sexy, but, man, could that cat put on a show.

He and the Comets, wearing their matching plaid dinner jackets, rocked that house, with theatrics that were as good as any I've seen since. The bass player, Al Rex, sat astride his stand-up bass, riding it like a stallion and slapping at its side, while Rudy Pompilli strad- dled him, leaning as far back as he could with his sax in the air. Lots of clowning, but plenty of great music. With Haley out front, they ran through all of the hits: "Razzle Dazzle," "Shake, Rattle and Roll," "Rudy's Rock," "Calling All Comets," "Dim, Dim the Lights," "Birth of the Boogie." By the time they segued into "Rock Around the Clock," Manchester had been launched into the rock 'n' roll era.

You could look around the theater that night and see it in ac- tion. The audience was made up of mostly kids my age, whose faces were lit with an eerie intensity. They bought right into the music. It was something new, something our own—not the crap they played on the BBC or fed us in school, not our parents' brand of postwar schmaltz. Rock 'n' roll spoke to us directly: teenage music, a totally different sound. It was like a new religion, and Bill Haley was deliv- ering the Word.

Clarkie and I were beside ourselves. The music, the showman- ship, the pulse of the crowd—we didn't say as much, but I know we were both projecting ourselves onto that stage. Even at fifteen, I was positive that was where my future lay. And I knew it that night: Nothing would stand in my way. After the show, when the crowd spilled into the street, I ducked around the corner into an alley- way and eluded a cordon of police in order to touch Rudy Pompilli's elbow as he climbed onto the tour bus.

I was looking for contact anyplace I could get it. Mostly I had to rely on the records we heard, those that made it to the stores in Manchester, because it was still pretty tough going in the north to hook into the sound that was starting to take root. We had *Saturday Club* on the BBC, which played the latest hits from America. But that was about it, as far as rock 'n' roll went.

One Saturday night in the fall of 1957, Clarkie and I headed over to a dance in the basement of St. Clements, a Catholic school in

Salford not far from Ordsall Board. It was a rival school, and we normally didn't hang out with those kids, but it was crawling with Catholic girls. Need I say more? We were dressed to kill. I had just bought a sharp red shirt with black flecks in it, no tie. A half gallon's worth of Brylcreem slicked our hair back—we were a couple of young James Deans, Clarkie and I.

We walked down the stairs and handed our tickets to the young lady who was collecting them at the door. Looking past her, I could see inside the darkened room: Maybe a hundred kids were already in the hall. We lingered by the door watching the action. "You Send Me" was crooning over the sound system and knots of lust-filled couples were grinding away. Here and there, teachers were crowbarring kids apart, and you could read the lips of the offended guys: "I wasn't holding my girlfriend like *that*." Man, we could hardly wait to get in there. Allan and I were besotted with girls. We weren't cool, but we hoped we had something going, and this crowd promised to raise our stock. As the song faded, the lights came up and the couples who had been feeling each other up during the slow dance scattered to opposite ends of the floor.

Across the hall we spotted Norma Timms and made a beeline toward where she was standing. Norma was a girl who, shall we say, developed early. She was from council houses that were a bit posher than ours; they had bay fronts instead of just flat entrances. Clarkie and I were definitely attracted to her on all fronts and vying to see who could get to her first. So there we were, making our way across the dance floor, kind of edging each other out of the way, when all of a sudden a sound came blasting out of the speakers that stopped us dead in our tracks.

*Bye bye love, bye bye happiness,*
*Hello loneliness, I think I'm a-gonna cry-y.*

I'd never heard anything like it before. The acoustic guitars going *chawng ki-chawng ki-chuk-chuk*. Barre chords layered one on top of each other. Two twangy voices harmonizing seamlessly as one. I'd never heard voices harmonizing in that way before. Whatever the power of that vocal blend, the magic, it *stunned* me. It was something else! "Whoa!" I gasped. "What the fuck is that?" We stood stone still and listened to it for a while, until we realized we were sticking out like sore thumbs. Kids had started crowding around us, wanting to dance, but I was transfixed. That is, until I saw Allan making headway toward Norma, which jolted me from my reverie.

But that moment was incredibly important, one of the turning points in my life. It was like the opening of a giant door in my soul, the striking of a chord, literally and figuratively, from which I've never recovered. From the time when I first heard the Everly Brothers, I knew I wanted to make music that affected people the way the Everlys affected me. That was *it* for me. I can trace it to that night at St. Clements.

I eventually nudged Clarkie aside and Norma later became my girlfriend, but the real victory was our musical conquest. We found the deejay a half hour later and demanded he tell us everything he could about that amazing record. He dug the disc out of a pile and gave us the lowdown: the Everly Brothers on Cadence Records. *Voilà!* He told us that they really were brothers who came from Kentucky and were fans of the Louvin Brothers, whose names I noted for future reference.

Allan and I started performing "Bye Bye Love" right away, copying their style as best we could. And we searched all over Manchester, looking for more of their stuff, figuring that if they had singles, they probably had an album. Within a month we hit the jackpot, *The Everly Brothers,* learned all the songs, and in no time had them down cold. "Brand New Heartache," "Maybe Tomorrow," "Wake Up Little Susie," and, most especially, "Lucille"—*wow!*

By this time, Allan and I were singing every chance we could get. There was a club in Manchester, the Plaza Dance Hall on Oxford Street. It was run by Jimmy Savile, an incredibly important

English compere who wore outrageous costumes and had dyed plaid hair. Years later, there were serious and shocking allegations that Jimmy had engaged in horrendous sexual abuses of children—it was a scandal that rocked the BBC and the country—but at that point in our lives, all we knew was that he was very supportive of us. We were totally unaware of his dark side. The only thing we were aware of was that every Monday evening the club held a talent contest that drew crowds. Well, Allan and I won it four weeks in a row, doing "Be-Bop-a-Lula" like the Everly Brothers did, and "When Will I Be Loved." Jimmy really encouraged us. He felt we had something special and could take it further than just being two kids with two guitars.

We played our hearts out at the Plaza and other dance halls in Manchester. For the time being I remained at Salford Grammar, but I thought long and hard about packing it in. Allan had already left Ordsall Board and was working a day job at Alexander Kenyon's, an electrical builder's supply store, and a gig at night with a Broughton skiffle band, the Riverside Rockets, as their lead singer, so he was making decent money. But it separated us for a while, and my mother was very upset with him for deserting her son. I did, in fact, feel abandoned and had no one to sing with for months.

As for my dad, he went to work as a warehouseman at Imperial Tobacco, by the Salford docks. It was a real comedown as far as positions went, but he faced the job in his usual stoic way. Two days later, he came home and said, "I've quit smoking today. You have no idea what goes into those cigarettes." He described opening up containers full of tobacco and finding rats, cockroaches, and all kinds of life-forms that had laid eggs in there, along with other kinds of shit too disgusting to mention. Instead of removing any of it, they simply closed the door and fumigated the works, leaving all the crap right in the mix. Small wonder why I never took up smoking! But in any case, my dad wasn't the same guy anymore. He'd lost his gregarious spirit, his inner glow. The change disturbed me no end, even though we never discussed it. The veil of emotional silence had not been lifted.

More grief befell me on February 6, 1958, as I was on my way home from another miserable day at school. I remember getting off the bus that day in a fog so thick that it was impossible to see two feet in front of me. When my eyes finally adjusted, I could make out the throng of newspaper hawkers who wore little placards across their shoulders announcing the day's latest headline. That day's big news was: MANCHESTER UNITED KILLED—and my insides seemed to drop right out of my body. The "Busby Babes" were my team. They were our local pride, on top of the world. My dad had taken me to dozens of their football matches, and some of their most celebrated players—Duncan Edwards and Eddie Coleman—had gone to my school. I grabbed one of the papers and tried to absorb what happened. From what I could gather, the team had been returning home from a European Cup match against Red Star Belgrade when their plane crashed on takeoff from a refueling stop in Munich. Gone . . . they were gone. It was impossible for me to digest.

So much shit was weighing me down that it was a relief when, a few weeks later, I ran into Allan on the street. It felt a bit awkward standing there, making small talk with my best mate, but we filled each other in on personal news. From what I gathered, he'd already left the Riverside Rockets and was looking for another musical outlet. "Hey, check this out," he said, flipping open a guitar case. Bending down, he lifted out a black thick-body semiacoustic electric guitar and handed it over as if it were the Magna Carta. Man, that baby felt good in my hands, and I have to admit I was jealous as hell. He had a small amp, too. That combination, amp and guitar, made him a rocker instead of a skiffle guy—exactly where I wanted to be. My envy aside, I was happy for Allan. He was heading in the right direction. And this time, I went with him.

We began doing shows around the Manchester area, billing ourselves as the Two Teens, Ricky and Dane Young. I was Dane—don't ask me why. Something about the name sounded flash and cool. If we were serious about making it in show business, we needed better names than Graham and Harold. As for Young, we were fresh-faced kids and thought it would be a fitting last name, which is weird when you factor in Neil later on. Looking back, it was all such a lark. Allan and I were trying on different personas, wanting desperately to be like James Dean.

The thing is, we were *good*. We could sing our asses off, and word about us started to get around Manchester. Pretty soon we were working coffeehouses and pubs, anywhere we could, earning a few bob and a leg up with the girls. Girls, we discovered, were a nice little perk that came with performing. It was all the incentive I ever needed. The first love of my life was Rose Oliver, a magnificent-looking creature with long, wavy blond hair and a body that was bursting into womanhood. She was beautiful and funny and not about to let me touch her. Didn't matter. Soon afterward, I got my first kiss from a girl called Sylvia. First sex, too (thanks, Sylvia), standing up in the alleyway out behind her house. I can't say that it was a transcendent experience. It was over before either of us knew what had happened. But you can be sure it whetted my appetite for what came later in the sixties.

As the Two Teens, Allan and I—make that Ricky and Dane—played local old-fashioned competitions that were a big part of northern England entertainment. We'd do talent shows that were right on the edge of vaudeville, where ten or twelve amateur acts would vie to see who would move on to the next week's contest. These weren't just singers, but jugglers, ventriloquists, mimes, accordion virtuosos, plate spinners, the whole gamut. One of the earliest of our escapades was at the Middleton Towers Holiday Camp, where we performed Conway Twitty's "It's Only Make Believe" to thunderous applause and were invited back for the three-day finale, which we lost to some crooner.

The hottest competition we entered was *Star Search,* at the Hippodrome Theatre in Manchester, on November 19, 1958. Carroll

Levis, a slightly overweight Canadian impresario who had seemingly cornered the market on amateur talent, was the emcee, which heightened interest from all across the north. It seemed like every act in Lancashire showed up to make their name. I recognized Johnny Peters, the frontman for the Rockets, whose coolness quotient was way off the charts. Ronnie Wycherley, who later morphed into Billy Fury, was slumped in a chair backstage, as was Freddie Garrity, a short guy with glasses who would have hits in the sixties with Freddie and the Dreamers. Most of the preshow buzz was around a group from Liverpool called Johnny and the Moondogs, who did a Buddy Holly number, "Think It Over." I thought they were pretty good, which confirms my taste, considering it was John Lennon, George Harrison, and Paul McCartney, with Johnny Hutchinson sitting in on drums. Allan and I decided to stick with "It's Only Make Believe" because we could wring every last ounce of emotion out of the lyric.

That evening the place was packed. Carroll Levis was a pretty famous guy, and the crowd came for him almost as much as for the performers. The acts, as it happened, were surprisingly good. The Harmonica Rascals were local favorites; they had a midget playing a big bass harmonica who was a cutup and mugged shamelessly for the crowd. And the Moondogs went over as you might expect. They'd probably have walked away with a win had they been able to stick around for the finale, but the last bus back to Liverpool was at 9:27, long before the show was done.

Allan and I had as good a shot as anyone. Our harmonies were airtight and we killed that ballad. When Levis dragged us all out onstage at the end, it was anyone's guess who would take first place. He lined up each act in a single row, then walked behind us and held a hand over our heads. If the crowd went crazy, you knew your chances were good. Billy Fury and Freddie Garrity had their friends out front, and the noise they made was deafening. The same with the Harmonica Rascals and Johnny Peters. But when it came time to rate Allan and me, there was no doubt we had won the night and would move on to the finals a week later in Morecombe.

Our star was rising, that was for sure. A manager even had his eye on us, a guy named Arthur Fee, who managed a band called Kirk Daniels and the Deltas. Fee was a real piece of work. He'd been a budding musician who hadn't made it and decided instead to develop pop acts in a way that was novel. His approach was that we'd become a show, an evening of cabaret, as opposed to just a band. So Kirk Daniels and the Deltas would open with us singing harmonies, followed by Ricky and Dane Young in matching green lamé jackets, then we'd all change into animal skins and be like the Flintstones, or some such stunt. And it worked—for a while. Dates for Saturday- and Sunday-night dances started rolling in, big reception halls in schools that could be converted into dance clubs where 150 kids would jive until curfew. And bigger pubs, like the Yew Tree in Wythenshaw. We'd do two forty-five-minute sets, no repeats. Needless to say, we learned a lot of songs. At first it was an interesting way to work, but we soon got pissed off at the gimmicky stuff and eventually decided to work on our own.

In any case, we were making twenty or thirty quid in some weeks, pretty good bread for a sixteen-year-old kid, especially when you consider my circumstances at home. We needed all the help we could get as a family. My parents were both working, but it was next to impossible for them to make ends meet, and the prospects in Salford were dim and dimmer. So I decided to leave school and go to work. This wasn't a very hard decision. I wasn't getting anything out of school, and I knew my future was as a performer, in music. It was time, I decided, to get on with my life.

My parents didn't try to talk me out of it. As usual, we didn't go for discussions about really personal stuff, but I knew deep down that they approved of my decision. I also knew they hoped I wouldn't take the standard Salford route, which was to work in the mine or the cotton mill until I was sixty, then get the gold watch—and just die. What a waste. That's the way most kids wound up. In fact, to earn extra money, Allan had started out working in the cloth mill in Salford. I went to visit him once at lunchtime, and it looked and sounded like hell to me. All these gigantic machines throbbing in the same rhythm, lots of shuttles flying around. And it was filthy, with bits of cloth flying all over the place. Amazingly, Allan didn't seem to mind, which made me realize that you could shut out anything if you wanted to. But it wasn't a place for me, I knew that right away. Fortunately, Allan left the mill for his position at Alexander Kenyon's, so he referred me there and I landed my first real job.

The two of us would go to work together, and it was insane just to get there. It was right outside Manchester, in Ardwick. We had to leave home about six in the morning, take two buses, and walk a bit. After work, at 5:30, a van would pick us up and we'd be driven to a town in the vicinity, where we'd play a gig and get home about three in the morning. I even had a job at a record store on Saturdays. It was a grind and a half that went on for years. But it felt great, at last, to earn a decent wage. I'll never forget my first pay packet—£2.10, about seven dollars US—which I took home to my mother.

I always contributed to the family pot, but I also managed to put away a few quid. Ever since laying eyes on Allan's electric guitar, I'd been saving up to buy one of my own. He was also trying to upgrade, and after a few months at Kenyon's we each had enough to buy matching Guyatones. Mine cost about fifteen pounds, which was a fortune at the time. But it allowed us, finally, to play rock 'n' roll.

We became—what else?—the Guyatones and began getting gigs at the network of coffee bars that was springing up across northern England. We did mostly Everly Brothers songs, with Buddy Holly stuff in two-part and a little Gene Vincent mixed in for good measure. One afternoon, we got booked into a show at the Bodega, a relatively small bohemian club just off Deansgate, by the Albert Square in Manchester. It was kind of a fake weekend-beatnik joint, with kids who wore striped shirts and berets and would click their fingers instead of applaud. We knew it was bullshit, but it paid cash money just the same.

After our set, a young, good-looking guy came up to us and introduced himself. He was Joe Abrams, the son of a man who owned the biggest newsstand in Manchester, about two hundred yards from the Bodega. At the age of fifteen, Joe had left school to help his father sell newspapers and magazines to the thousands of workers who passed by there every day. Joe happened to play the drums, and he came into the club to check out our act. "You and Allan are real good," he said to me, "but you need a band."

"What do you mean we need a band?" I said, getting defensive. "We're doing great together. Allan and I are each making five pounds a night. We don't need anybody else."

"Yeah you do. You need a drummer, a bass player, and a lead guitarist. Now, I happen to be the great drummer you need, and beyond that you need a bocking."

Now I was really getting in his face. "What the fuck are you talking about—a bocking?"

"No, no," he said. "You need *Pete* Bocking in your band."

"Oh yeah? What do we need this guy for?"

Joe Abrams smiled—he finally had me on the hook. "Because he can play every solo you've ever heard, every Buddy Holly solo, every Gene Vincent solo, all the Little Richard stuff . . ."

"Well, you know," I said, "let's go meet this Pete Bocking."

The three of us immediately made for a house in Didsbury, on the outskirts of Manchester. Even today it's hard to describe Pete Bocking. He was unlike any musician I'd ever met before—or since. He was shy and introverted, he rarely spoke above a whisper, and he was already bald at the age of seventeen. He wore sunglasses and a dark suit with sleeves that were too long and he smoked like a chimney. And he carried this rectangular case that he put on the floor in a ceremonious way.

"What's in the case?" I asked, without expecting too much.

Bocking didn't say a word as he flipped open the case, and—*Good God!* A *Stratocaster!* The first Fender Stratocaster I ever laid eyes on. I'd heard plenty about them, but that was about it. No one I knew in Manchester had one. They were too expensive—more than £170—but Pete had saved up and got this beauty, sunburst and sleek as a surfboard. I could tell from the way he handled it how special it was. And then he began to play. He didn't even plug it in, he just played it acoustically, but I could hear the magic in his touch. He played all the solos that we loved, and with style. He was everything Joe Abrams cracked him up to be.

I turned to Allan and said, "Joe is absolutely right—we need this kid." And I knew Allan felt the same way. We'd been very comfortable as a duo; we had two little guitars and a whole lot of gumption. But we saw what was coming. We wanted to have a rock 'n' roll band, and Pete Bocking on lead, Joe Abrams on drums, and their friend Butch Mepham, who played bass, were the guys who could help make it all come true.

We became the Fourtones, even though there were five of us. The Fourtones: *my very first band.* At the outset, we stuck to "complicated skiffle"—instrumentals and the Ventures kind of stuff. Soon enough, however, we drifted into American R&B: the Coasters, Barrett Strong, Arthur Alexander, artists like that, with our trusty Everly Brothers and Buddy Holly set mixed in. Allan and I loved the fact that Joe and Butch could keep a groove, but we were always waiting for Bocking's solos. He was one of those guys who never played the same solo twice. He was *that* good. And during our sets, Clarkie and I would glance at each other and go: "Oh *fuck*—solo time," then we'd edge over toward Pete and practically inhale his fretwork. What a feeling! With the Fourtones, Allan and I had finally tapped into some incredible energy. We'd still do Everly

Brothers and skiffle, but with a beat behind us and Pete Bocking's solos, we were on our way at last, ready to rock 'n' roll.

THE FOURTONES TURNED out to be a pretty good band. We played a lot of local gigs, almost every weekend, and began to draw a faithful following in the north. One of the benefits of being a good rock 'n' roll band in the late 1950s was that it was obvious that girls loved musicians. There was always a great-looking flock that clustered near the stage, and all sorts of eye contact would go ping-ponging back and forth. But one of the pitfalls was that if someone's boyfriend was watching his girl flirt with one of us, you usually stood a chance of getting the shit kicked out of you afterward. Bob Joy was one of those guys. He was an African American kid who had a habit of carrying around a silver dollar. He would look at you, flick it high in the air, and catch it . . . flick it high and catch it . . . over and over, flick it high and catch it, until he had your attention. Then he would flick it higher than before, and as your face went up to follow it, he would head-butt you as hard as he could. One night, Allan and I were carrying our amps to the bus as it was just pulling out, but somehow I got left behind. With Bob Joy, who was waiting there as well. That fucker was out to get me, and that silver-dollar-head-butt combo left an impression on my soul. It was dangerous, man. Jealousy was not to be taken lightly. It was a lesson, hard learned, that I wouldn't soon forget.

AS THE SIXTIES dawned, it was great being on my own, earning a decent wage, and playing music to crowds a few nights a week. Few eighteen-year-olds can claim as much. But sometimes all it takes is a chance encounter to remind you how much of a kid you really are.

Sometime after the new year began, I spotted an ad in the Manchester newspaper: the Everly Brothers, live and in concert, at the

Free Trade Hall. Oh, you bet I was going to be there. Allan, too. And we made up our minds that some way, somehow, we were going to meet our heroes. It was a dream of ours that wouldn't quit. Of course, we never thought it would happen. You know how those things go. But we talked out a plan that seemed logical at the time and determined to give it our best shot.

The night of the show we were eight miles high—adrenaline pumping, heart beating outside my chest. We had great seats, maybe eight rows back. My sister Elaine was with us. Word was floating around that Phil and Don weren't speaking to each other, and I had a fantasy of leaving Elaine there in the seats with Allan and taking Phil's part if he didn't show. But when the lights came up, there they were, together, just as we'd hoped. And they were fucking fabulous. Did all their hits. Two acoustic gray Gibsons, strumming them like mad. They sounded incredible. They sang around one mike, perfect balance. And those voices! C'mon, who did anything like *that*? They were just stunning.

Their drummer that night was an eighteen-year-old kid named Jimmy Gordon, who later played on "Marrakesh Express." Things do tend to come full circle.

After the concert, the place cleared out pretty quick. It was a school night for a lot of the audience, and besides, it wasn't cool for girls to be out that late, so we put my sister on a bus headed home. She didn't mind, she was on cloud nine. During the show Don Everly broke a string, and I darted to the stage and got it for her. I'm sure she stared at it all the way home, because I know she still has it to this day. After she was safely on the bus to Salford, Clarkie and I put our plan into effect.

There was no tour bus on the street by the theater. Okay, that narrowed things down. We figured the Everlys had to be staying in Manchester overnight, probably at the Midland Hotel. It was the best place in the city and a well-known rendezvous, where Rolls met Royce in the 1920s, about a hundred yards from the Free Trade

Hall. A uniformed doorman stood sentry on the front steps. In my best Mr. Cool guise, I approached him and said, "Are the Everly Brothers in?" Incredibly, he fell for it. "No, not yet," he said, and we knew we had them.

Clarkie and I took up position near the steps. I glanced at the clock tower across the street: 10:00. The next time I looked it was 11:45. The buses stopped running at midnight. It was typical north of England weather—pissing down and brutally cold—but there was no way we were giving up the quest. We knew we were going to have to walk the nine miles back to Salford in total darkness, but so what? It's the Everlys, man. Sometime after one o'clock, I spotted them coming around the corner. They were a little drunk; they'd been to a nightclub.

"There they are!" I hissed at Clarkie. "Oh my God, they're actually walking toward us. Fuck! Now what?"

It was obvious that they'd have to pass us because we were planted at the foot of the steps by the front door. One look at their faces and you knew they'd recognized us as fans.

"We don't want to bother you," I said, "but I'm Graham and this is my friend Allan, and we sing together. We sing like you—we copy your style."

"That's nice," Don said. "Are you any good?"

"We think we are," Clarkie told him. He explained about our band and how we played shows around Manchester.

"Hey, Graham and Allan, keep doing it. Things'll happen," Phil said.

*Graham and Allan.* Phil and Don called us Graham and Allan! It was Allan and me and Phil and Don standing on the steps of the Midland Hotel, talking music. Giving us encouragement. Instead of brushing us off and going to bed, they talked to us for what seemed like forty minutes, but it could have been forty seconds for all I know. Either way, it changed our lives. It was a big moment for me. After that night, I swore to myself that if I ever became famous and met fans, I would talk to them like the Everly Brothers talked to me and validated my very being. Today, if my bus is pulling out from a gig and I see fans standing there waving, I'll stop the bus and talk to them for a few minutes. Take it from me, you just never know!

Before we realized it, the Everly Brothers were gone, just like that. Clarkie and I were beside ourselves, clapping each other on the shoulder and hopping up and down. "Holy shit! Did that really happen? Man, I can't believe it!"

It kept us going for weeks. I was especially knocked out and took all their advice to heart. One of the things we talked about that night was writing songs, whether it was a cool thing or not. The Everly Brothers already had a stash of fabulous material to their credit, so obviously Allan and I were going to give it a try. They told us not to overthink it, just—you know, let it rip. A few months later, we finally got up our nerve.

We were camped out on a park bench outside the Regent Road Baths, a local swimming joint a few blocks from my home. We'd been across the street to a bakery, where we'd gotten some cheap day-old bread, and launched right into our first original tune. We didn't even have guitars with us, so we had to remember it: "Hey, What's Wrong with Me?" Not a masterpiece, but that didn't matter. It wasn't bad for a first shot at songwriting, and it eventually became the B-side of our very first record. It gave us enormous satisfaction to know that we could write a pretty decent rock 'n' roll song. I loved the whole creative process—combining personal feelings with poetry and music—and suspected that, in time, I could become a good songwriter.

Allan and I continued to work at it, to write together, and the Fourtones got really tight. There was a lot of great rock 'n' roll in our sets: "Mr. Moonlight," "Anna," "Mickey's Monkey," "You've Really Got a Hold on Me," "Stay," "Poison Ivy," songs that were so much fun to play. Eventually, in late 1960, we made our first acetate at the local record store, Johnny's Roadhouse. One Saturday morning, we dragged our equipment up to the second floor, where they had a paneled room with egg cartons on the walls to absorb and deflect sound. Strictly a rinky-dink affair. All five of us chipped in for the session, scraping together four shillings, and did three songs: the Everly Brothers' "Cryin' in the Rain," "Wimoweh," and a song we'd written called "Learn How to Twist."

But teenage bands don't last forever. In time, the Fourtones went their separate ways. Joe, Pete, and Butch moved on, and Allan and I began working with a different set of guys: Vic Farrell, who later became a pretty famous guitar player called Vic Steele; Eric Haydock, who'd played bass with Kirk Daniels and the Deltas; and Don Rathbone, a decent drummer to speak of, but, more important, his father owned a mortuary, and that allowed us use of its van.

One night in 1962 we were playing a gig at the Two J's on Lloyd Street by Albert Square. It was an incredible little place on the ground floor of an old building, one of the first coffee bars in Manchester to feature live music. In a later incarnation, it became famous as the Oasis, which is where the eponymous band got its name. Anyway, I was working there in the afternoon, serving coffee, cooking burgers, wiping tables, cleaning up. I'm not even sure I got paid for doing that; I just wanted to be part of the club. I told the owner, Jack Jackson, that our band was worth a listen, and he agreed to let us audition. Graham Clegg, who was the emcee, grabbed us just before we went on.

"I'm about to introduce you," he said. "What's the name of the band?"

Good question. We didn't have a name at this point and went off in the corner to mull it over.

"What about the Deadbeats?" Don said, taking a cue from the family business.

Deadbeats: I thought that sounded kind of cool. Clarkie, thankfully, didn't agree. "We're not Deadbeats," he said. "We're more fun than that."

Someone else—and I honestly don't remember who—thought we should name the band after one of our favorite singers. In an instant we all agreed, and I went off to deliver the verdict.

A few minutes later, we were gathered at the side of the postage-stamp-size stage when Graham Clegg stepped forward and leaned into the mike.

"Why don't you give a nice round of applause to a local band," he announced, "—*the Hollies!*"

THE HOLLIES HIT THAT STAGE AT THE TWO J'S AND we never looked back. Ready to go for broke as a band, we found our groove right away, and it transformed us into something intense and exciting. You put five guys onstage who can play together well, man, that's when all the planets align. It's like walking for the first time or riding a two-wheel bike. You get your legs—and you *go*. There's no stopping you after that. It's like a religious experience. Everything just clicks.

The sound we made onstage, the energy that came pouring off us, was fantastic. And our vocals—the harmony structure that Allan and I had perfected—pulled everything together in a tidy package. The songs we did weren't anything special—every band in England played the same basic set—but the Hollies managed to give them a unique sound. And besides, we were cool, we had a certain mystique. Allan and I had attitude up the wazoo, and Eric Haydock, our bass player, was a real piece of work. He was the James Dean of the band, moody and surly, but a real north of England lad. He had a *six*-string Fender bass, which was as offbeat as Eric, and all of that just added to our appeal.

The more clubs and dances we played, the better we got. We'd go anywhere, play anywhere we could. Nowhere in the north was off-limits. From Blackpool to Stoke, you name it, we played it. We had wheels, Don's van, that's all it took. It'd cruise by Kenyon's after Allan and I were done working, and we'd drive two or three hours to Stoke and play the King's Hall. Often we wouldn't get home until three in the morning, then do it again the next day . . . and the next. We did that for several years, didn't think anything of it. When you're young and playing rock 'n' roll, time becomes irrelevant.

So much music was storming through the north of England. Every town we rolled into, there were bands playing gigs. Those days, it seemed like there was one on every corner. Manchester had its share of good bands: Johnny Peters and the Rockets, Pete Mac-Laine and the Dakotas, Herman's Hermits, Wayne Fontana and the Mindbenders, Freddie and the Dreamers. But I think there were more bands per capita in Liverpool than anywhere else. They were louder and tougher than the groups we were used to in Manchester. More merchant seamen there, more violent street gangs, more Teddy Boys, all of whom were scary. You didn't fuck with kids from Liverpool. They'd beat the shit out of you. Even so, we kept our eyes on everything that was going on there. That city was crawling with bands who were already attracting attention in the south: the Big Three, Rory Storm and the Hurricanes, the Swinging Blue Jeans, the Fourmost, Kingsize Taylor and the Dominoes, the Searchers, and, of course, the granddaddy of them all, the Beatles.

I first saw the "Beatles" in Manchester of all places, which was an eye-opener as far as gigs went. It was at the Two J's, which had just changed its name to the Oasis. They were scheduled to play that night. They came through the front door about three in the afternoon to set up their equipment, and every girl in there stopped dead in their tracks. Man, it was like four Marlon Brandos had walked in: John, Paul, George, and *Pete.* They had an innate, primordial swagger. Aside from the raw energy they put out, they looked fantastic. They had just come back from Hamburg and were dressed in black leather with that Beatle haircut. What a sight! A total coolness emanated off them, like a *Young Riders* kind of vibe. You know, they'd swing the door open and they'd all be standing there while the dust settled around them. They hadn't even played a note, and the girls would swoon and faint. Fuckin' fantastic.

The Hollies played double bills with the Beatles a few times. In 1962, at Stoke-on-Trent, we shared a gig at the King's Ballroom. After soundcheck, I was standing around the ballroom backstage when John and Paul came up to me. "Hey, Graham, want to hear a new song?" Now, I'm always interested in a new song, but this was a new *Beatles* song. Interested?—take a wild guess. So they gave me what musicians call a total ear fuck: John and Paul on either side of me, with John playing the guitar, and they sang: *The world is treating me baaaaa-aaad, misery.* What a moment for me. John and Paul doing their trademark two-part harmony in the purest form, like the Everly Brothers, but different. The minute I heard it, I knew it was a smash hit. And later the Hollies went on tour with Helen Shapiro, for whom it was written—but she never recorded it because her manager turned it down! Misery.

The most unforgettable Beatles-Hollies double gig, of course, had to be at the Cavern, in Liverpool. It was in late 1962 and they owned that city. Meanwhile, the Cavern was like no place on earth. It was three tunnels linked by archways that made one room, wall-to-wall kids—hundreds of them—hot and sweaty, filled with dense cigarette smoke. No ventilation to speak of. Condensation streamed down the walls from the 100 percent humidity; circles of water pooled on the floor. The club was a cellar: literally underground. There was only one way in and one way out, via an endless flight of stone stairs that were always wet with sweat or urine. A real death trap. It was intense, a great rock 'n' roll scene. That was the first time I ever saw Ringo, who didn't even have a Beatle haircut at the time.

Ringo didn't change the sound of the band much, but he definitely changed the groove. Simpler and more understated than Pete Best's style. Ringo plays a heartbeat, which is a sound I love. It's one of the secrets of great drumming, because, in life, everything starts with the heartbeat. Your mother's heartbeat is the very first thing you hear when you are conceived, and that sets the rhythm for the rest of your life. There's no way around it. The heartbeat is the most important part of music if you want to connect on a personal level.

And it's very subtle: Ringo's right foot on that kick drum. He's an incredible drummer, one of the most underrated. And the Beatles were very lucky to get him.

In general, that band was flat-out amazing, and everybody knew it. They played a molten, scruffy brand of rock 'n' roll. And they had attitude in spades. They'd swear and smoke onstage, tell off the audience, all of which just added to their mystique.

The Hollies didn't have that kind of power. Oh, we had our share of loyal fans, we could put on a damn good show, pulled enough birds, but we hadn't hit our sweet spot, that point where you take the stage by storm and everything just falls your way. I'm not exactly sure why. Maybe we hadn't played enough gigs; perhaps we needed different material. Who knows? For one thing, there was still too much uncertainty within the band. We were playing more than a couple of nights a week and had gotten a residency at a place called the Twisted Wheel. A great little club, funky as hell, where you're on a stage the size of a skateboard and about as stable, no real PA system to speak of, jammed every night, the kind of room every rock 'n' roll band needs to cut its teeth. The money was respectable. Hard to believe, but I was making more with the Hollies than at my day job and could support myself pretty well. Most of us thought it was time to go for broke, to turn professional and just play music full-time. Unfortunately, Vic Steele didn't see it that way. In the north of England, there was a union hierarchy: You apprenticed at a job and worked your way up, the payoff being a lifetime gig to support your family. And Vic wasn't willing to give that up, which was too bad because he was a pretty good player.

That meant we'd need a new lead guitarist, someone willing to stick with us to the next level. We'd been hearing good things about the Dolphins, a group from Colne, a dozen miles from Manchester. Their lead guitar player was a guy named Tony Hicks who was supposed to be fabulous, much like Pete Bocking. So we sent word, inviting him to come play with us.

A few days later, during a jam-packed show of ours at the Twisted

Wheel, we heard there was a weird fucker lurking around outside, acting suspicious. This was our first encounter with Tony Hicks. He had come up on a bus from Colne and was too shy to come inside to see us. Instead he listened to our set through an outside air vent. From what he could hear, he knew the Hollies had their shit together and was intrigued about becoming a member of the band.

In retrospect, Tony was an ambitious lad. He also knew he could play rings around most guys in Manchester. The Dolphins were a band on the upswing, they had a rising reputation, which is why we went after Tony in the first place. As it happened, later, after Eric Haydock and Don Rathbone left the Hollies, we got Bernie Calvert and Bobby Elliott from the Dolphins as their replacements, so the Hollies were actually the Dolphins, with Allan and me as frontmen. But stealing Tony away was a real coup. In addition to being an incredible guitar player, he had a great set of ears. He could smell a hit a mile away. Also, he was an impeccable arranger, and his leads produced identifiable melodies before you even got to the first verse of a song. Just listen to the intros to "Look Through Any Window," "Stop! Stop! Stop!," and "Bus Stop," and you'll know right away how inventive this guy was. Plus he could sing, which meant that Allan and I could expand the harmonies to three-part, with Tony going underneath us for support.

Tony was a north of England boy through and through. Not particularly great looking; his nose was too big, teeth typically at odd angles. But his eyes were set on bigger and better stages. A couple of years later, we were playing just outside of London following a monthlong break that led into a new tour. Tony showed up and his nose was in a bandage, two beautiful shiners blackening both eyes. Of course, we all wanted to know what had happened to him. "Oh, man, I got into this ugly fight," he explained. "Some guy insulted my girlfriend. We exchanged a couple punches and he broke my nose." And we *believed* him. That was Tony to a tee. Like I said, he was an ambitious lad.

But he was also cautious, and before he agreed to join the Hollies there were certain assurances he needed, the most important being money in his pocket. In order to turn professional with us, he had to make an amount each week that at least equaled what he made as an engineer at the firm his father worked for. Hell, we were already pulling down more than that much. We made ten or twenty pounds night after night; my share alone was more than my father was earning, which allowed me to quit my day job. So we knew we could guarantee Tony a respectable income. But he also wanted to make sure we were heading in the right direction.

That issue would resolve itself soon enough.

WITH TONY HICKS on board, the Hollies started putting it all together. Basically, we were just a three-piece band: drums, bass, and Tony's guitar, with a little rhythm from me, but that was about it. Allan didn't play anything. Overall, we developed a solid, identifiable sound, crisp and cool, with vocals right out of the Everly Brothers playbook. Allan and I were tighter than ever. Our voices just wrapped around each other like a warm embrace. We were tighter than tight. Didn't even have to talk about it: We just sang and it came to the table perfectly cooked. I always knew where Allan was going and was *right there with him.* That doesn't happen often in life, when you wind up on the same unique wavelength as someone else. But I was lucky. I bonded twice: first to Allan and later to Crosby. What are the odds?

The Hollies hung out together most days, working on material, perfecting our sound. Adrian Barrett was around in those days. He was the son of the owner of Barrett's, the main music store in Manchester, where we bought records and a lot of our gear. Adrian was a very kind, stand-up guy. He was in charge of the store and gave us generous discounts, and occasionally he'd loan us a guitar to try out. We were always looking for places to rehearse, and he came to our rescue at a key time, getting us into a spare room above the Wimpy

Bar next to Barrett's on Oxford Street, where we could bash around to our heart's content. Before that, we rehearsed in a run-down Victorian house that belonged to an old woman who charged us a quid a week, so I guess we were happy to be saving the bread.

This was a pretty amazing time in my life. Gigs were rolling in and we were great for business, packing houses and getting kids off righteously. I was working with a great band, playing music full-time, and generally grooving on an excellent set of circumstances. Don't forget, I'd come from the Salford council estate and had only recently shed a Salvation Army wardrobe. You can't imagine the feeling of shaking that legacy. I have to hand it to my parents. They were in my corner every step of the way. Never gave me shit about leaving school or playing rock 'n' roll or forgoing a day job. They always seemed to know that I'd be okay in the universe. So many kids I knew—really talented kids—never got the opportunity to live out their dreams because of parents who insisted they stay the course. They lived and died in really shitty circumstances, working boring jobs, earning just enough to get by. "Yes sir, no sir," all their lives. My parents were so supportive. My dad was proud because I wasn't down the mine. They were really happy for me, and I was grateful for the chances they gave me. I knew how lucky I was. I used to take my weekly pay, which was in cash in those days, and give it to my family, no questions asked. I had everything I needed—and more.

Talk about things going my way—one day I walked into the Two J's and fell in love for the first time in my life. There, in a dark corner of the coffee bar, I noticed a petite raven-haired girl with eyes that mesmerized me from the very first moment. Her name was Angie Holmes, and she was a beauty on so many levels. Did I mention those eyes? Well, you get the idea. But beyond the obvious was a lovely spirit. She was full of life, funny and articulate. We started dating, and it got heavy pretty fast. We wanted to be together all the time, and I don't quite recall how this came about, but I ended up living with her and her family in Didsbury, just outside of Manchester. Give her parents credit: They were broad-minded people. They let us be together without laying a lot of crap on us.

In another respect, it allowed me to move out of my parents' house, which was a very big deal for an eighteen-year-old guy. Not that things weren't good at home. I loved my parents, never had a quarrel in that regard. But moving out was a rite of passage that I'd been looking forward to since quitting my day job. Living with Angie and her parents wasn't like being on my own, but it was putting one foot in that direction. Plus I got to live with my girlfriend, which was a lovely change of pace.

It seemed like no time before Angie and I got engaged at the Parrs Wood Hotel in Didsbury. That's what you did after leaving school and getting a job. It was the next big step toward the expected north of England life. Allan had already taken it with his girlfriend, Jeni, and I kind of liked the idea of a steady relationship. But I was starting to live the life of a rock 'n' roll musician and wound up being gone a great deal of the time. You know how it is. You come in wicked late—or not at all. "Where you been?" "Who were you with?" All reasonable questions, but better left unanswered. And, in time, Angie and I drifted apart. Sadly, the last time I visited Manchester a few years ago, I learned she had died from a brain tumor, and her husband told me he'd buried a great bottle of fine wine with her. That was Angie in a nutshell—a sip of fine wine.

Music and the Hollies started to consume me. There were so many great bands emerging and as many new places to play, so the scene in the north was incredibly vibrant. You'd play a coffee bar or club on a double bill one night, then meet a whole new group of musicians in another club the next. One of the most intriguing gigs was the lunchtime show at the Cavern in Liverpool. Bands were used to playing there at night, a grueling four- or five-hour stretch usually shared with a handful of local groups on the bill. We did a lot of those evening shows. But sometime around 1961 they instituted a little rock 'n' roll show from noon to one for the girls who worked in nearby offices. Instead of going to a fish-and-chips joint for lunch, they came to the Cavern with a bag lunch and paid a shilling for an hour of music before going back to work. It was always packed, a vigorous scene. And the girls locked right into us. They used to hang around and chat us up, wanting to form Hollies fan clubs.

It was great doing those shows, especially in the heart of Liverpool. The Beatles had just gotten a recording contract—the first northern group to break through the north-south divide—and we all hoped their luck would rub off on us. It was every band's dream to make a record with a major label, to hit the big time *just like the Beatles.* So playing at the Cavern, on their turf, we thought, brought us closer to that goal. At this time, we had a pretty good reputation going for us. The Hollies were fairly well known in the north. It hadn't filtered down to London, because we couldn't get past the social line: Everybody south of Birmingham was posher than we were. We were peasants to them. Probably still—that's the way it goes. All we had to do was to open our mouths; we had funny accents, we were almost like aliens in the south. But when the Beatles opened that door, we all wanted to run screaming through it.

One day, in February 1963, we finished a particularly energetic lunchtime show at the Cavern. The girls had left, the lights came up, and people were cleaning the place, picking up popcorn packages and cheese wrappers, wiping up piss. We were hauling our meager gear into the tiny side dressing room when a short, older man with glasses pushed his way into the cubicle.

"I'm Ron Richards," he said, thrusting out a hand. "I work at EMI and I liked your show. I especially liked the guy who was playing without any guitar strings."

Would the guilty party please step forward? Okay, that would be me. The night before, we had played at Colston Hall in Bristol, and during the show I'd broken my last string and couldn't afford new ones. So I did the lunchtime show at the Cavern with my Harmony guitar—and no strings. What did it matter? Tony, Eric, and Don made up the Hollies' dynamic rhythm section. I strummed along, except I didn't plug in, so it didn't make any difference whether I had strings on or not. Ron didn't care. In fact, he found it intriguing. He loved our energy, and we'd gone down great. That was all he needed to make the next move.

"I'd be very interested in recording you," Ron said. "What do you think?"

*What do we think?* Are you kidding! We were thrilled to death. Truth be told, we never saw it coming. Oh, we'd heard an A&R man was in the audience that day, and we'd turned up the heat, but that was about it. Still—*a recording opportunity?*

"How does that work?" one of us managed to ask.

Ron smiled circumspectly. "Well, you'll have to come down to London to record."

"When?"

"As soon as possible," he said. "I've got another week in the north, hitting various clubs and scouting new bands. Why don't you meet me in London in early April and we'll see what happens."

This was an incredible development. The Hollies wanted to make records—it was every band's fantasy—but we weren't actively searching for a label contract. Everything just kind of fell into our lap. Don't get me wrong: We were good, as good as any English band on the upswing. We had what it took to hit the big time. The offer to record, *now,* simply caught us by surprise.

*You'll have to come down to London.* I could have made that trip in record time, sprinted there if I had to. I was ready, ready for anything, but the band still had some loose ends to tie up. We were involved with a manager of sorts, a guy named Allen Cheatham, whose father owned a shirt factory just outside of Manchester where we used to rehearse. A nice guy, although not necessarily someone sharp enough to negotiate a major recording contract. The Hollies needed to move on and up, and we did, changing very quickly to a manager named Michael Cohen, who owned a store in Stockport called the Toggery. His father coincidentally also owned a clothing

My father during the war

My mother, 1953 *(© Graham Nash)*

My father singing at a holiday camp, 1954

My father and his sister, Olive, 1953. One of my earliest shots.
*(© Graham Nash)*

Me and Allan Clarke at school
*(© Graham Nash)*

With Allan Clarke, the Guyatones, 1957. We were fifteen.

Playing my black Epiphone guitar with "Hollies" lettering, June 19, 1965
(© 1965 Harry Goodwin)

The Hollies at the Cavern in early 1963

The Hollies in New York City, 1967 *(© Henry Diltz)*

The Hollies, 1983 *(© Henry Diltz)*

Stephen Stills, "Captain Many Hands,"
at the Caravan Lodge Motel,
San Francisco, 1969 *(© Graham Nash)*

David in Sag Harbor,
1969 *(© Graham Nash)*

Self-portrait; Plaza Hotel, September 1974 *(© Graham Nash)*

Singing the chorus of "Marrakesh Express" at Heider Studio 3, LA, 1969
(© Henry Diltz)

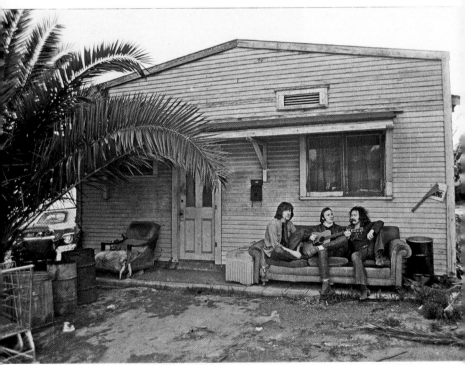

The infamous disappearing house, Santa Monica Boulevard, LA, 1969
(© Henry Diltz)

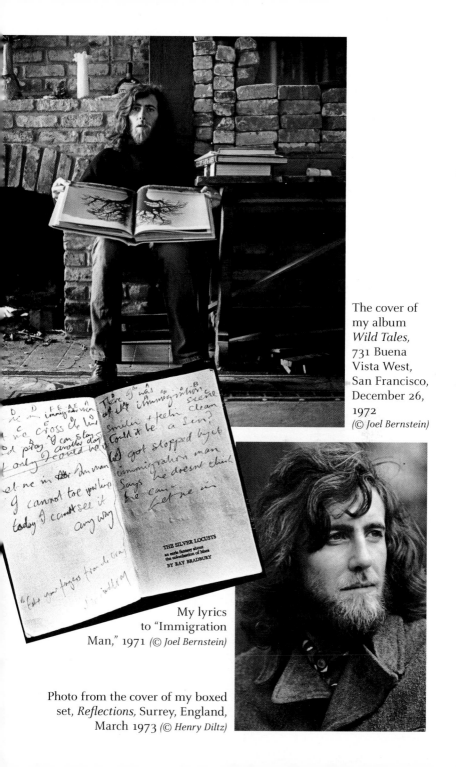

The cover of
my album
*Wild Tales*,
731 Buena
Vista West,
San Francisco,
December 26,
1972
*(© Joel Bernstein)*

My lyrics
to "Immigration
Man," 1971 *(© Joel Bernstein)*

Photo from the cover of my boxed
set, *Reflections*, Surrey, England,
March 1973 *(© Henry Diltz)*

Sculpting Crosby, Miami, 1977
(© *Joel Bernstein*)

The *Mayan*
(© *Bev Morgan*)

Tokyo, November
1975; the joint was
rolled in a copy of
the *International
Herald Tribune*.
(© *Joel Bernstein*)

factory, bespoke tailors, real stuff, and had given Michael money to open a boutique—teenage clothes, bright leather, rock 'n' roll wear. And I worked there to earn extra money. "Would you like that in black, sir?" Just like *Spinal Tap.*

Otherwise, everyone was on board. Tony Hicks still had a day job, but he agreed to give it up when we promised we'd pay him at least eighteen quid a week, which is what he was getting at work. Don worked for his dad at the mortuary in Wilmslow and was happy to escape that grind. And Eric had some kind of job, but not one that would keep him from going to London to record. Allan and I were all ready to go—we'd been there since we were six years old and sang the Lord's Prayer in assembly. We always knew this was where we were headed, so in our minds London was a fait accompli.

So we all drove down to London in Don Rathbone's Commer van, which had the mortuary name on the side panels. It was an incredibly upbeat trip; everyone's spirits were higher than high. And we stayed in some fleabag joint in Shepherd's Bush, a working-class neighborhood just outside the city, in one big room with seven beds in it, two sets of bunk beds and three singles. Decidedly cheap, since we were picking up the tab ourselves. We kept reminding ourselves, This isn't a record deal, it's only an audition. But somehow we knew this was our ticket to the top.

We made an audition tape the next day, not at EMI, but at a studio called Delane Lea at 129 Kingsway. Nothing very sophisticated. The tape was two-track, so basically we played live, no overdubs, which was okay because we knew what we were doing. We knew how to play and we had the energy, so when we did "(Ain't That) Just Like Me" and "Whole World Over," it went down fantastic. Ron ran a smooth ship, we were in and out of there in no time, and he had help from a London guy named Tommy Sanderson. Tommy was a piano player and bandleader who also happened to be a manager. Once you hit London, they immediately got rid of your north of England manager—"What the fuck do they know? You need a *manager*"—and hooked you up with someone who knew the ropes.

So Tommy came on board as our manager, and he and Ron had a business relationship with Dick James, who published John Lennon and Paul McCartney's songs. Should the audition prove successful, we were wrapped up for everything: recording, management, and publishing. A neat little package.

We got the word right away that EMI wanted to sign us. The deal was for a recording contract on Parlophone, the same label as the Beatles. The mechanism for hits was already in place, so it was like a cookie-cutter process, you just stamp 'em right out. "Let's put these boys in the studio and use the same energy and distribution that sold the Beatles records." Hey, I had no problem with that. It was exactly what we wanted, a shot with a proven strategy.

"Let's get right down to work," Ron Richards said. "Come to EMI and make a real record, on four-track."

EMI: That meant Abbey Road, the sanctum sanctorum. We drove back home that night after the audition, but we felt like we were flying.

THE HOLLIES' FIRST recording session was on April 4, 1963, only five short months after we formed the group. We rolled into Abbey Road studios, and it was like—*holy shit!* This was the place. Four amazing studios in a Georgian mansion that had recording history written all over it. It was like a factory, but an intimate factory, with so much going on that it was impossible to take in right away. Abbey Road: Now the Hollies would be written into its incredible history.

I remember how psyched the Beatles were the day before they went in to cut their first record. That night, they happened to be playing at the Oasis in Manchester, and the Hollies were around the corner at the Twisted Wheel. We all got together after our respective shows at this after-hours drinking place. When the pubs closed at 10:30, that was it, you were out of luck, but there were certain illegal places where you could drink after that, and we knew a good one. Three bands crammed into that little dive: The Big Three were also along for the ride. They were a kick-ass group from Liverpool with a couple of legendary characters—Johnny Hutchinson, a fearsome drummer with a short fuse whom I first saw play with Johnny and the Moondogs, and Johnny Gustafson, their bass player, an all-around head case. In fact, that night Johnny Gus plucked a rose out of the vase on the table . . . and *ate* it! After which he ate a cigarette, which blew my mind. Lennon was in an ugly mood that night. We'd all had a few pints, but John was feeling it from some other place. He was really unsettled about what the Beatles should record the next day.

"I want to do this fuckin' song, 'Anna,' by Arthur Alexander," he growled, "but I can't remember the fuckin' words."

"I know 'em," I told him, which was easy, because the Hollies did "Anna." So I wrote out the words, lifting the gloom. And I must say, the Beatles made a pretty good record of it.

Now we were about to get our chance in the studio. Not making an album, not yet anyway, but initially a couple of singles to test the market, like the Beatles did with "Love Me Do" and, later, "Please Please Me." Ron thought we should stick with "(Ain't That) Just Like Me," our cover of a 1960 Coasters song that the kids loved when we played it at gigs. *"Mary had a little lamb / Well, ain't that*—thunk thunk—*just like me?"* It was a little trifle, but catchy enough. Naturally, Allan and I hoped the A-side would be one of our songs. We played two of our tunes for Ron—"Whole World Over" and "Hey, What's Wrong with Me?"—but he wasn't in love with them; he didn't think they were commercial enough. And he was right, they were naïve and teenage. Even so, Ron encouraged us to keep writing. In fact he chose "Hey, What's Wrong with Me?" as the B-side, a nice gesture.

There was no fooling around in the studio in those days, no going in half-assed and waiting for inspiration to strike. It was all business at Abbey Road. The engineers wore white lab coats, and we couldn't touch anything, especially the board. Which meant we didn't really learn anything about the recording process at first. We were there to perform, and that was it. Sessions were only three hours long, a union rule. Then a woman with a tray of tea would come in and she'd hand out little brown envelopes with some cash in them to pay us, also a union rule. So we had to be fast: get the basic track down, lay on the vocals, and be out in three hours flat. Not a lot of wiggle room to make a great record.

Parlophone released "(Ain't That) Just Like Me" in May of 1963, and it went straight into the top twenty. Eventually, it stalled at number sixteen, but—*are you kidding me!*—our first record was an unqualified *hit.* We were on top of the world.

What do you do as a follow-up to that? Easy: another single just like it. With our new manager, Tommy Sanderson, on piano, we covered the Coasters' "Searchin'," a song all the bands in the north had in their set, and this one went to number twelve, with our own "Whole World Over" on the B-side. The Hollies were on a roll.

With two hit singles under our belts, Parlophone ordered up a Hollies album. Basically, we decided to take the best material from our two forty-five-minute sets and fuse it into one kick-ass hour. There were plenty of songs to choose from: "Mister Moonlight," "Poison Ivy," "Searchin'," "(Ain't That) Just Like Me" . . . The whole thing was done in one morning session. Then, after the lunch break and a cup of tea with some biscuits, we did the same set again—the entire album in two hours flat. That was it. Ron chose the twelve best songs. He could always find the true essence of our sessions. He had a great ear, and we relied on his judgment. The only thing he did that pissed me off was to tell us we couldn't record past 10:30 in the evening because the echo machines went off at that time. It wasn't until years later that I realized, *Wait a second!* Echo machines don't automatically shut off. It dawned on me that 10:30 was closing time at the pub. Ron and the engineers wanted to get a pint before last call, which is why *the echo machines went off.* In any case, they released our first album, *Stay with the Hollies,* on January 1, 1964, and the single from it, "Stay," a cover of the Maurice Williams and the Zodiacs hit, reached number eight, our first top-ten hit.

The Hollies were starting to carve out a groove in the nascent British rock 'n' roll scene. This was an amazing development for us. The British Revolution, as it was being called, had fired its first shot with Cliff Richard and the Shadows, a London act and bona fide stars, especially with Hank Marvin on guitar, but since early 1963 the scene had been dominated by northern groups: the Beatles, Gerry and the Pacemakers, the Searchers, and now the Hollies. For the first time in all of our memories, being from the north was an asset down in London, the Smoke. It didn't get any sweeter. Instead of walking around London feeling like lowly outcasts, we were suddenly *desirable* outcasts, treated with respect. The Hollies were a hit. We were all over the radio, all over the record stores, gradually edging our way onto TV. We'd even joined the Bobby Rydell/Helen Shapiro tour that was crisscrossing the country. No one recognized us on the city streets because by that time everyone had a Beatle haircut, even the girls. But we felt special, like we owned that fucking town.

Music was still the center of our universe. Our lives revolved around songs, finding the next suitable hit. Tony Hicks was our point man when it came to material. He used to troll the warren of publishers' offices along Denmark Street, looking for songs that we could record. One day, at lunchtime, we'd all gone down to a folk club called the Troubadour. Tony barged in while we were eating and said, "I've been to a publisher and found this song." He pulled an acetate out of his bag but couldn't figure out how to play it for us. One of the guys said, "They must be able to play music here. Leave it to me," and he disappeared with the record. A few minutes later, this incredible sound came blasting over the loudspeakers. It was Doris Troy singing "Just One Look." We knew right away. We could sing the shit out of this.

It was a sturdy, seductive ballad with a center of gravity: Everything else we'd done previously had been leading up to this. It captured everything the Hollies excelled at. We knew we could arrange it expressively so that it expanded on the original, while harmonizing beautifully, breathlessly, providing a soulful delivery, and giving it our own unique spin. We knew we could cover the song without apology.

We actually rehearsed it that same night. Allan and Tony belted out the refrain with an upbeat urbanity and I took the lead in the bridge, pleading the case of a determined lover:

> *I thought I was dreaming but I was wrong (yeah, yeah,*
> *yeah)*
> *But I'm gonna keep on schemin'* . . .

You can hear how I gave it an exuberant polish. Doris Troy's original Atlantic recording is almost subdued by comparison. Hers has a gorgeous moodiness to it, a vulnerability with an underlying sense of despair. The Hollies gave it an entirely different interpretation and, thus, new life.

Tony knew what he was doing when he brought us that song, and it became a smash hit in March 1964, eventually reaching number two on the charts.

This was turning into a storybook career. And I was having the time of my life. I moved to London at the end of 1963, bunking at the Imperial Hotel in Ladbroke Square. The city was just starting to take on its new spirit in the days before Carnaby Street exploded, and I loved everything about it. Tony also moved down, as did Bobby Elliott when he replaced Don as the band's drummer, but Allan stayed behind in Manchester after deciding to marry his girlfriend, Jeni. Eventually, I rented an apartment in a mews house on Kynance Mews in Paddington, right around the corner from where Alexander Fleming discovered penicillin. It was a great little place of my own, where I could get away from the hustling scene.

Well, not entirely away. Earlier that same year, I'd walked into the Two J's and smack into a scene that would change my life. Across the floor was an incredibly beautiful young woman, blond, tall, and well built, in a low-cut long-sleeve sheath dress that was as revealing as it was short. I kept an eye on her as the music started and a local guy asked her to dance. Man, could that girl move. No way was I going to let her get away from me, so I walked over in the middle of the song and cut in. Inconceivably, the fool she was dancing with turned her over to me, just like that. Her name was Rose Eccles. She was eighteen, she lived around the corner from my parents in Salford, and she was an independent soul. A no-bullshit girl with a big laugh and great sense of humor. I liked her immediately.

Really, I couldn't believe my good luck. Rosie was a head turner and smart, a powerful combination. Equally alluring to me was that she didn't know I was a budding rock 'n' roll star—and once she found out, she couldn't have cared less. We felt lucky to have found each other. Aside from the sparks we created, there was lots of laughing. We hung out together whenever I wasn't performing, haunting the coffee bars and clubs in Manchester, dancing at the Plaza Ballroom, listening to a lot of rock 'n' roll, making love always like it was the last time we'd get the chance.

We never talked much about our dreams, but I knew Rosie had always wanted to have a dress shop of her own, so Tony Hicks and I invested in one called Pygmalion in Backpool Fold, just off Albert Square. We rented the place and renovated it ourselves, my father put up the wallpaper, friends took care of the decorations. Rosie and her mate, Anne, were the resident fashionistas, so we left the style decisions and buying to them. It was one of the first boutiques in Manchester, with very hip stuff and a great vibe. I loved having a store where very pretty women would come in to try on dresses—and it was an instant hit. Rose was definitely behind its success.

Sometime in 1964, in the midst of all the Hollies' success, Rosie and I decided to get married. I know what you're thinking: Rock 'n' rollers whose careers are taking off are supposed to regard marriage like the plague. We were supposed to be available to all the girls who came to our shows and screamed their asses off. But Clarkie had been married to Jeni for a year, and it didn't seem to be affecting our popularity. And I loved Rosie, I wanted to be with her all the time, especially in London, where the scene had shifted. So we did it quickly and quietly, stealing off to the registry office in Albert Square in Manchester, no family or friends other than Pete MacLaine and his wife, Susan, and we spent our wedding night in the MacLaines' house—on their floor, of all places.

After that, everything changed. Rosie bowed out of Pygmalion and moved to London with me. We got a place of our own, a flat in a small high-rise in Shepherd's Bush, where Rosie painted the living room black. She came to all the Hollies gigs, hanging out with Allan's wife, and our scene felt snug and secure. For a while.

Everything kept coming our way, and in spades. The Hollies segued from "Just One Look" to "Here I Go Again," which went to number four, and followed that with "We're Through," the first A-side written by Tony, Allan, and me under the pseudonym L. Ransford, which we used on all our collaborations. Clarke-Hicks-Nash was too much of a mouthful, so we used my grandfather's name. The Hollies were consistently in the top ten, consistently featured in *Melody Maker* and *NME*. We were part of the prestigious Poll Winners Concert at the Empire Pool, Wembley, and were invited to play on the BBC's Light Programme, *The Talent Spot*. And our live shows were insane: wall-to-wall girls, screaming their heads off. Thirteen-, fourteen-, fifteen-year-old girls. They really went nuts when the lights came up, letting it all out, probably for the first time in their lives. There was a very real sexual undercurrent to those audiences, a by-product of young, good-looking guys playing loud rock 'n' roll. Those girls let themselves go. Total hysteria, wet panties. Incredible stuff. You could practically feel those twitchy girls exploring new sexual territory, casting aside all the taboos in their uptight English upbringings. Later on, guys would start turning up in greater number, but early on those eager young ladies ruled the roost.

At one of our shows at the Barrowlands Ballroom in Glasgow, where we backed a pop crooner named Johnny Gentle, seventy-five girls fainted during the Hollies set and had to be passed hand-over-head like in a mosh pit. Some of those gigs in the north had an eerie war-zone quality. The girls up there got us into a lot of deep shit. Look, half the reason I got into music was to attract women—who's kidding who?—but if some chick took a shine to the lead singer, you could bet he was going to get his ass kicked by her boyfriend and his thuggy pals after the show. Those fuckers were tough. I can't tell you how many buses I ran for after shows. Playing those northern provinces was murder. One time I got three front teeth shattered.

All in all, I got the better end of the deal. We'd get laid a lot, of course, mainly girls that you picked up at the shows. There were always adventurous girls who would find a way to get to us. They either had friends who worked as chambermaids at a hotel where we were staying or knew someone who could get them backstage. They'd find you if they wanted to. And once you were found, it usually led to sex. There wasn't any kind of courtship. It was fast. "Hello," and right to bed.

Another perk was signing breasts. Really. I'm not making this up. Girls would love you to sign their breasts. They'd just whip their shirts off. "Here, sign this!" So, naturally, I'd say, "Of course, yes, ma'am. How do you spell that? You don't, by any chance, have a longer name, do you?"

Once the Hollies hit the big time, our gigs took on a more respectable sheen. Instead of those piss-and-liquor-stained ballrooms, we graduated to cinemas and theaters, where the grime was more refined. There was a Top Rank theater in every town in England, and eventually the Hollies played 'em all: the Odeon in Manchester, where we'd seen Bill Haley; the Finsbury Park Astoria; places in Blackpool, Bristol, Scarborough, Stoke-on-Trent, Birmingham, Coventry, Bedford. They never ran out. You could literally play a different place every night of the week, and for a while that's exactly what we did.

We were going to ride that horse for as long as we could, not having the slightest idea where it would end up. We were babes in the woods as far as all this fame was concerned. Things were happening so fast; it was all so fluid. And the gig had changed since we'd burst onto the scene. It was something else entirely from the Billy Fury–Johnny Gentle–Marty Wilde–Dickie Pride–Vince Eager era, when a pretty-boy face and a dopey name got you fifteen minutes of English pop stardom. A whole new scene had exploded, grounded in talent, with great songs, versatile musicians, and bands that could put it all together onstage. Man, they were coming out of the woodwork. Kids from all over the country were making great music, often in the industrial cities where you'd least expect it. Liverpool, Newcastle, Leeds, Sheffield, Birmingham, Manchester—even those slick fuckers in London had a little bit of talent. No doubt about it, there was a new seriousness to rock 'n' roll, both as an art form and as a business. The kids knew it. Everybody knew it, even the Tin Pan Alley geezers who were fighting to hold on to their share of the rockpile. It was an undeniable force. The Beatles had started it all. They'd brought excitement and excellence to the mix and changed the ground rules.

The Hollies had earned their seat at that table. We'd come to play.

THE HOLLIES WEREN'T SATISFIED WITH NURSING OUR homegrown success. To make it—to have a long-lasting impact on rock 'n' roll—you had to crack the American market. That's where it all started, where Elvis and Buddy and Chuck and Fats and Ray and Richard and Phil and Don were. It's where Leiber and Stoller ran the factories, where Phil Spector built walls of sound and Berry Gordy cranked out hits on the Motown assembly line. Music history was being written in every major American city—by Allen Toussaint and Ernie K-Doe in New Orleans, Sam Phillips in Memphis, the Chess brothers in Chicago, the Ertegun brothers and Florence Greenberg in New York, Alan Freed in Cleveland, Dick Clark in Philadelphia, in Nashville, Los Angeles, Lubbock, even Hibbing, Minnesota. America was the holy land for any English band, and we were determined to pray at the altar.

It wasn't going to be that easy. Cliff Richard and the Shadows had gone there in 1962 and were treated like riffraff. No one took them seriously. Even the Beatles had been given the cold shoulder by three different record companies before they got a break. But once again, they had cracked open that door, and we intended to squeeze through after them.

Trouble is, we didn't have a huge hit out in the States. We didn't have a hit of *any* kind. The only record of ours that was released there was "I'm Alive," which failed to crack *Billboard*'s Hot 100. So we still didn't have an offer to perform there.

In April 1965, we finally got our chance. A guy named Morris Levy asked us to be part of a show he was producing at the Paramount Theater, in Times Square in New York City. Now, at the time, we didn't know Morris was one of the music industry's heaviest hitters, which was no exaggeration on several fronts. But he said the magic words "New York," and we sure knew the Paramount. It's where Frank Sinatra had played—and Buddy Holly. Where *Love Me Tender* had its premiere. It was Mecca, a very big deal. Don't forget, the Hollies were still basically Manchester boys; being in the Smoke was a big deal for us. Just to play for American rock 'n' roll audiences was enough of an incentive to make us salivate.

I couldn't wait to get over there. I was packed and ready to go weeks in advance. Except, as it turned out, international travel was outside of our expertise. We got to Heathrow, ready to roll, only to discover our visas weren't in order. You had to prove to American authorities that only you could do the job you were being hired for before they let you into the country. Somehow our handlers had overlooked that proviso. So we checked in to the Aerial Hotel at the airport, where we would be quarantined while they sorted it out.

Getting those visas stamped went right down to the wire. The Paramount gig was in five days' time, and after four days being cooped up in that airless room I was getting a little nuts, to say the least. Finally, with no time to spare, the visas came through and we took off for New York.

No need to tell you it was worth the wait. America was everything it was cracked up to be—and more. We arrived fairly quietly, not like the Beatles, no press corps waiting, no entourage. We took care of ourselves, carried our own luggage. When we landed, we got shoveled into the most enormous taxi I'd ever seen; it had like three doors on each side. The driver kept turning the radio dial and there were hundreds of stations, all playing rock 'n' roll, news, R&B, pop, classical, whatever you wanted. You could find it in an instant. We were used to the BBC's despotic monopoly of the airwaves, listening to whatever they wanted us to hear. Choice was never a factor. "You don't like Rosemary Clooney, too fucking bad. That's what we're playing at the moment." Not in New York. Spin the dial, you got the Ronettes, the Four Seasons, Gene Pitney, Sam Cooke, Dion, Nat King Cole, the Impressions, Jackie Wilson, the Beatles... It was a musical banquet, and we gorged ourselves on it all the way into the city.

We barely had time to check in to the hotel before soundcheck, but my head was spinning from the glitzy cityscape. Walking along Broadway gave me the chills. It was just like in the movies. The lights and the people were *insane.* I couldn't take my eyes off the Camel billboard that blew gigantic smoke rings into the air. And right across from it, just north of Times Square: the Paramount, in all its gaudy glory. This wasn't some shithole in Hoboken. It was the big time, and cavernous: 3,500 seats, with marble columns, a crystal chandelier like they had on the *Titanic,* a grand staircase, and balconies layered one on top of the other like a New York skyscraper. I immediately climbed to the top of the theater, the very last seat in the last row of the house, and stared down at that empty stage, contemplating who had played on it and how I had gotten there. I thought: If only my parents could see where I was sitting. They'd never even made it to London, and here I was, about to play the Paramount in New York.

The gig was the Soupy Sales 1965 Easter Show, with one of those Caravan of Stars–type lineups—the Hollies and eleven other groups. Half of the acts were less than forgettable, just schlock tacked on to pad the bill. But there was enough starpower to keep us interested: Shirley Ellis, Dee Dee Warwick, the Exciters, and King Curtis and the Kingpins. Bobby Elliott, a stone-cold jazz fan, was thrilled to meet Ray Lucas, who was King Curtis's drummer. But for me the payoff was playing opposite the headliner, Little Richard. That fucker was one of the greats, up there in the pantheon. I'd cut my teeth on "Long Tall Sally" and "Lucille" and "Good Golly, Miss

Molly." They were twenty-four-carat rock 'n' roll hits. Fifty years later, I still get off on them. Richard hadn't had a hit in seven or eight years, but no one gave a shit; he and his band still brought down the house.

The Hollies were ready to show America our stuff. I remember telling the stage manager, Bob Levine, "Our show is about forty-five minutes," and he went, "Yeah, well, that's not happening." *What?* "You're gonna do two songs." *What?* "That's right, two songs—for five shows a day." *What?* "That's the long and short of it, baby." They packed those screaming teenagers in there, trotted us out like beauty-pageant contestants, then right out the revolving door again—five times a day. The first show was at 10:30 in the morning. Try getting it up at that time of day. We played "Stay" and "Mickey's Monkey" over and over and over and over. And we didn't finish until nine at night, so when we walked out of the Paramount onto the street, Times Square was lit up like a Roman candle. We'd be rubbing our eyes just to get 'em to focus. *What?*

Even with all that, doing the show wasn't a grind. We were thrilled to be there, especially watching the master, Little Richard, five times a day. The guy was unreal. An incredible showman. He'd pound that piano as if it were a tough piece of meat and throw his head back and wail. And that band of his kicked ass, especially his guitar player, a young, skinny kid with fingers out to there. One night I was standing in the wings as Richard came off the stage and he was livid, his eyes bugging out like a madman, screaming like a motherfucker at that poor kid. *"Don't you ever do that again! Don't you ever upstage Little Richard!"* They got in the elevator, slammed the gate, and I could still hear him ten floors above, taking this kid's head off. *"You hear me, motherfucker! Fuck you—playing your guitar with your teeth!"* He was called Jimmy James then, but you don't need me to tell you it was Jimi Hendrix. Probably the only guy who could steal the spotlight from Richard.

New York, New York. I was in love with the place, and it kicked off my lifelong romance with the States. Every night, after the last show, the guys and I would head out onto the street, not knowing what to expect out there. It was a different town in those days, still something of an asphalt jungle. None of us ever went anywhere on our own. The Hollies stuck together out of camaraderie—and for protection. If anything were going to happen, you'd have to fuck with the five of us. The first day I got to New York, I'd opened the newspapers and there were like eight fresh murders on the front page. I remember reading about one guy who had been killed *for a fucking quarter!* So we were pretty cautious out there on our own. Walked all over Times Square, past all the girlie shows and tittie bars. There was a great record store on Forty-second Street where I bought Lord Buckley records and Lenny Bruce records and Miles Davis records. We didn't have access to that kind of edgy stuff in London, and that store was like hitting the jackpot. It was an adventure just walking into that place. Afterward, we'd lug all the shit we bought over to Tad's Steaks for a great dinner—$1.98 for a steak and a baked potato. Right around the corner from the Paramount was a little coffee shop, which was the first time I ever had corned beef hash with an egg on top. And if we felt flush, we headed to Jack Dempsey's bar for a bowl of Hungarian goulash. Just fantastic!

We were getting the royal treatment. We stayed at the Abbey Victoria on Seventh Avenue and it was the first time we each had our own room. Very posh. I couldn't get over how the taps turned on in the bathroom and hearing the phone ring like it did in the American movies and getting take-out food. *Take-out food!* There was no such thing in England, not even a hamburger stand. There was a black-and-white TV in the room and I watched Johnny Carson every night.

That is, if I wasn't already otherwise engaged. I have to hand it to American girls: They taught me a few things about sex that were outside of my advancing experience. It was obvious that American girls liked to fuck much more than their English counterparts. They were freer spirits and more experimental. English girls were shy.

You know that play *No Sex Please, We're British*? Well, that about sums it up. Trust me, it was a lot of work to get an English girl's knickers off. So I was a willing and dedicated student. My education started with Goldie and the Gingerbreads, the first all-female rock 'n' roll band signed to a major American label. They had a nice little groove. A lead singer with a big, throaty voice—Goldie Zelkowitz, who later changed her name to Genya Ravan and fronted Ten Wheel Drive. But I only had eyes for Ginger, the drummer, a fabulous creature who had all the right moves. She showed me what English women had only hinted at. Ginger couldn't wait to get her knickers off for me. And talk about playing rim shots! Yeah, there was a lot to learn about American women.

One night, before we wrapped up the gig, Morris Levy decided to take us out to dinner. He'd caught our show a few times and obviously liked what he'd heard because he'd staked us to a few hours in a New York recording studio, where we laid down demos for about twenty-five Hollies songs. I suspected it wasn't out of the goodness of his heart (a muscle insiders claimed had been left out of Morris's body), and that something else was going on. He had something up his sleeve. Now, at dinner, he was laying it on thick. We went to a pretty posh place, the Roundtable, a Turkish restaurant with a tasty little belly dancer with a bare midriff down to there, whom we later wrote "Stop! Stop! Stop!" about. Nothing like a little navel-gazing to soften us up. Somewhere between dessert and coffee, Morris played his card. In an effort to expand his business interests, Levy offered us $75,000 for our music publishing. Now, in 1965, that was a *lot* of money. Twenty-five grand each for Tony, Allan, and me. We weren't making anything that approached that sum. You can't imagine how tempting it was to take it. But having dinner with Morris Levy was one thing; getting into bed with him was another altogether. We'd heard stories . . . how he put his name as writer on all the records Roulette released, how at one point he owned the phrase "rock 'n' roll" and held the mortgage on Alan Freed's house, how . . . nah, better not go there. But we heard other things that scared the shit out of us. (He'd have cut off my dick and put it on a keychain had he discovered I was sleeping with his secretary, Karen.) So we weren't willing to sign with him, even for seventy-five grand, even though he was very kind to the Hollies. Later, he was eventually convicted of extortion and went to jail, so our intuition saved us from making an early mistake.

But, even so, it was cool meeting Morris. He was a gentleman thug, a great white, one of the early record sharks who put out a slew of legendary artists: Duane Eddy, Buddy Knox (check out "Party Doll," a brilliant rockabilly hit), Lou Christie, Frankie Lymon, Dave "Baby" Cortez, and Joey Dee and the Starlighters (who in 1966 changed their name to the Young Rascals). A few years afterward, he went on a tear with Tommy James and the Shondells, so say what you will about Morris Levy, he knew a hit when he heard one and got it on record.

Man, we soaked up American culture like sponges. I loved it instantly. On the plane back, I remember being thrilled that we'd held our own with all the acts on that show. The other bands really dug the Hollies. We'd put tremendous energy into those two songs and we had *done* it. Now it was time to go home and raise our game to the next level.

THE LOCAL MUSIC scene was on fire when we got back to London. The Beatles were still undisputed kings of the top ten, but the Rolling Stones, whom we toured with in early 1964, had finally pushed their way onto the international charts. So had the Kinks and Gerry and the Pacemakers, the Dave Clark Five, and a few of our fellow Manchester bands—Herman's Hermits, whose lead singer, Peter Noone, had worked the clubs with us, and Freddie and the Dreamers, whose lead guitarist, Derek Quinn, had been one of the Fourtones.

The tour we did with the Stones that year was a chilling experience. Hollies shows were pretty wild, but those Stones gigs were something else. Mayhem to the nth degree. The first time we played with them was in Scarborough, on the east coast of England, and that joint was jumping before anyone hit the stage. They were rough and loud—and fantastic. Different from the Hollies. There was a certain earthiness to the Stones. This was before Mick became *Mick*, before he started strutting and dancing. Didn't matter. They had that sound, that attitude.

At the time, Brian Jones was already separating himself from the group. It had been his band at the start, but Mick and Keith had taken over, and you could tell that Brian was looking for a way out. He traveled with us, instead of with the other Stones, so it had come to that. The end for him was near.

Sometime afterward, when the Hollies were recording at Abbey Road, we learned the Stones were in a studio over on Denmark Street. In those days, sessions were pretty loose affairs, nothing like today, with all the paranoia and security. So Allan and I went over there to see what they were up to.

It was just a closet of a studio, about as big as my kitchen, and pretty crowded with all of us jammed in there—the Stones, Andrew Loog Oldham, and an intense little guy in wild red leather cowboy boots who turned out to be Phil Spector. They'd just finished making "Not Fade Away" and were working on the B-side, "Little by Little." It was basically a throwaway, as most B-sides were, but they'd left a track open for percussion, so we all just started banging away on bottles and clapping. So for a few seconds, Clarkie and I were Stones sidemen.

We'd already toured with the Dave Clark Five in late 1964 and often, to my ears, we blew them off the stage. I didn't hang out with Dave—and I didn't particularly like him. He was aloof and condescending, just a mediocre drummer; Mike Smith was the standout musician in that band. They thought they were the Beatles—and they weren't. Their songs just didn't cut it.

The Dave Clark Five tour might have been a slog had it not been for the third act on the bill. The Kinks had just released "You

Really Got Me," and we loved the shit out of that song. All those power chords ripping through the intro, and Ray's nasal honk. It was obvious that record was going to be a smash, so we begged the promoters to put them on the tour. Lucky thing, too, because those guys were rascals. The Davies brothers were actually talking to each other then, and they were prodigious talents, lots of fun. They had a unique sound that was rough, raw, and edgy. And they were working-class lads, like us. Loved to join us for a few pints and raise a little hell. On the last night of the tour, the Dave Clark Five were in the middle of their big number "Bits and Pieces"—tits and wheezes—when Eric Haydock and Pete Quaife, the Kinks' bass player, took a huge bolt cutter to the stage power and cut those fuckers dead. Served 'em right.

We also did a tour with Peter Jay and the Jaywalkers, a Norfolk band that we loved playing with. They had a sixteen-year-old lead singer, Terry Reid, who became a dear friend of mine and a future songwriting partner. That kid had a great set of pipes. Terry, of course, turned down Jimmy Page's offer to be the lead singer for his new group after the Yardbirds disbanded, a band that he'd call Led Zeppelin. Hey, shit like that happens all the time.

In any case, in 1965 things were happening at lightning speed on the rock 'n' roll scene, and the Hollies shifted gears, heading into the fast lane.

Around this time, we got a call from our old friend and manager, Michael Cohen, the guy who owned the Toggery, where I had worked selling clothes. "This neighbor of mine says her son writes songs, and she's driving me fucking crazy," he said. "Every time I meet her, she asks if you'll listen to his stuff. Look, I know he's probably awful and it's an imposition, but I like this woman. We've been neighbors a long time. So would you do me a favor? Just go down there and see what this kid's about." Michael was always a decent guy, so we said, "Sure, leave it to us. We'll get her off your back."

So we go over to the address he gave us—a semidetached house in one of the better neighborhoods in Manchester—to meet this so-called songwriter, a fifteen-year-old Jewish kid named Graham Gouldman. Now, we're the Hollies—and we *know* we're the Hollies, so we're not going to make it easy on him, kid or no kid. We're sitting in this posh, middle-class living room, slipcovers on the sofas, nice art on the wall. I threw Mr. Songwriter one of my best stony stares and said, "Okay, kid—give it your best shot."

He picked up an acoustic guitar and started playing: "*Bus stop, wet day, she's there, I say, 'Please share my umbrella . . .'*" And it's fucking fabulous! Tony, Allan, and I are cutting glances at each other, and . . . we *know* this is a hit song. We know what we can do with it, too, putting a Hollies spin on the tune.

We were pretty excited, ready to rush out of there and get our claws into this song, when I said to him, "Uh, before we go . . . got anything else?"

Before the words were out of my mouth, he started singing, "*Look through any window, yeah, what do you see? / Smiling faces all around . . .*"

We just stopped and stared. "Okay, kid—that's two. We're definitely taking those two. No question about it." I shrugged out of my coat and sat down again. Obviously, we weren't leaving the house so fast. "One more time, kid—anything else in your songbag for us?"

He said, "Well, I do have another, but I'm afraid I promised it to my friend Peter Noone." And he launched into "*No milk today, my love has gone away . . .*"

Talk about being blown away. This fifteen-year-old kid wrote those amazing songs—I think they were the first three songs he'd ever written! It was incredible hearing them. And he eventually wrote "For Your Love" and "Heart Full of Soul" for the Yardbirds, "Listen, People" for Herman's Hermits, and later he started the band 10cc. Nice little career, wouldn't you say?

Before we even got back home, Tony had put a gorgeous twelve-string riff to the intro of "Look Through Any Window." The song was made to be sung by voices like ours. All the harmonies were *right there*, and in no time we turned it into a Hollies song.

We recorded it in less than two hours and knew we had an instant hit on our hands. Same thing with "Bus Stop." We cut it in even less time, an hour and fifty minutes flat. Tony Hicks and Bobby Elliott arranged it. Tony added that fabulous guitar intro, and we laid down the entire lead vocal and harmony just once. Reduced it to two tracks before putting on another set of vocals, followed by the solos—Tony, Allan, and me. In the can.

"Look Through Any Window" came out in September 1965 and shot right into the top ten. It also broke into the top forty in the States, which put us on the map there once and for all. The residual buzz from our performance at the Paramount in New York, coupled with a hit single, launched the Hollies into the forefront of the rock scene. We were frontline troops in the British Invasion, right up there with the Beatles, the Stones, the Kinks, the Animals, and the Yardbirds.

We decided we were through making our name strictly on covering American hits. We were writing our own stuff now, and in the process we were adding to the sound of rock 'n' roll. Okay, that might sound egotistical, but it's true. It wasn't just us, of course, but we were leading the way. There was a drift away from the simplest pop forms built on standard three- and four-chord progressions. New chord structures were being experimented with, innovative tunings, melodic patterns. We abandoned the trite moon-and-June rhymes, the hold-your-hand and just-one-kiss fluff that had governed lyrics for so long, in order to express ourselves musically. As songwriters, everyone's perspective was expanding, and with it their imaginations, their command of language, their facility with rhyme. Just listen to some of the singles released in 1965: the Kinks' "Tired of Waiting for You" and "Set Me Free," "It's My Life" by the Animals, the Zombies' "Tell Her No," "Satisfaction" and "Get Off My Cloud" by the Stones. Forget about where the Beatles were taking music. Creatively, the heavens had opened, and rock 'n' roll had morphed into rock.

My personal outlook was also in transition. I was starting to become political and socially conscious, which would alter my perspective forever. I had been sheltered all my life, not so much by privilege but by limited circumstances. I hadn't seen much of the world and I didn't have much education, so I hadn't read much about the world either. But living in London made it impossible to keep the blinders on. The people my age whom I encountered there were enlightened about the world situation, and I heard about it from all quarters: the escalation of the Vietnam War, of course, but also the first commercial nuclear reactor, apartheid and racial equality, the Profumo affair, military coups in developing nations, our diminishing environment, Rhodesia, Ghana, the Congo, Gambia. The postwar world was evolving in front of our eyes, and I found myself thinking about it in new and emotional ways. The issues at large began affecting me personally.

My initial response to this was music, expressing my views through song. And in 1965 we wrote "Too Many People" in answer to the Mau Mau uprising in Kenya, which the British had colonized in 1920. The situation there was a complete mess. So many innocent people had been slaughtered. It brought Jomo Kenyatta to the forefront of the African political system, and this scared England to death. Thinking about this, I began to realize that there were indeed *too many people,* too many rats, so to speak, and that population growth was an issue we'd better confront sooner than later.

With this song, I was starting to grow as a writer, starting to come round from the usual stuff the Hollies were writing and to view our stardom in an entirely new way. I felt we had a responsibility to use our public personae in order to speak out on important issues, to communicate them to our fans. It's one thing to rail and rant one's opinions, and quite another to put it across through music.

This was easy to do in 1965 as the city was changing into Swinging London. A full-scale cultural revolution was in progress, with youth and music dominating the scene, top to bottom. The boutiques on Carnaby Street catered to our lifestyle. Mary Quant was introducing miniskirts and Biba was around and Cecil Gee. The

King's Road in Chelsea had Granny Takes a Trip. Jean Shrimpton's face was everywhere, along with Veruschka and Penelope Tree. *Darling* and *The Knack* spoke to us from the screen, cynical and sexy and angry, and Radio Caroline was broadcasting off the coast. It was all happening at the same time, and I loved every minute of it. I immersed myself in the whole explosive scene, getting a new kind of education, something that filled in a lot of the gaps.

In between our gigs and recording sessions, Rosie and I made regular visits to Manchester. Both of our families were there, and we tried to spend time with them every chance we got. On one of those visits in 1965, something shocking happened. I got on the bus to go from Manchester to Salford. I was sitting on the upper deck as we pulled up to a stop outside of Lewis's department store on Regent Road. From my seat, I could see my mother at the bus stop. But not just my mother. She was with another man. They kissed passionately, at least more than in just a friendly, impersonal way. I ducked back out of sight while taking it all in.

That really threw me for a loop. I'd always assumed my parents had a pretty good marriage. They'd only ever had one argument that I recall, when my mother hit my dad with a wire brush and broke his skin. Otherwise, things were fairly routine in our house. I'd never seen real passion, but I'd certainly never seen signs of discord. I guess sometimes kids don't know all that's going on below the surface.

My mother got on the bus after the kiss, but fortunately she didn't come upstairs. I sure as hell didn't want her to know that I'd seen her. And since I knew where she was going to get off, I stayed on the bus a couple stops past our house and walked back to make it seem more natural. That gave me a chance to process what had happened, to reflect on events in my own chaotic life. I was kind of stunned that something like this was happening to my family, but it wasn't completely shocking to me. I'd been in rock 'n' roll for several years already, and I understood temptation. I'd sown a lot of wild oats. Hey, shit happens, people make mistakes. Including me, big-time. So by the time I got home, I thought, *You know, that's life.*

A couple years later, I encountered an incident that helped put some pieces in the family puzzle. During a series of interviews with me and a few friends about the Manchester rock scene, Alan Lawson, a journalist, discovered that my younger sister Sharon was not my father's daughter. You know how when siblings joke: "Look at her, she's not a Nash. Really, look at her and look at us. Sharon must have been adopted." It was a joke—but it turned out not to be a joke. Somewhere along the line my mother must have had an affair. It was absolutely shocking to me. So out of character for her. It was scandalous for those days, but my father always loved Sharon like his own daughter. Still, it had changed him. That and going to prison—I think he just lost his heart. He let his guard down and his immune system along with it, and he slipped into a steady decline.

In early 1966, my dad was in the hospital for some ailment or other. The Hollies were about to begin a European tour, but just before leaving I went to visit him, to give his spirits a boost. He was at Hope Hospital, but after canvassing the ward I was unable to find him. That place was ghastly, overcrowded with beds twelve deep on either side, and I walked up and down the rows like a commander inspecting the troops. Finally, I spotted a figure the color of an orange. Something was going horribly wrong with my dad's liver that was making his skin turn a hideous hue. He looked awful, so diminished, considering what a strapping guy he'd always been. I visited for a while, offered a few words of love, and promised to get back as soon as the tour was over in ten days' time.

A few days into the tour, we were playing in Copenhagen when I got a call from Rose. "Your dad's taken a turn for the worse," she said. "I think you'd better come home." I explained that we'd be home in three or four days, but she insisted. "No, it's bad. You've got to come home right now."

It was pretty late at night, and I couldn't find a commercial flight from Copenhagen to Manchester, so I hired a two-seater plane to fly over the North Sea. Rosie was there to meet me at the airport and just said, "He's dead."

I was in complete shock. I knew my dad was sick, but I never thought he was going to die. He was only forty-six, hard to imagine, twenty-two years older than I was then. His death changed my life in so many ways. It's why I believe, to this day, that you have to make every second count.

THINGS CHANGED MUSICALLY as well in 1966, as the Hollies' star kept shooting skyward. We were in a groove. We continued to have one chart hit after another. Our fourth album was already in the works, and every one of our live shows was absolute bedlam, screaming teenyboppers, kids jumping over balconies, girls attacking us on our way out of the halls. The only stumble, if you can even call it that, was a cover version we did of "If I Needed Someone," the George Harrison standout from *Rubber Soul*. I thought we made a damn good record of it. It was perfectly suited to our voices, with a smart three-part harmony that gave the song a soaring melodic virtuosity. Too bad George didn't share our enthusiasm. In his wisdom, he felt compelled to give a press interview, in which he called our version rubbish. "They've spoilt it," he said. "The Hollies are all right musically, but the way they do their records they sound like session men who've just got together in the studio without ever seeing each other before."

Sometimes, even Saint George didn't know when to keep his snarky views to himself. He felt as though he owned the fucking song and no one else had a right to interpret it. It wasn't as though the Beatles had never done cover versions in their career. I should have reminded him of toss-offs like "A Taste of Honey" and "Mr. Moonlight." Or his own anemic version of "Devil in Her Heart." I guess I also should have taken my own advice and kept my mouth shut, but two weeks after his outburst, I was still seething. So I spoke with a reporter at *NME* and fired back: "Not only do these comments disappoint and hurt us, but we are sick and tired of everything the Beatles say or do being taken as law."

In those days, tweaking a Beatle was like blaspheming the pope. But who the fuck cared. I was getting sick and tired of their holy status, the way they said whatever was on their minds, no matter whom it affected, right or wrong. All of London was in their thrall. And if you didn't know Popes John or Paul, or at least drop their names in conversation, you might as well take the next train back to the provinces, over and out. Keith Richards said it best in *Life:* "The Beatles are all over the place like a fucking bag of fleas." They were a great band and I loved their records. Every English group owed them a huge debt, but I had no intention of kissing their asses. (George and I became great friends later in life.) Besides, last I looked, the Hollies were holding down places on the same top ten as the Beatles, so pardon me if you don't like our fucking record but keep it to yourself, if you please.

Although we remained friends, George's outburst kind of cursed the record, and it stalled at number twenty-four—not a complete washout, but not our usual success. Pretty rare for the Hollies at this stage of the game. For obvious reasons, we needed to follow up with a killer single. There were plenty of things we'd written that were ready to go, but nothing that was a surefire hit. We kept coming up with songs like "When I Come Home to You" and "Put Yourself in My Place," decent album cuts, but ultimately rejected as singles by Ron Richards, who didn't think they were commercial enough to get instant airplay. We still hadn't reached the point where we could crank out our own singles. Thankfully, Tony Hicks was committed to trolling the Denmark Street publishing houses, and he fished another winner out of their files. He picked up a little gem called "I Can't Let Go," written by Chip Taylor, who'd had a smash with "Wild Thing" by the Troggs and later "Angel of the Morning" and Janis Joplin's classic "Try (Just a Little Bit Harder)." The song had a great hook we could work, and a verse with just the right touch of rejection:

*Feel so bad, baby, oh it hurts me*
*When I think of how you love and desert me.*
*I'm the brokenhearted toy you play with, baby . . .*

We made a classic Hollies record with it and shot right back onto the top ten, where it lodged all through the spring of 1966. You couldn't avoid "I Can't Let Go" if you listened to the radio. That March, we did a tour of Poland with Lulu. We opened in Warsaw, got into the Hotel Bristol, dumped our bags, turned on the radio, and the first thing we heard was "I Can't Let Go." That was mind-blowing, to start with. Then, a few minutes later, there was a tremendous commotion in the street below our window. I glanced out onto the square and saw a cordon of tanks, with troops massing on all sides and machine guns blazing. Holy fuck! We're in the middle of a revolution here. Assume the position, Nash. Save your skin! I was just about ready to dive under the bed when I got a closer look at one of the generals. Seemed to me he looked a lot like Peter O'Toole. In fact, that fucker *was* Peter O'Toole. In a Nazi uniform. They were shooting a movie called *Night of the Generals*. Hey, no need to tell the rock 'n' rollers in the hotel. Let 'em sweat it out behind the Iron Curtain.

The vibe wasn't that much better once we hit the stage. Lulu opened for us, and she was great, a ballsy, brassy, sexy Scot who could really belt it. "To Sir, with Love" was screaming up the charts, so the crowd was waiting for her and turned on the juice. Halfway through her set, a young kid ran up the aisle with a small bouquet of flowers for her, only to be intercepted by the cops, who beat the living shit out of him. And we were powerless to do anything about it. This just added to my rapid politicization. I naturally despise bullies and people who utilize power over others. And as far as the cops go, I distrusted them mightily since the incident with my father. The cops in Poland were bullies and fascists, which cast a pall over our visit there. Don't get me wrong: I have nothing against Poles, who were incredibly kind. In fact, I remember making love to an exquisite and quite adventurous Polish girl on that tour. But the police-state undercurrent creeped us out.

After Poland, I was ready for a little democracy on the half shell and welcomed another trip to the States. We got a tour there, about fifteen dates, playing ballrooms and doing some television stuff. I couldn't wait to get over there again and soak it all in.

First time over I'd been overwhelmed by New York, but this time around it felt more like home. Even better. You could lose yourself there, be whoever you wanted, no questions asked. "Hey, buddy, you want a girl?" "How about a boy?" "A chimpanzee?" I wasn't into boys or chimpanzees, but at least they were available if the urge arose. New York was one-stop shopping and incredibly discreet. Nothing like London, where everybody knew your business.

I hit the streets five minutes after we landed. *Zoom!* Right down to the Village. Just walked around, trying to soak up as much as I could. It was great. Nobody knew who I was. The club scene was amazing. It seemed like there was jazz on every corner. I hit the Vanguard and the Blue Note, caught shows with Mingus, Miles, Dizzy, and Gerry Mulligan. I went over to the Gaslight and saw the Spoonful. On Bleecker Street, I had my nose pressed against the glass outside the Village Gate, checking out the schedule, when I noticed some action behind me in the window's reflection. A group of guys dressed like freaks were lingering by a building on the other side of the street. I recognized them immediately—the Byrds, one of my favorite American bands. McGuinn, Clark, Hillman . . . and the guy in the cape and weird leather getup, David Crosby. Suddenly, they all walked into this head shop. Now, I don't presume to know what they wanted in such a place! But I didn't have the balls to introduce myself. "Hey, I'm in the Hollies. Love the band, man. 'Tambourine Man' is a great record." No one in America really knew who we were. Or if they did, they didn't really give a shit. Besides, Crosby intimidated the hell out of me. He gave off this don't-fuck-with-me vibe and seemed so unapproachable. I figured there was no point in knowing a guy like that.

We were staying at the Holiday Inn on West Fifty-seventh Street. A few days into our stay, I took a phone call from the concierge. "Mr. Nash, there's a man in the lobby who would like to talk to you. He says his name is Paul Simon." Now, the Hollies had just recorded "I Am a Rock" and did a pretty decent job of it. Paul liked it enough that he wanted to meet us. "Arthur and I are recording over at Columbia Studios," he said. "You feel like coming down to the session?" Are you kidding me! This was Simon and Garfunkel, for God's sake. They were putting together the *Parsley, Sage, Rosemary & Thyme* album and working on "7 O'Clock News/Silent Night," with a news bulletin mixed in with the music. Brilliant stuff.

I learned a lot watching Paul and Arthur record. They weren't just gorgeous singers, they were into the whole recording process. Nothing in that studio escaped their attention. One time, they said, "Hey, do you know this trick?" They would speed the track up and hit the snare drum in rhythm. Then, when they slowed it down, it produced a sound like *pch-oooooewe pch-oooooewe*. Brilliant. Another time, I watched their engineer, Roy Halee, take sixteen faders down at Paul's last breath at the end of "Hazy Shade of Winter." I'd never seen or heard anything like it before. Imagine how that looked to a rock 'n' roll star who once wasn't allowed to come within ten feet of the board at Abbey Road. The Hollies weren't allowed to touch the faders. If we wanted more of a kick drum, I first had to go to Ron Richards, and then to an engineer, who would bring up the kick drum. In America, everything was so hands-on. I couldn't take my eyes off what they were doing in the studio.

Later that week, Paul and Arthur invited me to accompany them to a gig at Texas A&M. On the plane down, I got a deeper understanding of who these men really were. They were far more worldly than I was. They talked about American politics, what was going on in Vietnam, about McNamara, about Dylan and his harmonica. Paul was reserved, but an intellectual Jewish guy who didn't mind saying what was on his mind, with very strong opinions. I'd never met anyone like him. He and Arthur were both political, very outspoken.

It wasn't like that in England. The freedom to express yourself was so foreign to me—and so damn attractive. And the shows they did, with just one guitar, were stunning. Simon's guitar work mesmerized me. Add to it those voices and those songs. I couldn't take my eyes off their stage presence, and how the audience reacted to them. Their timing was incredible. Everything about them was turning me inside out. It was a whole new ball game for me.

Before we parted company, I asked Paul what he was listening to. He told me about a record called *The Music of Bulgaria,* which was a live recording of the Ensemble of the Bulgarian Republic made in concert in Paris in 1955. The music originated in the fields—in this case, the ladies who worked farms in Bulgaria, cutting down huge sheaves of wheat. To alleviate the everyday tedium, they would sing together, usually solo or two-part. In the early fifties Philip Koutev had put together the National Ensemble, comprised of the winners of local, regional, and national competitions. Koutev featured a women's choir, for which he extrapolated these two-parts to many parts, producing a cappella harmonies unlike any I'd ever heard before: five-, six-, seven-part harmonies. As a lifelong student of such singing, it made my head spin.

I asked Paul where I could get this record, and he said, "I happen to have an extra one right here," and he handed it over. I took it home, and it instantly became my favorite record of all time in terms of musical harmony. In my London apartment, I had an incredible sound system: two Brunell tape recorders in each corner. And when I played this record, the music went from the turntable into the first tape recorder, then through the second tape recorder into the speakers, so that everything was a microsecond off—but brilliantly so. I would get loaded, get a couple brandies and Coca-Colas under my belt, and play this record—*loud.* I would lie in the middle of the floor listening, and that's how I turned people on to it.

I must have given away at least three hundred copies over the years. So in the early nineties, I got a call from Nonesuch Records to tell me that the Bulgarian Choir was going to do a short tour of America. Would I be interested in flying to New York to introduce them to the world's press? I said, "Absolutely, I'm there." There was a media event at the old Americana Hotel, where I got up and told the story of how Paul gave me the record and how, for thirty years, Croz and I had tried to spread this music throughout the world. Afterward, their translator came up to me and said, "Mr. Nash, the ladies would like to say something to you," and they all gathered around me. I was expecting something in pidgin English: "Thonk yu, Meester Nosh, for takink and showink us to Amerka." Instead, one of the leaders of the choir counted off, and they burst, in perfect harmony, into the end of "Suite: Judy Blue Eyes." *"Do-do-do-do do / do do / da-do-do-do."* It completely floored me. It was such an honor that this choir that I had revered for so long had learned that song and was singing it back to me.

After New York and Texas, my head was in a different place, but it was nothing compared to our introduction to Los Angeles. LA was uptempo, vivace: the Beach Boys, the Ventures, Jan and Dean, the Mamas and the Papas. Hollywood! Blondes! I was in love with it before I ever set foot there.

Flying over the city, I was already sold. There were turquoise-blue pools spread across the landscape, the ocean licking across the western shore, sunshine as bright as klieg lights. Minutes after we got out of the plane, I climbed to the top of the nearest palm tree and told Clarkie I was never coming down. It was a metaphor he should have heeded.

Things got off to a wretched start. We had to cancel gigs and an appearance on the *Hullabaloo* TV show because our work permits weren't in order. Again. A little cockroach from the musicians' union came up to us right after soundcheck and said, "Cards, please?" Of course we didn't have them. Tony told the guy to fuck off, but union guys are tough little bastards. "But we're *here*," we pleaded. "We're all set up. We can't play?" Nothing doing. We had to sit out those gigs, all of them, in fact, making the tour a complete washout. Fortunately, the Hollies were being thrown a party on April 27 by our American label, Imperial Records, and it promised to be a glossy affair.

The press party was the usual nonsense, lots of pretty strangers, too-fancy hors d'oeuvres, hearty corporate backslapping. A high-octane schmoozefest. But it was good to bump into Jackie De-Shannon, one of my favorite songwriters. And I recognized Burt Bacharach and Sharon Sheeley, Eddie Cochran's girlfriend, in the crowd. While we were refilling wineglasses, a young kid came over and started chattering at us. Hold on a second, squirt! With English people, you don't just start talking—you *introduce* yourself. Not this kid. He launched right into a rap about the Hollies and it became apparent that he knew everything about us: every B-side we'd done, our middle names, things we'd forgotten about, like an ad we did for Shell Oil in 1964. It was obvious this kid was a real fan.

His name was Rodney Bingenheimer, later to become a famous deejay at K-Rock in Pasadena. And he was about to change the direction of my life.

"What are you doing after this party?" he asked.

Where were this kid's manners? I didn't know him from Adam. And I wasn't about to tell him my plans. So I did what most English people do in cases like this: I turned the question back to him. "I don't know," I said. "What are *you* doing?"

"I've got these friends who are recording down the street, and I wanted to know if you'd like to come hang out in the studio?"

Turns out it was the Mamas and the Papas. Well, sign me up, baby. I loved "California Dreamin'" and "Monday Monday." I knew those records backward and forward, and what a brilliant arranger John Phillips was. And I knew how great Cass and Denny sang. Sure, I was interested in hearing what they were doing. But I really went because I had seen the album cover and wanted to fuck Michelle. Hey, I wasn't a bad-looking kid, and I was in the Hollies. I had as good a shot at her as any other guy. So off I went with Rodney Bingenheimer, ostensibly to check out the Mamas and the Papas.

As it happened, they were at Western Recorders in Hollywood, the scene of so many classic sessions with Nat King Cole, Elvis, Ray Charles, the Beach Boys, and Sam Cooke. Inside the studio, Michelle, John, and Denny were huddled around a microphone, putting an overdub on "Dancing Bear." Michelle was every bit as advertised: gorgeous and sexy—but otherwise engaged—so I wound up talking with Cass. She was hanging around outside the studio when I got there and seemed eager to talk about British rock 'n' roll, especially her idol, John Lennon.

"What do you think John would say about our music?" she wondered.

Loaded question. Lennon was a gnarly sort. Compliments from him were hard to come by. I wasn't going to bullshit this woman, so I put it to her straight.

"He'd keep you at arm's length until he'd trusted you enough to let you into his personal space," I explained. "So he'd probably put you down at first."

The minute the words were out of my mouth, Cass burst into tears. Holy shit! I'd only just met this woman and already she's crying. "What did I say? What did I do?"

Little did I know that Cass Elliot had a huge crush on John, and that was the last thing she'd wanted to hear. Carefully, I skated around the awkward moment, so much so that when Cass recovered she asked me: "What are you doing tomorrow?"

"What is it with you Americans?" I said. "You always want to know what we're doing? What are *you* doing?"

"I want to introduce you to a good friend of mine," she said. "I have a feeling you guys are going to like each other."

The next day, around noon, Cass pulled up to the Knickerbocker Hotel in a convertible Porsche, her long, honey-colored hair blowing aimlessly in the wind. She had the radio turned up loud: B. Mitchell Reed on KMET, one great song after the next. I slipped in beside her and off we went, snaking up Laurel Canyon Avenue to the top of the Hills, where Cass lived in a lovely ranch-style house, and we hung out for a while. Later, I would realize how much interesting hanging out went on there, but at the time I was just discovering what an incredible character she was—very complex, bright, talented, lonely, with a fantastic sense of humor that was at turns both sardonic and self-deprecating. Thanks to my meager self-education, I'd learned quite a bit about Gertrude Stein and her role in bringing people of different disciplines together, having meals, encouraging conversation. And Cass was exactly like that: Mama Cass. I got the feeling she sensed seismic shifts that were going on in my life—even before I did—and she immediately took me under her wing.

We jumped into the car and went halfway back down Laurel Canyon, pulling into a carport under one of those teetery stilt houses on Willow Glen. Upstairs, I could have sworn the place was deserted. There was absolutely nothing in it other than a couch, a chair, and a fabulous stereo system. There might have been a guitar leaning against the wall. Otherwise, there was a barefoot guy lying on his back on the couch, with the lid of a shoe box full of grass resting on his chest, and he was shaking it, separating the seeds and stems. I'd seen this guy before and suddenly realized: *Holy shit*—it's David Crosby! He didn't seem at all threatening, as he had in New York. In fact, he looked harmless and agreeable. (Probably the last time I could ever say that!)

Cass handled the introductions without telling him I was in the Hollies. I could tell he was slightly suspicious, wondering why I was with Cass, whether I was another starfucker trying to ride her fame. I could have been a roadie, for all he knew. David is, by nature, a suspicious man; you've got to really prove to him who the fuck you are and what you're up to before he'll even talk to you. And where Cass was concerned, he was overly protective. She'd been a dear friend for a long time, since she was a member of the Mugwumps and the Big Three back in her folkie days. Later, he'd gone on the Hootenanny tour with her as part of Les Baxter's Balladeers, a second-rate folk-pop group modeled on the New Christy Minstrels.

She, in turn, looked out for David, who was difficult, opinionated, stubborn, a punk, all the things that made it hard for you to make it in the business. But Cass recognized his talent and mentored him through the music industry. So they had a lot of history. He wasn't about to let some English gigolo fuck it up.

The entire time we were talking, Crosby continued shaking the shoe-box lid, which was quite impressive. And without taking his eyes off me, he rolled the most perfect joint I'd ever seen. Now, full disclosure: I hadn't seen many, and truthfully I'd never smoked one myself. The closest I'd come was at a gig we did in Morecombe, on the same bill with Donovan. I went over to Dono's dressing room to say hello, and he and Gypsy Dave were smoking something that smelled strangely enticing. So I went, "*Oh . . . sorry,*" while backing comically out of the room.

Crosby had a suspicion I'd never smoked dope before and he seemed eager to initiate me. Honestly, no one was more eager than I was. There was no controlling my curiosity in those days. Even today. I wanted to see where marijuana might take me, how it could open me up. I was ready for any new experience, real or pharmaceutical. Little did I know at the time that Crosby had the best dope in Hollywood. In fact, he had the first sinsemilla, which was two or three times stronger than anybody else's pot. And I proceeded to get ripped, from my tits to my toes. I was out of my mind. Man, I *loved* the feeling, and instantly I became a lifelong fan.

I'm not sure how long we hung out at Crosby's. It seemed like days, but it was probably an hour and a half. Afterward, Cass drove me back to the Knickerbocker, where the Hollies were waiting for me. I was totally wasted, but in an incredibly good way, and couldn't hide the fact that I was high. It was one of those cases, when you first smoke dope, where everything becomes insanely hysterical. "Look! A fly on the wall. A *fly!*" To their credit, the Hollies were amused—they were beginning to get used to my making left turns—but devoted to staying straight.

I didn't see Crosby for another couple months, but Cass stayed on my radar while we remained in LA. It was obvious she was someone I really wanted to know better, and I saw her every chance I got. I was fascinated by her, especially the sweep of her influence. She seemed to know everyone who mattered, and her take on them was delicious. She showed me many wonderful things in a very gentle way, opening my eyes and my mind. I loved hearing her stories about the various groups she was in—how the Mamas and the Papas, who were all longtime friends, had gone down to the Virgin Islands on John's American Express card and formed the group there, singing together while taking acid every day. I think she was always in love with Denny Doherty, but knew she didn't stand much of a chance. Broken hearts and egos continued to get in the way. Cass's life was a comedy and a tragedy and a life lesson all at the same time. If you really got to know her, it was impossible not to love her.

Crosby, too. I couldn't shake the guy from my mind. He was such a free spirit, so irreverent. Just a different kind of guy than I'd ever met, an incredible character. He hated the status quo, said whatever was on his mind. You didn't like it, tough shit. The energy he put out was incredible. Meeting Croz and Cass was a turning point for me.

And now things were about to get wild.

## chapter 6

NOTHING WAS THE SAME WHEN I GOT BACK TO LON-
don. My head, for one thing, was turned inside out, and I
began looking at my life in an entirely new way. Meeting
Paul, Cass, and Croz put a whole new spin on things. I loved the
guys in the Hollies, but they were . . . *content*—satisfied with the
type of material we were doing, grateful to play the role of happy,
bouncy pop stars, comfortable with their parochial north of England
sensibility . . . *content.* They wanted nothing more than what they
already had, whereas I was ready to devour the world. I had been
turned on by my encounters in the States, just turned on in general.
Smoking dope had had a profound effect on me. It jolted my curiosity onto an entirely higher plane. The Hollies, on the other hand,
were strictly pub guys; they had their eight pints a night to get their
jollies. I felt like we were starting to drift apart.

Professionally, things couldn't have been better. As soon as we
got back, we landed a truly important gig, appearing on *Sunday
Night at the London Palladium.* This was the show that everyone
in England stayed home to watch, like *The Ed Sullivan Show* in the
States, a revolving door of acts from across the spectrum: opera singers, ventriloquists, sword swallowers, comedians, dogs that barked
to "God Save the Queen," circus clowns, and the occasional tatty
rock 'n' roll group. It was the show where the term *Beatlemania* was
coined, so we knew its power as far as our career was concerned.

Incredibly, our bass player, Eric Haydock, didn't want to play it.

He claimed to be suffering from nervous exhaustion as a result of our trip to the States. *Nervous exhaustion!* We were workingmen from the north of England. That tour was a spa vacation to guys like us. What he really had was a gorgeous girlfriend stashed away in Manchester. He wanted to be with Pam, and that was the dodge. Eric flat-out refused to do the Palladium. He was done with us, which was a complete shock. Who the fuck do we get to play bass on such short notice? Klaus Voorman, who that year created the seminal album cover artwork for the Beatles' *Revolver*, was an excellent bass player. Best of all, we all knew him and he was willing to step in at the last minute. So at least the Palladium show would go on.

That Sunday night—May 15, 1966—Pete Seeger was headlining, and I was looking forward to hearing his set. We'd finished soundcheck around four o'clock and were hanging out in the wings, waiting for Pete to go on, when the phone rang backstage. Our road manager, Rod Shields, picked it up.

"Yes . . . yes . . . he's right here. Hold on." Rod cupped a hand over the receiver and waved the phone in my direction. "Graham, it's Phil Everly."

Wanker. He knew how I felt about the Everlys. No way I was falling for that one. "Hey, fuck off, Rod. Don't do this to me now."

"No, honest, man—*it's Phil Everly.*"

I shot him a sly, knowing grin and decided to play along. Taking the phone, I said, "Nash here."

"Hey Graham, it's Phil." And I couldn't help but recognize the *voice*, the voice I grew up on, with that thick, gorgeous Kentucky accent.

"Hi, fantastic. What can I do for you, Phil?"

"Don and I are in town. We're about to make an album here in England, and we wanted to know if the Hollies had any songs they haven't recorded yet?"

Allan, Tony, and Bobby had sussed out what was happening and were gathered around me, trying to listen in. Especially when I said, "Where are you staying? Oh, at the Ritz. And when would you like us to come? Oh, right after the show? Okay, see you then."

*The Everly Brothers!* Man, I must have sleepwalked through our performance at the Palladium. We did "Stewball," "The Very Last Day," a couple of our hits—a nice little show. But my mind was definitely on that suite at the Ritz. How could I concentrate, knowing the Everly Brothers were waiting? These guys were my heroes; I'd learned how to sing from their records. Everything I knew and loved about harmony came from them. The minute we finished, Allan, Tony, Bobby, and I grabbed a couple of guitars and made a beeline for the Ritz.

I knocked on the door to their room, it opened a few seconds later—and there was *Phil Everly,* ushering us in. Don was there, too, and I could see their two Gibson acoustics leaning on either side of a chair. Man, this whole scene was surreal. Of course I'm trying to be nonchalant, trying to be cool, but it's taking everything I've got. It's the Everlys . . . their suite at the Ritz, which was pretty posh . . . they want to hear *us* sing . . . my fucking head was spinning. They had no idea that Allan and I were the two kids they met on the steps of the Midland Hotel in Manchester. Later we told them and they said they remembered, but who the fuck knows. Didn't matter. That night, we were all just a bunch of musicians sitting around, playing songs and shooting the shit.

Did we have any songs for the Everly Brothers? Are you kidding me! We had tons of 'em. We were constantly writing. So we ran down about fifteen of them—"Hard, Hard Year," "Fifi the Flea," "Don't Run and Hide," stuff like that. And instead of choosing one or two, they took *eight.* "We want that one, that one, that one, that one . . ." It didn't occur to me until later just how much our songs suited their voices. They were custom-made for Everly Brothers harmonies, rich and resonant and loaded with pop ingenuity. Those guys knew what they were doing when they called us in.

We sat around with them all night, drinking tea and talking. They even played a few Everly Brothers songs for us, and I got up the nerve to ask Don a mechanical question that'd been haunting me for years: "How the fuck do you play the beginning of 'Bye Bye

Love'?" Those opening bars had changed my life, and I'd never managed to duplicate them entirely. When you hear them, it sounds straightforward enough, a few dominant chords that compress the rhythmic tension and give it that gut punch. Don demonstrated it a few times, but I suspect he may have double-tracked himself on the record because I've never been able to re-create that sound. Nothing's ever as easy as it sounds. There's always a master's trick, some little snag you can barely make out that alters the texture of the chord. Crosby claims they used an open tuning and just barred across the neck, but if so, that's not the way Don played it for me that night.

In any case, they invited us to their recording session. It was May 16, the *very next day,* at Pye Studios in Great Cumberland Place. The album they were making was called *Two Yanks in England,* and the session was remarkable for a multitude of reasons. First of all, so many great records had recently come out of that place: the Searchers' "Needles and Pins," "House of the Rising Sun" by the Animals, "You Really Got Me" by the Kinks, and the Spencer Davis Group's "Keep on Runnin'." Now the Everlys were going to cut eight of our songs there, and with us singing on them—*fuck* yeah! And then there were the session guys assembled for the gig: some kids named Jimmy Page, John Paul Jones, and Reggie Dwight on piano (he now goes by Elton John). They were all kids breaking in as session players, and for twelve quid you could have had them for days.

So there we were at Pye Studios, Clarkie and me, fresh from hearing "Bye Bye Love" at a school dance to standing on the steps of the Midland Hotel in a bloody rainstorm to helping the Everly Brothers make an album with our songs, in just eight and a half years flat. Nice little arc, wouldn't you say?

A FEW WEEKS LATER, "Bus Stop" was released and it exploded, the biggest hit we'd ever had. It even cracked *Billboard*'s top ten, which was a new, heavyweight milestone in our career. There was plenty of press and back-to-back gigs. The Hollies were doing something like 260 shows a year. It was everything we had hoped for—and more. One tricky aspect in the "more" column was fans. They'd turned up the heat in the last few months. Not as wild as Beatlemania, but a pretty hot scene. Man, those girls were fucking crazy. They'd grab anything they could get their hands on. Yeah, that too. At some shows, we had to make our getaway in small aluminum trailers normally used for food deliveries—five grown men crushed into a space not big enough for a dwarf. Another night, after the Poll Winners gig at Albert Hall, Tony Hicks nearly died when a fan grabbed his knitted tie and wouldn't let go. It was an ugly Isadora Duncan scene. The tie kept tightening and tightening until Tony had just about passed out. It would have been curtains had Rod Shields, our road manager, not managed to cut the tie, which probably saved Tony's life. It was bedlam. The Hollies got pretty good at moving as one. You never wanted to get separated. That happens, and you're dead meat. We'd learned that lesson on the Stones tour, where it was really fucking crazy. If they couldn't get to the Stones they would go for the next guys, and *we* were the next guys. Human shields for the Stones. Not my career goal.

But the momentum kept building. Our next single, "Stop! Stop! Stop!," came out in October 1966, and same thing: top-ten hit. The three of us—Allan, Tony, and I—wrote it in a cab heading to *Top of the Pops* about that Turkish belly dancer we fell in love with in New York and not being able to touch her. A stunning-looking woman who knew how to work it. Apparently, we couldn't get her out of our minds. We owe you that record, babe. And you, Morris Levy.

"Stop! Stop! Stop!" wasn't an obvious single at the outset. It took us some time to figure out how best to configure it. You can't just launch into the verse without some kind of lead-in, and the way that song was constructed, it was difficult to figure out an intro. Credit Tony with solving that problem. He came up with the banjo riff that imitated a balalaika, and that gave the record its inimitable sound.

He'd done the same magic for "Look Through Any Window" and "Bus Stop," with those unforgettable guitar riffs at the beginning of each. Tony was an incredibly tasteful guitar player; his playing carried the rest of the band. The singing was usually Allan and me, but Tony's riffs on guitar and banjo helped give the Hollies their musical identity.

We really hit the mark when it came to our next record. Tony, Allan, and I wanted desperately to write a monster A-side. So far, our biggest hits were Graham Gouldman songs, and, hey, you take 'em where you can get 'em. But we thought we were good enough writers to land the big fish. We knew the combination, how to come up with a universal theme, the right type of hook. So we went through a shitload of ideas until inspiration struck. I'm not sure which of the three of us came up with fun fairs. We had all been to them as kids: pulling ducks out of the water, a ring around a bottleneck, winning goldfish. We thought a love affair was pretty much like going round and round and round on a carousel. And before we knew it, the song just took shape. It was all there—the words, the tune, there was no stopping it. And Tony and Bobby wrapped it in an exceptional arrangement.

You ask me, "On a Carousel" was one of the Hollies' best songs. It's a pop song with an infectious chorus, but flirts with gorgeous shifts in rhythmic texture. The transition to "Horses chasing 'cause they're racing / So near yet so far-r-r-r-r" features a hook that keeps the melody from becoming predictable. Tony's barb-like accents that echo the phrase "on a carousel" demonstrate his subtle virtuosity. And the lyric captures the essence of young love without the usual moon-and-June clichés. We knew it was a hit from the get-go.

After "Carousel," it felt like we were on an express train. You couldn't avoid that fucking record. It exploded out of the box and ran right up the charts, so the gigs got better, as well as the money. This was the first time I'd made any serious dough. We'd made plenty steadily over the years, but after "Carousel" the bank vaults opened. Sometime around its release we got a check from Columbia for $250,000. A quarter of a million big ones! That made an impression. In retrospect, I handled it pretty well. I wasn't used to having a lot of money, so I wasn't a big spender. Okay, I did treat myself to a Rolls-Royce Silver Cloud, but a secondhand Rolls, which I bought from one of my dearest friends, Ronnie Stratton. We took it for a test drive down to London and when we came out of a show, it was covered in lipstick: I LOVE TONY, I LOVE GRAHAM, I LOVE ALLAN, all over the car. Otherwise, I sent money home. I tried to help my family as much as I could. One of my mother's dreams was to have her own pub, so I bought her one, the Unicorn in Pendleton. She ran the place and sat at the end of the bar regally, like Queen Elizabeth. But I didn't buy a lot of extravagant things because that kind of stuff never meant anything to me.

In December, I went out one night to Blaises, in the West End of London, to see a kid from America whom Linda Keith told me about: Jimi Hendrix. I sat directly behind John, Paul, and George. We were all stunned by his music; it was so primitive, so wild, so unbelievably rock 'n' roll. A few months later, in March 1967, the Byrds came to England for a short promotional tour to support their new single, "So You Want to Be a Rock 'n' Roll Star." This was the first time they'd been to the UK since 1965, when the promoter fucked up by billing them as "America's Answer to the Beatles." Utter blasphemy. It was absurd to make that kind of comparison. They'd gotten trashed by everyone all over London, the press, audiences, women, stray dogs—everyone except for the Beatles themselves, who sympathized and were incredibly kind to them. I remember catching the Byrds on the opening gig of that tour at Blaises, the same place I'd seen Jimi Hendrix for the first time. They came out and ... *they were smoking cigs onstage!* The Hollies would never have done that. We wouldn't have dared; we'd have gotten crucified for it. And they weren't particularly good. Their equipment was shitty. Two guys plugged into the same amp. No one was happy, onstage or off.

But this time around, all was forgiven. They were major stars trailing a ton of hits: "Mr. Tambourine Man," "Turn! Turn! Turn!," "All I Really Want to Do," "Eight Miles High," "Renaissance Fair." The Beatles invited Crosby to visit them at Abbey Road during a *Sgt. Pepper's* session. The Byrds' hotel was a hoity-toity affair called the White House in the north of London. I knew the place. It was full of blue-haired ladies and old fuckers in tuxedoes, the last place you'd expect to trip over a guy like Croz. So I gave David a call and said, "You've got to get out of that place. You can't smoke dope in the White House. Come stay with me." And he did. It was great to see him again.

Since our introduction in LA, he'd sent me a tape of stuff he was working on, including "Déjà Vu." Quite frankly, I'd never heard anything like these songs. I was used to writing in the standard pop format—an intro, first and second verse, go to the chorus, maybe do a bridge, do the last chorus and get the fuck out of there and get paid. I was trained to do that by the Hollies, and we were good at it. But "Déjà Vu" was a completely different beast. It was jazz-oriented; it never repeated itself. There was no first or second verse, no chorus. It just kept moving forward. I was completely blown away and, as a songwriter, quite humbled. I played Croz a couple sketches of my songs, and he was very encouraging. But I knew, at that point, musically he was miles ahead of me.

Crosby wasn't happy with the Byrds. They were refusing to put his songs on the albums, and in return David was behaving badly. He was being a dick, refusing to show for rehearsals, staging hissy fits, and acting out. (Little did I know, David had a PhD in acting out.) There was already talk about the Byrds getting rid of him.

Despite all that, he was the same ol' Croz I'd met with Cass. His irreverence and musical ability were extraordinary features. What amazed me most was the incredible amount of dope that this kid could smoke and yet still function. Still bright, still funny, still able to maintain his train of thought, still philosophizing, while I was still laughing at that fly on the wall. The guy was fucking immune to it all.

One morning soon after he arrived at my place, I woke him up with tea and muffins and said, "I've got to go to a press conference with the Hollies. Feel like coming along?" He was game. The event was in support of an artist named Keith, who'd had a hit with "98.6" and had just released a single of our song "Pay You Back with Interest." It was over at Pye Studios, where we'd recorded with the Everly Brothers, so it was familiar and comfortable turf. Crosby dressed for the occasion, in a cape with leather doodads and Borsalino hat.

The place was full of press, the usual guys who covered these events and asked the same meaningless, idiotic questions. Right off the bat, a reporter came up to us and asked some fucking stupid question like "What color are your socks?" or "What did you have for dinner last night?" Normally, the Hollies would have answered those questions. We were used to photographers saying: "Go stand in the doorway and put your elbows in your ears." And we'd do it, we played the game. That's the way things were done in England. But Crosby turned on the guy and said, "Hey, *fuck off!* Ask him a decent question." And the room went silent. He generated more publicity with those few words than the entire press conference.

His whole attitude was different from ours, but I instinctively knew that this was where I wanted to go. I was twenty-five and fed up with acting like a little moptop, no longer happy with being played for a fool by the press. It was time to move on, especially in the image department. And now I had a role model—of a sort. Crosby was a guy who seemed to be more in control, even though he was out of control. I loved his whole take on things.

AFTER DAVID LEFT, the Hollies set out on a package tour of the UK with Brian Poole and the Tremeloes and the Spencer Davis Group. In the few short years since our emergence on the scene, the quality of music had risen exponentially. Both bands were great onstage. They knew how to duplicate the high level of their records without losing the edge. Plus, everyone had learned to perform—to pace their shows, to make sure the sound was perfectly balanced, and to excite the crowds. Bottom line was: You had to be good. You couldn't get by anymore just by shaking your ass. Word got around if bands couldn't cut it onstage. The kids weren't gullible. You know: We won't get fooled again.

The Tremeloes were enjoying an amazing resurgence. They'd suffered serious blowback when word got out that Decca had chosen them over the Beatles in 1963. That was a hard one to live down. Then their lead singer, Brian Poole, left the group in 1966. Seems that a change of scenery was just the thing, because since then they'd had a string of three gold records: the Cat Stevens song "Here Comes My Baby"; "Silence Is Golden," the old Four Seasons hit; and "Even the Bad Times Are Good."

The Spencer Davis Group kicked serious ass. Spencer was a nice cat, and not a bad musician. But everyone knew that Stevie Winwood was the power behind that band. He was an enormous talent: a voice that mimicked Junior Walker's sax, same musical sensibility as the Mar-Keys. Only eighteen years old. Helluva combination. The last night of the tour in London, Dave Mason came backstage in a pair of foppy knee-length English riding boots. Stevie introduced us and told me he was leaving Spencer Davis to form a new band with Dave, Chris Wood, and Jim Capaldi. Gonna call themselves Traffic. I wonder if they ever got off the ground?

The pressure was always on the Hollies to stay on the charts, and as "Carousel" wound down its incredible run we struggled to come up with a follow-up single with the same kind of infectious groove. Tony had been playing with a melody influenced by the Byrds' version of "Mr. Tambourine Man." It was a three-chord progression dressed up with a strangely affecting refrain, but he couldn't put a lyric to it. As a placeholder, he kept singing, "Hey, Mr. Man," which not only didn't cut it but didn't spark any ideas. We tried forcing the issue, latching on to different parts of it as a springboard, but nothing doing. It wouldn't give.

Sometime that spring, we were rehearsing for a tour at Albert Hall. Marianne Faithfull was on the bill. We'd known her since she was sixteen, an insanely stunning woman. She was brilliant at image, pretty good voice. When she did "As Tears Go By," it was frail, vulnerable, projecting exactly the vision that stroked my Catholic schoolgirl fantasy. More than a few nights I went to sleep with her on my mind. Anyway, she turned up wearing a white blouse and gray schoolgirl's outfit. She was fabulous at playing that game. Man, it worked on me. The sight of her raised my fucking blood pressure, and gradually "Hey, Mr. Man" morphed into "Hey, Marianne . . . what's your game now, can anybody play?" But we chickened out. We didn't have the balls to sing, "Hey, Marianne," so we made up a name that we'd never heard before: Carrie Anne.

Needless to say, Ron Richards loved it. He could smell a hit a mile away and designated it as our next single. Listening to it today, you can hear its pull. The verses paint little tortured scenarios about the eternal conflict sparked when someone young and innocent confronts the sophistication that comes with growing up. The singer feels left behind when his childhood playmate takes on overt sexual appeal. He realizes she has to play the field a little bit, and for that he'll be rewarded: She'll be back once she's gained experience. Even so, his lament is downright painful: *You're so, so like a woman to me / So like a woman to me . . .* His attitudes are constantly shifting. The distance between heartache and resentment narrows: *When the lesson's over, you'll be with me . . .* Maybe, maybe not. Either way, the crowning touch is the irresistible chorus—*Hey, Carrie Anne, what's your game now, can anybody play?*—which weaves the scenes together in our signature three-part, right up to the dramatic climax, leaving her name echoing over the end.

We nailed that track in one session. You can hear the confidence in our voices in the way we pounced on those lyrics. The harmonies surge forward from the opening notes, building right to the crescendo that segues into the verse. It's a nicely polished performance.

And then we had the solo played by a steel-drum busker whom Ron Richards found on the street, that little calliope flourish that winks at the whole affair.

The Hollies had developed into a good little band. We'd become professional, efficient, and could always recognize a potential hit when we heard one. We could turn out hits like this in our sleep, again and again. We had the formula down pat (eventually we had seventeen top-twenty records in the six years I was in the Hollies). But I was tired of the routine. Sure, we could write a hit single to order, but the mechanics of it no longer intrigued. I was bored with the moon-and-June rhymes, singing about schoolboy crushes and forbidden sex. There were deeper things to be thinking about, other horizons to cross. I was listening to more intricate songs, like "Over Under Sideways Down," "Itchycoo Park," "Somebody to Love," "Strawberry Fields Forever," "Under My Thumb," "Hey Joe"—the radio that year was full of great songs. Their construction, lyrically and musically, showed off how far rock 'n' roll had come, and they served as a blueprint for where I wanted us to go, but we hadn't evolved like the Beatles had. Our material was fairly simplistic: We wrote pop songs. And the rest of the guys liked it that way. Me? I was smoking dope, opening myself up to new frontiers, growing creatively.

I'd been working on a few things intended to take us in a different direction. One particular number, "Sleep Song," threw the Hollies a powerful curve. In it, I wrote: *And when I awake, I will kiss your eyes open / Take off my clothes, and I'll lie by your side.* They freaked when they heard it. "We can't sing that. It'll never sell." Hey, different strokes. Except that poetry and mature experiences seemed to be outside their scope. My lyrics offended their provincial sensibilities and sent out signals that mine were on a different trajectory.

That summer, we were at Abbey Road, in the midst of recording our fifth album, *Butterfly.* The Beatles were in and out of the studio, putting the finishing touches on a long-awaited album, and in the course of things I became pretty friendly with their manager, Brian

Epstein. He gave me three gifts that rearranged my chromosomes: a 16 mm movie of the Beatles at Shea Stadium and another they'd made to promote their single "Strawberry Fields Forever." The final gift was an advance copy of *Sgt. Pepper's*. From the opening notes, I knew it was an incredible piece of work. Listening to it, there was wonderment, envy: "I wish we'd have been that smart." Musically, I was overwhelmed. I played it repeatedly for days, soaking it up. I knew every note, understood how beautiful it was, felt the power of the individual songs, and was stunned by the composition as a whole.

A few days later, my old friend Allan McDougall, BMI's publicity guru, called and wondered if he could bring the Turtles by my place. They were arriving from the States only that afternoon, and he thought a visit with me would help to acclimate them, get them into the groove. They'd been on a plane all night and were feeling pretty fucked up, but they weren't as fucked up as I was about to get them. I had a hash pipe that was eighteen inches long with a nice silver bowl that gave a good draw. At one point, after we'd been smoking it about an hour, I said, "You guys think you are high?" They said, "Yeah, we're totally fucked up." I said, "Well, good, because I want to play you something." And I threaded a reel of tape on the machine; it was the yet-unreleased *Sgt. Pepper's* album. I knew the album would wipe the floor with them. Very few had heard it, and everyone was anticipating it. Without telling them what I was going to play, I said, "Listen to this." And I turned it up *loud!* It was obvious from the first few bars that it was the new Beatles album, and the Turtles, Mark and Howard, duly shit their pants. They went directly from my place to Jimi's with news of what they'd heard. It was their first time in the UK. Welcome to England, baby!

ON SUNDAY MORNING, June 25, 1967, I was awakened by a phone call at my house in Kynance Mews . . . not my favorite way of waking up, but still I sleepily answered. It was Paul McCartney, and I was awake immediately. Paul invited me down to Abbey Road

Studios, where he and the boys were about to put on a live show for the whole world. Using the BBC and the Telstar satellite system, the Beatles were going to be singing a song, representing the best that Britain had to offer, to millions of viewers. The show was called *Our World* and John Lennon had written a special song for the occasion, "All You Need Is Love." Later that evening everyone gathered in Studio One, the big room at EMI. It was going to be the very first live worldwide television show—broadcast to about 400 million people.

I walked in with my friends Gary Leeds from the Walker Brothers, Allan McDougall, and my wife, Rose. Everybody was dressed to the nines in their finest hippie outfits: Mick Jagger, Keith Richards, Eric Clapton, Keith Moon, Marianne Faithfull, Jane Asher, Pattie Harrison, and many Beatle friends were there awaiting what was obviously going to be an incredible event. George Martin, who wrote the score, had the room set up like a live set with an orchestra conducted by Mike Vickers, who wrote some charts for several of the Hollies records. The Beatles played on a small stage set up to the right of the classically dressed musicians. The song started with the French national anthem and blended in two other Beatles songs, "She Loves You" and "Yesterday." You can even make out a Glenn Miller tune, "In the Mood," part of a Brandenburg concerto, and "Greensleeves," which was supposedly written by King Henry VIII. What a fantastic thing to be a part of, and I'm still thankful for Paul's kindness. You can actually hear me whistle during the fade of the record. It was such a special time in England—that hazy, crazy summer of love.

TOWARD THE END of summer, I was ready for a break. Rosie and I needed some time away from the madness and set our sights on a holiday to Morocco. I was drawn there basically by my fascination with the exploits of the Beat poets Allen Ginsberg and William Burroughs. Those were a couple of interesting cats, smoking dope all day, creating poetry, having a blast, living life, and I wanted to see if I could tap into that. Rosie's girlfriend, JoAnne, came with us.

She was a really lovely lost soul from Manchester who lived with us on and off, so it seemed agreeable to take her along.

To an Englishman like me, that African sun was a joy. I couldn't get enough of it. The women practically had to pry me off the beach in Tangier. Otherwise I haunted the cafés in the medina in Casablanca, drinking mint tea and people watching, once again just soaking it all in. My attempt to score a little grass got buggered by a cab driver who mixed it with too much other shit. But I was high enough just toking on that incredible country.

After Casablanca, we decided to catch a train to Marrakesh. The train was positively archaic, rickety and run-down, but coolly atmospheric. We climbed aboard with three first-class tickets and found ourselves sharing a compartment with two older American ladies whose hair was dyed blue. An incredibly stuffy scene. I got completely bored and thought, "I've got to get out of here." So I walked to the back of the train into the third-class compartment, and it was like Bedlam in there, totally insane. It was packed with people in djellabas and turbans, all smoky and hazy, with ducks and chickens and goats running around, people cooking on little stoves. Snake charmers, too. Just so fucking fabulous! The scene was way more exciting for me than the tea party at the front of the train, so I hung out in there for an hour or two, taking it all in. Then I went back to my first-class compartment, pulled out my guitar, and wrote "Marrakesh Express."

I just started playing and zoned. Words, melody—everything came at once. And I knew, the minute I finished it, that I'd turned a corner in my songwriting. It was an artistic breakthrough, more mature. Not about love, but about expanding your world. It was impressionistic, lots of black-and-white images. The characters were adult. It focused on travel to exotic, undiscovered places—and it was about dope.

That song excited the hell out of me. I thought, Now there's a hit song of a different beast. It was so different from what the Hollies were used to doing. The tone of it was smart and experiential, progressive. A step in the right direction. We could deliver it without compromising our ensemble approach. It was bound to transform us from a pop band to a rock band. At last, I thought, we'd finally come of age.

When I returned to London and played them the song, the Hollies didn't hear it at all. It didn't conform to their sensibility of what a hit song should sound like, and they didn't want to do it. We went around and around with it before they agreed to give it a try. There was a session at Abbey Road that went absolutely nowhere. The Hollies cut an awful track of it that I hope no one ever hears, but it gave me a clear view into our widening divide.

That picture was brought sharply into focus with our next single, and a specific moment when I started to separate from the Hollies. While we were off playing a gig in Split, Yugoslavia, I had written a song called "King Midas in Reverse." It was an introspective song about how my life was in turmoil. My marriage with Rose was starting to come apart (no real surprise considering the double life I was leading). I was outgrowing the band I loved and had spent my youth with. I was smoking dope while they were still doing their eight-pints-a-night thing. Turn and face the strange, *ch-ch*-changes. So the song was about a king who thinks everything he touches turns to gold, when it's really turning to shit.

The Hollies made a great record of "King Midas in Reverse." They liked the song, liked what it had to say, and it made us stretch in the studio. We laid down a really interesting track, starting with the opening riff on the bass strings of my guitar, and from there it took off into the stratosphere. We were actually on the road playing gigs and unable to finish it all at once, so in our absence Ron Richards added a full orchestra and sound effects and all kinds of interesting shit. The finished track he played for us was incredibly psychedelic. When I heard it, I was ecstatic, and so were the rest of the guys. It was innovative, a huge leap forward. I thought it signaled a real transformation. Once we put it out, the doors would be wide open again and the Hollies could do anything.

We had a lot of faith in that record. Its release on September 1, 1967, was greeted with a chorus of stunning reviews. Lots of approval focused on our evolution, how we'd grown as a band. But it wasn't the hit that we'd all expected. It was a so-so commercial success. It stalled at number eighteen instead of cracking the top ten, the first of our singles to do that in two years. In retrospect, I think "King Midas" was just too weird, not the kind of song listeners expected from the Hollies. It was more of a Graham Nash record with the Hollies on it, and that sound was still a few years off.

The worst backlash from the record was what it did to my relationship with the Hollies. Afterward, they no longer trusted my judgment. I suggested any number of songs to pursue as a follow-up, but they backed away from all of them. It was as if my miscalculation with "Midas" had cursed our hit-making prowess. Rationally, they knew that it wasn't my fault, but their minds were made up. And I literally gave up trying. Who wants to fight?

Another development contributed to our alienation. Just before "King Midas" was released we'd gone back to the States for a short swing of college gigs in the Midwest. A low-key bus tour, but nothing like the bus tours today, with built-in living rooms, kitchens, and wall-to-wall sound. This was on a regular Greyhound bus, with upright seats. There was hardly enough room to pull out a guitar, or anything else, for that matter. The saving grace was that Cass Elliot was on the road with us. She came along to keep me company, which was much appreciated. What I needed more than anything was a good friend who understood where I was at and could help me put it in perspective.

When we got to Chicago, at the Astor Towers, Cass came up with an interesting suggestion. "Do you want to take acid?" she asked.

I was game, willing to try anything. So she called her buddy, Spanky McFarlane, a kind of Cass character with the band Spanky & Our Gang. She sent us to a club called Mother Blues on Rush Street to score. Cass had done her share of acid taking and was the perfect partner for my first trip. We went back to the hotel that afternoon and dropped. Then we ordered fresh strawberries from room service and put Donovan's "Season of the Witch" on a small portable record player. Cass had given me a black enameled cane with a silver head on it, and I remember spinning it on my finger and seeing it turn into a musical nymph. What an intense experience, an utter delight.

It reinforced my feeling that I was just a speck, a grain of dust, and if you looked at the universe from that perspective, everything in the world was fucking meaningless yet incredibly meaningful. Acid really opened me up. It opened a door that was probably already there and put me in my place. An amazing drug. I think one of the reasons kids don't do it so much today is because I'm not sure society wants to look at itself anymore.

In any case, Cass and I were sharing the bed. I think she had hopes of seducing me behind the acid, but I wasn't going for it. She stroked my hair and asked, "Is this the way you want our relationship to be? Just platonic?" And I said yes. Friends, but good friends—no, *great* friends—nothing more than that. I'm sure it was difficult for her to hear. I loved her, but I couldn't will myself to be attracted to her. Afterward, I remember leaning over the bed and saw that the strawberries had turned into a plateful of hearts. And then a ringing . . . it was coming from the nightstand next to the bed.

The phone. It was Rod Shields, our road manager. "So are you ready to go?" he asked.

"What do you mean, ready to go? For what?"

Seems we had a radio station interview at WLS, with teenage fans of the Hollies. Somehow I got it together and did the interview, although on a rubber phone that dissolved into a rubber conversation. I was high the whole time, but thankfully I must have had it together, because no one seemed to realize I was out of my gourd.

Taking acid caused another crack in my widening rift with the Hollies. I was the only one of us experimenting with drugs, and it was obvious the effect it was having on the band. Once you start becoming more self-aware, more deeply attuned to your feelings and surroundings, you become more open to new experiences. Drinking beer didn't give the other guys a similar sensibility. Their perceptions about life were different from mine, and the more beer they drank—and the more dope I smoked—the wider the division between us grew.

Nowhere was this more evident than in our attitudes toward music. I started writing a lot of material on my own, deeper songs that were more intimate, more mature. A lot of it had to do with pushing myself after hearing Crosby's songs. I wanted to go there, where he'd gone, and beyond, if possible. The Hollies weren't interested in hearing what I'd done. They wanted another hit single. So Allan and I went over to Tony's flat in Chelsea and decided to crank one out.

We knew how to do it. Invent a situation, put a great little lick to it, give it a Hollies twist with vocal harmony, run it all through the Cuisinart: hit single, nothing to it. But it was getting old. And it never got older than the song we came up with. We cobbled the first name of Allan's wife onto the last name of mine and came up with "Jennifer Eccles."

> *White chalk written on red brick*
> *Our love told in a heart*
> *It's there, drawn in the playground*
> *Love kiss hate or adore*

Puppy love in the schoolyard again. I thought we'd grown up a little, that we were past that shit. But we were back to bopping around, singing: *"I love Jennifer Eccles / I know that she loves me . . . la-la-la-la-la-la-la."* It sounded like bubblegum, something Herman's Hermits might have done. The Hollies were better than that. But I went for it, which pissed me off big-time. I was angrier at myself than I was at them.

Listening to the radio around that time you heard "Magic Bus,"

"Sunshine of Your Love," "All Along the Watchtower," "Jumpin' Jack Flash," even "I Gotta Get a Message to You," which is where pop should have gone. And we're singing *"I love Jennifer Eccles / I know that she loves me."* It was fucking embarrassing. We were just repeating ourselves. We'd run out of steam.

The Hollies cut "Jennifer Eccles" in January 1968, then left for a tour in North America before it was released. We were doing the same old shit, Hollies songs, and my heart wasn't in it at all. I hoped my ambivalence didn't show. The last thing I wanted was to let those guys down. There was so much history between us—good history. But I'd be less than truthful if I didn't admit that I was sleepwalking through this tour. My head was in a really weird place. I was trying to figure things out: how to reenergize myself and the band, what I wanted, where I was headed.

I was turning all of this over when we rolled into LA a few days later. Crosby kidnapped me from a hotel we were staying at on Wilshire Boulevard and took me to a party at Peter Tork's house in the Hollywood Hills. Peter was winding down his service with the Monkees and was very much a part of the scene. His parties were legendary, days-on-end affairs with great Sunset Strip and Laurel Canyon characters, plenty of music, sex, dope, the whole enchilada. I was looking forward to checking it out. Plus there was someone there Croz wanted me to meet.

The house was at the top of the Hills overlooking the city. We banged on the front door, the usual cloud of smoke drifted out, and suddenly we were in a living room filled with all sorts of people jamming. My eye went right to a kid pounding the shit out of the piano, playing a fabulous boogie with Brazilian overtones.

"Wow! Who's that?" I asked, half listening, not wanting to miss a note.

David smiled. "That's the guy I want you to meet—that's Stills."

I knew all about Stephen Stills. I was totally into Buffalo Springfield. Allan Clarke had given me their album, which I'd carried throughout our tour of Canada. I practically played the grooves off that record. The word on the grapevine was the group was about to break up. The problem, apparently, was with their lead guitar player, Neil Young. He often turned up late for gigs, or not at all. He didn't show at Monterey Pop, flat-out refused to play an important showcase on *The Tonight Show*, all of which frustrated the hell out of Stephen. He'd had enough of Neil's shit. Besides, Stills was a guitar virtuoso in his own right and wanted the lead guitar position of the Springfield for himself. Looking back, it's doubtful Neil ever wanted to be part of a band. Here's an illustration that'll put it in perspective: David and Stephen saw *A Hard Day's Night* and knew exactly what they wanted to do. Neil didn't give a shit about *A Hard Day's Night.* He saw *Don't Look Back* (twice) and took that as his role model. Neil always wanted to do what Dylan did: be an individual, a great songwriter, an interpreter of his own music. You couldn't do that in a group, a lesson I'd learn about Neil much later in the game.

As a musician, Stephen was coming into his own. He could sing. He played practically every instrument with style and finesse, and he was an exceptional arranger. And he was a damn good writer. He'd written "For What It's Worth" and "Bluebird."

Stephen was a guy in the Crosby mold. He was brash, egotistical, opinionated, provocative, volatile, temperamental, and so fucking talented. A very complex cat. And a little crazy, because he grew up in a very fucked-up family. His father was a hustler and his mother devoted to booze. His two sisters had their own issues. And all that shit rolls downhill. Stephen was the one that it all landed on, and that had a profound effect. He felt "less than" throughout his youth. The first time he felt "more than" was when he picked up a guitar, so he often mixed bluster with insecurity.

Crosby loved the way Stephen played—and lived. They were both on the make, ready for anything. Both brilliant, innovative musicians, competitive as a result of both coming out of bands that stifled them in some way. Even then, I got the sense they'd wind up doing something together. And though I never articulated it, never allowed myself to so much as entertain the thought, I longed to be part of whatever they ended up doing. There was something incredibly magnetic about those guys. I had never met anybody like David Crosby. He was irreverent, funny, brilliant, and a hedonist to the nth degree. He always had the best weed, the most beautiful women, and they were *always* naked. He'd be having a phone conversation with somebody while getting a blowjob—from *two* women. This was completely alien to me, and *so* attractive. I was pretty much of a straight arrow. Even when I smoked weed, I was relatively straight. I'd had my share of women, but I wasn't anything like Crosby. He was out front about it and didn't give a shit what anyone thought.

I invited them both to a gig we were doing on Valentine's Day 1968. The Hollies were in town anyway and happened to have several days off, so I called Elmer Valentine, who owned the Whisky A Go Go, and said, "Why don't we just bring all our gear down to the club and do a show?" And he went for it, no questions asked.

Word got around town that the Hollies were playing. That night, the audience was mostly musicians. All the great bands in Hollywood showed up: the Monkees, the Mamas and the Papas, the Beach Boys, the Springfield, the Spoonful, the Doors. And we didn't disappoint. We were at the top of our game. For "Carrie Anne," we prerecorded the steel-drum solo and the bass part from the record and played along to the tape, long before bands did that. The same for the string section in my song "Butterfly," and the horn sections on "Games We Play." That was pretty technically innovative for 1968.

Afterward, I left with Stephen and David, which the Hollies thought was a little strange. We spent an hour or so tooling around in Stephen's secondhand Bentley, which he called the Dentley, everyone smokin' it, talking about the show. They'd loved the Hollies, how we had it all together onstage, but they especially loved the way I sang harmony with Allan, seemingly able to hit any intricate note. Finally, stopped at a red light, Stephen turned to David and asked the question on everyone's mind.

"Okay," he said, "which one of us is going to steal him?"

THE HOLLIES CONTINUED OUR TOUR, AND ON March 15, after our show in Ottawa, Canada, I went to a party thrown by our record company's local rep at our hotel. It was the usual corporate affair, impersonal and aimless. I grabbed a ginger ale and was about to make my escape when I noticed a striking woman sitting in the corner by herself. Absolutely beautiful: great face, long blond hair cut in Cleopatra bangs, extremely short pale-blue dress, sapphire eyes. There was a Bible of some sort on her lap—one of those old jobs, with tooled leather, embossed, big, maybe half the size of a night table. That interested me right there. Who the hell carries something like that around? She wasn't reading it because she was looking at me . . . and I was looking at her. Man, I *wanted* that woman the moment I laid eyes on her.

Our manager, Robin Britton, started yapping in my ear. Experience told me it was something about business, how much we made that night, which hands I had to shake, where we're going the next day. I wasn't listening to a word he was saying. This woman had hypnotized me; she was a stunner, period. Finally, I said, "Robin, fuck off, I'm trying to check out this woman."

Instead of backing away, he slapped me on the side of the head. "Hello! *Hello!* If you'd just shut up for a second, I'm trying to tell you that this blonde wants to meet you. She's a friend of David Crosby's. Her name is Joni Mitchell."

Oh. *Fantastic!*

I remembered Crosby telling me something about her. He'd met her in the Gaslight South, a coffeehouse in Coconut Grove, heard her sing, and felt he was hit by a grenade. He was absolutely gone forever. "If you ever run across her in Canada," he said, "mention that we're friends because I've already told her about you." So I shuffled over and introduced myself.

"I know who you are," she said, slyly. "That's why I'm here."

Oh. *Fantastic!*

I sat down next to her and asked about the Bible business in her lap. Joni pulled back its ornamental cover. "It's not a Bible, it's a music box," she said. And it played a funny little melody with a broken note in it: *dee-da, dee dee-da, da-doink*. It cracked us up in a way that only people succumbing to infatuation could find funny, and we played it—and laughed—over and over again. Eventually, she invited me back to the place where she was staying, the Château Laurier, a beautiful old French Gothic hotel in the heart of town. Her room on the seventh floor was out of this world, literally: It had a beautiful steepled ceiling, walls made of stone with gargoyles hunched just outside the windows. Flames licked at logs in the fireplace, incense burned in ashtrays, candles were lit strategically, and beautiful scarves had been draped over the lamps. It was a seduction scene extraordinaire.

That was all any healthy man needed, but Joni wasn't done, not by a long shot. She picked up her guitar, sat in front of the fireplace, and *started to play songs:* "I Had a King," "Marcie," "Michael from Mountains," "Song to a Seagull," "Nathan La Franeer," "Urge for Going" . . . She played fifteen of the greatest songs I'd ever heard in my life, and I'm *dying*. She killed me with those songs, each one a gem. I never knew anyone could write like that. There was pure genius sitting in front of me, no doubt about it. I was awestruck, not only as a man but as a musician. I thought I knew what songwriting was all about, but after listening to Joni's masterpieces, one after the next, I realized how little I knew. She was twenty-four years old. My heart opened up and I fell deeply in love with this woman on the spot.

We spent the night together. I'll never forget it for the rest of my life. It was magical on so many different levels. The next day we woke up at two in the afternoon and I realized I was in hot water. I'd put in a wake-up call with the hotel's front desk, but somehow misplaced putting the receiver back in the cradle. The Hollies had already checked out of their hotel without leaving details about our itinerary. I only knew they'd be somewhere in Winnipeg. I had no idea where they were staying or playing or how to get there. Our gig was only a few hours off. Somehow, I got the details and found a flight to Winnipeg. Traumatic, but worth every minute of it.

BUT YOU CAN'T process an experience like that without conse-quences. Meeting Joni did a number on my head that reverberated through my entire life. It affected the way I thought about music. Hearing her songs opened another door in my head, just the way acid had earlier, and Crosby's influence had before that. I was in transition, rethinking everything I knew, or *thought* I knew. It's hard to describe how I felt hearing Joan's songs and playing a set with the Hollies later the next night. Impossible not to draw com-parisons. I enjoyed our music, we'd made some great rock 'n' roll, but, man, had I moved on.

I remembered David telling me about a similar situation with the Byrds. They had a musical parting of the ways, didn't want to do his more ethereal songs, weren't supportive, started undermin-ing him onstage. Tensions blistered on June 18, 1967, when David finished his set with the Byrds at the Monterey Pop Festival, then sat in with Buffalo Springfield as a replacement for Neil Young. The Byrds went apeshit. After a while, he realized it just wasn't fun any-more. But David didn't take shit like that lying down. He was a provocative cat. He fought back, trying to make his point, and at times was a real asshole about it. In his case, the situation became so combustible that, in August 1967, Roger McGuinn and Chris Hillman had enough and just sacked him. That wasn't the case with the Hollies, whom I loved, but my dissatisfaction was real.

WHEN WE GOT back to England, "Jennifer Eccles" was clawing its way up the charts. That was the straw that broke the camel's back. It embarrassed me to hear that fucking song on the radio. Now we had to promote it as well. I felt like such a whore, especially after hearing some of the new stuff Crosby was working on, like "Tamalpais High" and "Wooden Ships." Talk about stretching out as a writer! He and Stills were experimenting like mad, exploring new musical forms, summoning new imagery with words, while we were making bubblegum singles. The guys wanted to protect their little fiefdom: more hit singles, more club dates, more tours, more *Top of the Pops* appearances, more fans, more-more-more of the same. I couldn't do it anymore.

My mind was on fire. Ideas were flowing. I couldn't put the brakes on, not now, not with all this stuff coalescing around and inside of me. The drugs were pushing me in all kinds of interesting directions. Weed unlocked my mind and my emotions, which had to be awakened for me to start writing meaningfully. I'd spent too many years in the Hollies creating songs from situations that weren't very real. I didn't want to find myself ten years from now singing the latest version of *"I love Jennifer Eccles / I know that she loves me."*

In some way, the Hollies knew that wouldn't work. Those guys had ears. They knew when songs weren't cutting it, and they knew I was dissatisfied. Something had to give. Then they started making noise about doing an album of Dylan covers. I had nothing against giving it a try. Who the fuck doesn't like Bob Dylan songs? People tend to think you can't cover his stuff unless you do a high-gloss

Peter, Paul and Mary number to it, but just play a Byrds album. Roger McGuinn and Crosby had a gift for translating Dylan, and that band took his songs in a whole new direction. They sewed a different set of balls on them. I figured the Hollies could cook up something tasty. But an entire album of Dylan covers? Something about it sounded cheesy.

I talked it over with Ron Richards. He liked the idea. In the past, we'd done some folk-inspired material—"Stewball" and "The Very Last Day"—and he believed putting the Hollies and Dylan together was a logical step. Okay, I get it, count me in, I'm with the band. But once we got into the studio, everything went wrong. The guys decided to make Dylan swing. The arrangements whitewashed the songs, giving them a slick, saccharine, Las Vegasy feel. They emasculated them, obliterated their power. We did a version of "Blowin' in the Wind" that sounded like a Nelson Riddle affair. It was a hatchet job, just awful.

That was it, as far as I was concerned. No more Dylan. I put my foot down.

I was convinced the Hollies had lost their focus. I thought we weren't getting anywhere and perhaps we needed some time apart. The same thing was happening to my marriage. Rosie had met someone on a trip to Spain, and you know how those things go. I was a little angry, but I completely understood. I was a musician on the road. I was gone every night. And quite frankly, I could never keep it in my pants. It was difficult to stay out of trouble after those gigs. The girls were beautiful, available, willing to do anything. And when you spend a couple hours being adored and then go back to an empty hotel room with its dreadful wallpaper, you want to do something to warm the place up. So I couldn't blame Rose. We were both kids trying to get out of Manchester. And we'd done it, too, but that was as far as we were going. Besides, I was in love with Joni.

I had moved out of our flat into a sweet little mews house in Kynance Mews. An old converted stable, two bedrooms, simply decorated, washed pastel walls. Typical new bachelor pad. Furnishings were limited to a good stereo, several guitars, and a drum kit that belonged to Mitch Mitchell. I'd met Mitch on a TV show the Hollies did in Bristol with Ravi Shankar. Bobby Elliott had taken ill and ended up in hospital, so we replaced him for a couple of gigs with Mitch. He was a great kid, more of a jazz drummer, in the Charlie Watts mold. Our respective groups were on the road all the time, so whenever Mitch was in town he stayed at my place. As a result, we hung out together and went around to Jimi's quite a bit.

All that time, I never saw the fucker sleep. Mitch was always up, always zoning. With all due respect, we smoked a lot of dope, but Mitch was higher than that most of the time. He loved to greet the morning with a half tab of acid, just to see what the day brought.

Another guy who came around was Eric Burdon. I was drawn to Eric because we were both in bands from the north of England. The Animals were from Newcastle, one of the toughest towns in England. Eric knocked on the door of my new digs one night in the spring of '68. "Hey, how ya doing? C'mon in. Want a beer? Here, snort this." Same shit—musicians, right? He was pretty high already, and so was I.

"You ever seen this?" he asked, shoving a book into my hand.

It was a collection of work by M. C. Escher, the Dutch graphic artist whose architectural constructions and geometric grids explored infinite space. Encountering Escher under normal circumstances was challenging enough, but Escher on acid was a mind-blower. I was into his vision from the moment I laid eyes on the worlds he'd created. I loved the irony, the light and dark opposites, the division of space. Seeing the images in that book was like another form of acid. I thought, "Jeez! Somebody sees like that? Well, then I can see like that, too."

Escher turned me on to art in general. Remember, I was a guy who never read a book or had any image on his walls, never went to museums. But I had a bottomless supply of curiosity, and Escher tapped right into those reserves. I began educating myself, studying the European expressionists—Erich Heckel, George Grosz,

Karl Schmidt-Rottluff, Henri Gaudier-Brzeska, and especially Egon Schiele. Later I amassed a large collection of Eschers, including the twenty-one-foot *Metamorphosis III,* which I still have, the only extant print in the world. I was searching for something, and I found it in art. Just like that, another door had opened wide.

At the same time, I seemed to be closing one on the Hollies. My dissatisfaction with our direction became an untenable tug of war, with each faction pulling in opposite extremes—me on one side, Allan, Bernie, Bobby, and Tony on the other. To ease the tension, I suggested I take some time off in order to work on a solo album. I'd stockpiled a nice little set of songs that either the band had rejected or I didn't feel like sharing. But the other Hollies were completely opposed. They didn't feel I could make my own music while remaining a member of a band. They were being dicks. It was like: "What in the bloody hell are ya tryin' to do?"

We prided ourselves on keeping internal struggles private, but it was hard to mask my frustration. Even harder to keep a secret in that incestuous scene. That May, as we were leaving on a tour with the Scaffold and Paul Jones, *NME* broke the news with a headline: GRAHAM NASH MAY SPLIT HOLLIES. I must have shot off my mouth to a predatory reporter, because they had the whole story, with a fat quote from me: "I believe in a completely different musical direction to that in which the Hollies are going, and right now I feel as if I'm letting myself down not doing as I want."

That was a nice little grenade lobbed into the works. Once that happens, it's almost impossible to hold things together. Out on the road everybody's in such close quarters. You've got to keep your cool, not let that stuff interfere. But, man, everyone was feeling it. I was so bored, trying not to let it show. I'm sure the other guys were resentful in their own way, wondering what was going to happen to the group. There was a sense that things were getting away from us. The marriage was on the rocks.

Looking at us onstage, you'd never know we had problems. It was always such a joy singing with those guys, so for a few hours each day the Hollies were a happy family. But afterward, something would spark the fires. Business moved to the front burners. Recording would come up. "You know, we need another single." "Time to start thinking about a new album." Boom! We were back on that bandwagon.

I remember talking this business over with Mickie Most. He was a damn fine producer, knew a hit record within the first two bars. A couple years back, he'd been recording Donovan, and if the session was booked from four to eight, Dono would be done by six. With the leftover time, Mickie worked with my friends from Newcastle, the Animals, and in a couple of takes "House of the Rising Sun" became the cheapest hit record in history. I hung out with Mickie and his wife, who were encouraging me to go solo. He offered to produce me. We'd do an album together, no strings attached. And Dono's manager, Ashley Kozak, agreed to take me on: He was ready to go. It was tempting, but my mind kept flashing on Crosby in the States.

Finally, in August, I went back to LA to visit Joni, which was the first time I sang with David and Stephen. And then I had to face the music with the Hollies

IT WAS HARD to hear what I heard that night and not start thinking about the future. There was no doubt in my mind that the Hollies and I were finished. They were my past. It was obvious that David and Stephen were my future. Not only were they writing great songs; they were great players, great singers, and they thought differently. On top of that, they recognized my talent.

Nothing concrete was discussed. There weren't really any plans. Everything was kind of half-assed, up in the air. The Springfield had broken up. Neil had gotten a solo deal with Reprise Records; Richie Furay was making plans with Jimmy Messina to put Poco together. Stephen and David were just hanging out, writing and singing songs. They actually made demos of a few things—"Guinevere," with Jack Casady on bass, "49 Reasons," and Croz's startling tribute to Bobby Kennedy, "Long Time Gone." Los Angeles radio deejay B. Mitchell Reed played these demos on the air, referring to the two of them as "The Frozen Noses." But that night at Joni's gave everyone ideas. It was one of those moments when lights go on and everything begins to make sense. We had discovered something fantastic and were willing to let it speak for itself, to let it gestate a little. We knew we had to sing together in some way, but I was still with the Hollies. Even though I was unhappy, we had dates to do, records to make—but my heart wasn't in it anymore.

On the way back to London, I tried working things out in my head. I didn't have anything to keep me from cutting ties with the Hollies. There were no legal papers apart from our recording contract with EMI. Nothing internal with the boys themselves, other than a verbal agreement in which we shared songwriting credits and publishing equally. That was another bone of contention. Allan, Tony, and I had a long-standing deal that our names would all go on songs that we wrote, no matter how large or small the contribution. Credit where credit's due. If you put two or three words in there—fine, we've written it together. But at some point that no longer made sense. "King Midas in Reverse" was a perfect example. Allan and Tony didn't write any of it, but all three of us are credited on the record. That started to piss me off. I had several fine songs that the Hollies were reluctant to sing and I'd be damned if I'd share publishing with them. It was time to put things in order.

I made an appointment to see our publisher, Dick James. He was a character, an old music-hall soft-shoe guy who'd bullied his way into Tin Pan Alley. Everything about him was old school: navy-blue blazer with gold buttons, ascot at the neck, pompous schoolboy accent. In business, Dick had the reputation of being a first-class prick. John and Paul were less than thrilled with him because he had a standard fifty-fifty deal with them. That meant that every time a song of theirs got played or a record got sold, he put 50 percent of their publishing royalties in his pocket. It's a terrible deal for songwriters, one notch above slavery. However, once artists got big enough they'd usually renegotiate the percentages down to something more equitable: say, 80 for them, 20 for the publisher, maybe less, depending on the artist. But not Dick, he wouldn't budge, even with the Beatles. And he did the same thing later with Elton John. So I wasn't expecting much when I went to see him because the Hollies had the same standard fifty-fifty deal.

But I'll say this for Dick, he may have cracked the whip over his artists' backside, but he was a man of his word. When we were in the throes of signing with him, and hesitated, he did a little grandstanding. "If there is ever a problem, just come and talk to me. We'll work it out, and blah-blah-blah. Now sign right here." His ability to sweet-talk us was one of the reasons we eventually signed. And I reminded him of that when I went back to see him.

Dick was shocked to hear that I was thinking of leaving the Hollies. He clearly thought I was another crazy kid on my way back to nowhere. Soon enough, I'd be working in the coal mines.

"No, I've found something else," I assured him. "I'm probably going to America to sing with two men. Now, remember when I first signed with you? You said that if I was ever unhappy, we'd work it out."

"Yes, I remember that," he said.

"So, how are we going to work it out?"

"Like this," he said. He picked up his phone, buzzed his secretary, and said, "Doris, bring in Graham Nash's contract." A few minutes later, the agreement landed on his desk. "So, you see your contract? This is what we're going to do with it." And Dick proceeded to rip it into shreds. "You're free. Good luck to you, my boy."

He didn't try to talk me out of it or get a piece of my new music. He was a real mensch. I hate to think what that gesture cost him. I've made several million dollars from my post-Hollies publishing. But that wasn't the point in 1968. It was only a step, a first step toward freeing up my obligations, but a step nonetheless in the right direction.

It was harder, however, to keep up pretenses with the Hollies. After our gigs, I would simply retreat, head back to a hotel room, and write songs. It was the only way I had of keeping my head together, reaching inside and expressing my emotions. In August, we were doing a residency at a nightclub in Leeds. At the Oulton Grove Motel, after one of the shows, I hit the trifecta. I had a chunk of hash that I was secretly smoking and wrote two songs that would take my writing to a different dimension: "Right Between the Eyes" and "Lady of the Island," and the beginning of another, "Teach Your Children," one right after the other.

"Right Between the Eyes" was about the wife of a friend of mine, a gorgeous White Russian woman I was attracted to from the moment we met. Beautiful women are hard for me to resist. We just fell for each other, simple as that. And during a period when she and her husband had separated, we ended up having a brief but torrid affair. I felt a little guilty, even though their relationship was over, so this song was kind of a confession. *"And the pain that we could bring to him I don't think I could beat / Please don't ask me how I know, I've just been up that street."*

"Lady of the Island" was about two ladies: the woman from "Right Between the Eyes" and my wife, Rose, who'd moved to the island of Ibiza, in Spain. All the dreamy desires of my subconscious blended with the aching loss and I was inspired to write this heartfelt lyric.

> *Holding you close, undisturbed before a fire,*
> *The pressure in my chest when you breathe in my ear;*
> *We both knew this would happen when you first appeared,*
> *My lady of the island.*

The afterglow of those relationships left a deep-rooted impression on me, and I was caught up in memories that refused to let go. In my solitude, they haunted me. The images those lyrics create are forever etched in my soul. You can almost hear the effect the recollections are having on me. In any case, I thought both songs raised the bar on my writing abilities and I couldn't wait to share them, although I wasn't sure with whom—the Hollies or my new American friends.

As for "Teach Your Children," the origin of the song came from my recent infatuation with art. I had begun collecting photographs around that time, powerful images that had an emotional effect on me. One, in particular, was a Diane Arbus image of a boy in Central Park. It spoke volumes to me. The kid was only about nine or ten years old, but his expression bristled with intense anger. He had a plastic hand grenade clenched in a fist, but it seemed to me that if it were real the kid would have thrown it. The consequences it implied startled me. I thought, "If we don't start teaching our kids a better way of dealing with each other, humanity will never succeed."

The song I wrote was slow and eerie, not at all like the recording that everyone is familiar with. The words and melody were pretty much intact, but the feel was all wrong. It was sluggish, too sluggish for the message I wanted to convey, so I put it aside until I could approach it with a fresh ear.

No matter; that night in Leeds was an artistic bonanza. Credit the mood or the hash or a combination of the two, but it was a blessing to get three great songs out of a sitting like that. Finally I was convinced I had songs the Hollies would love. Surely this would break through our differences. Certainly Allan would hear it right away. Maybe it would send us down a new and vital path.

Ah, no such luck. The Hollies weren't interested in any of my new songs. Nothing was going to dissuade them from doing that album of Dylan covers. Crosby weighed in with valuable advice. He told me, "Those are pretty good songs you got there, Willy. You've got a nice wide palette. If someone listens to those songs and doesn't appreciate the fact they've got a world-class writer in their midst, then the group is no longer seeing clearly." He'd hit it right on the head. Seems as though I was at a complete loss with the band. That did it, I decided. We were through.

That September, we fulfilled some previously canceled shows, a short tour of Sweden, Finland, Holland,' and Belgium. Then as soon as we got back, it was right into the studio, where we cut a new single, "Listen to Me," but in my head, I'd already left the Hollies. Crosby and I kept in touch through the upheaval. He told me that he and Stephen were waiting to make music with me. In fact, Stephen had taken the demo they'd made to Ahmet Ertegun, the founder and president of Atlantic Records, and hyped him on the fantastic sound the three of us had come up with. Ahmet loved Stephen's ass. Ever since the Springfield disbanded, they'd talked about doing something else together. I could tell Crosby was getting impatient—and nervous. No matter what I told him, he and Stephen had little faith that I'd ever leave the Hollies. They figured that my loyalty to and friendship with Allan would go a long way toward mucking things up.

"Hey, man, we don't want to wait any longer," Croz told me during a phone call at the end of October. They wanted to gauge my seriousness about putting something together with them. "Stephen and I are gonna come over to England as soon as we raise some cash." Almost as soon as those words were out of his mouth, Stills walked into the room, pulled out his wallet, and fanned fifty one-hundred-dollar bills in front of Crosby's eyes. "There should be enough for some airfare here," he said, chucking the bills into the air like confetti. Ahmet had come across with a little seed money. David and Stephen decided to strike while the iron was hot. The next day, November 1, 1968, they were on a plane to London.

They came prepared and with plenty of artillery. They had guitars and enough money to rent a flat on Moscow Road with a little upstairs studio in it. I moved right in with them for three weeks. We went to local stores and stocked our refrigerator, we had ladies come by, plenty of dope. And we sang our asses off. It was a musical riot.

Each of us came loaded with songs. David had "Guinevere," "Long Time Gone," "Almost Cut My Hair," and "Wooden Ships." Stephen brought "You Don't Have to Cry," "As I Come of Age," "Helplessly Hoping," "49 Reasons," "My Love Is a Gentle Thing," and fragments of a song he was working on about his relationship with Judy Collins. And I had "Marrakesh Express," "Lady of the Island," "King Midas in Reverse," "Right Between the Eyes," and some of "Teach Your Children." Not a bad lot to start with—the songs, I mean, although I could say the same about the guys.

The three of us fell in love all over again. Our voices blended gorgeously on every song. It was as if they knew exactly where to go without having to be told. We didn't have to break things down, work out harmonies or individual parts. We found the groove the moment we opened our mouths and those songs evolved organically, just like that.

We established a democracy early on that featured a reality rule: If I play you a song and you don't react to it, you'll never hear that song again; if you go, "Fuckin' cool!" then I've got you. Simple as that. That meant we'd only do songs that the three of us really loved, and that was a good basis to start from. There were other rules, too, silly ones and send-ups. Of course, we were so high on hash half the time that I barely remember the specifics. It was a wild three or four weeks. We just didn't want to stop singing, hearing that incredible sound. At some point, *Rolling Stone* asked Crosby to describe it for them. His answer paraphrased Jackson Pollock but was typical Croz: "There's a whole bunch of it that just don't make it with words—it's like trying to describe fucking."

We knew what we wanted: a record deal with a company that left us completely alone so there was no outside bullshit, no one who tried to mess with our sound. Sure Ahmet put up dough to get us moving, but that didn't buy him a free pass. In fact, we really had our hearts set on Apple Records. It was a happening label. They had James Taylor, Jackie Lomax, Delaney & Bonnie, Billy Preston, the Iveys (who later became Badfinger), and Mary

Hopkin. And, oh yeah, I almost forgot—they were the Beatles, no small fact. In the midst of our rehearsing, they'd put out *The White Album,* and when we heard "Blackbird" we jumped all over it with three-part harmony. It's one of those tunes we've sung steadily over the years.

One day in early December, George Harrison and Peter Asher (then the head of A&R for the label) came by Moscow Road to hear what we were up to. By that time, we had nearly an album's worth of material and ran down everything we knew on a couple of acoustic guitars. We really nailed it, we were on our game that afternoon. The music, sung in its entirety, sounded glorious. To say nothing of which, we had created a new sound. I could see on their faces the effect that we had. Or so I thought. A few days later we got a formal reply: "Not for us." Turns out they just didn't hear it at all. As a matter of fact, the same thing happened sometime later, when we played it for Simon and Garfunkel at Paul's apartment in New York. We thought, "They understand this kind of sound. They're going to *love* it." But they didn't love it, which was shocking at the time.

Hey, have it your way.

No matter, I knew we had something incredibly special and I was more than ready to make it official: The Hollies and I were parting company. Unfortunately, I handled it badly. I didn't have the balls to tell Allan or the other guys. They were my mates; I'd grown up with them. I'd been joined at the hip with Allan for most of my life. We'd been best friends since we were six and we relied on that friendship. Both of us assumed we'd be involved with each other for the rest of our lives. So I knew how he'd take it. He'd be hurt, completely pissed, especially since I was moving on and, in effect, leaving him behind. So instead of settling things man-to-man with Clarkie, I turned chickenshit and just told Ron Richards. The Hollies got the news from him and the music press.

Obviously, things were a little, shall we say, awkward, but I agreed to finish my obligations with the Hollies, which amounted to a final charity gig, the Save Rave for the Invalid Children's Aid Association at the London Palladium on December 8, 1968. The band still didn't believe I was splitting from them. It didn't seem real—that is, until Crosby showed up in our dressing room backstage. His presence made for a pretty tense scene. He was in his fuck-you dark green leather cape, Borsalino hat, twirling a cane like Bat Masterson, joints in his pocket. And there was that loaded Crosby swagger you couldn't avoid. I can only imagine the effect it had on the other guys. Tony Hicks says he knew at that moment it was over between us. Allan . . . I'm not so sure. He took it really hard.

I didn't stick around to soothe frayed nerves. Two days later, I was on a plane to Los Angeles. I was twenty-six years old and came with basically nothing, just my guitar, a small suitcase, and a few of my favorite things: an albino turtle shell and a mirror in the shape of a jester that I'd found on the King's Road. I had no money to speak of. My financial people didn't want me to be taxed by two governments, so for a few months I couldn't touch my bank account. Crosby told me not to worry about a thing. "What do you need?" he asked me when I arrived at his house. I didn't know. I had no idea what it cost to live in the States. He said, "Let me lend you a little dough just to tide you over," and he wrote me a check for $80,000.

Ostensibly, I was going to crash with Croz. He'd moved into a house on Crater Lane in Beverly Glen. When I arrived there just off the plane, a party was in full swing: Who knows, maybe it was an ongoing affair. Beautiful young women all over the place, some clothed, some not so clothed. Plenty of weed. Music pulsing through the place. I was in hippie heaven. After ten years of playing with a stick-straight band, I wind up in the middle of this blissed-out mayhem. It was *insane,* and I loved every minute of it. Too bad I couldn't relax and enjoy it. I wasn't feeling that well. I had jet lag and a nagging cold. Suddenly, like in an acid flash, Joni Mitchell appeared. Taking me by the arm, she said, "Come to my house and I'll take care of you."

America! What a country this was!

~~~

I MOVED INTO Joni's and somehow never made my way back to David's. Do I have to explain this? No, I didn't think so.

She had a great little place, a quaint one-bedroom wooden cottage nearly as small as my Salford home but so incredibly charming. It was built in the 1930s by a black jazz musician, lots of knotty pine, creaky wooden floors, warped window sashes, mismatched carpentry. Crosby had brought Joan to Los Angeles to record a year and a half earlier, and she found the house, which cost about $40,000. She was not a rich girl at that point, so Joan used her artistic sensibility to dress that place in her inimitable style. She could transform a shack and make it look chic and gracious. The living room felt like a safe, snug refuge, welcoming, toasty, warmed by sunlight. There was some great furniture mixed with Craftsman pieces, a couple of cabinets full of beautifully colored glass objects, a stunning Tiffany lamp, Joan's artwork leaning discreetly here and there. Against a wall beneath the ripple-paned windows were bookshelves with little vases and knickknacks, a wooden pig from a carousel. And, of course, a piano. Around the corner, a useless, simple kitchen. Joan wasn't much of a cook. Soup and salad and that was it.

The house was well situated for peace and quiet. Standing on the porch, we could barely see the neighbors—a cabin on the corner that used to belong to Tom Mix and where Frank Zappa and his family now lived, and just beyond that, up the hill, a house rented to Joan's manager, Elliot Roberts.

So Joan and I lived together in this lovely place, with its garden out back, one of the dreamiest sanctuaries in Laurel Canyon. What a gift to land here, even with all its twists and complications. Once again, the instigator was Crosby. He knew Joan and I would hit it off, even though his place in Joan's bed was still fairly warm. Didn't matter to Croz. He didn't get hung up on shit like that. He wasn't territorial or the jealous type. He wasn't possessive. The way he saw it, women were made to be loved every which way, and without any strings attached. Long-term relationships were fine, as long as you played by his rules, which meant monogamy was out of the question. He was going to make love to whomever he pleased, whenever he pleased, wherever he pleased, however he pleased. And he was up-front about it, just so you knew. There was no doubt David had been in love with Joan, but they were already breaking up during the recording of her first album. Their relationship had turned turbulent, according to Crosby. Anyway, he knew I would be better for her than he was. And what happened was probably one of the most civilized she's-not-my-girlfriend-anymore-and-now-she's-yours swaps that had ever taken place.

In the meantime, David had fallen in love with a beautiful young woman named Christine Hinton. An army brat with a freethinking worldview, she'd started a David Crosby fan club with her friend, Debbie Donovan, when she was fourteen, and variously—and often together—they'd been David's lovers. David, of course, wanted both of them. He even wanted me to enjoy, so one night when I'd crashed at David's house, he asked Christine to go downstairs to be with me. What a wonderful woman. Rock 'n' roll, huh? Christine accepted his ground rules for an anything-goes relationship; to a large extent she felt the same way he did. And in a curious way, they were devoted to each other. So these tangled issues had a way of resolving themselves.

Ten days after I'd moved in with Joan, David, Stephen, and I took the red-eye to New York to try to put something more concrete together. We were three guys who sang harmonies incredibly well, but we needed to get the machinery rolling, with a band, a record deal, and other incidentals that go with the gig. It was time to find out exactly where we were headed. We didn't want to rehearse in LA because Laurel Canyon was too damn social and we wanted to get out of the scene. Leaving was the only way we'd get any work done. Our good friend John Sebastian came up with an alternative. He proposed that we relocate to Sag Harbor on Long Island.

"Nobody'll bother you there, man," he said. "I'll rent you a house. You'll be totally fine."

Sag Harbor, a funky little hamlet on the lip of the Hamptons. Dead of winter, no one was there. Perfect. Sebastian rented us one of those wooden chalets, just outside of town on a lake. We invoked the "no women" rule: NO WOMEN ON THE BUS. That meant Joni and Christine remained behind in LA. Judy Collins, who lived in New York, did manage to infiltrate our strategic defense shield, but she came and went before it became an issue.

Before we moved out there, however, we stopped off at the Record Plant in the city, where Sebastian was in the process of recording his first solo album. It was December 21, 1968. Paul Rothchild was producing the session—nice guy, the house producer at Elektra Records, with an impressive track record: the Doors, the Butterfield Blues Band, Tim Buckley, Love, and later Janis Joplin's *Pearl*. David knew him socially in LA, they used to hang together, and Croz had made a demo a year earlier with Paul at the board. Seemed like he might be a good producer for us. He had some time left in the studio after one of John's sessions, so we went in and put down two tracks, "Helplessly Hoping" and "You Don't Have to Cry."

Paul doubled our voices to give it a rich, resonant sound. Stephen played guitar, bass, and piano. Instead of drums, we substituted tambourine.

Nothing like a test drive to realize the vehicle wasn't up to speed. We knew right away that Rothchild wasn't right for us. He was too precise, too rigid. We were so much looser than Paul. If one of us moved away from the mike, even an inch, he went apeshit, and that started to piss us off. We'd do what we thought was a great take, and he'd cut us off midstream: "No! You moved!" So what? We cared more about how it felt. There was a lot of testosterone flying around that session. Paul wanted control, and that was the last thing we needed from a producer. Meanwhile, he was chemically on the same trip we were on, so he couldn't counterbalance the adrenaline in the studio. He couldn't say, "You guys are too coked up and are singing too fast." Crosby recognized that right away. The demos we made are frantically fast and high-strung, not the way we wanted to hear ourselves.

More than anything, it taught us that we didn't need a producer. With Paul Rothchild, we'd have to give up artistic control as well as financial points, which would cut into our profit. We had the songs, we knew what we were doing. Give us a skillful engineer and leave us alone, we'd deliver the goods.

Despite our misgivings with the two-song demo, Ahmet Ertegun managed to hear the magic. We gave him the Rothchild tape and he dug it right away. He was a true music lover, he had great ears and knew what he was listening to. He thought we had the best sound since the Everly Brothers, maybe better, more dynamic, with the same cutting edge as Buffalo Springfield. Sign us to Atlantic? He'd love to, baby, but it wasn't as easy as everyone thought. Legally, I was still tied to a label. Not Parlophone, which had let me walk away, but Epic Records in the States, to which the Hollies had recently moved. Epic wasn't particularly willing to release me contractually, not after shelling out a small fortune for us a year or so earlier. Croz walked me through a few possible deal-breaking scenarios, none of which would have worked in my case. He'd been craftier. After the Byrds canned him, he called Clive Davis, president of Columbia Records at the time, and went ballistic, putting on an act to rival Pacino in *Scarface*. "I'm here in Miami, man. I'm sitting on my boat, and I'm leaving the music business—*screw all you guys!*" Laying it on thick. "I'm giving up the music business. I want my contract canceled. Fuck you! Good-bye!" Clive bought that crackpot story and let him go, free of charge. Since Epic and Columbia were both CBS labels, there was a better than good chance he wouldn't fall for it twice. I knew this much: It was gonna cost me. So we decided to consult the oracle for advice.

David Geffen was a notorious piece of work, and I liked him immediately. He was a natural bully: brash, fast-talking, intimidating, fearless, a punk, all of it odd, considering he was a skinny little guy.

Anyone could have shut him up with a swift one across the cheek. But Geffen was smarter and sharper than the assholes running most record companies, and he didn't take shit from them despite being half their age. I'm not sure where he got the stones to play that game, but he had them, and we wanted him on our side.

A former talent agent of the *What Makes Sammy Run?* variety, Geffen had morphed into a self-styled manager for Laura Nyro, whom he adored. Took care of everything she needed so Laura could roost at the piano day and night and write those dark, moody beauties. It made sense for us to court a guy like that. Croz insisted that was the way to go. He wanted a street fighter like Geffen, a shark, as he called him, but he didn't trust David enough to handle it alone. He thought we needed someone to balance the equation, so we convinced Elliot Roberts, Joni's and Neil's manager and an old friend of Geffen's, to team up with him as managers.

As it turned out, adding Elliot was a brilliant move. Geffen was the muscle; he made grown men cry. You'd never want to be on the opposing end of a negotiation with David. But Elliot also had our backs. He was funny and a scoundrel—a head, one of us—with an innate sense of holding things together. Every time a situation looked like it would blow us apart, Elliot knew how to defuse it, keep everyone cool. And that wasn't easy, even in the beginning, when things were still relatively calm. David and Stephen were guys who could explode in an instant; you'd never see it coming and then—*BOOM!*—a stereophonic shit storm. Whereas I simmered like an English teakettle before letting off serious steam.

Anyway, Geffen took on the job of getting us a record deal. Since Stephen was already on Atlantic and loved Ahmet Ertegun, that label was at the top of our list. But early on, we got a reality check. Atlantic wasn't breaking down any doors to sign us. Seems Ahmet thought we sounded a little like the Association, but without that group's pop hits, like "Along Comes Mary" and "Cherish." Damn right, we didn't. Plus 1969 was the Year of the Guitar Player, the year of Hendrix, Clapton, Jeff Beck, Carlos Santana, Jimmy Page.

But, like I said, Ahmet had ears and heard the echoes of originality. And as guitar players went, Stephen had few peers. Anyway, he had no intention of letting Stephen out of his Buffalo Springfield contract with Atco. But eventually Ahmet and Atlantic came across with the goods.

That still left me dangling out in the cold, tied to Epic Records. But Geffen and Ahmet figured out that Epic wanted Poco, a country-pop group featuring Richie Furay. Richie's situation was almost identical to mine. He was tied to Atlantic via his own Springfield contract with Atco. So they made a deal to swap me to Epic for Richie. It was that simple. I was free to sign with Ahmet, which David did as well, and suddenly all three of us wound up on Atlantic.

All that was left was for us to make the music.

I THOUGHT WE WERE GOING TO MAKE AN ACOUSTIC album, just the three of us, our guitars and those voices. But as soon as we moved out to Sag Harbor, the game plan changed. Stephen had other ideas. Suddenly, a band materialized out of nowhere: Harvey Brooks on bass, Paul Harris on keyboards, and Dallas Taylor, a drummer who got on with Stephen much the way I did with Croz. Stephen was also a unique bass and piano player. He felt he could take care of it all between us.

Sag Harbor played an important part in our development. We were finally free, we had a shitload of incredible songs to rehearse, and we were smokin' it and snorting like crazy. We'd get up at various times, have breakfast and coffee in the kitchen, and sometime around two o'clock we'd head into the living room, where the drums were set up, and get to work. All told, this was rock 'n' roll ecstasy.

Our goal was to coordinate an album's worth of material. There were plenty of songs to choose from. We already knew we had the sound. The Everlys were always in the back of our minds when we approached each vocal, but adding that third voice, that third harmony, really broke new ground. Two-part is a snap; most decent singers can do it in their sleep. It comes almost naturally. One voice carries the melody and the other hits an interval somewhere above or below that. There are really no restrictions on where you place the harmony. You can move around wherever you like on the scale.

The choice is more emotional than technical; it creates the feeling. But three-part gets trickier with guys like Stephen, David, and me. Normally, you'd go directly to the triad, the three sequential notes that make up the arpeggio in a chord. In a C chord, that meant breaking into a standard C-E-G harmony, which for a singer is basically going on automatic pilot. Not us. We were flying free-form, doing it by feel. Our voices had range and pinpoint control, which allowed us to locate the tension in the harmonies. We experimented with melodic dissonance, modal chords, and irregular arpeggios, using flexible notes that combined in unusual ways. And that's what gave us our unique sound.

One of the first songs we tried was "Wooden Ships," which David and Stephen wrote with Paul Kantner. Man, we were dipping and looping all over the place. When we segued into the chorus, it was obvious we were in uncharted territory with the harmonies. The last phrase of each line soared to new extremes.

> Wooden ships on the water, very free and easy,
> Easy, you know the way it's supposed to be.
> Silver people on the shoreline, let us be,
> Talkin' 'bout very free and easy . . .

We knew from that moment what our harmonies could do.

The same thing happened with every song we tried. We marched right through 'em: "You Don't Have to Cry," "Long Time Gone," "Marrakesh Express," "Guinevere," "Helplessly Hoping." Constantly experimenting, exploring subtle new sounds. It was a remarkable couple weeks in early January 1969. We hardly did anything but rehearse. Outside it was snowing like crazy, we had a fire blazing in the fireplace. Everything was working; it was an exhilarating feeling.

All of us were inspired—and wired. Croz, as always, had stocked his Ice Bag, so called because his initial pound of sinsemilla came in a bag that used to have ice in it. Now it bulged with weed and coke. We were movin' on up. Coke had become a mainstay of the LA scene. Stephen and David *loved* cocaine, and I wasted no time acquiring their appetites. What was not to love? Things go better with coke, right? It made you feel even better than you felt, and I was feeling pretty fucking good to begin with. I loved cocaine, too, no doubt about it, and for a while it became a real part of my social life.

Of course, three hippies wired to their eyeballs in a snowbound cabin for a month—sooner or later, someone's gonna snap. We decided to clear out of that joint at the end of January, before the mood changed and we chewed off each other's limbs. Besides, we'd done what we'd set out to accomplish. We had an album's worth of great songs by the time we left for Los Angeles. Now all we needed was a name.

Rest assured, we weren't going to name ourselves something young and dopey. We'd already been Byrds, Springfields, and Hollies, faceless entities. This time around we were going to use our last names, but we didn't know in which order they would appear. I spent some time sounding them out in my room and figured out that "Crosby, Stills & Nash" rolled off the tongue better than any other configuration. Trouble is, that didn't go down well with Stephen. Stephen wanted his name first. I understood why. He'd just come off *Super Session*—with Mike Bloomfield and Al Kooper—which boosted his reputation, and when push came to shove he was the leader of the group. He was a master arranger; he was going to play every instrument on the album other than the drums. And that's a strong position to be in with Crosby and me. Stephen insisted we call ourselves Stills-Crosby-Nash, with hyphens, but the way I heard it, it just didn't sound right. At the time, we decided that this was a democratic group, and if two of us decided on one name, the other guy would just have to deal with it. It wasn't hard convincing David that CSN sounded more musical. That's two to one on my scoresheet. I hadn't been in America all that long, but there was a lot to like about this democracy business.

We had a helluva time in Sag Harbor, cementing our friendship, getting wasted together, just hanging out, enjoying life. But I was especially looking forward to reuniting with Joni. We'd only had short bursts of time together since starting our relationship. And both of us were going through incredible changes. Mine, of course, was a whole life reversal, an upheaval, but Joan's was every bit as transformative. Since her debut LP, *Songs for a Seagull,* a cult following had risen up around her. Artists were lining up to cover her songs, and Judy Collins had a top-ten hit with "Both Sides Now." Joan was working on a new album, which would be called *Clouds,* that promised to solidify her reputation, and things were taking off for her at a fantastic clip. The fans were starting to attach all kinds of significance to her songs. Plenty of accolades, but a lot of weirdness, too. It was pretty intense, a lot to handle, but we had each other, which kind of kept everything in check.

We decided to meet in New York City the last week of January. And on February 1, 1969, the night before my twenty-seventh birthday, Joni played a solo gig at Carnegie Hall. It was a typical Joni moment. She came dressed as always in eclectic secondhand clothes, wearing what I learned was a parade skirt, an enormous flared thing with a sequined American eagle on the front, and on the back, an artichoke. Her mother, Myrtle, took one look at her and said, "You're not going onstage at Carnegie Hall wearing *that,* are you?"

I'd met her parents, Bill and Myrtle Anderson, a few months before this. Joan and I had gone to visit them in her hometown, Saskatoon—a nice suburban house, not posh but very clean, stark white walls. I can't describe what Joan's room looked like because I wasn't allowed within twenty feet of it. Bill and Myrtle were a very straight, religious couple, and they weren't about to let a long-haired hippie sleep with their daughter under their roof, that was for sure. It surprised the hell out of me. It wasn't like she was a virgin, not even close. But just to make sure, they put me in a downstairs bedroom, separating us by a floor, and made it clear I'd need an army behind me if I intended to sneak up there.

Carnegie Hall was a very big night for her. Joni absolutely killed that New York crowd. She was stunningly brilliant. The audience loved her. She was one of them—she talked about stuff that touched their hearts, real life, and they knew it. *Reverence* is not too much to describe the vibe in that place, which was a pretty heavy thing for Joan to take on. It was quite a moment for me, too, watching her on that legendary stage. Just Joan, a piano, and a guitar that sounded like an entire orchestra. The Hollies knew how to work a crowd, using showbiz techniques to build a performance. But this was different from anything I'd ever seen before. It was the kind of excitement that built from the inside out, nothing artificial or put-on about it. As far from showbiz as one could possibly get. Joan's audience was emotionally moved. Clearly, she was on her own trajectory.

There was a great backstage scene after the show. Crosby was there, and David Blue, and Joni's Canadian friend Leonard Cohen, and Harold Leventhal, and Joel Bernstein, her photographer, who later became one of my very best friends. It seemed essential that everyone mark a turning point in Joan's career. Afterward, we all piled into a cab and went downtown to the Bitter End. Turns out it was Don Everly's thirty-second birthday. Even Dylan showed up to celebrate that milestone. He slipped in quietly, sat in the audience, and brought three songs to the Everly Brothers—who didn't like any of them. I knew exactly how that scene should have gone down.

In any case, it was time to put up or shut up. We began to record our first album on February 8, 1969, at Wally Heider's studio at the corner of Selma and Cahuenga in Hollywood. I didn't know much about studios in America, but Stephen and David felt it had the right vibe. Heider's was a beautiful little dump of a place. We recorded there because it was private, off the beaten track. Very few people knew anything about it. Nobody would be hanging out, there'd be no buzz. We wanted to be left alone to do what we had to do. We didn't want the musicians' union in there, no record company honchos or hangers-on. We knew we could never have been as private or as invisible at Western, A&M, or Goldstar, and besides, Stephen and David had recorded at Heider's before.

We wanted total control over everything we did, and we made sure of it. We told Ahmet, "Leave us the hell alone!" and for some inexplicable reason he did exactly that. Originally, he'd wanted Tom Dowd to produce us, and both of them wanted Jerry Wexler involved. Those were his guys. But they were New York guys, and we were LA guys. It wouldn't have worked. The environment in the studio had to be exactly right, or we couldn't do what we set out to do. We knew what we were doing. And somehow we convinced Ahmet that our vision would work. He trusted us. It was like turning the asylum over to the inmates, but we were brilliant inmates. The place was ours. This was a strictly creative affair. Friends stopped by—Joni, photographer Henry Diltz, Cass, Peter Fonda, Garth Hudson, John Sebastian—people we loved and trusted who would not interfere with the vibe. But that was it. Enter at your own risk.

The engineer was a guy named Bill Halverson, the studio manager, big blond dude, a very complicated character. He drank a lot, his marriage was on rocky ground—excellent credentials, he'd fit right in. Word was that he would listen but basically stay out of our way. And he knew how to get vocals and stack them. That was all I needed to hear. Apparently, at some previous session, Halverson had gotten a great sound on Stephen's acoustic guitar—by accident. He'd left some compressors in the loop that shouldn't have been there, and Stephen considered it an act of technological genius. Go figure. I didn't know Bill Halverson from a hole in the ground, but I trusted Stephen to make the right choice.

There was no great preamble to making our first album. We just turned up at the studio, got our guitars out of David's Volkswagen van, tuned up, and launched right in. There was no great mystery to our recording process. We put Stephen in a chair, miked his D-45, and angled a Neumann microphone to his mouth. David and I stood to the side, each with our own Neumann mike. We sang through each song to get the essence of it down, then overdubbed more vocals as the situation demanded. But it felt like a live performance, right through the album.

From the get-go, there wasn't a lot of wiggle room. We only had ten or eleven songs between us that we all felt would work for the album. Not too much weeding out of material. I think Stephen already had "Change Partners." There was a song he'd written at our Moscow Road flat in London called "The Doctor Will See You Now, Mr. L"—Mr. L being John Lennon—but we'd been so wasted at the time that none of us could remember it. Years later, John Colasuardo, a musician from New York City, gave me a tape of a demo session that Stephen had recorded in August 1968 that featured this and twenty-one other songs (twelve of them appeared on Stephen's *Just Roll Tape* in 2007). John had found the tape in a trash bin behind a defunct studio he'd been rehearsing in and kept it all those years.

We tried John Sebastian's "Darling Children" and considered cutting a version of the Beatles' "Blackbird," which we loved to sing, but we were very careful about shaping the overall record, crafting the musical journey from start to finish. In my Hollies days, an album consisted of your twelve hits lumped together to sell mass quantities of consumable music. But *Revolver, Sgt. Pepper's,* and *Pet Sounds* had changed all that. The new approach was to view an album as a tabula rasa. "Let's draw this beautiful picture on it." It no longer had to be twelve familiar but unrelated pieces of music. And in that sense, we could develop a flow, make sure the feel was right, get our chemistry across.

We realized the most important track would be the opening number, because it would set the tone for the rest of the album. It's the track where you can't take the needle off the record after you've heard it. And we had one. Man, did we have one.

The first time Stephen ever played me the "Suite," I knew exactly what our record would sound like. It was back in December '68, right after we'd been at the Record Plant with Paul Rothchild. We went over to David Geffen's apartment, where Stephen explained how he'd been working on four different songs that were unfinished, but connected by their subject matter. All of the fragments focused on his relationship with Judy Collins, whom he loved even though she often exasperated him. He was trying to say something to her through these songs about their relationship and her career—as a folk troubadour, a cabaret chanteuse, an interpretive singer. The various identities were perplexing her, Stephen claimed, and his lyric intended to reassure her that, no matter what, he'd be there for her.

> *This doesn't mean I don't love you*
> *I do, that's forever*
> *Yes, and for always.*
> *I am yours, you are mine*
> *You are what you are*
> *You make it hard.*

I was gobsmacked as he segued from one song fragment to the next, knitting each of them together seamlessly with ingenious instrumental bridges. Each one entirely different in structure, each one beautiful in its own right.

> *Chestnut brown canary*
> *Ruby-throated sparrow*
> *Sing a song, don't be long, thrill me to the marrow.*

When he came to the end of it, I kept shaking my head. The brilliance of it was overwhelming. I'd never heard anything like it before. The suite: indeed. Stitched together, it was seven and a half minutes long and intensely different. The lyrics were beautiful, the melodies unforgettable. Layer upon layer of rhythmic textures. It was *stunning,* just a stunning piece of music. I knew we could sing that and slay people with it. It was all there, the opening track of our first album, and from that moment on, I knew we were making a smash hit record. What are you going to do, take the needle off the record after you've heard "Suite: Judy Blue Eyes"? *I don't think so!*

It took us something like eleven hours to get the song down on tape. With all the different parts, it was a ballbuster to sing and play through. The length alone was a challenge. But listening to the playback, I knew we'd pulled it off, especially the end, which erupted into liberated mayhem. The string of ad-libbed hollers, birdcalls, and fractured Spanish put the finishing touch on a balls-out masterpiece.

Stephen sat there stone-faced through the playback. When it was over, he said, "I'm not sure we got it."

I practically leapt off the chair. "Are you fucking kidding me? It's fantastic. We killed it."

"I'm not sure," he said. "I want to do it again."

Goddamn perfectionist.

So we did the entire "Suite" again. Painstakingly. Diligently. Tirelessly. Endlessly—for another ten hours. Afterward, when we listened to the playback, Stephen said, "Nah, the original's still the better one."

Goddamn perfectionist.

Almost everything we did went down with ease. Those sessions were an absolute joy. For one thing, we were properly wired. We smoked a joint and snorted a line before every session—a CSN ritual. It put us in a rapturous mood. And the rapport we had together was unbelievable; we were emotionally and psychically connected. You could see it in all of our eyes. We knew what we had and how we were relating. It gave us room to experiment and create, to get really out there and let ourselves go. No one's ego got in the way. We were in love with each other because we were like-minded, we were funny, we were hippies, we smoked dope together, and we shared a commonality of music. We were as tight as our harmonies. And we were loose—man, were we loose.

There was a lot of horseplay in the studio at Heider's. We threw "air pies" at anyone who hit a vocal clam. And when any of us lost it, we turned to our alter egos, the Reliability Brothers, who bailed us out of crazy situations. No matter how joyous those sessions were, at times we tended to hit a wall. Then one of us would yell, "Hey, we're the Reliability Brothers, man. We can do anything!" And the next take would be right on the mark.

Our normal routine: We would go into the studio at two in the afternoon and not come out until around four the next morning. Then we'd head to Norm's restaurant on Sunset Boulevard, have breakfast, and head back into the studio for another few hours. We were *maniacs*. It was intense, but exhilarating. I'm not sure how Joni put up with me. But she understood what the process was because she was involved in her own similar process. We were both in the midst of making albums: me, up to no good at Heider's with Croz and Stills; Joni, working with Henry Lewy at A&M, the old Charlie Chaplin studios on La Brea, finishing up *Clouds* and writing new songs for what would become *Ladies of the Canyon*. I started hearing snippets of "The Circle Game" and "For Free" during the hours when she concentrated on new work. We both wrote whenever the spirit moved us. It didn't matter to Joan when she worked, morning or night. Same with me. But in that tiny house, with dueling creative artists, the dynamic was interesting when the muse hit us at the same time. In Joni's house, when it came to the piano, I always gave way, allowing her to have first dibs. If she was working at the piano or playing guitar in the living room, I'd head into the bedroom with my guitar or often take a walk. Occasionally, I lingered in the kitchen, just listening to her play.

I loved hearing Joan developing those songs. From the moment I first heard her play, I thought she was a genius. I happen to be good at what I do, but genius? Not by a long shot. She was on another planet in terms of her songwriting ability. Her acoustic guitar was the entire orchestra. The bass strings became the cellos and double basses, the middle strings the violas, and the high strings, violins. And everything she played was in strange tunings and picking patterns. The way she'd gotten to them was through a childhood brush with polio. As a result, her left arm was a little weaker than the rest of her body, so forming an F chord, which required some strength, presented real problems. To get around it, she learned to play in the open tunings that blues players had used for years so she wouldn't have to play that damned F chord. Later, she began to write using unique tunings that she composed herself.

Those tunings mesmerized me. I was merely a rhythm strummer, but Joni played with what is called an indicated arrangement, with hints of bass lines and counterpoints that balanced the vocal with the instrument. Over time, I convinced her to show me some of those tunings and used them liberally to work out new tunes. Once, I heard her playing in a gorgeous new configuration. After she was finished and had gone into the kitchen, I picked up her guitar and the notes that cascaded out were like shooting stars; they astounded me. I figured out a couple of ways to play interesting sounds with it, and then I finished "Lady of the Island" using Joni's special tuning.

Music aside, I was deeply in love with Joan, and I believe, even now, that she felt the same way. For me, our relationship was a dream. She opened me up to so many experiences—musical, intellectual, romantic, and artistic. My marriage had been such a scattered affair; I was always on the road, preoccupied with my career. I'd clearly been too young to deal with commitment. Recording the first CSN album offered a period of satisfying creative ferment, but it also let me stay in one place. Living with Joni allowed me to put down roots—and those roots went deep. I loved the routine, but also the exquisite freedom. We respected each other's work, but didn't intrude. We were careful never to step over respective boundaries. Give her credit: Despite her being in another league completely, she was gracious enough not to criticize my songwriting. She never gave me advice, never said, "If you went to an A minor there . . . " or "That line isn't so great"—she never said any of that.

Joan's feminine side—and what a side!—brought me back in touch with my own emotions. I'd forgotten how to trust after my marriage to Rose and after my breakup with the Hollies. Joni and I shared everything: all the baggage, all the fantasies, as well as our strengths and insecurities. We held nothing back. She was a free spirit, a complicated woman, but it was an attractive complication. She was like an Escher drawing, with all its sharp angles, unexpected turns, and mysterious depths.

The other side of Joni was the girl-next-door persona, a relaxed, playful side that was so easy to fall in love with. In many ways, Joan was one of the boys. She was at her most comfortable around men. She *really* liked men. She liked to repair cars, play guitar, and hang out with the guys. We could always count on her arriving at Heider's, mixing easily with Stephen and Croz. And during playback, she'd grab me and we'd jive in the studio. It was that exuberance, that joie de vivre, that lit her like a bouquet of sunflowers.

I started painting when I was with Joan. She was an accomplished painter with a ravishing style. Mostly figurative images, influenced by Van Gogh, Gauguin, and Picasso, lots of fiery colors and blunt textures. She considered herself a painter first and a musician second, and you can see that emphasis reflected in the album covers she designed: the self-portraits on *Clouds, Ladies of the Canyon, Turbulent Indigo,* and *Dreamland,* and the line drawings on the covers of *Song to a Seagull, Court & Spark,* and *The Hissing of Summer Lawns.* I used to watch her paint in the backyard, where she'd put up an easel and go right to work. She had such fun, enjoying the expression and the solitude when she painted, so she got me into it, just by example. I would use some of her paint, experiment with texture. Having paintbrushes in my hand, I discovered, was the same energy as having a guitar in my hands. Just a different tool. And I could express myself in a different way with those brushes.

My first painting was from a childhood memory. Our two-up-two-down in Salford was overrun by cockroaches. My sister and I used to tap the wallpaper and hear them scurrying, and when we came home at night and turned on the light, you'd see them scatter like politicians. So I have an inherent dread of those guys— cockroaches and politicians. As a result, I painted a self-portrait, me sleeping in a bed in a room with no ceiling, with two giant cockroaches coming over the walls. Over the years my subject matter improved, and I've had gallery shows all over the world. But at the time, I was still trying to find my artistic footing.

One morning in March, while we were still working on the first CSN album, Joan and I went to breakfast at Art's Deli on Ventura Boulevard. We'd parked the car down the street, and on the way back we passed a small antiques store that drew our attention. In the window was a vase that took her fancy, clear glass with little enamel flowers on it. Joan rarely bought anything for herself. It just wasn't her style to blow money on something frivolous, but this time I suggested she treat herself. "Go on," I said. "How much can it be? It's not Gallé or Steuben, it can't cost thousands of dollars." In fact, it was pretty cheap, between eighty and a hundred dollars, so Joan bought it and took it home.

It was one of those gray cloudy days in Los Angeles that foreshadows the spring. When we got back and put our stuff down, I said, "I'll light a fire"—she had an open fireplace with a stash of wood in the back—"why don't you put some flowers in that vase you just bought. It'll look beautiful. It's kind of a bleak day. It'll bring some more color into the room." Then I stopped. I thought: Whoa! That's a delicious moment. How many couples have been there: You light a fire, I'll cook dinner. I thought that in the ordinariness of the moment there might be a profoundly simple statement. So Joni went out into the garden to gather ferns and leaves and a couple flowers to put in the vase. That meant she wasn't at the piano—but I was! And within the hour, the song "Our House" was finished.

> *I'll light the fire, you place the flowers in the vase*
> *that you bought today.*
> *Staring at the fire for hours and hours*

> *while I listen to you play your love songs*
> *all night long for me, only for me.*

I turned the second verse—*Come to me and rest your head for just five minutes, everything is done*—from an English phrase that signals the dishes are washed, the washing's been taken in, the chores are done. It was that simple. We all have a song—the first time you ever kissed someone, the first time you got laid in the back of a car—so the instant you hear it, it takes you *right back* to the moment in a very real way, the same way that a smell or taste reminds you of someone. I think that's why "Our House" was such a popular song, because we've all been there, all felt that tug. And the refrain summed up exactly where I was at.

> *Our house is a very, very, very fine house,*
> *with two cats in the yard, life used to be so hard.*
> *Now everything is easy 'cause of you.*

MIDWAY THROUGH THE sessions, we realized it was time to start thinking about an album cover. I'd known Henry Diltz since 1967, when he photographed the Hollies in New York City, so we enlisted him to take his best shot. Not some slick paste-up job or psychedelic mumbo jumbo. We wanted him to capture us in a natural setting, to convey the intimacy of the group and the music we'd made. On a recent walk through the neighborhood with Henry, we'd spotted an abandoned house on the corner of Palm Avenue and Santa Monica Boulevard that had exactly the right feel. It was a funky joint with a beat-up old couch out front. This was promising. He rounded up the guys and we sat on the couch. Easy as that; everyone happy. When we got the proof sheets back the next day, one image was obviously *the* shot. Only problem was, we were sitting out of order: Nash, Stills & Crosby. So we went back there the next day to reshoot the picture . . . and the house was gone. It had been bulldozed into the back lot. Screw it, we decided to use the picture anyway. So Crosby's name was above my head and a lot of people wound up thinking I was Croz.

When CSN got back to the studio, there wasn't a whole lot left to do on the album, so we relaxed our no-visitors policy a little. One night, just after we'd recorded the "Suite," Ahmet brought Phil Spector in to hear us. Very spooky guy, didn't say a word to anyone, but his eyes darted everywhere, observing everything, taking it all in. Another night, Ahmet came in with Garth Hudson, who loved what we were doing. He definitely picked up on the vibe in that place. Recording with David and Stephen had such a different feel. Even though I'd enjoyed making records with the Hollies, we'd done it for so long that it had lost its excitement. With Stephen and David it was a brand-new sound, with songs that meant something, songs we thought could change people's lives, songs that could break hearts, get people thinking about shit, such as "Long Time Gone." David had written it the night Bobby Kennedy was assassinated. He was too disturbed, couldn't sleep, anguished by the senseless tragedy, and scribbled throughout the early hours of dawn.

> *Speak out, you got to speak out against the madness*
> *You got to speak your mind*
> *if you dare.*
> *Don't, no don't try to get yourself elected*
> *If you do, you had better cut your hair.*

As a lyric, "Long Time Gone" rolled right off the tongue, but our tongues were tied when it came time to record it. We tried it over and over and couldn't get the track. You know what *the track* is when you hear it, but it wasn't happening for us. Who knows why. We'd worked all night on it, never coming close to anything that satisfied. Frustration started to cloud our objectivity. About three o'clock in the morning, Stephen said, "Hey, why don't you guys get a burger and go home?" So we did . . . no use beating a dead horse.

When we came back the next day, Stephen said to David, "Want to hear your song, man?"

In the hours after Croz and I had left the studio, he, with Dallas Taylor on drums, had created the entire track. It had an incredible arrangement—dark, moody, ethereal, sonically beautiful. There was space in it, a lot of space for David to sing his ass off, space for the vocals to come in on the choruses. The track was *right there*, it spoke for itself. And Stephen earned a new nickname: Captain Manyhands.

It was easier with "Lady of the Island." That was a three-track record on an eight-track tape that we got on one take. Me singing and playing guitar, with Crosby sitting right next to me, blending in that beautiful cellolike fugue. We also got a gorgeous take of "Guinevere," which is a motherfucker to sing. Years later, it was catnip for a cat like Miles Davis. He was working on *Bitches Brew* at the time and bumped into Crosby in the Village. "Hey Dave," he said, "I recorded that tune of yours, 'Guinevere.' Want to hear it?" Miles had his arm around a tall leggy blonde he wanted to screw, so all three of them went back to his apartment to hear "Guinevere." Miles put on the song, a twenty-minute version that riffed in myriad cosmic directions, and went into the bedroom with the blonde, leaving David there to smoke it and listen to the track. A half hour later, Miles emerged from the bedroom rendezvous. "So, Dave, what do you think?" Crosby threw him one of his trademark glares. "Well, Miles, you can use the tune, but you have to take my name off of it." Miles was crestfallen. "You don't like it?" he asked. Crosby refused to temper his opinion, even for royalty like Miles Davis. "No, man—no. I don't like it at all."

About ten years later, I was at an after-party event for the Grammys at Mr. Chow in LA and saw Miles come in with Cicely Tyson. He caught my eye and started waving insistently at me. I looked over my shoulder, certain he must be gesturing to somebody else.

CSNY performing at the Fillmore East, New York City, June 1970
*(© 1970 Joel Bernstein)*

CSNY in the dressing room, Metropolitan Sports Center, Bloomington, Minnesota, July 9, 1970 *(© 1970 Henry Diltz)*

CSNY with Dallas Taylor and Greg Reeves; Studio City, California, July 1969 *(© 1969 Henry Diltz)*

CSN at Criteria Recording Studios, Miami, March 1977 *(© Joel Bernstein)*

Taping the *Daylight Again* television special at Universal Amphitheatre, Universal City, California, November 28, 1982 *(© Henry Diltz)*

CSNY performing, 2004 tour *(© Joel Bernstein)*

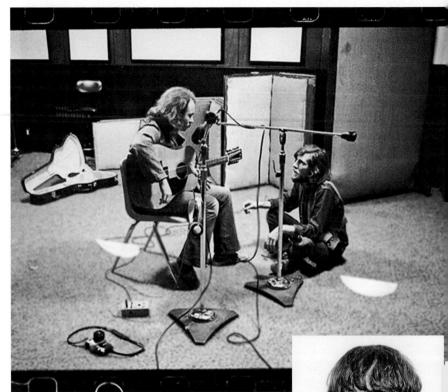

With David Crosby, during the recording of the *Graham Nash/David Crosby* album, November 1971 *(© 1971 Joel Bernstein)*

David Crosby, early days of the Byrds
*(© Harry Goodwin/Michael Ochs Archive/Getty Images)*

Performing with Croz *(© Henry Diltz)*

David Crosby onstage with Crosby, Stills, Nash & Young, Campus Stadium, University of California at Santa Barbara, November 9, 1969
*(© 1969 Henry Diltz)*

With Neil Young, Fifth Avenue Hotel, New York City, June 1970
*(© 1970 Joel Bernstein)*

Backstage at Roosevelt Stadium, Jersey City, the night Nixon resigned,
August 8, 1974 *(© Joel Bernstein)*

Me on the big screen at Live Aid in Philadelphia, July 13, 1985
*(© Philadelphia Enquirer)*

No Nukes concert at Madison Square Garden *(© Lynn Goldsmith)*

Chipping the wall down in Berlin, 1989 *(© Stanley Johnston)*

Occupy Wall Street event; David's son James Raymond, playing melodica, 2011 *(Getty Images)*

At the White House: John Hartmann, far right; Michael John Bowen, far left

Me and David with Jacques Cousteau and his son, Philippe

Receiving the Office of the Order of the British Empire from Her Majesty, 2010. The emerald was gigantic.
(© Buckingham Palace)

"No, no, c'mere, man," he insisted. When I got within earshot, he leaned close and asked in his low, gravelly voice, "Crosby still pissed at me?"

I said, "You mean about 'Guinevere'?"

"Yeah." He nodded. "He still pissed?"

"I don't think so, Miles. He was either too high or he wasn't in the right mood to hear your take on it. He probably expected the chords to be the same as his, but I don't think he's pissed at you one bit."

Miles pondered this with Socratic intensity. "Okay. Tell David hello. Tell him I hope he's not still pissed."

In any case, we put the finishing touches on the album, delivered it to Ahmet at the beginning of April, and reveled in his reaction to it, which was sincere and emotional. He was genuinely delighted, even a bit overwhelmed. He recognized right away that we had made a stunning piece of music. It was *exactly* the album we wanted to make, no second guesses, no regrets. *We* knew! Everything we wanted to say was on that tape. And we were pretty full of ourselves for pulling it off.

Over the next couple weeks, we took our acoustic guitars everywhere, went to visit friends, our musical peers, and sang the entire album live for them, start to finish. We covered the entire Laurel Canyon circuit: Cass Elliot, Peter Tork, Peter Fonda, Elliot Roberts, Paul Rothchild, Jennifer Warnes, Barry McGuire, they all got a private performance. We gave them what we called an ear fuck: put one of them in the middle of us and sang in their ear, which never failed to blow their minds because the music was great, it was something brand-new. The feedback we got was pretty spectacular. They were stunned at how beautiful we sounded. So we knew—we knew we had something special.

The weight was off our shoulders, but I missed the studio. It was, in many ways, where I felt most at home. So for a few weeks I went to observe at A&M while Joan finished work on *Clouds*. After one session with Paul Rothchild, she too decided that she didn't need a producer. Sound familiar? History may not repeat itself, but it does echo. It was fun watching her do her thing without having to worry about the critical consequences. Joan was a happy girl in the studio, and extremely capable. She knew exactly what to do, how she wanted to sound. There was always a fully formed arrangement in her head, a perfect structure for each song, a suitable accompaniment, when other voices should come in—which were all hers, of course—and how to shape each song so that its essence was preserved. Recording is, for the most part, a solitary endeavor, and Joan enjoyed that. She had the same attitude as CSN: "Stay out of my way, I know what I'm doing." And for Joni, it never failed to pay off.

On April 11, 1969, David, Stephen, and I found ourselves in New York, at David Geffen's apartment on Central Park West, ready to review the acetate of our first album. Tommy Dowd had remastered it from a 15 ips EQ'ed copy. We hadn't given Atlantic the master two-track tapes, because we didn't trust record companies, even with Ahmet involved, to take care of something so precious. And lucky thing, because Dowd had remastered the entire album, which pissed us off righteously. Suddenly, Tom's fingerprints were all over our record, way too much bass on "Suite," for instance. It sounded slicker, different from what we'd struggled so hard to do. Bottom line was that it wasn't what we delivered, and that alone—didn't matter who did it, could have been Saint Spector himself—was enough to piss us off. We wanted it to represent us, not what Atlantic thought we should be. Croz threatened to break Tommy's legs if he ever did anything like that again, and we remastered it ourselves at Atlantic Studios.

Afterward, we all went our separate ways. Stephen hightailed it to England for a music special of blues performances, filmed for broadcast and featuring Buddy Miles, Eric Clapton, Jack Bruce, and Buddy Guy. A music junkie of the first order, Stills couldn't tear himself away from the scene. David and Christine Hinton made a beeline for Fort Lauderdale, where his boat, the *Mayan,* was anchored.

The *Mayan* was a two-masted Alden schooner built in 1947 that Croz had bought in 1967 with $22,500 borrowed from Peter Tork. It was where Croz went when he wanted incredible peace, where he could be the master of his own destiny. And I joined Joni for a few of her concerts, at the Philadelphia Academy of Music and the Fillmore East in New York.

On April 30, 1969, we flew to Nashville for Joni and Bob Dylan's appearance on *The Johnny Cash Show* on ABC-TV. The night before the show was taped, Johnny and June had a dinner at their house outside the city for every performer on the bill. Just so happened that Bob was a guest. He'd had his motorcycle accident and hadn't been seen or heard in public for over a year. He was in town, making *Nashville Skyline,* so this was a very big deal.

The dinner was the kind of event I wasn't used to. It was fancy, affluent, gorgeous plates, gold cutlery, maids and waiters scurrying around. At one point in the evening, Johnny rose, picked up a gold knife, and tapped it against a glass to get everyone's attention.

"Here at the Cash house we have a tradition that you have to sing for your supper," he said in that lush, gravelly growl. "So—there are some guitars. Let's go."

Nobody moved.

Bob was sitting on the stairs with Sara, and both of them looked uncomfortable. Mickey Newbury, a famous Nashville songwriter, was there; so was Kris Kristofferson, and of course, Joni and me. Everyone stared at those guitars as if they were radioactive. My confidence level was ridiculously high as a result of our recent studio hijinks, so I thought, Fuck it—I'll get up.

Of course, nobody there knew who Crosby, Stills & Nash were. I doubt anyone knew who I was or that I'd been with the Hollies. I was merely Joan's boyfriend, along for the ride. So I grabbed a guitar, sat on the stool, and whipped off a version of "Marrakesh Express." *All abooooard . . .* I hit the last chord, knew I'd killed it, put the guitar back on the stand . . . and walked right into a standing lamp that went crashing to the floor.

That broke the ice! Everyone thought it was funny as shit. So, promptly, I think Kris got up and sang "Sunday Morning Coming Down," Joni played "Both Sides Now," and even Bob got up and did "Lay, Lady, Lay," "Don't Think Twice," and a few other songs. His performance that night was overwhelming. Everyone was in tears. This was *Bob Dylan,* for God's sake. No one had known if he'd ever sing again. It was an incredible moment, especially for me. I revered Bob, but I was pretty confident, too. The *Crosby, Stills & Nash* album was about to be released, and I knew how special it was, even in front of this crowd. "You don't know it now, but you just wait," I thought. Yeah, pretty confident—and I had the girl of my dreams with me. What an incredible moment in my life.

THE ALBUM DID everything we thought it would. From its release in May 1969, it immediately caught fire and went burning up the charts. "Crosby, Stills & Nash" was on everyone's lips. The music hit hard; it was a definite game changer. You could hear our songs on almost every station in America, out of every student's dorm-room window. We had a giant hit on our hands.

Exactly as we'd expected.

Now we had to promote it. It was one thing to sing it acoustically for friends, quite another to play it in a large venue. We could sing it live brilliantly. No problem where that was concerned. And we had Dallas on drums. But Stephen had played bass and keyboards on the album. And he was our lead guitarist. So we knew a bass player was going to be in the cards. I'd be able to cover some of the keyboard parts because Stephen had taught me how to play some simple piano. But even with that, there was a lot of discussion about adding another member to the core.

Stephen and Dallas went to England to ask Stevie Winwood if he'd join us but he didn't want to. The same with Al Kooper, who'd recently been kicked out of Blood, Sweat & Tears. John Sebastian actually made a lot of sense. He was our friend, someone we knew we could have fun with and get along with musically. He had a sweet voice—just think of the Lovin' Spoonful—but there was no room for John, vocally or writing-wise. And truthfully, we didn't need another voice. We weren't looking to be a choir.

Ahmet appeared to have the answer. One evening at the start of that lazy, amazing summer, he invited Croz and Elliot Roberts to dinner at his house. There was a lot to celebrate. The CSN album was selling like mad, and requests for concert dates were starting to pile up. Ahmet knew he had a smash on his hands. After the plates were cleared, Ahmet began playing music on the stereo and reminiscing sentimentally about Buffalo Springfield. He loved the magic that band had created, especially loved the tension in the guitars, the way they balanced each other.

"You know who you ought to talk to?" Ahmet asked. Who was the one guy who could do it all, bring the chops, the songs, the heat? And give CSN the missing elements it needed for an unbeatable live performance? His answer: "You guys need Neil Young."

(© Joel Bernstein)

NEIL YOUNG: IT WAS LIKE LOBBING A LIVE GRENADE into a vacuum. Croz knew too well the potential blowback. Neil was a guy with immense talent who was utterly self-centered. Bands for him were merely stepping-stones, way stations to a personal goal. That's the way it had gone down with Buffalo Springfield. They could never count on him at crunch time, never be sure he would turn up at gigs. But Ahmet knew the core of the Springfield was unbeatable, and he longed, in some way, to hang on to that value. He also realized what Neil's presence did to Stephen. It not only kept him off-balance, but prodded him to rise with his guitar licks: "Follow *that*, motherfucker!" In which case, Stephen usually did. Neil brought out something in Stephen that was animal-like. They were like two longhorn stags on either side of a stage.

Stephen's reaction was predictable. *"Are you fuckin' kidding me, Ahmet?"* he huffed. "I just spent two years with the guy. He's disruptive, doesn't turn up. You want me to go back *there*?"

It was obvious from the stories around town just how explosive their relationship was. But it was hard to say no to Ahmet because you knew he was coming at it from a purely musical point of view, and when Ahmet talked, you listened. He was a very influential and persuasive cat where we were concerned.

The situation got thornier after Croz recalled an incident. One day, he had been sitting on the trunk of his car in Joni's driveway when Neil drove up the street, saw him, and pulled over. Crosby, in his suspicious way, asked, "What are you up to, man?"

Neil shrugged and said, "I wrote some new songs. Wanna hear 'em?" And he whipped out a guitar and sang "Country Girl" and "Helpless."

Croz thought to himself, We've gotta have him.

The first I heard about it was in New York, during the remastering of our album. Stephen mentioned, "Maybe we should just get Neil." I was totally against it. I didn't want Neil in the band—I didn't want *anybody* else in the band—and I said as much.

"What the hell are you doing?" I asked. "We created this beautiful sound. Why fuck with it?"

Crosby emphasized our need for a lead guitarist when Stephen played keyboards in a concert situation. And, of course, those songs. "This guy is writing some of the best shit I ever heard," he said. "He's the guy who wrote 'Expecting to Fly' and 'Clancy.' When he sings those songs, you want to listen. I want him in the band."

Stephen was equally adamant. He knew how great Neil really was. And he wanted what he had in the Springfield, which was Neil the writer, singer, and guitar player who had an aura, real mojo. David and Stephen were two thirds of a democratic band, so it was really a fait accompli.

"Look, I don't know Neil Young," I said. "I don't know if he's anyone I can hang out with, like I can with the two of you. I don't know if I can confide in him, if I can go to him and say, 'I've got this tune, what do you think?' I don't know *anything* about him. Let me at least meet the guy before we make this gigantic decision."

I got really worked up over this. We were so personally involved with each other. Did we have room, time, and space for another person in the mix? Another time-bomb personality? I didn't think so. From a vocal point of view, I was totally opposed. Four-part is very different from three-part. Besides, I felt Stephen played great guitar; he was four times the guitar player Neil was. Wasn't that enough?

I put my foot down. "I've got to meet Neil Young."

He happened to be in New York at the time, and we arranged to meet at a coffee shop on Bleecker Street, just the two of us. I didn't want anyone else to influence what I thought about this cat.

I remember walking in, seeing a guy with this dark cloud about him, and strangely enough, a lightness at the same time. Hard to explain. The guy was that sphinxlike, tough to read. It was obvious from the get-go that he knew what he wanted. We talked about what he could bring to the group. Unafraid, I got right in his face.

"Why am I talking to you about this fucking band I happen to think is already complete?" I asked.

Neil threw me one of those inscrutable stares. "Well, man, ever hear me and Stephen play together?"

I'd never heard the Springfield live, I admitted, but I'd heard plenty of stories.

"Yeah, man—we've got it, man. And I've got the songs, too."

"I don't doubt that," I told him. I'd heard "Expecting to Fly" and "Nowadays, Clancy." Songwise, he could pull his own weight. But my concern was more about chemistry. Crosby, Stills & Nash was a stable compound; adding another element was potentially combustible. Like Crosby said, "Juggling four bottles of nitroglycerin is fine—until you drop one . . . "

Turns out Neil Young was a funny motherfucker. I knew he had this dark, looming presence, a scowl and a loner tendency. But Neil was *funny*. Now, maybe he understood that I was the group's lone holdout where he was concerned and he was on his best behavior, but at the end of breakfast I would have nominated him to be the prime minister of Canada. Based on his personality and my intuition, I went back to the guys and said, "I get it—he's in. Let's give it a shot."

It so happened that Neil was managed by Elliot Roberts, same guy who managed Joni and us. So, first, we ran the whole business thing by him. Because we were Crosby, Stills & Nash, the question was whether Neil would become one of our band members or part of the corporate entity. Elliot insisted that Neil have his name up there with ours: Crosby, Stills, Nash & Young. It sounded more like a law firm at that point. I lost my ampersand and Neil got it. But that made sense, and I admired Neil for his attitude, which was: "If I'm going to join this band, I want my name up there and an equal share." He was joining us *after* we'd made the first album, so we agreed to give him an equal cut of the gigs and anything else we recorded together, but nothing from the first record.

In any case, we had to move fast putting something together. The timing was delicate. The album was riding high on the charts and it was necessary for us to get out there and promote it. We wanted to be out in front of an audience while the record was fresh and hot. There were already a few upcoming gigs on our dance card. So we rented out the Village Gate in New York for a few days in June and rehearsed there, to get a feel for CSNY.

I hadn't been inside the Village Gate since I'd first come to New York in 1965 with the Hollies. Back then, I was really into jazz, so I'd already seen Miles Davis at the Vanguard. Richard Alpert, who became Ram Dass, opened for him in a suit and a tie. He just walked onstage and talked about a new psychedelic era that was coming and turned on a strobe light—the first one I'd ever seen—with his tie swinging as the light hit it, just like acid. It was also the first time I ever saw a musician blow an incredible solo and just walk offstage, still playing, and go to the bar to have a drink while his bass player soloed. I later learned that was *so* Miles. Entering the Village Gate again brought back many fond memories.

Otherwise, there was a lot of work to be done. We had to slot Neil into what we were doing without losing the essence of what we'd created. Tough to do musically. It was going to change the sound of the band. And it was going to change the sound of the first record, live, because we were about to sing those songs in concert. We showed Neil what the vocals were, CSN style, then asked, "How do you fit into this chorus?" When we did a Neil Young song and came to the chorus, it was: "This is what we would do here, but we need to make room for your harmony." He had an unusually high voice, so often I would go under him to make it four-part, but there were also times we agreed to double the high part, which gave the harmonies an extra edge.

We began rehearsals at Stephen's house on Shady Oak, a beast of a place he was renting from Peter Tork on the Valley side of the Hollywood Hills, in Studio City. It was a big, strange sprawling structure that had originally belonged to the actor Wally Cox, with a music room covered in oriental carpets and a swimming pool and a storehouse of drugs that kept everyone mellow. Stephen had a studio on the premises, with a B-3 and an ever-ready drum kit. I'm not sure how many people lived there. Lots of very nubile young women. Friends who needed a place to crash for a while. It was an all-purpose hippie haven. We spent lots of lovely days there, using the sauna, feasting on steak dinners, indulging ourselves on the food and various other tasty treats.

Jimi Hendrix stopped by when he was in town. And Eric Clapton. David Geffen and Elliot Roberts came to hear us rehearse. Man, Geffen was so full of himself at the time. He'd done the record deal and worked out the trade of me for Richie Furay. There was the whiff of a Woodstock deal in the air. He was strutting around like a dandy peacock, so we threw him into the pool. Stephen and Croz picked him up and did the dirty work. He had this expensive white shirt on, a pair of designer slacks, patent-leather loafers. "You think you're full of yourself? Well, watch this!" He was completely soaked, and then we chucked a bunch of roses in after him. I took a photo of him standing there, soaked to the skin.

He came out of the water with a rose in his teeth. He had to know it was a joke and that we grudgingly loved him. When you have someone like Crosby in your band, you have to play it nice and loose, otherwise you're not going to survive. And Geffen, if anything, was a long-term survivor.

Those rehearsals went better than anyone expected. Musically,

Stephen was on fire. He and Neil picked up right where they'd left off with the Springfield, playing amazing barnburner solos together. Stephen made room for Neil in the solos, and Neil expressed himself accordingly, just as we hoped, saying, "Follow that, motherfucker." Stephen's riffs would say, "No problem, listen to this. Take *that,* motherfucker." At the end, they'd be *right there* together, building to a brilliant crescendo.

I've got to admit that Neil added an element to Crosby, Stills & Nash that we didn't have: that dark edge, that biting Neil Young thing. It was obvious after those first few days at the Gate that we had made the right decision. The music went somewhere else that was equally great, if not better. We were smart enough to realize what was happening. It wasn't like we did this because our manager or record guy thought it would be a good idea. We did it because of the music.

Our coming-out party, so to speak, was at the Chicago Auditorium Theatre on August 17, 1969. It was a warm-up date before we played Woodstock, which we heard was going to be a giant thing, maybe twenty thousand kids. Joni opened for us in Chicago—how ballsy was that? Our album was in the top five; the buzz on both coasts and everywhere in between was enormous. It was the first time I'd performed since being with the Hollies. I could hardly wait.

Everyone knew this would be sensational. Geffen and Roberts were antsy. When your artist has that kind of buzz, it makes your job that much easier. You can now say to promoters: "I'm sorry, they won't go for it." And whether we did or not, that was their attitude. "We don't need you. These guys are going to be gigantic. Do you want a taste or not?" It gave the managers great power when the buzz was that undeniable. And the attitude spread throughout every manager and record company. Ahmet was bragging like a proud parent about having this new supergroup on his roster. Atlantic, for the most part, was still considered an R&B label (a term their legendary producer, Jerry Wexler, had coined in 1949), with a primarily black audience. They already had Led Zeppelin and Cream—and now Crosby, Stills, Nash & Young. We helped push them right over the edge, into the world of young, white record buyers.

The Chicago gig lived up to everyone's expectations, including ours. Stephen, David, and I walked out and hit those kids with the "Suite." *Bam!* Right between the eyes. Then we introduced Neil, and the crowd went crazy. We did three and a half hours: all the stuff on the first album, stuff that would later be on *Déjà Vu,* all of Neil's songs, some Springfield stuff. And we would talk. A lot. It felt great to finally put it all together and to hear the crowd's reaction, which was beyond delirious. From that first show in Chicago in 1969, we were Crosby, Stills, Nash & Young. Believe it or not, after that tour, apart from one concert, an anti–Vietnam War benefit in San Francisco's Golden Gate Park, Crosby, Stills & Nash didn't play as a trio again until 1977.


WE MOVED ON TO New York after Chicago. We kept hearing great things about the Woodstock festival. It was going to be monumental, transformative, a cultural flashpoint. Rumors coming out of upstate New York were "Now it's a hundred thousand people," "Now it's two hundred thousand . . . " Joni was supposed to go up there with the rest of us, but she was scheduled to appear on *The Dick Cavett Show* on the Monday after the festival. That TV show was considered a very big deal. So Geffen and Roberts made a decision. If we got held up upstate, she'd blow a big career move. Rather than risk Joni being stranded at Woodstock, they pulled her off the festival roster and she sat it out in a New York hotel room.

On Sunday evening, August 17, a limo drove us out to Teterboro Airport in New Jersey to get a helicopter to the festival. The rumors now were beyond belief. It was a nation, a disaster, a *revolution*; they were calling out the National Guard. We never thought of not going. In fact, we couldn't wait to get there. Dallas and I went up in one helicopter, David, Stephen, and Neil in another right behind us, and we tandemed in. It was pretty wild. We flew up along the Hudson River and then over this . . . *sight*! David's description of it was the best. He said it was like flying over an encampment of the Macedonian army. There were a *lot* of people there. It was more than a city of people—it was tribal. Fires were burning, smoke was rising, a sea of hippies clustered together, shoulder to shoulder, hundreds of thousands of them. The focus of it was the well-lit stage. We could see it all from up there. It was intense, a very special moment.

About fifty feet from the ground, something went wrong. The tail rotor on our helicopter failed, and the craft started to spin in opposition to the rotation of the blades. The pilot had to—*land it now*! Hard. He thumped it down. Dallas freaked out. Later, he said he wanted to punch me in the face, but those feelings dissolved the moment we touched down.

John Sebastian met us with many rolled joints. He, of course, had the best dope at Woodstock. We went straight into his tent at the right-hand side of the stage and got incredibly wasted. "This is crazy, man," he told us. "Just take a look." Outside, it was muddy and a little drizzly. Hard to get a grip on the enormity of the scene.

It was such a tumultuous smoke-ridden cocaine-driven moment that it's hard to remember everything as it went down. I think that Santana was on immediately before us. It was their national debut, as well as ours, and no one had seen Joe Cocker live in the States until then either. And as we shuffled onstage to do our set, we could see all our peers watching from the sidelines: the Band, the Airplane, Richie Havens, Janis, Blood, Sweat & Tears, Jimi . . . When Stephen announced that we were scared shitless, it was because of all those heavyweights—artists we loved—ready to check us out. They'd heard our album and thought, Okay, now show us. But, truthfully, I wasn't nervous in the slightest. I didn't give a shit how many people were out there. I'd already been through six or seven years of madness with the Hollies. The kids at Woodstock were stoned and placid by comparison.

The stage sound sucked. We could hardly hear ourselves, and the sound of the audience was enormous, even if they weren't saying anything. It was their energy, which thrummed like an engine. So we had to wing it. It was cold, and the guitars immediately went out of tune. Stephen was tuning madly throughout the opening of "Suite: Judy Blue Eyes," even as he was running down that incredible riff. David and I were on one mike. We knew how to balance our voices. I'm always eight or nine inches away from the mike head. They call me Razorthroat for a good reason. I thought we sounded fabulous. Man, I was getting higher and higher on that stage. The energy was fierce. And we *killed* 'em.

We played about an hour, beginning with "Suite," then going on to "Helplessly Hoping," "Guinevere," "Marrakesh Express," "Long Time Gone," and some of Neil's songs, including "Mr. Soul" and a new tune of his, "Sea of Madness." At the time, we had no idea that Neil had refused to have his songs filmed or recorded, something that the rest of us would never have thought of, let alone agreed to. That's the main reason many people don't realize that the four of us performed at Woodstock. We only knew that we had done well. We could sense it. And understand: It was only the second time we had ever played together, which was *insane* (our first performance was at the Chicago Auditorium Theatre just days before). We felt triumphant.

Afterward, we went back to Sebastian's tent and proceeded to get even higher. By that time, we'd watched a couple of other acts and, sometime just before dawn, it was Jimi's turn. I got to see most of Jimi's set, and as we were leaving he was launching into "The Star-Spangled Banner." Woodstock was coming to an end. And what an end—a brilliant piece of musical history.

When we got back to New York City, Joni was waiting for us at our hotel, not at all happy that she'd missed the festival. Frustrated, she'd watched the whole thing unspool on TV news, which had covered it practically from beginning to end. Our babbling and rambling about the experience didn't make it any easier for her.

Instead she'd put all her energy into writing about it and had a good 90 percent of the song finished before we arrived. She played it for us before we even got settled.

> *I came upon a child of God*
> *He was walking along the road . . .*

It was a beautiful, gentle ballad, rather smoky, folky and moody. I noticed Stephen listening intently with that strange look in his eyes. When Joni had finished, after delivering that magical refrain—*We are stardust, we are golden*—he didn't hesitate. "Can we have that song?" he asked her. "I know exactly what to do with it. But I'd like to change it a little."

Because Joni was one of the lads, to say nothing of being my girlfriend, she merely shrugged and said, "Sure." And, of course, Stephen turned her ballad into a balls-out rock 'n' roll song. He took that songbird, dark-purply approach of hers and attached electric jumper cables to it, with Neil adding that killer of a riff at the top.

Crosby, Stills, Nash & Young returned to LA after that. Our next shows were at the Greek Theatre, back on our home turf. We asked Joni to open the shows for us (I found out later that Neil had told Joni that we should be opening for her). The shows were rather special for us . . . not only was Joni a fabulous writer and performer but the atmosphere she helped create was electric. One might even say magical. One night a rainbow-colored contrail from a rocket—fired from the Vandenberg Air Force Base—illuminated the skies. Even the fans who couldn't get tickets filled the trees behind the theater every night.

From the very start of our relationship, it was obvious to me that Stephen Stills was a hugely talented man. He played nearly every instrument on our first album, everything but drums. Croz and I played our rhythm guitars but there was no question it was Stephen who was the driving force. I recently heard an audience tape of our performance of "Suite: Judy Blue Eyes" from the Greek; to my ears, it is one of our very best performances ever of that great song. It still thrills me to remember the moment that Stephen first sat me down and played me the "Suite." I was astounded by the melody and structure of the piece . . . Four completely separate movements blended into one ridiculously fine song. We were most definitely on a roll.

A couple of weeks after that we played the Big Sur Festival on the grounds of the Esalen Institute, overlooking the Pacific Ocean just off Highway 1. It was an intimate affair, nothing at all like Woodstock. Joni was on the show, as were Joan Baez and her sister, Mimi Fariña, Cass Elliot, the Flying Burrito Brothers, John Sebastian, and Dorothy Morrison, who sang "Oh Happy Day" (my friend Stanley Johnston recorded that record when he was a young engineer at radio station KPFA). The thing I mostly remember about that event was that there was a swimming pool in front of the stage. Some guy kept screaming something unpleasant at us. People were trying to shut him up, and Crosby delivered one of his best rejoinders: "Peace. Love. *Kick his ass!*"

Joni and I weren't very happy together at that point. I think she recognized that our relationship was starting to wind down. Somewhere along the way, the bloom had gone off and, in retrospect, she may have already been looking for a way out. A lot of it stemmed from my inability to make a larger commitment. Sometime before Woodstock we had talked about marriage, but I'd already been in a marriage that ended after three years. And I was recently divorced from Rose and wasn't sure the time was right—or, even though I was in love, wasn't sure if I was ready for more. I was very hesitant, and Joan picked right up on that. Some of it also had to do with Joan's grandmother, Sadie Jane McKee, who had wanted to be a performer but wasn't able to because, as a mother, she had to take care of the kids. My sense was that Joan thought if she married me I would want her to stay home and be a wife, as opposed to a writer and performer, which had *never* crossed my mind. Never. That's not what I wanted from a partner. I was too respectful of Joni's talent and wanted only for her to fulfill her dreams. In any case, she wanted more from me. She didn't understand how committed I was—but in my own way. I was completely in love. I would have been with her for the rest of my life. I'm certain that she saw it the same way.

All of these conflicting emotions crystallized when she completed her song "Willy," which she'd begun writing back in March, in a limo we'd taken to Big Bear. I guess that even then she understood that things were coming to an end. That song really pinned what was going on between us. It's an incredibly sad but truthful song. She first played it for me on the piano in the Laurel Canyon house.

> *Willy is my child, he is my father*
> *I would be his lady all my life*
> *He says he'd love to live with me*
> *but for an ancient injury that has not healed*

The song took my breath away. She put it right there in my face and it made me very uncomfortable. I remembered specifically *looking through the lace at the face on the conquered moon,* which dates the moment—and Joan's growing dissatisfaction—to the days following the historic moon walk, three weeks before Woodstock. I'd told her then that I felt I'd given my heart too soon. And it was true, I could not *hear the chapel's pealing silver bells.* I was scared to hear them, even though I was completely in love. Nor did I heed the warning that I was *bound to lose if* I *let the blues get* me *scared to feel.*

Instead, I read her mood as a growing wariness of the incestuous LA scene. Joni—and all of us—craved a change of scenery. In Los Angeles, we were always in a hot white spotlight. There was too much attention on everything we did, too much backbiting, too much gossip and adulation. Joni felt that if she moved to another city, perhaps people wouldn't look at her as closely. So I decided to buy a place for us to live in San Francisco.

When I first came to New York in 1965, I realized just how magnificent America really was. The city in all its grandeur swept me right off my feet. Moving on to LA confirmed that impression, adding sunshine, palm trees, and a great feeling of freedom to the equation. San Francisco did the same thing to me, but more on a musical level. The Grateful Dead were there, the Airplane, Boz Scaggs, Santana, Steve Miller. And Crosby, too. He, Christine, and Debbie Donovan had moved up to Novato in a rural part of Marin County, with the *Mayan* anchored in Sausalito. Neil was to buy a three-hundred-acre ranch in Woodside, and Elliot Roberts would live nearby.

It was the spirit of the city I was ready for. The neighborhoods were young. Music poured out of the buildings. Everywhere you looked there were hippies, head shops, record stores, fortune tellers. The weather was different from the heat of LA, more windy and damp, like English weather. And the people were more relaxed because *everyone* was wasted *all the time.*

I kind of fell in love with Haight-Ashbury. The neighborhood was coming out of its seamy, post–"Summer of Love" period and slowly undergoing a revitalization. A real estate broker took me to a beautiful little oasis, Buena Vista Park West, overlooking the Haight. On the west side of the street that ringed the park was a four-story Victorian that had been built in the 1890s and had made it through several earthquakes and the Great Fire. That was it for me. It would need a lot of work, a top-to-bottom gutting, but I was more than willing to take on the project. So I bought it immediately for $59,000, the first serious purchase I'd ever made. For a kid from Salford, it was an incredible leap. I didn't tell Joan right away about the house I'd bought for us. I was going to surprise her with it once the renovations were under way.

CSNY began getting serious about our first album together, which would ultimately become *Déjà Vu.* We all had songs. We'd started recording in Los Angeles, but the scene shifted quickly to the San Francisco environs. David and Christine were settled in Novato, hanging out with the Grateful Dead, most of whom lived just down the road. My house wasn't ready yet, so I checked in to the Caravan Lodge Motel, a funky joint in the Tenderloin district, but convenient to Wally Heider's San Francisco outpost. David took a room there as well, and so did Neil, who moved in with two bush babies, Harriet and Speedy. They looked like rats, with gigantic eyes and big long tails. Invariably, one or the other was always clinging to Neil's neck, and they would *sproiiiing* off his shoulder and cling to the wallpaper and *sproiiiing* to the carpet, a crazy fucking scene indeed.

A couple days into the rehearsal period, I went up to Novato to visit David and Christine. They were in a big old country house with Debbie Donovan and a number of hippie chicks who came and went. We used to get up around one or two o'clock and go sit by the pool, trying to figure out what we were going to do that night. One thing for sure, there would be plenty of drugs. We were all stoned and pretty well coked out of our minds—everyone, that is, but Christine, who was never a druggie. She was the joint roller; she made sure the boys had enough to smoke. Christine ran the whole show.

On the last day of September in 1969, we were vegetating at David's in that near-perfect hippie setting, feasting on the vibe of that perfect day. It was warm and beautiful. The summer was grinding to a halt; a change of spirit was definitely in the air. Mickey Hart, the Dead's percussionist, had sent a horse over to the house for Christine that afternoon, and there was a communal joy watching her ride across the grounds. I was especially happy for Croz. He was a self-proclaimed satyr with insatiable lust, but Christine had somehow captured his heart. She was a very beautiful woman, such a great spirit, full of laughter.

Later that afternoon, I was by the pool when Christine sidled over and handed me three joints. "I just rolled these for you," she said. "Enjoy, enjoy, enjoy."

That was the last time any of us ever saw her.

She drove off in David's van with her friend Barbara Lang, taking the cats to the vet. On her way there, on the main street in Novato, one of the cats jumped into her lap, scratching her. She leaned down to take the cat off her lap and veered into the opposite lane, where she was hit by a school bus and killed instantly.

I watched a part of David die that day. He was a strong guy, no doubt about it, but Christine's death was too traumatic for him. When she died, a piece of him was gone. She'd been one of his muses—more than that. He loved her much more than he admitted. He wondered aloud what the universe was doing to him. And he went off the rails; he was never the same again.

After that tragedy, we somehow continued to make *Déjà Vu,* but David often wound up in tears in the studio. Drugs helped him mourn—or so he thought—but, of course, they only made things worse. He was inconsolable, falling apart. The love and sunshine that was in the first Crosby, Stills & Nash album had disappeared from *Déjà Vu* because, in one way or another, we were all tormented, all miserable, all coked out of our minds. David had lost Christine, Stephen had broken up with Judy Collins, and my relationship with Joan was deteriorating. Neil was also having problems with his wife, Susan. Sometime during these sessions, I remember going to Neil's house in Topanga. I had given him a straight-on portrait I'd taken of him that looked like it was printed on canvas. His wife had posted it on a bulletin board next to the refrigerator—attached with two thumbtacks straight through the eyes. When I saw that, I knew something drastic was going on in that house. So we were all struggling with romance, confused that the universe suddenly wasn't going right, which is why *Déjà Vu* is so much darker than the first record.

Ahmet knew what kind of shape we were in, and he definitely disapproved. He wondered about the longevity of this band, and I think he felt he'd made a mistake by recommending Neil in the first place. The tensions between Neil and Stephen were becoming more obvious, reverting to those games they used to play in Buffalo Springfield. Stephen doesn't play on "Country Girl," and the only reason he's playing on "Helpless" is because we recorded it at

Heider's. We were all irritated with each other to some extent. I had hoped the sessions would at least be pleasant, but it was turning into a fucking nightmare.

We were losing it, that was for sure. Even the technical stuff was starting to come undone. I would do a mix, Crosby would do a mix, both of us would get those songs right. We'd come back to the studio a day later, play back the mixes we'd done—and they would be completely different. Stephen and Bill Halverson would stay up until five in the morning remixing what we'd done, *after* takes had been agreed to and finalized. That happened constantly. And, again, we were snorting too much coke. At one point, I went into the studio, got everybody together to talk things over, but became overwhelmed by what I was going to say—and burst into tears.

"We're fucking losing it," I said, weeping uncontrollably. "It's over. This isn't any fun."

Even though we had great music in the can, it was too much of a struggle. We were battling ourselves. Making the album was turning way too dark. I was twenty-seven years old. I was supposed to be a man, and here I was, crying my eyes out because we were losing it—whatever *it* was. David's reaction was to cry with me. He was still dealing with Christine's death. Very often, I found him sitting against the studio wall, crying. There was nobody to take care of us. Elliot Roberts wasn't around all that much, and Geffen wasn't there at all.

The scene in the studio was all kinds of unstable. A lot of cocaine. A lot of Neil being-in-the-band but not-being-in-the-band. He recorded "Country Girl" in a different studio or at his ranch and brought in the tracks for us to sing on before taking it away for a final mix. He didn't sing or play a note on "Teach Your Children" or "Our House," although he was great with David on "Almost Cut My Hair." He was also great on the live tracks—"Everybody I Love You," "Helpless," and "Woodstock"—but wasn't really a part of the group, which pissed me off big-time. What I suspected from the start.

The amount of cocaine we snorted during those sessions was ridiculous. On "Helpless"—a very slow song and a beautiful piece of work—there were four guys snorting cocaine and yet trying desperately to slow things down. But it was impossible for us to record that song until two in the morning, after the coke had worn off and we'd wound down enough. Meanwhile, we had to get the song down fast before our dealer would come by and replenish our stash.

The Dead and the Airplane were also at Heider's, but in adjacent studios, working on new stuff. I didn't know Jerry Garcia too well, although I knew he was a fine musician, so Crosby suggested I approach him about playing on "Teach Your Children." I had played the song first for Stephen after completing it at the Caravan Lodge Motel. He listened distractedly, then said, "Okay, I've got it, but in all due respect I think this is the way it should go." And he gave it a country arrangement that ultimately turned it into a hit. In any case, I'd heard Jerry had just started playing pedal-steel guitar and asked if he would add a pedal track to my song. After the first take, I said, "Thanks, Jerry, you're done."

"No, no," he protested, "I fucked up that part when we go right into the chorus. Can I do another?"

"Absolutely, do it," I told him, "but I'm never going to use it. The first one was exactly what I wanted."

And, of course, his pedal steel was one of the defining elements in that recording.

About three quarters of the way through the *Déjà Vu* sessions, I cornered Stephen and said, "Our problem with this record is we don't have 'Suite: Judy Blue Eyes.' "

He looked at me as if I were nuts. "I know, man—we did it already."

I said, "No, we don't have what it represented—a kicker, an opening track that stuns you and keeps you glued to the rest. I'm talking about what the 'Suite' did for the first record. We don't have that song!"

David's contributions—"Déjà Vu" and "I Almost Cut My Hair"—weren't the "Suite," and neither were Neil's "Helpless" and "Country Girl." Nor was "Everybody I Love You," which Neil cowrote with

Stephen. I knew "Teach Your Children" and "Our House" were going to be hits, but they were nowhere near the opener we needed to make a bold statement. The same thing with "Woodstock," which rocked out but lacked the necessary grabbing power.

The very next day, Stephen found me outside the Caravan Lodge Motel and said, "Hey, Willy, remember yesterday how you were telling me we didn't have a great opening track? Well, listen to this." And he played "Carry On."

*Get the fuck outta here!*

He'd gone back to his room and whipped out that song. All there, completely intact.

We made a great record of "Carry On," but things were deteriorating much too fast. I was worried about David's emotional state. He was in shock, no doubt about it. He also seemed suicidal, and I feared greatly for his life. He needed a change of scenery, pronto. So David and I made a pact: to drink together around the world. You don't snort coke or smoke dope to forget such a tragedy—that's a drink situation. Courvoisier and Coca-Cola, a horrible drink, but we didn't care; it did the trick. We talked about where we wanted to go, but wherever he chose, whatever he did, I wanted to be with him. And however he got fucked up, I would get fucked up with him. What are friends for?

On October 10, 1969, we flew to New York and stayed at the Chelsea Hotel. I took a picture of David standing in the doorway under a pull-down fire escape. There's a window behind him with a big EXIT sign over it, and I caught Croz staring out, looking worse than miserable. I knew for sure at that point, he was contemplating not being here.

From there, on October 14, we took off to London and the go-go music scene that was nearing its peak. We didn't give a shit what kind of music we heard, though. We didn't go to clubs to hear bands. We went to get fucked up and to pick up women. Anything to distract us from Christine's death. I was sticking by my friend, still worried for his life.

But a two-week binge had to be enough to distract Croz. Besides, we owed it to the rest of the guys to get back to Heider's and finish the album. There were also a number of dates to play interspersed on the schedule: Detroit, Chicago, Cleveland, Pittsburgh, Sacramento, Phoenix, San Antonio, Salt Lake City, Denver, we hit all of those places in just under a month, all arena shows, wall-to-wall kids.

John Sebastian opened our show in Honolulu on November 22, the anniversary of the assassination of JFK, and it was unfortunately marked by the death of a female fan who fell from the balcony of the HIC Arena. The gulf between Joan and me was getting wider by the moment. I believe that "Big Yellow Taxi" and her song "River" were both started during this tense time. "Big Yellow Taxi" was really one of the first "environmental" songs, becoming a worldwide hit.

The weirdest date was on December 6 at the Altamont Speedway in Northern California. We got a bad vibe from the moment we arrived. Electronic music blared over the PA that was loud, obnoxious, and irritating as hell. That put us in an itchy and distracted mood. More than two hundred thousand people were packed onto that track, most of them ripped on amphetamines and LSD. The Hells Angels were drunk and unruly. It was an ugly scene, and unpredictable.

The only reason we did Altamont was because Jerry Garcia had called Croz and prevailed on their friendship. But by the time we got there, the Dead had refused to go on after Marty Balin, lead singer of the Jefferson Airplane, got punched in the head. That left it to Santana, the Airplane, the Flying Burrito Brothers, the Stones, and us to keep a lid on that crowd. Woodstock had been our gig. Altamont was Mick's gig, and we were cool with that. The Stones were headlining; we'd be long gone by the time they went on.

Our set went down smoothly and was incident-free, but Stephen was freaked out from the moment we went onstage. He took the temperature of that crowd and sensed the danger in the air. Later, he said he feared that some nut was going to try to shoot Mick, which distracted him from the get-go. And, of course, during the Stones' set a fan was fatally stabbed by a Hells Angel *a short distance from the front of the stage,* which more or less signaled the end of the Woodstock era. The minute we finished, we grabbed our guitars and took off for the helicopter at a dead run. We were out of that scene before the applause died down. We flew down to LA and appeared that night at UCLA's Pauley Pavilion, where Stephen fainted from exhaustion.

WE FINISHED *DÉJÀ VU* BEFORE THE END OF 1969. The last week in December, the album was mixed at Heider's in LA and San Francisco, and the four of us said our good-byes. We were glad to get away from one another. We needed space—not just from each other, but from the business, from the music, from Elliot and Geffen, from being CSNY. We left, although briefly, and planned, individually, to scatter throughout the world. Stephen was set to do a "reverse Nash," moving to England, where he'd purchased a 350-year-old Tudor manor house on a twenty-acre estate that had belonged to Ringo Starr and, before him, Peter Sellers, and Spencer Tracy and Katharine Hepburn. Neil was headed out on tour with Crazy Horse, while David and I planned to resume our debauch.

As always, however, there were dates to play before escape plans could be put into effect. We had a short tour in Europe, with Joni. That wasn't as strange or as awkward as it sounds. She and I managed to remain friends, even though my heart had been broken. I've always been able to compartmentalize, emotionally as well as professionally. The only time I remember it turning weird was in Copenhagen on January 11. A few days earlier, we did a show in Stockholm and, as usual, we engaged our audience in a brisk repartee. The fans considered us a political band. Every chance we got, we rapped about politics onstage with a gentle anti-American slant, especially when it came to the Vietnam War and the myth behind the Kennedy assassination. It upset Joan. The next day, I sensed there was something wrong. We were in our hotel when I asked her what was up.

"You keep slagging America after it gave you all this opportunity," she said. "Why are you biting the hand that feeds you?"

Like us, Joni was opposed to Nixon and the war, but she didn't think it was fair to throw hand grenades from the side of the stage. We argued, and she ended up pouring a bowl of cornflakes and milk over my head. I was stunned—to say nothing of being pissed.

There was a maid in the room. I turned to her and said, "Would you kindly leave?" Then I put Joni over my knee and I spanked her.

Needless to say, it was one of the more interesting moments in our relationship.

WHEN WE GOT back to the States, Croz said, "Hey, Willy, my boat's in Fort Lauderdale. We should head down there."

Sure thing, I was game. David was a different person when he was on the *Mayan*. He's an expert sailor, loves the high seas. As captain, he had certain responsibilities that would distract him from feeling so impenetrably blue. Sailing would give him something to occupy his thoughts rather than obsessing about Christine day and night. He had tortured himself for months over her death. "Could I? Should I? Would I?"—all the questions one asks oneself. He needed to process Christine's death, and to deal with it in terms of his own responsibility. And he needed to let go. He *had* to let it go.

Honestly, I was expecting a weekend getaway. We'd go to Florida, have dinner, spend the night in a hotel, and then go out the next day for a light, breezy sail. Not a chance. David had other ideas. He was going from Fort Lauderdale to San Francisco. Three thousand miles, seven weeks on a boat.

"Okay." *Aw fuck!*

We took our time provisioning the *Mayan*. Lots of food and water were stowed on board. A steady supply of weed and a bottomless reserve of coke. And a crew that rivaled the one on *Gilligan's Island:* Leo Makota and Steve Cohen from the CSNY road crew, singer-songwriter Ronee Blakley and her boyfriend John Haberlin, our friends Bobby and Gay Ingram from Coconut Grove, and Anita Treash, a friend from Big Sur who paired up with Crosby. I certainly wasn't going to be of any use. I'm English. I knew about Francis Drake, but in no way was I anything resembling a sailor. Of course, David and I both had our guitars, with grand intentions to write songs galore on the open sea. And Joni planned to come down for part of the trip, so there was going to be plenty of music in the air.

Once we boarded the *Mayan,* David's ghosts were tamed. He was transformed on that boat. All the pain and anguish began melting away as he slipped into the role of an emotionally healthy person. Captain Croz. Man, he was in his element, pulling up sails and coiling the ropes, navigating through treacherous shoals. He needed to deal with the ocean every minute of the day, never knowing if it would do something he didn't expect. It could turn nasty at any moment. A storm could come in suddenly, with forty-foot waves, and you're like a cork floating on the ocean. Amazingly enough, we didn't have any lifeboats, but I trusted Croz. He was as confident and comfortable with the boat as he was with his guitar and music. He put everything he had into it. It was heartening to see him come around like that, taking the edge off a perilous couple of months. The *Mayan* saved David's ass, no doubt about it.

We left Fort Lauderdale on January 23, 1970, and sailed through the Windward Passage, between Cuba and Haiti. It was fabulous weather, warm and sunny. We all had our watch, which was four-hour stretches. David always took the dawn and the sunset watches, more salve for his weary soul. In the Caribbean, we sailed over to Jamaica, which is when things started getting wild.

The Jamaican authorities didn't like the long-haired hippies with this beautiful boat. Something about it felt wrong to them. They assumed we were running drugs from Jamaica back to Miami. Croz told them, "Hey, man, we don't need to smuggle weed. We're rich rock stars." But that didn't wash. So when we docked in Kingston, we were kept on board while the police confiscated our passports. I started arguing with a Jamaican cop. "That passport's the property of the Queen of England. Don't you know *blah, blah, blah . . .*" I got fucking righteous. Silly shit, in retrospect. A team of eight men—five from customs, two from immigration, and a cop—searched the boat thoroughly, in the hold, everywhere. They never found anything, because our stash was in a milk carton in the refrigerator. I'm not sure where David had stored the firearms, a couple pistols and a few rifles that were kept in a guitar case, but they missed those, too. Shit, man, this was Jamaica, where they've got some of the best pot in the world. Why were they looking for our stash?

Eventually they realized who we were. A police check reported our identities as famous rock 'n' rollers, so after a week they returned our passports and sent us on our way with no apologies. Of course, their suspicions weren't *totally* wrong.

As we sailed toward the Panama Canal, my sea legs kicked in. David taught me a lot of basic boating knowledge, which sails did what, from bow to stern. He said, "Notice how the wind is coming from such-and-such direction. You need to pull up a staysail so that it will catch the wind and take us in *that* direction." And I have to admit that I enjoyed it. It was an incredibly different feeling. I started acting and doing as I thought sailors did, like carving a whale on a piece of wood in scrimshaw fashion.

There were incredibly peaceful nights, great sunsets, the ladies cooking dinner, the lobster and fish we just caught, and the dope we were smoking and the music we were making. *Idyllic!* And incredibly therapeutic. We sang every day. Nothing like it in my lifetime.

Joni met us just outside of Panama, and that altered the dynamic. I knew she was coming, and it was anything but pleasant. Some kind of argument broke out, with Joan yelling that I hated all women. Coming from anyone else, I would have dismissed such an irrational remark, but from her I had to think about it, and it hurt, for sure. In the end it was nothing more than a way to strike out at me. She really knew how to get to me. She had come to Panama to have a nice sail with David and me, but things had turned too ugly between us. It got pretty tense. So she decided to leave us and fly back to LA. I must confess that I was somewhat relieved.

Moving through the Panama Canal was a thrilling experience. It was banked on either side by a lush rain forest, with parrots and monkeys swinging through the trees. At the western end of the canal, David went ashore to arrange for Joni's flight home. Some drunken asshole in a bar started giving him grief about hippies, and wondering why David wasn't in Vietnam, defending his country. He hated that guys who looked like us had this beautiful boat. Turns out the guy was the FBI's head of security at the docks. So he intended to stick us with a lot of regulations that would normally be forgiven. This guy pissed David off so much that Croz said, "I wish that fucker would drop dead." Be careful what you wish for. The next day, when David went back to pay our fuel bill, we learned the guy had had a heart attack during the night and was dead.

Talk about bad juju. Nothing like a curse to spook the shit out of us. Fortunately, Croz had scored some Panamanian Red while ashore, which took the edge off the news as we sailed up the west coast of Central America and Mexico, trying to recapture the previous spirit of the trip. We were off the coast of Guatemala, on Crosby's watch, when suddenly he cried out, "Willy! Holy fuck! *Look at that!*" I squinted to see where he was pointing, and there was a whale. It was the biggest animal I'd ever seen *in my life.* Now, we were still smoking a lot of dope, so who knows? But I could swear it was at least one and a half times the size of the *Mayan,* maybe a hundred feet long, with a blowhole the size of a table. And *blue*—a rare, near-extinct blue whale. The sound it made when it took a breath made my heart stop. Then a *whoooosh,* with steam spewing out. Dolphins played off its nose, making it all the more surreal. Another day I saw a bird, two or three feet tall, standing on the ocean. "Hey, Croz," I said, "how is that possible?" Now, we were pretty fucked up, but not all that trashed. As we came around, I realized the bird was standing on the back of a giant sea turtle.

Anyway, after we saw the whale I started writing "Wind on the Water." It's not so much a song about a blue whale as it is a portrait of Crosby. At the time, he was taking a lot of heat from critics; he was an easy target. *"Over the years you have been hunted, by the men who threw harpoons . . . "* It was David I was talking about in that first verse. *"Over the years you swam the ocean, following feelings of your own . . . "* Later, I segued into the issue about the shoddy treatment of whales, how they were slaughtered to make lipstick and eye shadow, but the song served a dual purpose. I also wrote "Southbound Train," "Frozen Smiles," and "Man in the Mirror" during the voyage. And I wasn't alone in my productivity. David wrote "Where I Will Be," an incredibly sad song, and "Whole Cloth." The songs were dark, because our lives were dark.

It was a long journey, past Costa Rica and Honduras. Coming up the coast was an unusually hard slog, and we were battered by waves seemingly the size of skyscrapers. At one point, when we got caught in a storm, I watched David physically pick up the anchor, which must have weighed 250 pounds, and throw it overboard to keep us from drifting toward a giant rock face. That saved our ass. I had to trust Croz with my life, literally. We had taken that hairy route because the only other option was to go from Panama all the way out to Hawaii, in order to catch a wind that would blow us to San Francisco. But *Déjà Vu* was about to be released, and we knew we needed to get back into the business end of things. Otherwise, no one would be around to promote the record. I'm sure Geffen and Elliot and Ahmet were freaking out. So we decided to power right through.

From Cabo San Lucas it was all upwind, so the boat ran on power, motoring the last leg of the trip. The wind was in our faces all afternoon long as we hit it head-on, pushing to get home. Just outside San Diego, we ran out of fuel and tacked up into San Diego Harbor. David delighted in cutting off the engine and sailing into port, dropping the sails, knowing how the inertia would steer the boat so that we pulled up to the dock slowly, perfectly. We were pretty full of ourselves. We had brought the *Mayan* three thousand miles without a scratch. As we prepared to tie up to the dock, another boat full of blind-drunk newspaper people with hookers on board rammed into the *Mayan* and ripped out the bowsprit. *We'd come all that fucking way!* It's a good thing our guns were stowed, out of Croz's reach. Man, they scattered like rats off that boat. Luckily, we'd been in the process of filing our papers with customs and immigration, so the feds witnessed the entire incident and ID'd the culprits, making them pay up.

Everything was different when we hit dry land. At home, things between me and Joni were still fragile and tense. During the sessions and touring for the *Déjà Vu* period, she'd recoiled from all of the cross-pollination with the four of us, getting too sucked into our scene. Our last fight in Panama hadn't helped. It began to disturb her that her life and career were so intertwined with ours. She just needed a break from everything. Immediately.

A week or two later, while I was busy laying a new floor in Joan's kitchen, a telegram arrived from her, from Matala, Crete. It said: IF YOU HOLD SAND TOO TIGHTLY IN YOUR HAND, IT WILL RUN THROUGH YOUR FINGERS. LOVE, JOAN. And I knew at that point it was truly over between us.

I was brokenhearted. Joan had affected me on a very deep level. She had every quality I found attractive in women—amplified to the tenth degree. She was not an ordinary woman, but rather complicated and philosophical, a musical genius, a great lover, and a wonderful companion. With Joni, it went deeper and wider and higher—and consequently lower. I sank into an impenetrable gloom.

I decided to move out of the Laurel Canyon house as fast as I could. I didn't have much there, just a few things in the closet. I didn't want to be there when Joni got back from Greece. What was I going to say? What could I do—try and convince her to reconsider where we were at? No, it was over, and I wanted out.

My San Francisco house wasn't ready for occupancy, so I checked in to one of the bungalows at the Chateau Marmont, a prestigious showbiz hotel at the foot of the Hollywood Hills, where some incredibly wild scenes were always under way. I kept to myself for the most part, trying to nurse my broken heart. I had to deal with it, and my way of making sense of the situation was to write—so I knocked out three songs: "Simple Man," "I Used to Be a King," and "Stranger's Room."

After I got that telegram from Joan, and knowing that she thought I might want to hold her down if we married, I tried to say what was really in my heart.

> *I just want to hold you*
> *I don't want to hold you down.*
> *I hear what you're saying, and you're spinning my head*
>     *around,*
> *and I can't make it alone.*

I came up with those lines first and put them together using the idea that my approach to love—and life, in general—is a simple one. I wasn't the same kind of deep thinker that Joan was. Even though I'd spent years educating myself about photography, politics, beat poetry, art in general, and, well, the world at large, when you scratch the surface I'm a pretty simple man. It's most obvious in my music. Simple constructions seem to have a powerful impact. The band always laughs because any song of mine can be learned by them in thirty seconds flat. I don't use complicated chords or intricate word patterns. I couldn't possibly write things like "Guinevere" or "Déjà Vu." "Our House," for example, is a very simple concept. So the verses of "Simple Man" evolved from who I was, and what I was feeling.

> *I am a simple man, so I sing a simple song.*
> *I've never been so much in love and never hurt so bad*
> *at the same time.*

In "I Used to Be a King," King Midas (in reverse) was the king I used to be, where everything he touches is supposed to turn to gold but doesn't. Yeah, I know, it's somewhat self-pitying, but that's where I was at. At least three songs came out of the breakup blues.

There was really no place for me to settle in at that point. During the *Déjà Vu* sessions I'd lived variously at the Chateau Marmont and the Caravan Lodge Motel, and before that at Joni's in Laurel Canyon. A battalion of workers overseen by Leo Makota and Harry Harris were still in the throes of tearing my house in the Haight apart. But with few viable options, I moved in, living in a sleeping bag on one of the floors. I also needed wheels, a way to get around. The whole time I was with Joan, I never had a car. She was my full-time ride in LA. So Croz and I went to a Mercedes showroom in San Francisco, where I had my eye on a posh new model, the 6.3 liter.

David walked around a blue one on display while I looked over an identical car in maroon. Two scruffy long-haired hippies ogling a gleaming Mercedes—you gotta know the salesman wasn't particularly thrilled. The vibe I was getting from him was: Don't even *touch* that fucking car. So I walked right over to this pencil dick and said, "I think my friend is buying the blue one—and you can wrap this baby up for me right now."

David was feeling better; he was ready to rock. The music and the *Mayan* had literally saved his life. I wanted to rush right into the studio and start cutting a Crosby-Nash album. It's not that we decided we could do without Neil and Stephen. From the get-go, we designed Crosby, Stills, Nash & Young to be a mothership, where we could all come together, make music that would keep the ship afloat, and then branch out and play with anyone we wanted. To this day, we operate much the same way. So we knew that we didn't have to ask Stephen and Neil if we could make a record. Besides, Stephen was in England recording a solo album, and Neil was recording tracks for *After the Gold Rush*. Frankly, I was glad the two of them weren't around. I'd just been through a couple of weeks of binge drinking and a seven-week sail with David. I didn't care much about Stephen and Neil at that point. Croz and I were both in great shape, tan and trim, clear-eyed, all those good things. We were closer than ever. We had the songs, as well as the love and trust of each other. Working together just made good sense.

Before we could get started, however, *Déjà Vu* was released on March 23, 1970, although "released" is a bit of an understatement. It exploded out of the box, with two million advance orders. Promoters immediately jumped on the CSNY bandwagon. A tour was proposed that was every bit as immense as the market for the LP seemed to be. We'd be performing at arenas, with huge advances. And we'd be self-contained, not leaving anything to chance, which meant carrying our own PA system, speakers, monitors, microphones, the works. It was ambitious as hell, and wildly lucrative. All four of us were ready to rock.

Stephen came back from England, ostensibly to sing on *After the Gold Rush,* but also to edge back into the fold. Living abroad had done a real number on him. He'd jammed with Jimi Hendrix and Eric Clapton. He'd played on Ringo's single "It Don't Come Easy." And he'd done twenty-five sessions in twenty-seven days, working on his own album, on which he played an incredible variety of instruments. So his ego was the size of Uranus—and, no, the pun is not unintentional. He was also pushing the limits of cocaine madness.

Driving to rehearsal one afternoon, he was distracted by the sight of a cop in his rearview mirror and veered into a parked car, fracturing his wrist. So, suddenly, the tour was on hiatus while Stephen took most of April off to recuperate in Hawaii.

Then, in May, a real-life drama threw us a wild curve. I can't remember where I was when I first heard about the students shot by National Guardsmen at Kent State in Ohio, but I know damn well where Neil and David were. They'd been hanging out together in a cabin in Pescadero, in Northern California, that was owned by Steve Cohen, the guy who did our lights. The two of them went out for a drive through Butano Canyon, smoking a fat one and grooving on the redwood trees. In the meantime, Steve Cohen had been to the market for groceries and came back waving a magazine with John Filo's legendary image of the girl kneeling over the body of a dead fellow student. Croz looked at it with mounting dread before handing the magazine to Neil, who grabbed a guitar, walked out into the woods, and came back a half hour later with a stunning new song, "Ohio." He didn't modify or polish it. The final song was what came right out of him. Croz immediately called me and said, "We need to be in the studio right now."

"What is this all about?" I asked him.

"It's a song we've got to cut immediately," he insisted. "Round up the guys and book us into Record Plant. Neil and I will get down there right away."

The next night CSNY were in Studio Three, with Bill Halverson poised at the controls. We cut "Ohio" very quickly but also needed something appropriate for the B-side. Eventually, we decided on "Find the Cost of Freedom." Recording it was an amazing moment in our career. We sat on four chairs facing each other in a square, doubled the voices, and had a master track finished in less than a half hour.

Coincidentally, Ahmet Ertegun happened to be in Los Angeles. He was in the studio that night right after we'd finished recording, and understood what we were doing as soon as he heard playback.

"Listen, man, we want it out now," we told him. "This is too big a deal. The country has started shooting its own children. Things have spun out of control."

"But you've got 'Teach Your Children' going to number one," he said.

"Pull it!" I told him.

He was incredulous. "Graham, you're going to have a *number one hit*!"

"I don't care. Pull it."

Very few record guys would have honored that request. But Ahmet was an extraordinary cat. He took the tape with him, caught the red-eye back to New York, and personally pushed it through the machinery, getting it out in two weeks' time. The single went out with a cover of the Bill of Rights (an unused mockup had four bullet holes through it).

Needless to say, I'm goddamn proud of that record. It was us at our best, as troubadours carrying the news, being town criers, saying, "It's twelve o'clock and all is not well."

NOR WAS ALL WELL within our own little circle. The feeling between us after *Déjà Vu* wasn't exactly what I'd call lovey-dovey. We had a really meaty tour that was set to roll out in May 1970, but there was all kinds of friction brewing within the group.

Our bass player, Greg Reeves, had been leaning on us heavily to give him a solo spot in the show so he could showcase a number of songs that he'd written. I was completely opposed on many levels. Mainly, I thought Greg's songs just weren't good enough. It had taken me fifteen years as a writer to reach the point where my stuff really shone. CSNY agreed to sing any song if it was great, but not just because our bass player demanded it. And then there was his attitude: Greg refused to take no for an answer. He got weird about it, bent out of shape. So a few days before our first gig in Denver, we decided it was time to part ways with Greg. As luck would have it, Stephen had worked in London with a Jamaican cat named Fuzzy Samuels, who flew to LA, stepped right into Greg's role, and learned our entire set in no time.

But Stephen and Neil weren't helping matters much. They were slipping into a phase I called "Stephen and Neil: the Dark Side," and it was affecting the equanimity of the group. Neil was growing pissed at Stephen's overindulgence with cocaine. Things boiled over during our opening gig in Denver. Stephen had hurt his leg riding a horse in San Diego and hobbled onstage using crutches and a cane. Personally, I thought he was a little over the top, because he hadn't been that badly injured. And Neil concluded he was doing it for sympathy rather than need. We played a couple of songs at sound-check and they were fucking horrible. David and I were hoarse from back-to-back rehearsals. Stephen had done too much coke and was fucking up, so Neil put his guitar down and left the stage. During the show itself, things got worse. The electric part of our set was ragged as hell. And Stephen was showboating, making it seem like a Stephen Stills concert, with David, Neil, and me as his backup. He was just *dominating* us—or at least trying to. He was so overbearing. And Dallas's drumming fed right into it. Toward the end of the concert, Neil walked off in the middle of a song and refused to come back for the encore.

"I've had it with Dallas," he said backstage after the gig. "He's fucking up my songs on purpose. Either he goes—or I go."

Neil's sense of rhythm is incredibly simple, but Dallas wasn't that kind of a drummer. He often played fills, which were distracting. Neil absolutely hated them. Plus, Dallas was Stephen's guy. They hung together, did drugs together, got up at four in the morning to go into the studio together. When Neil looked at Dallas he saw Stephen as well, and a double dose at this point was lethal medicine.

Things reached a head the next day in Chicago. Once again, we did a soundcheck that was just awful. Afterward, David, Neil, and I huddled and agreed we couldn't go on like this.

Neil said, "Not only do I not like Dallas—and he's gone, that's for fucking sure—but I don't like Stephen right now, either. I can't play with him when he's this out of it."

Neil and Stephen are both great musicians, but when Stephen's out of it he's not the great musician he should be. Neil wasn't taking that many drugs. He liked to snort occasionally and smoke a nice joint, but by no stretch of the imagination could you have called him out of it. So after soundcheck, the three of us fired Dallas, called off the tour, and left Chicago on the first plane out. We didn't even tell Stephen, who had wandered off by himself. He came back for the show—and there's no fucking show! We were gone.

We were completely pissed at him, and he wasn't in any kind of state to hear that. What can you do with someone who's blasted out of his skull? You can't start discussing details with him. Meanwhile, we weren't relating to each other on a rational level. There was too much head butting and dick measuring, too many strong individuals insisting they were right. All those dates and commitments—it never made any difference to us. We lost a fortune by blowing off a $7 million tour. Elliot and Geffen had to fix it with the promoters by rebooking the tour, but they couldn't fix our internal struggles.

Back in LA, we immediately began rehearsals with a new drummer, Johnny Barbata, who'd played with the Turtles and had been at my London apartment when I'd played *Sgt. Pepper's* for them. He fit right in. We set up in a sound stage on the Warner Bros. studio lot where they'd recently filmed *They Shoot Horses, Don't They?*, about marathon dancers. I remember looking at the sign over the stage door that said HOW LONG WILL THEY LAST? and thinking, "How appropriate." The way things were in LA, you could never predict who might turn up. In the middle of one of our songs, the stage door slid open and Bill Cosby came in with a bullwhip. He started cracking it around us, shouting, "C'mon, you fuckers, get to work!" *Ke-raaaack!* "Get rehearsing!" *Ke-raaaack!* And Laura Nyro showed up to check us out. In many ways, she reminded me of Joni. There was a piano on the stage, and when she started playing "Eli's Coming," you just shut the hell up and experienced it for what it was.

Somehow, we regrouped in June for a five-night stand at the Fillmore East in New York City. Stephen was in better shape, though no less humble. This time, we were prepared to go on. We were well rehearsed, getting along reasonably well, and writing new material that really cooked. Neil, especially, was in top form. A few weeks earlier, when I hadn't been feeling as charitable toward him, he'd cornered me and said, "Hey, Willy, listen to this, man." *Old man lying by the side of the road / with the lorries rolling by* . . . On top of that, he'd also just written the incendiary "Southern Man." Holy shit, I thought, what a prodigious talent. Songs like those are the very essence of who Neil Young is.

I had put the finishing touches on "Simple Man" and decided to preview it at the Fillmore on opening night. Before we went on, word came backstage that Joni was in the audience. Obviously she had good seats, close to the front, which made it that much more emotional for me. It was hard to get really personal when I knew she was sitting right there. I can still remember playing the song that night, walking onstage in a dark-green velvet vest with a carnation in the buttonhole. I was feeling entirely exposed, even though no one in the auditorium knew that Joni and I had broken up. While I'd never gotten the chance to talk to Joan about it, the song allowed me to say what was in my heart.

We also performed "Man in the Mirror," which I had written on the *Mayan* as we sailed past Cuba; acoustic versions of Neil's "Down by the River" and "Cinnamon Girl"; Stephen's Buffalo Springfield standout "Bluebird" as well as his new songs, "Black Queen" and "Love the One You're With"; and, of course, "Ohio," which had just hit the airwaves. An interesting moment for both the audience and me was my rendition of "King Midas in Reverse," which was the only time I'd ever attempted a Hollies song in a CSNY concert.

During the Wednesday night show, word drifted back that Dylan was in the audience—which is when things began to get dicey. I did my solo, then Croz and Neil did theirs. But because Bob was there, Stephen did *three* solos, and that pissed us all off, me in particular. I confronted him as he came off the stage. "We're supposed to be in a fucking band," I said. "We all have plenty of songs we want to sing. C'mon, man, what the fuck!" The whole time I was giving Stephen a piece of my mind, he was standing there with a can of Budweiser in his hand, getting angrier and angrier because I was busting his balls. As I talked, he stood there, crushing the can of beer, which foamed all over his hand and onto the floor of our dressing room.

Somehow things cooled down a bit and we played the rest of the show, but afterward the audience refused to leave. We'd delivered, and they wanted more. It was crazy, they just kept cheering in their seats. So we hit the dressing room, relaxing and smoking dope.

Roughly twenty minutes later, they were still there, going crazy, which is when Bill Graham slipped a note under our door. It said: "Your audience awaits you." We'd done our three-hour show, with two or three encores. We had very little left in the tank.

"We're not coming out, no matter how much you pay us," Neil told Bill. The next thing we knew, a hundred-dollar bill came sliding under the door. As soon as Neil saw that, he shouted, "Not enough!" Seven more hundred-dollar bills came sliding through at regular intervals. We were all laughing our asses off about it. Neil scooped those bills up and we went out to do another encore.

On the way to the stage, I had to talk Neil out of throwing the money into the audience. I knew if he did it, it would start a riot. I reminded him of how the first night I came to New York, someone had been murdered on the subway for a quarter. "You throw hundred-dollar bills out there—man, we're dead!"

I don't know what happened to the eight hundred dollars. Maybe Neil pocketed it. I don't remember seeing my share of it, anyway. But the audience got their money's worth, that was for sure.

No doubt about it, we had recovered our form. The band really cooked, we were loose and spontaneous, in exceptional voice, and our audience soaked up as much as they could get. Those audiences really loved what we were doing: not only the music, but our political raps. We were determined to engage our fans in meaningful dialogue from the stage. We railed against the war—all wars—Nixon, police brutality, environmental pollution, racial inequality, overpopulation, and politicians in general. We did a lot of amazing music in that short stretch and decided to release the best of it on a live album, *4 Way Street*. We were making an astounding $50,000 a night. Sitting at the top of the charts. Even with all that, we couldn't save ourselves from self-destruction.

As the dates tumbled on—through Providence, Philadelphia, Detroit, Portland, Oakland, LA, St. Louis, Chicago, and Minneapolis—the delicate CSNY fabric got even more frayed. The electric portions of our show brought out the best and worst in us, particularly when it came to Stephen and Neil. Their old competitive shit started frothing up onstage. The guitar breaks were like duels. Ideally, those guys should have been inspiring each other, picking up on a riff and playing it right back. Instead they were squaring off, trying to show each other up. Stepping all over each other. Afterward, in the dressing room, we'd almost have to separate them before they lunged at each other, ready to draw blood. It was a huge fucking mess.

It didn't help that we were smoking insane amounts of weed. Fair to say that none of us ever went on without being high and *then* some. Fuzzy Samuels was so freaked out by the gigs, I heard that he took acid every single day of the tour. And we all had our eyes on our own personal shit. I was gathering songs for an upcoming solo album, David was mixing *If I Could Only Remember My Name,* Neil the same for *After the Gold Rush,* with Stephen still working on his eponymous album. It was that last album that eventually sealed our fate.

In July 1970, while I was camped out at the Chateau Marmont, Stephen called and said, "You remember that song of mine, 'Love the One You're With,' that I cut in London? Well, I've brought the track back and we're in Wally Heider's with it. I need voices for the choruses. Any chance you and David would come down? I'm getting a couple of girls I know to sing, too."

Considering this was Stephen and it was his first solo record, we were only too happy to oblige. I happen to love that song. Stephen got the title from Billy Preston, who was playing with the Beatles at the time. They were at Stephen's house in Surrey, hanging with Ringo. Apparently, Stephen spotted some girl and made a comment to Billy about how great she was. Billy responded, "Hey, man, if you can't be with the one you love, love the one you're with." To which Stephen replied, "Excuse me, can I borrow a pen?" In any case, we went to Heider's that night and met the other singers: Rita

Coolidge, her sister Priscilla, who was married to Booker T. Jones, and Claudia Lanier, all incredible voices. Needless to say, I flashed heavily on Rita. She was a startlingly gorgeous creature: part Cherokee Indian, part Southern belle with pigtails, lithe body, incredible in jeans, frills, feathers, exotic, the whole package. And a fantastic singer—smoky voice, really distinctive. All of which hit Stephen the same way as me. He was coming on to Rita all session long, but I beat him to the punch. I invited her to go to a concert with me the next day at five o'clock. Unbeknownst to me, Stephen called her to say I couldn't make it. "Graham's a little sick today," he told her, "but I'll pick you up around three." So she ended up living with Stephen for a couple weeks.

I felt that Rita wasn't where she wanted to be, but where she belonged—for the time being. Stephen was an attractive man, musically and physically. Realistically, I understood what was going on. But I didn't think Rita's heart was in it 100 percent.

Due to the circumstances, Rita was hanging out with CSNY all the time. I saw a lot of her, and we became very attracted to one another. Very. Now, as an Englishman, I consider myself somewhat of a gentleman. There was no way that I was going to put the move on Rita behind Stephen's back. But we fell for each other hard; our mutual attraction was almost unbearable. "You know I want to be with you," I said to Rita, "and I believe you feel the same way. But I can't even kiss you without dealing with Stephen. He's my friend and partner—and he's obviously in love with you."

I had to do the right thing. So I showed up at Shady Oak with Rita and found Stephen in his studio. "I really like this woman," I told him. "I think I like her more than you do, and I think she likes me more than she likes you. So having told you this, I'm going to be with her."

What transpired was one of those moments when no one said a word—and then Stephen spit at me. Although he missed, this was hardly going the way I'd hoped, so I made a beeline for my car. Rita followed closely on my heels. She just grabbed what few clothes she had in a closet and left along with me. That same day, I moved out of the Chateau and into her house in Beachwood Canyon.

Needless to say, Stephen and I didn't speak for a while. I'm not so sure that he's forgiven me to this day, even though I tried to handle it the best I could. If someone steals your girl—although to me it didn't go down that way—you're bound to hold a monster grudge. I'm sure Stephen has his own version of what went down, but in the end, it put another strain on things between us.

Living with Rita was a sweet little interlude, the perfect antidote to my crazy lifestyle. She was a straight shooter, very quiet, not gregarious at all. She had a very religious upbringing; her father was a preacher and her mother was a community organizer who raised Rita to be a thoughtful, considerate person. Rita understood what had happened to Joni and me. I was still greatly affected by the end of that affair. Rita was incredibly sensitive to my feelings and made things easy for me, especially with the vibe she'd established in the house. We had the upper floor of a two-family structure. Downstairs, her friend Annie shared a flat with two songwriters who were pretty good, so there was a lot of music in that place coming from the top and bottom floors. I was busy writing material for my solo album, *Songs for Beginners,* and Rita was writing, too; she was always on the piano. That woman could play: She played it way better than I did. In fact, she wrote the famous coda—the piano bit—to the end of "Layla." Jimmy Gordon got the credit for it, but it was actually all Rita's.

I wrote a batch of songs at Rita's house: "Better Days," for what we experienced during that time, and "Wounded Bird," which was about the aftermath of Stephen's relationship with Judy Collins. Another song, "Military Madness," helped to get a lot of things off my chest. England had been bombed by the Germans, and when I moved to America I realized that the same issues were going on in Vietnam. The battle was raging, and I wanted to say something about the madness of the military agenda waging preemptive war—which is what happened later in Iraq and Afghanistan. I also finished "Chicago," which stemmed from an incident following the Democratic Convention in 1968. The Chicago Eight had been busted for disrupting the event and desperately needed money for their defense. Hugh Romney, the beat poet and alter ego of Wavy Gravy and my hero, called to ask if CSNY would come to Chicago to raise the funds. David and I wanted to go; Stephen and Neil also wanted to, but had other commitments. As a response, I wrote the song to them, asking, *"Won't you please come to Chicago just to sing?"* Later, when I learned that Bobby Seale had been bound and gagged and chained to a chair in the courtroom, once again I was deeply affected. It didn't matter to me whether he was guilty or not. In my book, you don't get to call that a fair trial. So I finished that song with a renewed intensity.

I also wrote "Frozen Smiles" for Stephen, because he was too busy listening to people who filled his nose rather than his heart.

The first show Croz and I ever did as a duo was in Detroit in January 1971. Jane Fonda and Donald Sutherland had been doing a series of shows called "FTA," which was nicknamed the "Fuck the Army" shows. Mac Holbert was the tour manager, and he put me in touch with Jane, who recruited me and Croz to get involved. I traveled by train to Detroit and we managed to raise money to help fund the Winter Soldier Investigation. John Kerry, our present secretary of state, had a certain credibility, being a decorated veteran, and he became an eloquent spokesman for the movement.

My song "Oh! Camil" was written for Scott Camil, another spokesman and a highly decorated vet, who had earned two Purple Hearts, a Combat Action Ribbon, two Presidential Unit Citations, a Good Conduct Medal, a National Defense Service Medal, a Vietnam Service Medal with three stars, a Vietnam Cross of Gallantry with Silver Star, a Vietnam Cross of Gallantry with Palm Leaf, and a Vietnam Campaign Medal during two tours in Vietnam with Charlie Company, First Battalion, First Marines, First Marine Division. Another hero of mine.

He decided that he would have to raise his voice and speak out against what he and his fellow soldiers had been doing, and became a founder of the Vietnam Veterans Against the War organization, after seeing the many atrocities our soldiers had committed against Vietnamese civilians.

I'd been cutting tracks for my solo album for some time and finally had enough good material to give it the requisite weight. I cut most of *Songs for Beginners* in early 1971 at Heider's in LA, which was like old home to me, while producing two other albums at the same time, for my friends Seemon and Marijke, half of the Fool, and for the poet Charles John Quarto. All my supertalented friends turned out to help: Croz and Rita, who played piano and sang all the voices with me on "Simple Man." Phil Lesh, Jerry Garcia, Dave Mason, Dorian Rudnytsky, Johnny Barbata on drums, and Chris Ethridge on bass. Clydie King, Vanetta Fields, Brenda Lee Eager, and Dorothy Morrison sang backup. Most great backup singers know instinctively when—as well as when *not*—to sing; they had it down to a science and managed to turn it into an art.

All told, I was pretty proud of that album. As a writer, I thought I'd come a long way since the Hollies. In the interim, I had learned a lot about myself, and working with these accomplished people taught me a damn sight more. My engagement with what was happening in the world had become more sophisticated, and I felt the confidence to express my political and social opinions. All of it fed the music, and the music fed me, which is right there in the grooves of that solo record.

At this point, CSNY were all caught up in our individual projects. David was involved with the Dead and the Airplane in a mash-up called the Planet Earth Rock and Roll Orchestra, and he was working with Paul Kantner on Jefferson Starship's *Blows Against the Empire.* I had the acid-drenched pleasure of mixing the entire second side, which included "Have You Seen the Stars Tonight." Neil was out on tour and writing material for *Harvest.* And Stephen was up to his eyeballs in a second solo album, cutting it in Miami, presumably as far away from us as he could get.

Our double-record live set, *4 Way Street,* was released in February 1971 to mostly mediocre reviews. None of us was happy with the way it sounded: spontaneous and *authentic,* which meant occasionally out of tune. Stephen had pressed us to fix the mistakes, arguing that the album would still be live as long as it maintained the live *feel.* But Croz and Neil argued for a warts-and-all approach . . . It had to be *pure.* And they won.

Even though it sold millions of copies, the album didn't bode well for our long-term future together. With each of us off in his own little world, rumors were flying all over the place: We weren't talking to each other, it was the end of CSN, the end of CSNY, the end of the innocence, the end. But that's all they were at that point: rumors. Although I knew better. In our hearts, we all did.

CROSBY, STILLS, NASH & YOUNG NEVER DISBANDED. Ever. We fought, splintered, swore vengeance and swore off each other, declared fatwas, placed ancient curses on a member, sabotaged each other, you name it—if there was a way to thwart our collective mission, we've done it, and in spades. But despite all that, to this day we remain a group. That doesn't mean we haven't strayed from the marriage. Oh, baby, have we strayed, and often. Then again, CSNY is the most successful open marriage I've ever encountered. Any one of us was free to work outside the band, either by himself or with other musicians, recording or touring. No questions asked, no permission necessary. However, as CSN or CSNY we contractually owed Atlantic Records a lifetime of product, which more or less guaranteed our dysfunctional marriage.

As 1971 rolled on into summer, and *Songs for Beginners* came out, David and I both wound up living in the San Francisco Bay Area. David was restoring a house in Mill Valley while crashing part-time aboard the *Mayan,* which was docked in Sausalito harbor. I was entrenched in the Haight. My house then was finally habitable. Two hippie friends, Leo Makota and Harry Harris, had gutted the place and rebuilt it. The structure included a sixteen-track studio, a dark room, and a billiards room in the basement. David had his own room there, too—the Crosby Suite—on the second floor, where he kept a lot of his stuff.

Croz and I wound up hanging out a lot, singing together, and working on myriad music projects.

I love singing with David. There's an intimacy between us that's hard to describe, a kind of vocal shorthand, but more than that: something deep and warmer, like a comfortable old leather shoe. It's easier to make music with just the two of us. I understand where he wants to go and I can shadow him insanely well. Croz has a beautiful Welsh voice. I don't know what it is about those singers from Cymru—Tom Jones, Bryn Terfel, Dave Edmunds, Duffy (okay, maybe not Duffy). Maybe it's the coal dust in their voices—who knows? But they have a beautiful tone, a natural vibrato, that resonates like a cello, rich and luxurious. That's David's sound, not mine. I have a north of England voice, very simple and uncomplicated, perhaps with greater range than his, which makes our voices a little bit like oil and vinegar. That combination is not supposed to work, but, you know, if you shake it up, you get great vinaigrette.

In any case, we're very comfortable singing with each other. We don't have to think. We know instinctively that we'll make each other shine. David was a huge fan of the Everly Brothers and the Louvin Brothers, as was I, so we share the same kind of ear where harmony is concerned. But what really makes it work is the trust we have. He can go anywhere he wants with his voice, and I'm *there*. So often, from the way he's breathing before a vocal line, I know just where he's headed. And many times I've sensed him about to sing the wrong words, and I've sung the same wrong words, so the audience can't tell we've made a mistake. On a couple of occasions, we've listened to playback of us singing together, looked at each other, and gone: "Who the fuck is singing that third voice?" When we isolate our voices, there is no third part! Together, the air and wave generation of our voices create a ghost harmonic, a third harmony, that is only sometimes evident when we sing duet.

Voices aside, I just happen to love the guy. He's a really fascinating cat: curious, confident, complicated, imaginative, tasteful, generous, romantic, with a huge heart. He's also reckless, audacious, hotheaded, and cheeky, which are also attractive in their own Crosby ways. Once again, it's the whole package, take it or leave it. I've always been inclined to accept him for who he is.

June 22 was the date that Croz and I started recording what I hoped was going to be a hit single. I'd heard the Tom Rush recording of Joni's song "Urge for Going" and I was excited to begin translating the song to our style. Cass Elliot and Geffen came by for support, and I remember watching Geffen as he put on headphones and looked like he was going to sing to the track we had just cut. I dove quickly over to the tape machine, managed to press the Record button, and captured Geffen in the only recording he's ever made. He was awful, truly dreadful, and I have the tape to prove it.

The next day Cass came by again to introduce me to a beautiful lady friend of hers, but got into a huge argument with Croz about some petty matter. Croz ended up yelling that Cass was a parasite and throwing both women out of the studio. This completely shocked me, not only because he was being so rude to someone we both had loved for so long, but also knowing how important Cass had been in getting Croz together with me in the first place. I was so angry that I went to hide out at Joel Bernstein's place in Topanga Canyon for three days, avoiding even speaking to David. Not a great start for us as a twosome.

But, as usual, all was forgiven. We really did want to sing together and, also as usual, that's what mattered the most. So we agreed to book our first tour as a duo.

Beginning in September, we took our act on the road for a two-month swing, hopscotching merrily around Canada and the United States like two stoned Pied Pipers, doing medium-sized halls.

Our repertoire was a vast songbook of CSN standouts, individual solo tunes, and stuff we just happened to love, which included some of Joni's songs and Beatles favorites, whatever we felt like. If you listen to any of the tapes or bootlegs that are floating around of those shows, it's clear the stripped-down versions of the CSN songs are remarkable for their intimacy and power. We brought a rawness to them that reinterpreted the old standbys, allowing you to hear different emphases and harmonic elements. Another highlight of those shows was the way we interacted in front of a crowd. Turns out Croz and I were natural comedians. Who knew! Our spontaneous, stony dialogue between songs was funny as hell. The audience loved it—and so did we. It provided a nice counterpoint to the intensity of those songs, taking the edge off and giving the shows a laid-back, understated feel.

We opened our tour in Vancouver. Normally crossing the border was routine, but not for me, not at this particular checkpoint. I'd played Vancouver with CSNY in early 1970. At the airport, on our way back to California, we got one of those classic fascist lines: "Show me your papers, please." A few minutes later, a guard began waving us through. "Mr. Young . . . Mr. Crosby . . . Mr. Stills . . . you can go. Mr. Nash—not so fast." So I got left behind. Now, we were pretty famous at this point, and a number of people standing around there recognized me, asking for an autograph. But this asshole gave me the runaround for another half hour while they checked through all my stuff. It was bullshit, and it infuriated me. I don't like being left out, and I especially don't like bullies, so steam was coming out of my ears. I fumed the whole way back to San Francisco. The minute I got to the house I went straight to the piano, carrying a book I'd been reading, *The Silver Locusts* by Ray Bradbury. I just folded the cover back and began writing a song on the pages, trying to express my disgust with people who always want your papers.

> *There I was at the immigration scene*
> *Shining and feeling clean*
> *Could it be a sin?*
> *I got stopped by the immigration man*
> *He says he doesn't know if he can*
> *let me in. Let me in immigration man.*
> *Can I cross the line and pray, I can stay another day . . .*

At the end of October, when we got to New York for our concert at Carnegie Hall, Stephen walked onstage with an acoustic guitar about an hour into the show. This was an interesting development. There was a residual edge, and we both felt it because of what had transpired with Rita. I had been with her for almost a year, and he had to deal with it, making it awkward to be in our presence. I don't think he was in another relationship at the time. I do recall two insanely gorgeous sisters who were staying at Shady Oak and were always naked. Jaw-droppingly beautiful girls. Those girls were incredible playthings. They were available to whomever they fancied fucking. It wasn't like they were with Stephen or Dallas. They were with the *house.* It was a crazy time.

In any case, Stephen played a few CSN songs with us. And the next night, in Boston, we did the same thing—but the three of us were joined by Neil. We did excellent acoustic performances (fortunately recorded) of "Ohio" and "Find the Cost of Freedom." All four of us on one stage, completely unrehearsed. It's hard to explain how enjoyable it was to play with those guys. We launched into it beautifully together, no rehearsal, no set list, no band, no egos, nothing but music. Our four voices in their purest form. So informal and relaxed. Nothing like it. It felt so good that we did it again the next night, when we returned to Carnegie Hall, with more or less the same result, although amazingly we forgot the words to the "Suite" and stumbled hilariously through it. For a while we toyed with releasing a live album from those three shows, but following *4 Way Street,* it wouldn't have made sense.

On October 10, 1971, Croz and I played an acoustic show at the Dorothy Chandler Pavilion in LA. What made it interesting was that Croz had a temperature of 104 and was also suffering from the "Lebanese" flu. His mother was in the audience and he had to be on his best behavior. This concert eventually became the bootleg record *A Very Stony Evening.* Funnily enough this was the very same hall in which I became an American citizen many years later.

The tour behind us, in early November, David and I began recording sessions at Wally Heider's in San Francisco for our first album together. We put together a dream band: Russ Kunkel on drums, Leland Sklar on bass, Danny Kortchmar on guitar, Craig Doerge on piano, and the multifaceted David Lindley, incredible musicians whom we called the Jitters. Every musician longs to play with an outfit like that. It's a true joy working with creative stylists. Once we decided what key the song was in, we left everything up to them. There was no need to tell them what to play; they were innovative and exploratory. Occasionally, we had a preconceived arrangement in our heads, but within that, a certain spontaneity took place, especially in the solos, where we just said, "Fuck it—let them express themselves however they want." Onstage, that makes it fresh every night, and in the studio it creates unexpected energy, offering up all kinds of interesting alternatives. We took advantage of everything that band gave us, and you can hear the result on every track. The album, which was dedicated to "Miss Mitchell" for many reasons, wasn't the all-out commercial success we'd hoped for, but it represented exactly where we were at, which, at the time, was a very agreeable place.

Back in March of 1969, David and I had been in the studio doing some mixing on the first CSN album. David had a nasty habit of taking out a buck knife and cutting little notches in the desk next to the studio board. You could gauge the progress of the album in those little nicks. On this occasion he was doing exactly that when the door flung open and a young, good-looking kid charged inside. Crosby leapt up and pointed the knife at the kid, who boldly grabbed it out of David's hands.

"That's *my* fucking knife," the kid insisted.

I thought, "Wow! Who talks like that to Crosby?" David was a pretty formidable character, and he didn't take shit like that from any skinny, cocky kid.

Croz grinned. "Aw, that's just my friend Jackson Browne."

A couple of years later, I'd been hearing about this guy more and more. Word was all over the LA music scene about what a great songwriter he was. A huge talent in the rough. Plenty of artists had already covered his tunes, and recently he'd been convinced to record his own material. In fact, Geffen had signed him to his label, Asylum Records.

Now, in November of 1971, Joni and I, with David and Joel Bernstein, were driving to Neil's ranch for Thanksgiving dinner with him, his wife, Carrie Snodgress, and Stephen. Croz had that "I just ate a goldfish and you didn't" look on his face. "So what is it?" I asked. "None of you have heard *this,*" he said, and whipped a cassette out of his pocket. "This is the new Jackson Browne record." Joni asked, "Who's Jackson Browne?" Joel and Croz said, in unison, "Only your next boyfriend!" How true indeed. Later, Jackson invited me to sing a high part on his single "Doctor, My Eyes."

THERE WAS A LOT of pressure on us to reunite as CSNY, but throughout 1972 the four of us were too busy working the margins. Stephen was in Europe with his eight-piece band, Manassas; Neil was shooting his first movie, *Journey Through the Past,* and promoting *Harvest,* his follow-up to *After the Gold Rush,* which became the top-selling album of the year. Croz and I were marching from theater to theater, entertaining joyous audiences, as well as ourselves.

One show in particular gave me a rush of significance. We played a benefit, along with Neil, for the Prison Inmates Welfare Fund at the Winterland Ballroom in San Francisco, and I couldn't help flashing on my father's incarceration. All these years later, it remained one of the most affecting events of my life. The memory of it still haunted me. That night, departing from our usual onstage banter, I made a special plea for funds. "The prisoners—they don't want luxury in there," I told the audience. "They just want to be able to live like decent human beings." Later, I said, "A man shouldn't spend four years in there and be exactly the same when he comes out, maybe even less of a human being. He should be able to improve himself . . . C'mon, man, this is the world."

My father had gotten a really shitty deal. He was never the same after he came out of prison, and his death, at forty-six, can be traced to that event. But his business with that camera wasn't the whole story, as I discovered only recently. My father was one of eleven kids, and he had a sister, my Auntie Lily, who later became my Uncle Tony. I loved her/him dearly. But unbeknownst to me, she'd been stealing things all her life and storing them at our house. We had a cupboard under the stairs that was always locked, which was where her swag was stashed. So my father didn't go to jail for the camera, as I thought. He was protecting his sister. He was convicted of receiving stolen goods—not just the camera, but all the stuff they found locked up in our house.

Things aren't always what they appear to be. That wisdom was driven home again and again as circumstances evolved over the next few years.

In the fall, Neil's career took an unexpected tumble. During rehearsals at his ranch for an extended arena tour, he fired guitarist Danny Whitten, who used his paltry fifty-dollar severance to score drugs—and overdosed. Danny's death had a devastating effect on Neil. The rest of that tour was marked by a series of listless, uneven shows, and he called David and me to step in and help. We joined him on the last seventeen shows of the tour.

While the tour was in progress, he issued *Journey Through the Past,* a double-soundtrack album to his film. After four spectacular solo LPs, the album failed to deliver and both it and the film were trashed by the critics.

Stephen also experienced a slide of sorts. Manassas kind of withered away. It was too expensive a band to keep on the road, and the unending tour bled piles of cash. A second album, *Down the Road,* reflected Stephen's condition. It was sloppy, disoriented, not a solid effort. "Things were moving too fast," he told an interviewer about that period. "I got a little crazed. Too much drinkin', too many drugs." We nearly lost Stephen a couple of times. I remember one occasion in particular, at his house in Surrey. He OD'ed that night, and we had to get a doctor there pronto, who pounded on Stephen's heart while Crosby and I anticipated a bad ending. Luckily, we were wrong.

Croz and I were also chasing personal ghosts. David abandoned a reunion tour with his old group, the Byrds, and dealt with resurfacing depression, watching helplessly as his mother, Aliph, died from an agonizing bout with cancer.

All kinds of shit was raining down on us lads. It was time to get together and think it all over.

In the summer of 1973, Neil rented a funky wooden beach house by Mala Wharf in Maui, where the *Mayan* was anchored, which seemed like a lovely place for us to reconvene.

The house Neil rented was rather large, so there was room in there for all of us. Everyone except me brought family with them: David had Debbie Donovan, Neil came with Carrie, Stephen had just gotten married to French chanteuse Veronique Sanson, and Elliot Roberts brought his girlfriend, Gwen, and her two sons along. It was a great place for all of us to hang out. It was within walking distance of the nearest burger joint. Nobody knew we were there, and anyone who did left us alone. Talk about paradise! There were palm trees, sandy beaches, beautiful sun, friendly people. I loved the place from the moment I set foot on it. And for a while, I thought Hawaii would solve all of our problems.

One day, soon after we got there, David said, "We're gonna go diving."

I said, "Who's this *we*, Masked Man? I'm not going diving."

"Why?" he asked.

"Because there's a fucking shark down there with my name on it, and I'm not going in. Screw you! Good-bye."

He gave me some macho shit. "Hey, man, if I can do it, you can do it." Anyway, we smoked a big one and thought about it.

Now, I'm not an ocean guy; I'm English. My fear of sharks came from seeing the movie *Tabu* as a child. When the young kid wants to marry the prince's daughter and doesn't have any money, even when he knows he's got to give the chieftain a dowry, he dives deep into the lagoon to where the giant clam is and steals its pearl—except the giant clam closes over his leg and a shark gets him. Ever since, I've been terrified of sharks. Ironically, Crosby's father was the cinematographer of that film, so I can lay blame directly at David's flippers.

Anyway, my first dive was about 140 feet, no training, completely mad, almost suicidal. There was a submarine off Lahaina that had been decommissioned and sunk to do paint experiments. We went down and swam around and inside it and came up—and I'm still alive. So Crosby's father gave me the fear, and his low-down son took it away.

We all came to Hawaii with tons of songs. There was "Time After Time" and "Carry Me" from Crosby, "Human Highway" from Neil, and "Wind on the Water," "And So It Goes," and "Prison Song" from me. There was definitely an album in that musical bounty. Rehearsals started almost immediately after we got there, seesawing between the deck of the *Mayan* and Neil's house. Plans were to iron out the material before heading back to California, where we'd record at Heider's. The album was going to be called *Human Highway,* after the song Neil had written. Everyone was getting along like a house on fire. Until the last day, when it was time to leave.

I'm still not quite sure what happened—and I'm not sure if anyone exactly knows. The four of us had gathered on the beach in front of the house. It dawned on me that we'd need an album cover, so I grabbed Stephen's Hasselblad, stuck it in the sand, worked out the exposure and framing, walked into the shot, and had my friend Harry Harris snap the shutter, which produced a juicy color portrait that was absolutely fantastic. A cover in one shot! We could hardly believe our luck, but that was as far as our luck would go. Right after that, some business, some cocaine thing, went down, and suddenly we weren't talking to each other. The energy just fell out of the project. We broke up and left Hawaii separately.

This is the kind of shit we put ourselves through. Music, drugs, talent, ego, excess, stubbornness—mix them together and it's a powerful explosive.

One night after rehearsals, Croz and I were at my house in San Francisco, smokin' it, when Croz looked out of the window and saw a guy trying to steal the hubcaps off his Mercedes. Because my bedroom was situated under the eaves, the huge, triangular windows didn't open, so Croz grabbed a handgun out of his bag, hustled downstairs to the front bedroom, and fired at the guy out of the open window to scare him off. Worked like a charm. The guy stopped what he was doing and fled. But David assumed the guy had a getaway car nearby and would come back for it, because you can't very well go running down the street with hubcaps.

Sure enough, not ten minutes had passed before the guy came back to retrieve his car, and David took a few more shots at him, putting one directly in the trunk of the car, just for good measure.

Two days later, I'd returned to Neil's ranch, where we'd resumed CSNY rehearsals for *Human Highway*. That meant my house was empty. But Joel Bernstein, who by this time lived in an apartment next door and had never been told of the earlier shooting incident, noticed a suspicious guy who had pulled over in a VW and seemed to be casing the joint. Joel came over to make sure that the guy knew that the house was occupied, and got the shock of his life when two bullets came screaming in through the window. Obviously, the guy had come back and mistaken Joel for David. And he must have been a pretty good shot, because those shots were close, way too close for comfort.

Crosby always had guns around. Later, he would say it was because of what happened to John Lennon, but he's been fascinated with firearms since he was a kid. And the Manson murders helped fuel his point of view. Those killings occurred in a house owned by Terry Melcher, who had produced the Byrds. Croz had been there often and lived less than a half mile away, which prompted him to add a twelve-gauge shotgun to his arsenal. I grew up in England, where no one, neither police nor criminals, had guns, so to me the gun thing was a pretty bad scene. Personally, I believe that the gun lobby—along with the tobacco lobby, the alcohol lobby, and the pharmaceutical lobby—will be seen as major criminals in years hence. But as far as Croz and CSNY went, it wouldn't be the last time that guns played a role.

That was CSNY in the summer of '73. And it's been a trait of ours repeatedly through our entire existence. Put all of us in a room, and anything could trigger a fatal blast. We were our own worst enemy. What a partnership!

For a while, we kicked around in splintered variations. I actually went on before Neil when he played the Roxy's opening in Los Angeles when Cheech and Chong had to cancel, and Croz and I continued performing as a duo in slightly larger settings. Stephen attempted to jump-start Manassas. Meanwhile, in the fall of 1973 I decided to stretch out on my own, putting together material for another solo album. *Wild Tales* was a good collection of songs but dark and moody, which was where I was at the time. Even the cover was pretty stark; Joel Bernstein's black-and-white shot of me looking intense, forlorn, caught the vibe perfectly. For whatever reason, the public wasn't ready for it. The album never caught fire and Atlantic didn't promote it. The whole affair left me in a deep emotional hole.

Around this time, I was out doing something in Los Angeles with David when we drove back to his boat in Newport Beach. The plan was to spend a nice night having dinner, then go to the *Mayan* and smoke one, enjoying ourselves. David had his stash in the big shoulder bag he always carried. As we pulled into the shipyard, we noticed a convoy of black sedans in the surrounding parking lot.

"Ah, the fuzz, the feds, I can smell them," Croz said. "They must be here to bust me. Maybe I should leave my bag in the trunk. There's a lot of stuff in it."

We both laughed, writing it off to paranoia. So we parked and climbed onto the boat. Simultaneously, a US Customs agent came up the steps from the main cabin and pointed a gun at us. "Stop right there. You're under arrest."

Apparently, someone aboard the *Mayan* had been smoking dope. A person in the next boat had smelled it and called law enforcement. So big deal, they'd found a couple of roaches on the boat, but we hadn't been there in a week or so. The cop didn't want to hear it. He was only interested in making a bust. The way I saw it, he had no right to do that and I gave him an earful, a real bunch of shit. In my English way, I said, "This is not good manners. Why are you treating my friend like this?" I grew outraged at the way he treated Croz like a criminal. In retrospect, he *was* a criminal, but the way it went down wasn't right—and I said so. Why *I* didn't get arrested, I have no idea. But they took David off the boat in handcuffs.

Incredibly, they didn't find David's stash in the shoulder bag. He just casually hung it over a chair and everyone forgot about searching it. Lucky thing, too, because inside the bag was plenty of incriminating evidence. In any case, Elliot Roberts was called and Croz was bailed out, costing him a cool twenty-five grand to a lawyer to avoid a jail sentence.

But the allure of drugs was beginning to take its toll. When Croz and I did our acoustic gig at Carnegie Hall, an incident with dope cost us a powerful ally. For some reason, David didn't want to travel with his stash. Instead, he had given an envelope filled with dope to Reine Stewart, one of the wonderful, beautiful naked women who were always around David. Croz learned that David Geffen was on his way to New York and insisted that Geffen bring it with him before we did the show. Geffen, of course, refused. He didn't do that kind of shit, it was the last thing in the world he'd be involved with. Croz went ballistic. He told Geffen that if he didn't bring the grass to New York, we weren't going on that night, so begrudgingly Geffen relented. He put the envelope in his briefcase, got stopped at LAX, the envelope was found, and Geffen was promptly arrested and taken to jail. On Yom Kippur, of all nights. Even with that,

Geffen managed to make bail and get to New York in time for our concert. He actually showed up at our hotel before we went on, at which point Croz demanded the dope. Geffen couldn't believe his ears. "I was arrested and put in jail!" he explained, completely exasperated. "I don't have it." Croz was apoplectic. "I'm gonna fucking kill you!" he screamed. It was a standoff, but Geffen eventually had the last word. He figured that handling us was a nightmare and promptly ditched us and all his other rock 'n' roll clients, dissolving his management business.

I once again realized the power of drugs and excess.

Another potent drug was CSNY, one whose habit I just couldn't kick. No matter how much bullshit had gone down between us, making music with that gang was too much of a temptation to resist. So when a tour was proposed for the summer of 1974, I was in. We all were, and then some.

The idea was Bill Graham's. He'd already put out feelers to national promoters and convinced Elliot that we could fill arenas and stadiums—about thirty-five of them, in fact—the first tour ever of that magnitude. Nothing under twenty thousand seats, with many topping fifty and eighty thousand strong, and one, the Ontario Motor Speedway, in California, clocking in at two hundred thousand. The Beatles had played Shea Stadium and the Stones had done some isolated big dates, but at that point it was unheard of that a rock band could put that many people in a facility to hear music, night after night, for two and a half months.

Things hadn't ended great between us in Hawaii, but—*so what*? We'd make it work. We knew there was a lot of money to be made. We hadn't been out on the road for a while and all of us had expensive lifestyles. The financial incentive was definitely there. And, in that respect, I have to say we sold out. Generally, we liked to play small venues, where you could see the audience's eyes, gauge their body language to know if they were connecting with you. But that's too difficult with fifty thousand people. So we did it for the money.

Everything was going to be first-class. Travel was in private planes, helicopters, and limousines with police escorts. Hand-embroidered pillowcases in every hotel with Joni's drawing of the four of us silk-screened in five colors on the front. That same logo was burned into teak plates that we used at all the shows. We stayed in huge suites at the best hotels, with the most amazing food every night: sushi, champagne, lobster, caviar, all endless. We had our own guy who supplied each of us with a gram of coke every day. Once, I called my friend Mac and asked, "What happens if you swallow an entire gram, because I think I just took the coke capsule along with my vitamins?" He said, "Don't worry, just watch TV. You'll be fine." Incredible decadence.

The music was another thing altogether. We'd perform our preshow ritual: snort a line and hit the stage. Sometimes we were great, other times we weren't. There were a couple nights we were ragged, out of tune, lethargic. None of us was really on top of his game. There was just too much cocaine around. I don't think that when you're smoking the amount of dope and snorting the amount of coke that we did—and staying up to all hours of the night—that it's possible to be on top of your game. We were out there, constantly stoned—*constantly*—and glad of it. It was madness. We were so incredibly loud that it was difficult to keep pitch. (I'm sure we did major damage to our hearing on that tour.) The monitors weren't great. And it's hard to sing "Guinevere" to tens of thousands of people.

We knew how to shift onto automatic pilot, and there was a certain amount of that taking place. Onstage, Neil stood to one side, Stephen to the other, with Croz and me in the middle, all those hardcore egos colliding like nuclear fusion, but as soon as the lights hit and Stephen kicked off the riff to "Love the One You're With," our opening number, all that flew out the window. It didn't matter how much you despised the guy who didn't want to be part of the band or another guy who is so out of it that it's hard to bring him back. The moment the music started and the lights hit us, everything was okay.

Despite all the craziness, our shows were often incredible: four- or five-hour extravaganzas that didn't end until well after midnight. Joni was part of the festivities, not our opening act—she was too big for that, but she alternated with Jesse Colin Young, the Beach Boys, even the Band occasionally. It was a different combination every night. You'd never know who was going to shine. As far as CSNY went, we all wanted our songs in there, so there was plenty of group and solo stuff. Neil would blow the crowd away with "Pushed It Over the End." He was telling the tale, and he was an angry mother-fucker, really emotional and extra-powerful. David performed "The Lee Shore" and a new song called "Time After Time," during which Stephen would wander out to sing with him, holding his newborn son, Christopher, then do "Word Games," a killer of a tune. I'd do the "Prison Song," sometimes "Chicago" or "Our House." We'd do whatever we felt like on whichever night. I once played a new song that I'd just written for my girlfriend Calli and had to teach the guys the chords, live, right there onstage.

We were good at making everything appear seamless. Onstage, our image was the Four Musketeers. Still, we each had our indi-vidual personas. I'm the guy who tries to keep us all together, care-ful not to isolate any of the parts. Neil needed no hand-holding, he took care of himself. He knew how to do it. But Neil usually followed his muse. If the music wasn't good he checked out early, and you'd feel the hole where his energy should have been. Crosby was also pretty strong on that tour, so I didn't have to worry about giving him a boost. Stephen was my main concern. If Neil was the added fuel that made the locomotive go faster and blow more steam, Stephen was still the driving force in the band. And if he was failing, then we were failing. It all had to do with his delicate approach. He tended to overblow when he got insecure or when he was out of it, in which case the subtleties—those fabulous Stillsian subtleties—would not show up in his touch. So you had to mother Stephen onstage for him to play at his best. During a song, I usually walked over to encourage him, smiling even when he, or any of us, made a mistake. It was important, if that happened, that we laughed and said, "Fuck it. Next song. Who cares? Carry on."

If you looked behind the scenes, there were cracks in the facade. Neil was up to his old isolationist tricks, being in the band, but not a part of the band. He kept his distance every chance he got. He'd turn up for soundchecks but disappear until showtime. He didn't hang, even at some of the ridiculous parties after the concerts. And he showed up for the gigs in mirrored shades. The rest of us usually traveled together, but Neil had his own Winnebago with Carrie and their son, Zeke, a symbol of independence, which had everything but a no-trespassing sign on the door.

Crosby was engaged in his own sexual divertissement. He took two beautiful young women on tour with him: Nancy Brown, a stunning young girl from Great Falls, Montana, and Goldie Locks, from Mill Valley, not as pretty as Nancy but, shall we say, way more adventurous. Those ladies totally took care of David all through that tour. Crosby had *incredible* sexual energy. It got to be such a routine scene in his room. I'd stop by with someone and go, "Aw, fuck, he's getting blown again. Oh, dear, let's give him a minute."

It was a wild, profligate, orgiastic, self-indulgent couple months, loaded with crazy scenes and often wonderful music. On that tour, Neil Young hit a patch of brilliance in his songwriting: "Don't Be Denied," "On the Beach," "Hawaiian Sunrise," he brought all of them to the act, great, great songs, and we did our best to play them all brilliantly, too. Stephen had moments when no one could touch him, not Clapton or Bloomfield or Beck or Santana or anyone in that league. And we all sang our hearts out, the CSNY magic. Those were the highlights that I try to hang on to. Some nights after the show, we celebrated our triumphs. We'd have great parties with strange people all taking the weirdest drugs and eating the best food—all paid for by us, of course. Other nights, the excess would overwhelm. Tensions between us crept up all the time. The petty bickering was so damn debilitating. The ups and downs, the highs and lows, were emotionally unrelenting. For obvious reasons, Crosby took to calling it the Doom Tour.

There were other symptoms that contributed to that name. In Houston, Texas, during a rare day off, I was chatting on the balcony of our hotel with Russ Kunkel, our drummer. We went into the living room of my suite to catch the evening news—Walter Cronkite said: "Singer Mama Cass dies in London." Holy shit! We'd lost Cass. I never saw that one coming. Nor had Russ, who was married to Cass's sister, Leah. It was shocking to both of us—and to learn of it that way was devastating. We were all heartbroken. Words cannot describe it. She'd meant so much to me. I loved that woman in ways I never fully understood or expressed. It seemed unbelievable that she was gone. July 29, 1974. Life hasn't been the same since that date.

Cass's career had been on an upswing of late. She'd had a big hit with "Dream a Little Dream of Me" and was in the midst of headlining a week of sold-out shows at the London Palladium. We were thrilled for her. She was finally getting to do what she'd always wanted: be a cabaret-type star. She had *made* it, at last. But after one show, she went back to Keith Moon's apartment and died. The official story was that she had eaten a sandwich and choked during the night, but that was the same official story we got about Jimi, so it was probably drugs. Ironic that she had been the first to turn me on, and I know there were times she'd done heroin with Crosby. But last I heard, she was doing fine. I'd been pulling for her, my longtime muse.

Afterward, Russ and I went back out on the balcony to commiserate about Cass's death and one of those incredible things that always comes up in my life happened: A giant butterfly flew slowly by. A butterfly, Cass's favorite image. Russ and I both whispered, "Cass!" Spooky how those things occur.

And sometimes our political past caught up with us. No doubt CSNY was branded a political band. We were flamethrowers in the best democratic sense. We'd always intended to be in front of audiences, speaking our minds. We wanted our songs to make people think, and over the years we'd given fans a whole smorgasbord of them: "For What It's Worth," "Long Time Gone," "Chicago," "Military Madness," "Immigration Man," "Ohio," and "Teach Your Children" to a certain extent. All four of us followed the Watergate hearings like a soap opera, outraged that the administration's leaders were lying to the American people and screwing with the Constitution. I think that everybody knew Nixon was somehow involved. And, of course, the famous eighteen-minute gap on the Oval Office tapes—we knew it was a lie, just another cover-up. In response, I wrote "Grave Concern," in which during the guitar break were overdubs of Haldeman, Ehrlichman, and Nixon saying: "I don't recall." "I don't remember." "I wasn't even there." "I'm not a crook."

We'd already fired up the cannons when we went out on tour. As Dylan said, "The battle outside was ragin'." Everyone knew what was going on. So on the evening of August 8, 1974, we were laying it on thick at the Roosevelt Raceway, where fifty or sixty thousand people had come to hear us sing. We'd heard rumblings that Nixon was on the verge of resigning. We had a television backstage so we could watch the proceedings. The four of us were huddled around that set during intermission, when we learned that he had resigned. I went onstage and delivered the news. "Guess what, folks? He's gone!" We didn't have to say who. Everybody knew. Huge cheers erupted through the crowd. *Tin soldiers and Nixon coming / We're finally on our own.* No more. Justice—finally!—and vindication. Time to celebrate. It's the essence of who we are as a band. We didn't let this shit go by. We had to say something.

The mood swings on that tour were dizzying, mad. Through it all, I tried to stay loose and sane the best I could. Ping-Pong became a regular diversion. Mac Holbert, our tour manager, and I would play behind cocaine for five hours at a clip. And Bill Graham would challenge me before every gig. He was a powerful man, ridiculously competitive, but so was I, and often our games would be brutal contests of the will. I had incredible respect for Bill. He was a great character. And I knew his personal story—that his family perished in the concentration camps and how he'd walked halfway around the world to avoid the Germans. He'd built and supported the San Francisco music scene and had a certain amount of integrity—emphasis on *certain*—because his edges were rough when it came to business. He'd scale the house and say, "We have forty thousand people in here tonight" when the place held sixty thousand and we knew damn well every seat was filled. That happened time and again during that tour. I wonder who made out on the missing twenty thousand ticket sales?

When it was over, the entire tour made close to $12 million, but David, Stephen, Neil, and I only got $300,000 each. That left $10.8 million unaccounted for, by my arithmetic. Where did all that money go? Plenty of people took their cuts off the top, plus any side deals they had going, while we picked up the tab for all the decadence. We were having too much fun at the time to take notice, but it caught up with us later on.

It could have been the perfect situation that all bands dream of: four great musicians at the top of their game, playing to adoring audiences in sold-out arenas across the country. But it wasn't, because we fell for the rock 'n' roll bullshit in a big way. We fucked it up. Crosby was right: the Doom Tour, indeed.

A FTER THE FINAL SHOW AT WEMBLEY STADIUM IT WAS obvious to me that relationships were being reshaped, as were the dynamics within the group. Neil invited me and my girlfriend Calli, Joel Bernstein, Leslie Morris, Sandy Mazzeo, and Ranger Dave (David Cline) to head out on the road with him, with no real destination in mind. Neil's mode of transport was his newly acquired 1934 Rolls-Royce, which he immediately named "Wembley."

Our first stop was the coastal town of Southend-on-Sea. We were all so pleased to be out of the chaos and frustrations of the tour that it was easy to fall into a familiar pattern: We smoked a lot of hash and hung out, deep into our own creative proclivities. Leslie and Calli and I were drawing, Joel was photographing the moments, and Sandy and David were making sure we were all taken care of (including Wembley). We were very comfortable in each other's company and I remember watching Neil write the first draft of a new song, "Daughters," in the oddly named Boston Hotel. The cover of my first book of photographs, *Eye to Eye*, was taken in a photo booth in the arcade in town.

After a few days, all of us (with Wembley in the hold) flew across the North Sea to Rotterdam and then drove through the cold driving rain to Amsterdam, where we settled in at the equally oddly named Memphis Hotel. During our stay there Neil wrote "Deep Forbidden Lake" and "Vacancy." It was fascinating to me to watch his creative process. I learned much about just being open and spontaneous

Playing my Fender Stratocaster during a CSNY show in Norfolk, Virginia, August 17, 1974 (© *Joel Bernstein*)

while writing. I must confess that I never felt closer to Neil than I did on that road trip. I got a further glimpse into just how complicated a human being he is, and I also realized how much I admired and respected him.

Neil continued to write, on a typewriter, as he and Sandy had done throughout the tour, about all that was happening. Calli and I and our friend Constant Meijers visited Constant's painter friends Karel and Mathilde Willink. That visit definitely started me thinking again about painting, and my inner thought processes helping to wipe out all the negative feelings about what had happened in the last few months.

When Calli and I returned from Europe, Stephen, Croz, Neil, and I reconvened in my living room in San Francisco to discuss the possibility of resuming the *Human Highway* album that we'd abandoned a year and a half ago. Crazy, eh? Yeah, I thought so too. But we decided to record in my small home studio in the basement. Man, it was crowded but functional. Things didn't go so well, however. Neil walked out on us rather quickly. Something was not right with him but we didn't know what it was. It shocked the three of us that once again things seemed to be falling apart before we even got going. I was feeling down and Stephen wasn't doing much better. After Neil left, Stephen asked me to put a vocal on a song of his, "My Angel." He was pretty out of it at the time, and he wanted me to sing a minor set of changes through a major chord, but my body refused to do it. I came to the chorus and I couldn't get it. It didn't work. *I just couldn't do it,* which didn't satisfy Stephen. He insisted I try again. I got so pissed at him that I just quit, and I walked out after many, many tries.

Stephen was so upset that he went to my tape closet and took a razor blade to the master two-track of a demo I'd done with Joel Bernstein on guitar of my song "Wind on the Water," slicing it in half.

I went nuts. All that work—and he'd destroyed it in a fit of rage. I ran up to my bedroom at the top of the house and called down to the CSN tour manager, Mac, in the studio. "You have to throw

Stephen out of the fucking house!" I insisted. It put Mac in a precarious position, because he was a key part of the glue that was supposed to hold the unit together. In the meantime, I was incensed, getting crazier and crazier. I had just mixed that tape and now the master was gone. When you fuck with a master tape, it is fucking with the gods. Calli got me to lie down and listen to some calming music. The track she put on was Bob Dylan's "Idiot Wind." Not so calming, really, but it helped to bring me out of my funk. I didn't speak to Stephen for months after that.

If CSNY was on a downward slope, as Croz and I felt it was, we were determined not to follow. We loved singing together and enjoyed each other's company. There was never any bullshit between us, no competition. We're only competitive in wanting the best from each other. Okay, he was doing way too much cocaine, more than was good for any three human beings, but then so was I. We were a matched set of bookends. But it was clear that we wanted to make music together. We had plenty of songs left over from the aborted *Human Highway* album. So Croz and I had a record to make.

Our former business manager Jerry Rubinstein had become president of ABC Records and offered us a two-album deal. We felt Jerry would take care of us. Ahmet would, too, but we'd been with Ahmet for six years and he wasn't the force at Atlantic that he used to be. Plus, David and I wanted to separate ourselves from everything that had to do with CSNY, including our record company. So we signed with ABC.

David and I sifted through our material. He had "Carry Me," one of my favorite of his songs. I had "Wind on the Water," and I was writing like a crazy person. "Take the Money and Run" was, of course, a paean to our well-padded tour partners. And there was always something to write about Joni. When we were still a couple, I'd spent some time with her in British Columbia, where she had a little stone house on a beach. It was a place where she was indeed bouncing off boulders and running on the rocks, so I wrote "Mama Lion" to capture that snapshot.

In the midst of this creativity, I got invited to a birthday party for David Geffen in Beverly Hills. It was an incredibly swank, borderline decadent affair: lots of chicly dressed people, a lavish array of food. I took a good look around and flashed on an upcoming benefit I was doing in support of Cesar Chavez's boycott of the lettuce and grape industries. At that time, I had a hundred-acre parcel of land just north of Santa Cruz, from which I could see the *braceros* working in the fields. The bosses prohibited them from using long hoes, because you could rest on them. Not cool. I had also driven with Leo to the food store of the *compissanos* in Delano, and there was nothing in it aside from a few cans of beans. So I went straight home from Geffen's party, with the juxtaposition of those two worlds in mind, and finished "Field Worker" the very same night.

I also wrote "Cowboy of Dreams" around that time. David and I had given Neil a present of two black swans for the lake on his ranch. I don't know where we got them, but they were stunning creatures—and they were immediately eaten by coyotes. Those are the birds in that song. But there were other messages woven throughout. Crosby and I have been influenced by those announcement boards outside churches that include inspirational sayings on them. On one, Croz had seen: "If you smile at me I will understand, because that is something everyone does everywhere in the same language," which David used for "Wooden Ships." I spotted one that said something about coming together as a nation, which became incorporated into "Cowboy of Dreams." But the song was also my take on Neil, about how insane it was to be so wary of this man and so attracted to his music at the same time. He scared me because I could never count on him. Once, when I was playing "Cowboy" for my friend Larry Johnson, we talked about the relevance of a key line: *And I'm tired of the heartache and scenes / with the cowboy of my dreams.* He said, "Tired? Aren't you really scared of this shit?" So I changed it to: *And I'm scared of the heartache and scenes . . .*

Making the album *Wind on the Water* was a pleasure from start to finish. It was one of our finest efforts. David was in excellent session shape and the band were consummate pros, the Jitters again. You work with guys like that, the sky's the limit. It's amazing what they contribute to the creative process. They played right there in the same room with us, so it was like mimicking a live performance. We all fed off each other. The energy it created was inspiring. One afternoon, at Village Recorders in Westwood, we cut four masters in the same session: "Margarita," "Wind on the Water," "Carry Me," and "Mama Lion." Very little overdubbing, maybe on a couple of the choruses, but the lead vocals were pretty pure. Four *masters* in one day—in our world that's unheard of.

Plenty of friends rallied to the cause. Carole King came by to help out on a couple songs, playing organ on "Bittersweet," and we recorded several things of hers—"I'll See You in the Spring" and "I'd Like to Know You Better," both of which are still in the can. James Taylor played acoustic guitar and sang on "Wind on the Water," and Jackson Browne provided backup vocals on "Love Work Out." And we repaid favors for years by singing on James's recording of "Mexico"; "Breakaway" for Art Garfunkel; "You Turn Me On, I'm a Radio" and "Free Man in Paris" for Joni; "All the Pretty Little Ponies" for Kenny Loggins; "Every Woman" for Dave Mason; Elton John's "Cage the Songbird"; and Gary Wright's "Love Awake Inside." Most of our friends were making great music, and we seldom turned people down. If the song was great, David and I loved singing backup vocals. We were good at it. It was in our genes. And in the years that followed, we sang together on "Another Day in Paradise" for Phil Collins, Bonnie Raitt's "Cry on My Shoulder," Michael Hedges's "Spring Buds," "She's Becoming Gold" for Marc Cohn, "These Old Walls" for Jimmy Webb, and Carole King's recent live version of "You've Got a Friend." And in 2012 we sang with John Mayer on "Born and Raised," and most recently, we sang with Jason Mraz on Jimi Hendrix's "Angel" for an acoustic album of Jimi's songs.

▲▲▲

WHILE WE WERE making *Wind on the Water*, David and I shared a bungalow at the Chateau Marmont, the same bungalow in which John Belushi later died. Arthur Garfunkel lived right next door. The Chateau happened to be a wonderful place to live. You never knew who was going to be at the pool, which star would appear when the elevator doors opened. One day, I got on the elevator with no less of a legend than Groucho Marx. I was paralyzed. Couldn't say a word, not even "Good morning, Mr. Marx." The Chateau was one of those places. It let people be who they wanted to be. It's the place where rock 'n' rollers went when life wasn't treating them so well, which is where I felt I was at the moment. Sure, I was making an album with a guy I considered my very best friend. But my life, for the most part, was unending chaos. I was thirty-three years old, constantly on the go, living here, there, and everywhere, in a dysfunctional relationship with Mr. Stills and Mr. Young, and doing way too much cocaine. Living at the Chateau brought this all into focus, and truth be told, all of it, including the drug use, had begun to feel old.

David and I tried to make the best of our arrangement. We concentrated on the music we were making, keeping the Chateau's distractions at bay while coordinating our crazy-quilt schedules. David ate earlier than I did. He's a breakfast person, and I'm not. Breakfast, for me, comes around noon. So I would walk over to Schwab's drugstore on Sunset Boulevard, where one of the Bowery Boys—Huntz Hall—ate every day. One day, I slipped into a booth there with Leslie Morris, who had once worked for Elliot Roberts but was handling our affairs. Sitting at a table adjacent to us was a very lovely, interesting-looking woman, whose beauty and energy captured my attention. She was a blond beauty, wearing a pale-blue sweater, and she had an incredible light in her eyes. Naturally, I wanted to talk to her. She was sitting with a coke dealer named Skip who I didn't know, but Leslie did. One wave of her hand and I had an immediate in.

The woman's name was Susan Sennett, and she fascinated me

from our introduction. She was an actress, one of the two "college girls" who moved into Ozzie and Harriet's house after David and Ricky had moved out, in a TV show called *Ozzie's Girls*. I laid the usual rock 'n' roll number on her: "I'm a musician, we're making an album and staying at the Chateau." She was completely unimpressed; it didn't mean a thing to her. She didn't have a clue who either CSNY or I was. This made her even more intriguing, so I invited her to visit us at the Chateau the next day. Because I wanted her—desperately.

Skip smiled through it all. He saw the whole thing going down, but couldn't derail it. Nothing could. I was determined.

I spent most of that night trying to figure out how to make myself a little more attractive to this woman. At Schwab's, she had explained that she'd just been to an Asilomar conference on self-exploration, on the Monterey Peninsula. Aha! Now I knew what to do. I'll get up in a tree, I thought. (Don't even attempt to follow this reasoning.) So fifteen minutes before she was supposed to show up, I climbed into a tree outside our bungalow at the Chateau. It was quite fascinating up there, overlooking Hollywood. It reminded me of the peace I'd found in the tree in Ordsall Park all those many years ago. I'd smoked it heavily and was feeling pretty good about everything. And, believe it or not, this stunt actually worked. I could feel that she was attracted to me as soon as she arrived. The next day, I invited her to a session at Village Recorders, to show her what I do. Afterward, she said, "Would you like to come home with me?" Are you kidding? I was already packed.

She had a kind of energy about her that I'd never experienced. I loved that kind of woman, provocative and complex, but Susan was something else. She was very complete, self-possessed, and alluring. On one of our first dates, we were driving down Sunset Boulevard in her '69 convertible Karmann Ghia that she owns to this day. I spotted a hooker on the corner who was stunning, a knockout. As we drove past, I was checking her out, but being as discreet as possible to avoid being noticed. Susan slammed on the brakes and pulled to the curb.

"Don't you *ever* not look at a beautiful woman if you're with me!" she fumed.

I was stunned. She already had my heart, but that flat-out floored me. No woman had ever been confident enough to say that before—to allow me to be me, whoever the fuck I am. *She just wanted to hold me / she didn't want to hold me down.* As a result, I became serious about love. I'd been in love with Joan, but that wasn't the same. I *adored* Joan. I *loved* and became *bonded* to Susan. Susan is without doubt the love of my life.

Crosby liked Susan from the start. He went with me to check her out at a little store she owned with her mother, Ginger, called Babes in the Woods. It was an eclectic boutique, candles, women's clothing, costume jewelry, those sorts of things. Her grandmother had been W. C. Fields's secretary for fourteen years, so they were selling his personal phone book, a leather cosh, his will, and a police badge he used when he was caught speeding, all of which I bought. Afterward, we got Susan and her mother insanely high on hash oil, and that appealed to Croz, who liked anyone game for a new drug experience. Boy, was I infatuated with Susan Sennett!

Meanwhile, back at the Chateau, some of David's psychosis had to do with his unresolved love for and loss of Christine, and a lot of it had to do with his current domestic situation. David was in an intractable scene at home. He was alternately living with two women—Debbie Donovan, now mother of their daughter, Donovan, and Nancy Brown—in an arrangement that put the squeeze on him. Both women were in love with him, and each was getting increasingly possessive.

In his way, David loved Debbie—and in his way, he didn't. They were good friends. She was motherly toward him. She took care of him, everything from washing his clothes to lovemaking to giving him advice. And she had been Christine's best friend. He knew her long before he knew me. But while we were making *Wind on the Water,* he'd started to disconnect from Debbie, and he was racked with guilt, which triggered more drugs.

Coke, in large doses, makes you suspicious. It's supposed to make you feel fantastic, on top of the world, daring, invincible, but in excess, as with any drug, it turns to the other side. Croz was having trouble sleeping at the time; it's difficult to sleep behind massive doses of cocaine. During this period, a prowler invaded his Mill Valley home. David routinely kept a loaded Colt .45 on his night table, and if he hadn't been awake enough at the time to roll over, grab his gun, and fire it, he and Debbie would most likely be dead. On another occasion, he picked a fight with a garage attendant at the Chateau and ended it by sticking his gun in the guy's ribs. That is the kind of behavior he was exhibiting then.

All this behavior came at the wrong time, because *Wind on the Water* proved a critical and popular success. The album was finally released in September 1975, catching fire right out of the box. It got tons of airplay, a tsunami of buzz. David and I and the entire band with whom we made the record went on the road as the record climbed steadily up the charts.

Even though David and I were coked to the eyeballs, we managed to kick ass on that tour. It was an excellent scene, in every respect. We were both in great voice and enjoyed working together. There was no competition, no egos interfering with the act. No bullshit, no weird trips. The energy we put out was incredibly focused. This time, we were also in a better financial situation. Because of the '74 tour fiasco, from which we'd netted only a fraction of the gross, we fired our manager, Elliot Roberts, who was Neil's man to begin with and never entirely in our corner. Everything he did was always colored by how it would affect Neil's career—and God bless him for that: To this day, he remains Neil's man. But we needed someone looking out for our best interests, and Elliot was definitely not that guy. Instead we hired his assistant, Leslie Morris. She took over everything for us—management, publishing, recording schedules, the works—and hired new accountants and lawyers. Out with the old, in with the new. In our fragile way, we were on the right track.

That tour took us right across America, and in December we wound up performing in Japan. Our performances were mostly acoustic—David and I on two guitars, with Craig Doerge on keyboards and David Lindley playing anything with strings, with Joel Bernstein on guitar occasionally as well. The musicians were there to gently amplify what we were doing. Croz's and my songs shone in that kind of intimate setting. We believed that if you couldn't play a tune on an acoustic guitar and move someone's heart, it was a useless song.

Working there was a little unsettling. Each time we came to the end of a song, the audience applauded wildly—and then *stopped,* as though someone had flipped a switch. Followed by *silence,* like a vacuum. It unnerved me, until I realized it was an act of politeness, and even then it took some getting used to.

Once, during our soundcheck at the Budokan in Tokyo, an accident occurred that reconfigured our shows. Our four Martin guitars always sat on stands at the side of the stage, and when David Lindley launched into an extended violin solo called "Reel of the Hanged Man," his playing caused all of the guitars to resonate on the same note; they were shaking and buzzing like crazy. Instead of stopping, Lindley played right along with them, expertly altering the melody of his riff. Needless to say, it floored us. We already knew the guy was a brilliant musician, but this was a display of extreme virtuosity. It became a regular part of the show, and he could make the fillings fall out of your teeth the way he accompanied himself with those phantom guitars.

Another aspect of those shows was the way our focus changed. A few weeks earlier, Jackson Browne had introduced David and me to a man named Tom Campbell, who runs the Guacamole Fund, a not-for-profit foundation that deals with relevant social issues: antinuke, environmental, energy, and wildlife stuff. We had dinner in my bungalow at the Chateau Marmont to discuss how our appearances could benefit his efforts and people in general. Jackson had been doing benefits from the moment he started performing. His dedication to the human condition is staggering and inspiring. I wanted to do my share. In the course of this dinner, I learned that Jacques Cousteau was coming to town. He was in the States trying to figure out how to get the *Calypso* down to the Amazon. I was a huge fan of Jacques's and I wanted to meet him, so Tom arranged a get-together at a restaurant in LA, along with Linda Ronstadt, another admirer of Monsieur Cousteau.

In the course of our discussions, I asked Jacques what he thought was the biggest problem facing humanity. Admittedly, I was expecting some standard fish answer: how we're fucking up the oceans (which we are) or the near extinction of whales (which we are doing little to contain). But without batting an eye, he said, "Nuclear police." That took me by complete surprise. He explained that he foresaw a time in the not too distant future when federal authorities would be able to enter your house without a warrant to discover whether you had any nuclear material. With help from Tom Campbell, he proceeded to explain how the nuclear power industry resembled a snake: from the head of the snake being all the miners dying from radon poisoning, to the mining of uranium and its transportation, to the enrichment, to the storage of nuclear waste, to the threat of nuclear terrorism, to the dangers of nuclear explosions and the nuclear-war scenario. I must confess, he got my attention, although I'd already had some awareness of this issue. In the 1950s, Bertrand Russell led a famous march from Aldermaston, the seat of Britain's nuclear facilities, to London. I had followed it with great interest. But Jacques and Tom drove home to me how important it was that young people should know what was going on at present, as well as the problems they'd be facing in the future.

Croz and I agreed to make a serious effort to educate our audiences about the world's enduring social ills, particularly the antinuclear and environmental issues. We immediately initiated a process known as tabling—sponsoring tables in the foyers of all the theaters we perform at, where we, through Tom Campbell's auspices, invite local grassroots activist organizations to disseminate information about their ongoing social projects. And we gave the Cousteau Society a table to sign up new members and promote their cause. We've been "tabling" religiously for almost forty years.

Jacques loved the whole theme of *Wind on the Water,* to which Croz had added his a cappella song "Critical Mass" as an introduction. So Mac Holbert and a few of our friends at the Cousteau Society cut together a lovely six-minute film with footage that detailed the absolute beauty of the whales balanced against images of them being harpooned and slaughtered. It played behind us on a screen as we sang the songs and was extremely effective and emotional for everyone involved.

The whole time on the road, Croz and I were writing like mad, and when we got back, at the beginning of 1976, there was enough material for another album, to be called *Whistling Down the Wire.* In order not to lose the momentum, we immediately set to work, getting the songs down in the studio. We also cut a slew of spontaneous tracks with the Jitters—things we just vamped on that will never be released, like a jam called "The Dirty Thirty," a funky blues of Croz's called "Drop Down Mama," and a thing of mine, "Taxi Ride." It was as loose and groovy a session as I'd ever been involved in, just smokin' it and playing. The music was great, creativity was raging, things in general were pretty peaceful.

And then Neil came calling.

I was pretty surprised to hear from him. Last I'd heard, he was in Europe with Crazy Horse and churning out albums, *Tonight's the Night* and *Zuma,* one right after the other. When he stopped by my house it was ostensibly to say hi and catch up with me and Croz. I say "ostensibly" because it's never straight-up with Neil. Same ol' shit: "Hey, Willy, I want to play you something." Out came a cassette with four of Stephen's latest songs, one of which was "Black Coral," and all of which were amazing. Of course, Neil is never going to play you four songs of someone else's if he doesn't have eight songs of his own.

"Aw, man!" I sighed. "Why are you playing me this?"

The long and short of it was that he and Stephen had been holed up in a studio in Miami, working on an album together. They'd already cut about twelve songs. Just the thought of those two working together sent a shiver down my spine, but, as I said, the output sounded incredible.

"Listening to it, though, isn't there something missing?" Neil asked.

Croz spoke right up. "Yeah—*us.*"

Neil continued: "Because I'm heading back to Miami tomorrow, man. You guys want to come?"

Aw, fuck—here we go again. Croz and I put our session on hold. The next morning the three of us were on a plane to Miami.


I KNOW WHAT you're thinking: Didn't we learn a thing or two about four superegos trying to coexist in one studio? Why in heaven's name were we gonna do that again? But it's the music. It's *always* the music. It's like a drug, irresistible. And we're both smart enough—and dumb enough—to recognize that.

There was plenty of music to listen to when we got to Miami. Lots of great songs were already in the can: "Midnight on the Bay," "Human Highway," "Long May You Run," "Ocean Girl," "Black Coral," "Guardian Angel," "Make Love to You"—one right after the next. I was duly impressed. Croz and I barely had time enough to drop our bags before we were propped in front of microphones, putting harmonies on those babies. It was like an assembly line—*bang! bang! bang! bang!* Yeah, we were banging 'em out like the pros we were, with none of the residual bullshit to sidetrack us.

We also knew this: The minute we put the vocals on those songs, it was going to be a CSNY record. David and I were already making

*Whistling Down the Wire,* but we had a few extra tunes that we could contribute to the cause.

For the time being, everything flowed beautifully. We were working at Criteria Studios, which was a great little studio. And we were all staying at the Mutiny Hotel in Fort Lauderdale, an *unbelievable* place. If it was eighteen floors, it seemed like there were seventeen floors of coke dealers. It was one big scoring emporium.

Unfortunately, by mid-May David and I had to get back to LA to finish our new album on time. "We're sorry," I told the others, "but we have studio time booked. We have to go. Let's figure out when to continue this baby."

That's the moment when the shit hit the fan. Stephen insisted we stay and finish their album, and suddenly all the positive energy began to shift. You could feel it just get sucked out of the room. Something else was driving this sucker, and it didn't take us long to learn what it was. Elliot Roberts had a Stills/Young Band tour booked and ready to roll. They *had* to have an album to support the tour and were counting on us to make sure it got done. Hey, too bad. We had just as important a deadline, and we weren't about to scrap it for their tour. Everything would get done in due time.

We only had a few days left in Miami, but things were heading perilously downhill. One morning, I couldn't get any reply from Neil's room. I called the front desk of the Mutiny and said, "Am I out of it? Am I dialing the wrong number?" The receptionist said, "Oh, no—Mr. Young has checked out." *Whaaaaat?* "Yes, Mr. Young checked out earlier this morning."

"Going where?" I asked.

"Back to San Francisco."

We were supposed to be in the studio in four hours. Man, some things never change. It was another case of Neil having had enough—whatever enough was supposed to be—and he'd split without telling anyone.

I went straight back to my room and began writing "Mutiny."

*With the ice man cooling the wind the coastline can't be
    very far,*
*With the shore man rowing behind we'll find our way
    beneath the stars.*
*But the captain sat there and grinned, and he set the sails
    for Shangri-la*
*Mutiny at Sail Boat Bay*

I was disgusted with the whole situation. Just when it seemed
things were rolling along, all the old demons rose up to embrace
us. To make matters worse, when Croz and I went back to LA, with
every intention of returning to Miami, I heard that Neil and Stephen had come up with the brilliant idea to take David's and my vocals off the tracks and turn it into a Stills/Young record. When word
of it got back to us, we totally flipped out. I couldn't believe anyone
would be crass enough to wipe our voices off those tracks, and, if
true, it was disrespectful to us and, much worse, to the music. All
of our good work unheard and wasted. Just completely wrong and
unjustifiable. I swore I would never work with them again.

Admittedly, I got some satisfaction hearing war stories about
the Stills/Young Band's tour. Seems that it was snakebit from the
start. With too little time to rehearse, the band never felt comfortable onstage. A review in the *New York Times* called the show "an
ill-conceived evening," blaming the sound, which was "rough and
overly loud." The tour needed work. Stephen wanted to stick to a
single set list until the band got tight, but that apparently bored
Neil. And eventually, Neil reverted to being Neil. Heading to a gig
in Atlanta, he was traveling in his bus down the highway when the
driver put on his left turn signal to go to the gig. Neil insisted they
go right instead. "But, Neil, the gig is to the left," the driver assured
him. Neil got right in his face. "*I said turn right!*" The next day, at the
gig in Atlanta, Neil just never turned up. Instead he sent everyone
in the band a telegram: FUNNY HOW SOME THINGS THAT START SPON-
TANEOUSLY END THAT WAY. EAT A PEACH. LOVE NEIL. He'd gone home

and left the entire company—the band, roadies, support staff, and promoters—holding the bag.

I felt relieved not to be part of that scene. Instead, David and I tunneled into and completed *Whistling Down the Wire,* which was released in July 1976. It was a softer album than our previous records, without the obvious hit singles, but it showcased where we were at in a fine, effective way. I was extremely happy with it. And our subsequent performances, to support its release, were unusually energetic; we were in a terrific groove. Our onstage work with the Jitters was particularly dynamic. Lots of free-form jams, variations on old standards like "Déjà Vu," and yet still intimate, an informal, personal affair. The show took on new life every night. Great way to work. I was enjoying myself again.

On August 10, before heading off to Europe, we began a three-night gig at the Greek Theatre in LA. It was one of those hot-ticket shows where everybody turned out—people we'd worked with, musicians we admired, friends, lovers, the music-business cognoscenti. I was dreading the possibility that Stephen might show up. At the time, he was really down on his heels. His marriage to Veronique had broken up, his band had disintegrated. The guy was watching his life come apart at the seams. Even so, I didn't want to see him. I was still fuming about the master he'd taken a razor to and his part in wiping our vocals in Miami. Before the show began, I pulled Susan aside and said, "If you see a guy in a football jersey trying to get backstage, keep him the fuck away from me." Stephen was a big-time Colts fan and had taken to living in the team jersey. I didn't want him anywhere near us that night. David and I had earned our moment in the spotlight—it was our night to shine.

But, sure enough, on the third night, Stephen managed to talk his way backstage. During intermission, I caught sight of him in the crowd as he walked toward the stage. It was one of those tense, potentially explosive moments: What happens now? Part of me wanted to turn and make tracks, but he seemed kind of sheepish, out of sorts. I couldn't ignore him. The guy is just too much a part of my life. We'd made too much great music together. So—fuck it. I grabbed him and gave him a hug. And pretty soon Crosby joined the embrace—a threesome, just the way David likes it.

Croz and I went out and finished the show. We ended with "Wooden Ships," took a few bows, and left the stage to thunderous applause. A few minutes later, we wandered back onstage, this time with Stephen in tow, and sang an acoustic version of "Teach Your Children." I hated to admit it, but it felt great singing that way, in a trio, just like that fateful night at Joni's. There's something so magical and irresistible about it. I'm a sucker every time.

Meanwhile, instead of keeping Stills away from me, Susan pulled him aside and invited him back to our place for dinner. Smart woman. She thought he seemed shy and sweet, not the two-headed monster I'd made him out to be. In fact, it was Susan's version of Stephen who showed up that night. He was easygoing, agreeable, the Stephen Stills it was easy to love. We got mightily drunk, talked well into the night, deciding *once again* to put the old group back together. Here it was the summer of 1976, and we hadn't made a record as CSN since 1969. It was time—time to see if it worked, to see if we still had the magic. Just the three of us: Crosby, Stills, and Nash. We were headed into the studio.

God help us one and all.

I N DECEMBER OF 1976, CROZ AND I VISITED STEPHEN in the studio at the Record Plant in Los Angeles. He was recording songs of his like "Run from Tears," "See the Changes," and "Dark Star" with his engineer Michael Braunstein. As usual, David and I weren't just observers, we got right in there and tried to put down several new songs. I'd written "Just a Song Before I Go," "I Watched It All Come Down," "Mutiny," and "Carried Away." David brought "In My Dreams," "Jigsaw," and "Anything at All" to the party. We all decided that maybe we had enough songs together to start a new CSN record. We ran down Stephen's "See the Changes" in our old formation, Crosby, Stills & Nash singing around one mike, and it was *all there.* Everything we knew how to do instinctively coalesced in that inimitable three-part blend. All the pieces fell into place. We decided to move everything—lock, stock, and barrel—to Criteria Studios in Miami. Off we went again.

I knew damn well what Neil brought to the equation, but without him the session had a more collaborative feel. The vocals were easier to negotiate with three. There was none of the tension that prevailed, for better or for worse, none of the gamesmanship that gave CSNY its edge. Sure, there'd be plenty that we'd miss by Neil's absence, but the advantages were stacking up for doing it this way.

The situation in Miami was certainly a bonus. We booked in with a company called Home at Last, two lovely young women who rented out semipalatial, multibedroom homes to bands recording

(© Henry Diltz)

at Criteria so that everyone could stay together. We had a fabulous Spanish-style villa just a short drive from the studio. The women got the groceries, did the cooking, changed the beds, cleaned the house. All we had to do was show up and go to the studio. And that made it a very attractive setup. The studio was also a contributing factor. Criteria was an out-of-the-way outpost for the West Coast music scene, which meant we could work undisturbed. And the guys who worked there constantly—Ronnie and Howie Albert—were great engineers and producers. All the elements were on our side.

Of course, nothing was more powerful than the music we brought with us. Croz's "Shadow Captain" was a monster of a song, lyrical dreamlike poetry set to Craig Doerge's fine music, and "In My Dreams" was another of David's beauties. While his stuff was typically image-laden and descriptive, Stephen's songs were unusually personal and confessional. He was in tip-top shape as a writer, but an emotional mess, and it all came tumbling out in the music. "I Give You Give Blind" and "Run from Tears" are so fucking powerful. And "Dark Star," about his relationship with Joan Baez, was achingly self-revealing.

> *Forgive me if my fantasies might seem a little shopworn*
> *I'm sure you've heard it all before*
> *I wonder what's the right form*
> *Love songs written for you have been going down for years*
> *But to sing what's in my heart seems more honest than the*
> *    tears*

I hadn't heard Stephen operating at this level in some time. He was on top of his game, churning out great rock 'n' roll tracks, gorgeous arrangements, heart-wrenching vocals. And he wasn't drinking, which kept him focused on the music.

I'd also had a run of good luck where songwriting was concerned. A few weeks earlier, I'd been on vacation in Hawaii. Leslie

Morris was with me, and in an effort to score some grass we met up with a dealer named Spider at his house near the beach. This was around one in the afternoon, and I had a four o'clock flight back to Los Angeles. Spider was a cheeky little bastard. He said, "You're supposed to be some big-shot songwriter. I bet you can't write a song before you go."

"Oh, really," I said. "How much?"

"A hundred bucks."

I finished "Just a Song Before I Go" in a little under forty minutes. Turned out to be the biggest hit Crosby, Stills & Nash ever had, on the charts for twenty weeks. The original lyric I'd scribbled on school composition-book paper is currently in the Rock and Roll Hall of Fame.

I also brought "Cathedral" to the session, which I'd begun writing back in 1971, around the time we played the Royal Festival Hall. After that gig, Leo Makota, my road manager, and I decided to drop acid around six in the morning. We hired a 1928 Rolls-Royce and a driver because neither of us had any business being behind a wheel. Two hippies tripping. "Let's go see Stonehenge!"

Back then, you could actually touch the rocks, embrace them, which I did, perhaps excessively so. The site still had an anything-goes policy. And so I lay on the grass, on acid, in the middle of Stonehenge, *for hours* (although maybe it was twenty minutes). It was an incredible trip. My big revelation was that I was as insignificant as a speck of dust in this vast universe of ours. Acid can be good for perspective.

On our way back to London, we stopped in Winchester, first at the Great Hall to see where the fabled Round Table of King Arthur and his knights was kept. Now, I knew that it was probably bogus, more mythical than real, but that myth has tantalized English schoolboys for four hundred years, so I wanted to see it. As I approached the building, there was a man standing in front of me dressed in something resembling a beefeater's outfit, holding a small tray in his hand. On the tray were small horn beakers of water and little squares of bread.

"Here ya go," he said, pushing it toward my face.

Now, I was peaking, so I didn't quite grasp his intention. "What do you mean, 'Here ya go'?" I asked.

He gazed into my eyes and said, "Don't you know it's just okay to *be*?"

On acid, it was the most profound thing that anyone had said to me *in my life*. Don't I know it's just okay to be? All this posing as a rock star, musician, famous hippie, millions of seats, hit records—*it meant nothing*, if you could just *be*.

From there, we took the five-minute walk to Winchester Cathedral. Leo and I made our way to a side chapel with an aboveground grave resting on a huge marble plinth, where one of England's early kings was buried. As we entered the church, the sun had been blocked by clouds, but it eventually appeared, shining through the stained-glass windows, which, on acid, was a mind-blowing effect. I started to walk down the nave toward the cross of Jesus. I was still peaking, and I felt a strange, unworldly presence at my feet. It stopped me in my tracks. I looked down and my legs began wobbling. I was standing on the grave of a soldier who died on my birthday, February 2, but in 1799. I'm not sure if it was real—I was on acid, what did I know from reality? But that's what I *think* I saw, and it became part of my song "Cathedral." I found out later that, in fact, I was not hallucinating. Someone sent me a photo of the actual grave. Go figure.

I wrote the song during the ongoing experience. Afterward, I realized that if I was going to criticize religion, I'd better have every fucking word right. It's a serious song and I wanted to be sure of what I was saying, which is why it took me six years of intermittent work. Obviously, I was writing other songs in the meantime. But I kept coming back to that song, remembering a "cobweb on a face" and a cleaning lady trying to swish it off with a cloth. All those images came floating back to me: *flying in Winchester Cathedral / sunlight pouring through the break of day.* How, walking down the aisle, *expressions on the face of the Savior made me say, "I can't stay."* And feeling like I wanted someone to *open up the gates of the church and let me out of here!*

After we recorded "Cathedral" at the beginning of February 1977, I took a break to visit my mother, who wasn't well. She was never a very healthy woman, suffering from mitral stenosis, the blocking of the mitral valve. In 1953, she had one of the first heart operations in the north of England to try and correct it. To get to her heart, the doctors had to break every rib, lift her left arm up, cut through tissue, poke around and clean out the valve, put the heart back in place, sew her up, and make sure the ribs were in the right place. It was a big operation, easily life-threatening. I remember sitting in French class in Salford Grammar when someone knocked on the window, signaling our teacher, Mr. Chadwick, out. They had a long conversation before Mr. Chadwick walked back into class and said, "Graham"—his face was solemn, and I was sure my mother hadn't made it—"your mother's okay. She made it through." Here it was, nearly twenty-five years later, and she was still grappling with the operation's aftereffects.

While I was there, I took a walk around Manchester and found myself standing on the steps of the Midland Hotel, in the very spot where Allan Clarke and I had waited for the Everly Brothers on April 22, 1960. It was snowing, blustery, a typical north of England day, almost like a Lowry painting. I stood there watching people come and go well into the evening, and goddamned if they didn't look exactly the same as they had when I was a kid. Bundled up in their overcoats, with their red noses and flat, dead stares. I thought, There but for the grace of God. That's me, if I had not had the instinct or made the decision to get out of there. I would have been one of those people hating their fucking lives, pissed off at their bosses, trying to find a bus, breathing toxic air from the industry around Manchester. I felt relieved, thankful that I'd been fortunate enough to enjoy experiences that weren't available to someone like my father. I immediately went to the hotel and wrote "Cold Rain" and finished it on the plane back to Miami.

Crosby often tells people, "If you really want to know about Graham Nash, listen to 'Cold Rain.' That's who he is." When I sing, *Wait a second, don't I know you? / Haven't I seen you somewhere before?* I'm talking about myself. *You seem to be like someone I knew / Yes, he lived here but he left, when he thought that there was more.*

Usually, with my songs, Crosby has heard them in advance of a session. But this time I came to the party with "Just a Song Before I Go," "Cathedral," "Carried Away," and "Cold Rain" without playing them beforehand, so I think they may have impressed him more than hearing dribs and drabs up front. They were four fine pieces of music, if I say so myself. I felt like I'd come a long way since writing "Hey, What's Wrong with Me?" with Clarkie. Working with Stephen and David made me stretch as a writer, trying to be as profound lyrically as I thought their songs were. Writing, I discovered, was basically a muscle that needed exercise. If I'd have been a plumber for thirty years, I'd have been a fantastic plumber.

When I got back to Miami, things started getting weird. No surprise. Our routine was the same: getting up late, having lunch, and recording from five o'clock to four or five in the morning. But drugs started to get in the way. David's drug taking was a full-blown obsession. He and Nancy Brown were not in great shape. In fact, they were both quite a mess, doing an ounce of coke a day. Nancy looked terrible. The drugs were destroying her. She had gone from being an extremely beautiful woman, knocking everybody on their ass, to looking like a witch, with sores covering her body. And it was hard to get David to concentrate. He was getting up later and later, avoiding the sunlight.

Croz had always been able to handle drugs better than anyone I'd ever met, but by the time we got to Miami they'd gotten the better of him. I'm a pretty tolerant man. I'm also pretty private, and what David does with his private life is his business. But it now affected the music and our studio time. We'd head into a session waiting for him to show. "Where's David?" "He's in the bathroom." "Where's David?" "He's doing business." He and Nancy were holed up for hours in their room, not communicating with the rest of us. Fortunately, we were rich enough to have Criteria on hold twenty-four hours a day, so it didn't matter when we went to the studio or when we finished. But in an effort to bring some sort of efficiency to the process, we needed everybody to be awake at roughly the same time. And drugs were definitely interfering with that.

David was deteriorating before my eyes. Like Nancy, he was covered in sores, but he kept telling me it was a staph infection. Because he's an expert on every disease known to man, I believed him. But it wasn't staph. It was a result of massive amounts of cocaine. I heard he'd spent a small fortune on coke that year.

Somehow, we were able to hold everything together in the studio. We scraped those sessions together into a cohesive piece of work. At one point, while we were mixing "Shadow Captain," the assistant engineer looked out the window and noticed a shadowy figure lurking about out. He said, "Hey, there's somebody pissing in the bushes." We wanted to see who it was, so we ran outside to discover—*it's fucking Neil Young!* He's back, and he's pissing in the bushes.

"I was just down here, man, recording in Fort Lauderdale, and thought I'd pop in."

Uh-huh. There was no room for Neil on this album, but we invited him inside to hear what we'd done, and I could tell he was pretty impressed. Still, it was a long way to come just to check out our scene. Even today, I can't tell you what he had in mind. Neil Young is a weird cat. I remember a bunch of us were playing poker in his living room one day. He came in, took a look around, and got so pissed about not knowing half the people there that he *walked out the window.* It was only four feet off the ground, but four feet is a long way to go when you walk out of a window. He kind of stumbled when he landed and continued walking down the path toward his lake. Like I said, Neil is a weird cat, and he's never changed. That's the beauty of it, I suppose.

~~~

DURING THE MIXING of the album, we took a break for a week and sailed to Bimini, in the Bahamas, just to air things out. We rented a boat from a sailing friend of David's, a beautiful vessel: the *William H. Albury,* a schooner like the *Mayan,* but bigger and fancier. Right off the bat we ran aground, but the rest of the trip was an all-out hoot. We got high, went diving, and almost lost Joel Bernstein, who had come along to shoot an album cover. He'd been chasing us around the studio for a couple weeks, trying to frame an image that showed us off at our best. Unfortunately, Croz looked like shit in Miami, but out on the water he'd recovered his glow. The boat was the perfect setting to get a cover shot. Stephen was wearing a knitted cap from the Cousteau Society, David was in a T-shirt, and I had on a dark red top, all three of us trying to look our coolest. Joel pounced. He got a shot of us on deck, looking like serious hippies. "Yeah, I think that's the one," he said. Then, a moment later, we burst out laughing—also a great shot. So the first run of covers depicted the serious side of CSN, and when that sold out we replaced it with the laughing pose.

In spite of everything—or perhaps because of it—the album came together at the very end. There was a lot of last-minute conflict: between David and Stephen, David and me, me and Stephen. The same old shit. But so what! What went on between us was nobody's business. All the public needed to know was: What the fuck does the music sound like? And it was a fine, fine record, one of our best. Called simply *CSN,* it came out in June 1977 to superb reviews and just as superb sales.

Of course, we had to tour to promote the album, but before we left, I married Susan, on May 4, 1977, at the Church of Religious Science on Hollywood Boulevard. I knew then what I know even more now: that she was too rare and beautiful a person not to have in my life. Okay, I'll admit it: I was wildly attracted to her, but Susan meant so much more to me than the physical charge she put out.

She was wisdom, the voice of reason, my emotional anchor. She kept me grounded. I don't know how many times she said about one of my partners: "This guy's a little weird right now, but you've got to be forgiving. Don't fly off the handle. It's not going to get you anywhere." Somehow she enabled me to function in my own crazy way. She understood and supported my idiosyncrasies, how I'm often not there, even when I'm present, off in my own little world. Instinctively, she knew to drive the car when I was daydreaming, spacing out, thinking about songs, looking at images, checking out girls. She loved me enough to let all of that slide. I'd never met anyone like her, then or since.

CROSBY, STILLS & NASH toured all summer and through the fall of 1977, the first time we ever appeared in concert as a trio. It was a turbulent time in the music scene. *Frampton Comes Alive!* dominated the charts and would sell an unheard-of ten million copies. Disco was taking over the pop airwaves: Donna Summer, Gloria Gaynor, and *Saturday Night Fever* (to which, believe it or not, Stephen contributed, laying down those inimitable percussion parts). Reggae was a brand-new force to be reckoned with. Elvis Costello and the Attractions were ushering in new-wave rock, David Bowie was poncing about with glam and Eno. Critics were trying to determine where we fit in. Who, they wondered, would come to our shows? Would the music be fresh, or nostalgia? Were we still relevant?

Crosby, naturally, told them to calm down. "We never worried about coming together because of external forces that we had no control over," he told a journalist. "We've just tried to concentrate on the music and let everything else fall where it may."

I sure as hell wasn't worried. The new album was a smash, and our shows sold out in a matter of hours. Were we still relevant? Are you kidding! Ninety percent of the acts in the world would have killed for the type of demand we were creating. We still attracted our share of heads and hippies, but they were older hippies who brought their kids. College students always seemed to discover us, no matter what era they were at school. And as for the music, old and new, I defy anyone to pack three or four hours with the songs or intensity we were putting out. Stephen seemed more relaxed without Neil hovering over him. As a guitar player, he was a monster. Crosby was in decent enough shape. All three of our voices were as tight as they'd ever been.

Those were some of the most satisfying shows of my career. We kicked ass, big-time. The megavenues—Madison Square Garden in New York and the Forum in LA—were huge successes, with standing ovations before we ever sang a note. Everywhere we went, the crowds were incredible. Those audiences were on their feet from the first note to the last encore, and even when someone yelled out "Where's Neil?"—which occurred like clockwork every night—it failed to put a dent in the all-out rave. Considering the size of those arenas, mostly twenty-thousand seaters, they were pretty intimate affairs. We did a lot of rapping with those audiences, talking about the songs, current affairs, things that were on our minds. It was a special connection we had with our fans, an almost personal rapport that few bands were able to pull off.

Toward the end of summer, before the second leg of the tour, Stephen arranged a visit to the Oval Office for us. Turns out he was a Jimmy Carter fan. He thought Jimmy was "cool." Hey, to each his own. It seemed like a bit of a farce, considering who we were. How many times had we trashed the government from the stage? When you took our politics into account, it's a wonder they'd let us set foot in Washington, let alone the White House. But we had a couple of dear friends who worked there in some capacity, and when the tour rolled into DC, a meeting was set.

Five of us went: Stephen, David, and me, along with another guy and Harlan Goodman, our managers at the time. John had taken a joint with him, and when no one was looking he took a hit by the open window. I was pretty nervous about the whole deal. It was the White House, for God's sake, just a tad out of my comfort zone. And all of a sudden, the president of the United States came striding through the door, holding his hand out to me. Imagine that! I'm the kid from the Salford council estate, and here comes the leader of the free world. You can't make this stuff up. But Jimmy Carter was incredibly friendly. He knew our music and was a big Allman Brothers fan. I couldn't help recalling that great *Saturday Night Live* sketch with Dan Aykroyd as Carter talking someone down from acid. "Just put on some Allman Brothers music. You'll be fine." Of course, his chief interest was in getting us to do a benefit concert for him, which was never going to happen. Trust me on that. Still, it was an experience I'll never forget.

When we went back on the road to play eighteen more shows, something had changed. It's hard, even with some distance, to put my finger on what had taken place, but something had shifted in the chemistry of the band. We weren't communicating the way we had been at the outset of the tour. Individually we'd turned inward, and it became evident onstage. Our voices were still strong, but there was no joy in the delivery. Everything felt forced. We were phoning it in.

This affected me more than the others. I was having such a great time singing with Stephen and Croz. Every night, I couldn't wait to get onstage, to feed off the audience's love and harmonize with my friends. It was the best high I ever got. For the three or four hours we were out there in front of a crowd, there was nothing like it. But the tension between us was palpable. It was insidious, it cut through everything good. After the intermission at one show, I was in tears. David and Stephen came offstage arguing about the length of a chord. It was ridiculous, not even an issue, but they needed some petty grievance to tear into each other. Really! *The length of a fucking chord!* Everything we'd worked so hard to achieve: It was dissolving in front of my eyes. Something in me snapped. I grabbed both of them and put them up against a wall. "Don't you know that you're fucking blowing it here?" I cried. "You guys are arguing about the length of a chord. What the fuck does that matter! We've got twenty thousand people out there waiting for us. For *us*! We've got to go out there and be *good*!"

Another night, in Oakland, in the middle of "The Lee Shore," some glitch in the equipment sparked feedback from Stephen's guitar that cut right into David's searing vocal. Stephen just shrugged, which Croz took the wrong way. He assumed Stephen was stepping on his spot, and that touched off even more tension. Things got really ugly onstage, so much so that the audience could tell.

We all seemed to be at one another's throats, and for no good reason. One night, after a welcome day off, we were hanging out at a hotel bar, just letting it rip, drinking ourselves into oblivion. Everyone was there, the crew, our ol' ladies. We got so shit-faced that around two in the morning Susan and I ripped off our clothes and jumped into the pool, stark naked. Soon everyone followed suit: Stephen, David, the entire gang. There must have been twenty of us in there. It was one big skinny-dip. I don't know who started the singing, but we all chimed in. And that was the incident that broke the tension. It just disappeared, from that night forth. The rest of the tour was a flat-out pleasure.

In an interview that Stephen did with *Crawdaddy,* he managed to nail exactly how we interact. "We make up for each other's stupidities," he told them. And I suppose he was right. The three of us were thorny little fuckers. We'd been together for practically ten years, through our unstable twenties, in the spotlight for all of that time. All three of us were complicated, intense, headstrong, talented, unpredictable—qualities that came with risks. Add money, women, drugs, and alcohol to the mix, it's a wonder we weren't in high-security lockdown. No question, CSN was a rocky marriage. Maybe that's the key, what gave us our edge. Who knows?

I loved Croz and Stephen without question, yet spent many a night swearing off them for good. The older we got, the longer we were together, the more difficult our relationships had become. David's addiction had become precarious and Stephen infuriated me to no end. Whenever I thought things were heading toward a meltdown, something would remind me of their better sides. Like Croz's humor and generosity. He never failed to come through in a pinch. And Stephen—just when I was ready to give up on him for good, he'd deliver something straight from the heart. For instance, in late 1977, after we finished the CSN tour, I needed a vacation from Stephen something fierce. I can't put my finger on any one reason; it was an accumulation of things, the usual bullshit. Susan was pregnant with our first child, and I wanted to be away from, well, our stupidities. I really had to pitch in at home. We were living in Susan's old house, at 1508 Sanborn Avenue in LA, and there were thirty-two cement steps up to the front door. One night, the doorbell rang. It was Stephen Stills. He'd made an entire lamb dinner for two, with potatoes, carrots, mint sauce, the works, handed it over, and left before we could even thank him. And that summed Stephen up in a nutshell. Regardless of how many drugs he's taken or whether he's straight, whether he's crazy as a loon or totally sane, it comes down to the fact that he's a damn good man.

Nevertheless, I wanted to put some distance between us. The tour had worn us down so much that, in January 1978, when we attempted to make a new album at Criteria, the session disintegrated into an unstructured jam. The material felt forced—there weren't enough good songs for an album—and our energy level was pretty low. Some of this could be attributed to me. I was distracted by the birth of my son, Jackson, in February 1978, and wanted to be at home with Susan. And Croz was flirting with his old buddies McGuinn, Clark, and Hillman about the possibility of launching a Byrds reunion.

I was also looking for a more suitable place to live. I was fully committed to raising a family, but not in the middle of that crazy fucking scene. I was also worried about the world's dwindling water supply. When I lived in San Francisco, there were billboards everywhere that said: SAVE WATER—SHOWER WITH A FRIEND, which started me thinking about my relationship to the environment. We were doing a number on the Columbia River, diverting it and turning it into mud. San Franciscans were upset about how they were bailing out Los Angeles: "Why are we sending all our water reserves down to this desert?" So I projected thirty or forty years into the future and decided that water was going to be more precious than oil. If I was going to move my family to a new locale, it needed to have certain criteria: a stable government, an abundant water supply, and places that would accept my credit card.

I knew just the place.

In 1969, Joni and I had gone to Kauai, the westernmost of the Hawaiian Islands, to visit our friend, the folksinger Buffy Sainte-Marie. Later during our stay, I drove from her place in Kappa'i to Hanalei, with its incredible Bali Ha'i scenery, beach, mountains, waterfalls—paradise. Average rainfall at the peak of Mount Waialeale, the extinct volcano that is Kauai, is about 450 inches a year. Needless to say, water was never going to be a problem. I fell for the usual tourist urge: I must buy something here. Then I left and promptly forgot about it, until later, when land there was ten times the price.

In any case, I went back to Kauai with Susan, knowing it might be where I'd eventually settle. We were at the Ebert house on Hanalei Bay, later owned by Michael Crichton. I was getting stoned with the Ebert boys, playing Ping-Pong, and falling in love with the island. In the course of a game, I mentioned that I was interested in buying some land on the island. One of the guys said, "Talk to Jack the Fisherman—talk to Fat Jack."

It took me a while to locate Jack Ewing, a character right out of the movies. Big guy, six feet tall, 280 pounds, just like my dad. He said, "If you're interested in property, I'll see you at eight o'clock in the morning."

"Are you kidding!" I said. "I'm a musician. I haven't been up at eight in the morning unless I was still up from the night before."

"Too bad. I'm a fisherman. Eight o'clock or no deal."

Let me tell you, eight o'clock in the morning was pretty interesting. If you've never seen it before, you ought to give it a try. Once.

Jack showed Susan and me a beautiful acre on the beach, but I didn't want to live close to the ocean. It left me too vulnerable to the elements and to the public. Instead he took us up into the Wainiha Valley, drove a mile in, and . . . it was *spectacular*. There was only a funky little house, just a shack, really, not more than five hundred square feet, no glass in it, just screens. But gently rolling hills, lots of trees, plenty of privacy. Nothing around it as far as the eye could see. Jack got out of the car, whipped a papaya off a tree and sliced it in half, whipped a lemon off another tree, squeezed it on the papaya, and handed it to me. God, what a mouthful! There were dozens of types of fruit on the land, which came to slightly over four pristine acres. I wanted it desperately.

"Is there anybody else interested in this property?" I asked him.

Turns out one of the Beach Boys was in the process of closing a deal for the land with the owner, a champion surfer named Joey Cabell. The offer was for eighty grand down and payments for another 170 grand spread out over a few years.

"How about I give you all $250,000 immediately?" I proposed.

I bought that place within an hour of seeing it. A lot of dough, but the best money I've ever spent.

I immediately brought my family to live in this place. For years, we lived in that tiny shack. The kids slept in the garage on the cement floor. What did they know? It was paradise. They had everything they needed. And we still had the house in San Francisco and Susan's rental on Sanborn, in LA. All three of my kids—the two boys, Jackson and Will, my daughter, Nile—were born at the Sanborn house, where I cut each of their umbilical cords. But they went to school primarily in Hanalei. Later we traded the Sanborn house and the San Francisco house for a home in Encino, where we lived on and off for the next twenty-five years. I had to be in LA, which is where my managers, the musicians, and the studios were, so we wound up splitting our time between Encino and Kauai. But ask any of us Nashes where we live, and all of us will pipe up: Hawaii.

MONTHS WENT BY before I had any contact with my partners. Stephen was off doing what he always did—playing and jamming with the best musicians available. Without David and me, he turned up the juice, veering from harmonies to roots rock, which is where he felt liberated. And Croz was often at sea, on the *Mayan*. For some reason, it became harder to get in touch with him; he was often unavailable when I called, a symptom I found particularly ominous. Our lives were so bound together, inextricably so. "Unavailable," I feared, meant wasted on drugs.

In the meantime, I pursued plenty of personal projects, trying in earnest to be a good husband and father. Things other than music were becoming more important to my life. It was inevitable that I turned my attention elsewhere. My love of photography gave me hours of pleasure. The collection of important images I had amassed was considered museum worthy, with over two thousand photos by Diane Arbus, Edward Steichen, Peter Emerson, Weegee, Manuel Álvarez Bravo, W. Eugene Smith, and Paul Outerbridge, among many others. I was thrilled to be at both ends of the history of photography, from my collection of daguerreotypes to the first digital studio. In 1978, I curated an exhibition of my archives at the University of Santa Clara and published a companion catalogue, *The Graham Nash Collection*. I also became an American citizen.

I loved the States from the moment I set foot in it. At the time, the country made absolute sense to me: land of the free, home of the brave. The people, its customs, the lay of the land: I wanted to become part of it and to make it a part of me. I'll never stop being English—that aspect of me was stamped from the womb. (I still can't go to the beach without turning lobster red.) But the American way of life held such a carefree appeal. Everything about it suited me to a tee.

There were other reasons for my becoming an American citizen. I've always thought of myself as a fair person. Hard as it may be, I try not to be hypocritical. So if I was going to mention how great the people are in the States, while continuing to criticize the government from the stage—as I did with "Chicago" and "Immigration Man," and as Crosby did with "Long Time Gone"—it seemed only just and honorable that I did it as a citizen. I also wanted to vote, to exercise the rights and privileges of everyone else. I owned property in three states. Heaven knows I've paid my share of taxes, so it was time to put my mouth where my money was.

The process was easy. I hired an immigration lawyer out of DC and did all my homework, took and passed the requisite tests. So on August 14, 1978, Crosby's thirty-seventh birthday, I joined fifteen hundred other immigrants in the audience section of the Dorothy Chandler Pavilion in Los Angeles. It was a stage I had played on several times in my life. In fact, Crosby and I had done a famous show there together in 1971, which became a bootleg called *A Very Stony Evening.* Oh, we'd been stoned all right, feeling no pain. But this time, I was extremely nervous. I knew that I had passed, but until the moment when the officiator instructed us to stand and said, "I now pronounce you American citizens," I was sweating it out. And I must confess, when the crowd broke out singing "The Star-Spangled Banner," I was deeply moved. It meant that much to me. I had made it! I let out a deep breath and gave Susan a kiss. Stephen had also come, for moral support, and afterward he took us to celebrate at Pink's, an amazing hot dog stand but not exactly gourmet cuisine.

"You want to be an American citizen?" he said. "Then, here, eat this." And we polished off a couple of hot dogs and Cokes.

I consider myself very lucky to be in a country where I can speak my mind as freely as I do. What an incredible country this is! But I have to admit that the America I live in today is not the country I set out to join, it's not the country that I fell in love with, and that's a shocking thing for me to say. I fear America has become a police state, with a military that uses heat weapons against suspected enemies, a police force that pepper-sprays protesters exercising their inalienable rights (I told you I did my homework), and a justice system that fails to treat its prisoners humanely. So I will continue to speak out against what I consider objectionable and to crusade for justice and equality, only now I do it as an American citizen. God help me—God help us all.

With Jackson Browne at Abalone Alliance concert,
January 29, 1979

A T THE START OF 1979, I TURNED BACK TO WHAT I deeply loved: making music, expressing myself through song, photography, art, and activism.

I did a number of benefits with Jackson Browne for an antinuclear group called the Abalone Alliance. They were to protest and shut down the Pacific Gas and Electric Company's power plant near San Luis Obispo. Since my dinner with Jacques Cousteau, I was totally opposed to nuclear proliferation and its potential to annihilate the planet. It didn't make sense to me, what with all the inherent risks and dangers. We knew about the problems at the plants: how they have pipes that crack and stretch from leaks, releasing radiation into the atmosphere and ocean. We knew that containment domes, after thirty or forty years, get brittle and tend to crack. It was time to rally public opinion and to take a stand.

This was the first time I'd ever led a band myself. A kick-ass collection of musicians: Russ Kunkel on drums, Tim Drummond on bass (one of my favorite rhythm sections ever), Craig Doerge on keyboards, and maestro David Lindley on many stringed instruments. I'd never been onstage before without someone to play off of, whether it was Clarkie, the Hollies, or Crosby, Stills, or Young. Carrying a show on my own was a very gratifying experience. It enabled me to place a different value on who I was and what I'd accomplished.

I went on to do more No Nukes shows with Jackson, Bonnie Raitt, John Sebastian, John Hall, and others, in California. One concert, on the steps of the nation's Capitol on May 6, also included Joni and Dan Fogelberg; it was the first large-scale antinuclear demonstration after the partial meltdown of one of the reactors at Three Mile Island in Pennsylvania, the worst accident in the history of commercial nuclear power in the United States. (By May 1983, solar-power technology had advanced to the point where I could perform in San Luis Obispo at the first benefit concert at which the electricity for sound and lights was provided by a solar-powered generator, nicknamed the Solar Jenny, that had been put together by Tom Campbell.)

On a clear day from my kitchen in San Francisco, I could see the Faralon Islands, just off the coast. I learned that, to get rid of nuclear waste, the Nuclear Regulatory Commission would take barrels of the stuff and throw them off a ship, close to those islands. But the barrels were watertight and didn't sink, so they shot them with rifles until they went under. Later, someone sent me a picture of some giant mis-gened sea anemone, some weird distortion of the normal growth pattern. The radiation was affecting the way plants grew, a very bad scene, so I wrote a song called "Barrel of Pain."

> *I can see the sea begin to glow*
> *I can feel it leaking down below*
> *I can barely stand it*
> *What you're doing to me.*
>
> *And in the morning will you still feel the same?*
> *How you going to keep yourself from going insane?*
> *With glowing children and a barrel of pain*
> *I don't want to hear it!*

My music was becoming more topical and uncompromising. I'd always been committed to taking a public stand, but it was time, I decided, to turn up the heat. The nuclear madness was a direct threat to my family and me. Singing was the best way I knew to put myself on the line.

I wanted to record "Barrel of Pain" as soon as possible. There were also other songs—"Innocent Eyes," "Love Has Come," "In the Eighties," "Out on the Island," and a number of songs I was working on at the time. While I was collating the material, Joel Bernstein brought a photo to my attention that he had taken while we were vacationing on Kauai. I'd been standing on the lip of Waimea Canyon, a miniature Grand Canyon on the island, holding an old bright-green plastic Imperial Flash Mark II camera I'd been fooling around with. The lens wasn't that great, but when you got lucky it took really interesting blurry pictures. Joel took a panoramic photo with his Linhof Technorama 6 × 17 against that dramatic background. When we checked out the proof sheets, there was a double rainbow that I'd not been aware of in the sky behind me. A gorgeous picture. At that moment, I decided to make an album to fit that photo, *Earth & Sky.*

As it happened, David and I both had deals to make solo albums for Columbia Records. So in February 1979, I booked time at Britannia Studios in LA and assembled a fabulous band: Danny Kortchmar, Tim Drummond, Chocolate Perry, Craig Doerge, David Lindley, Joe Walsh, and two drummers, Joe Vitale and Russ Kunkel. For vocals, there was no one better than Crosby, who agreed to come down and give me a hand.

I hadn't seen David in a while. He'd been holed up in Mill Valley, spending time with Jan Dance, the lovely young woman he'd met at Criteria Studios in Miami. So when he showed up at Britannia, I wasn't prepared for his appearance. He looked horrible—pale, sweaty, dirty, suspicious, slit-eyed, covered in sores. "A staph infection, you know." Yeah, right. I'd heard that one before. It was obvious to me he was heavily into freebase. I could see how it was dragging him down. Jan was a mess, too. Just two years before she'd been this adorable, sweet creature with a lively disposition, but those features had practically disappeared. What had happened to Nancy Brown was now transforming Jan. Nancy had managed to escape. She'd finally bolted from David's clutches to get some help. Jan had obviously taken her place. It was sad—and infuriating.

From the beginning, things went badly. David kept nodding out during breaks, then he'd disappear, presumably to hit the pipe. He didn't seem to be working hard enough, and it was showing up, especially in the playback. His voice was rough, husky; our harmonies were strained. I couldn't vibe him out, I couldn't anticipate him anymore. The communication between us had stopped.

I tried broaching the subject with him, explained that the music was suffering, but he blew me off. "Hey, I'm fine," he insisted. "I'm on top of it." End of discussion. And I tried pleading with Jan to get him some help. I told her that David was in shitty shape, killing himself. If he was incapable of turning it around, she needed to do something about it. I'd help them in any way I could. I was watching my friend's drug addiction destroy everything great that we shared—our love of music, to keep playing and change people's lives. Our careers! It was going down the drain.

Look, I was no Boy Scout. I was snorting, but drugs weren't a problem for me. I didn't have an addictive personality, especially when it came to cocaine. I'd done my share, taken enormous amounts. There is a Polaroid picture I have of a rock of cocaine that was bigger than the eight ball sitting next to it in the shot—and Tim Drummond and I finished it in three days. So I've been there, I've been out of it at times, but I could walk away from it. And if coke wasn't around I didn't go searching for it, and that's the situation Crosby was in. He *needed* drugs, and he needed the money to pay for them.

David and drugs were always spiritually intertwined. But lately the drugs had become seriously problematic. Ever since Christine's death he'd been more and more drug dependent, slipping into a state he called "cocaine psychosis," the paranoia that comes with being too high most of the time. He was so heavily into cocaine that most of Croz's waking moments were spent figuring out how to score, where and when to get it, how much he had left, and how much to share with his friends. Behavior like that puts you in a lot of freaky situations. Like this one: David sold his Mercedes for crack. Yes, the very car he'd had since the afternoon he and I both bought Mercedes together. The guy he sold it to promptly OD'ed, and David broke into the guy's house—while the body was still in the bed—and stole his pink sales slip back. Freaky. Then he had the balls to resell the car to someone else. Like I said: freaky.

He was broke and constantly on our managers' backs: "I've got to find more money. You've got to sell this. Find money. I need money fast." We'd made a lot of dough, millions upon millions. But he'd gone through it all. *All* of it. It was inconceivable to me. But it was all too real.

One evening at the studio, we were working on "Barrel of Pain." While Stanley Johnston and the other engineers were setting up and balancing the sound, the band eased into a warm-up jam. That was our usual way of kicking off a session. Someone starts a riff, another musician joins in, the drummers know what to do—and it begins to cook. We had a great jam going, it was rocking like mad. Crosby's pipe was sitting on one of the amps, and because the jam was going so well, the amp was shaking . . . and the pipe was slowly but surely moving toward the edge. Both Stanley and I could see what was happening. And sure enough, at a certain point when the band hit a particular chord, the pipe fell off and shattered.

David got very upset about his broken pipe and stopped the jam, trying to put the pieces of the pipe back together. He was angry because it meant he couldn't get high that day, and he needed the crack to stay awake.

I shot a look at Craig Doerge and saw the disbelief on his face: What happened to the music? Which is when it all came clear to me. It's the moment I realized that drugs were more important to David than music. He was in deep shit. And I'd had it, I had to do something. "Fuck you, I'm done," I told him. "This is not making me happy at all. This sucks. I can't work with you anymore."

I wheeled away from him, but before I did, I pulled Jan aside and told her: "If I were you, I'd get that son of a bitch to a doctor right now."

I was hurt and angry. Resentful that this fucking drug was more powerful than our music. Up to now, the music always saved our asses, but not this time. This was a tumultuous event in my life, moving away from Crosby like that. I was strong, but it terrified me. I figured that my relationship with David, on a musical level, was probably over. It was the end—of Crosby/Nash, Crosby, Stills & Nash, the end of Crosby, Stills, Nash & Young. The mothership had a huge, gaping hole in the hull.

Crosby was in much deeper trouble than I thought. I learned that after the blow-up, when he'd left the studio, he refused to let Jan drive him home. Instead he sped off in his Mercedes, up into the densely packed hills, with Jan desperately pleading with him to slow down. Inevitably, he nodded out at the wheel and plowed into the back of a parked car. No one was hurt, but when Jan insisted they get out and find the owner, David refused and took off. That's the kind of nightmare he was living. There was nothing else that I could do.

I SPENT THE next couple of months finishing *Earth & Sky*, keeping my distance from Stephen and David as best as possible. I loved making that album. All the songs were close to my heart. In the middle of the session, I moved my home studio from the basement of my house in San Francisco to LA, a beautiful old Hollywood place called Crossroads of the World, on Sunset Boulevard. The space had previously been a restaurant that failed. The minute I saw it, I knew it would make an incredible studio, so I leased it, added soundproofing to the walls and ceiling, redid the floors, built a control room, and moved all my equipment down there. I asked Rick Griffin, the well-known underground artist, to design the logo, a silhouette of Leo Makota's dog Rudy howling, with the name RUDY RECORDS coming out of its mouth. Stanley Johnston and I finished and mixed *Earth & Sky* there.

While Columbia Records was working on the album, I got proofs of the cover back from their art department, with Joel's double-rainbow image on it. And there at the end of the rainbow was . . . a bar code! I couldn't believe it. I'd made the entire album on the strength of that photograph. I picked up the phone and called Walter Yetnikoff, the president of Columbia at the time.

"Good record you made, kid," he said.

"Thanks, but I have a problem, Walter."

He grew impatient. "Oh, yeah? How can I help? What, what, *what*?"

"You know what's supposed to be at the end of a rainbow?" I asked. "A pot of gold—*not a bar code.* Physically, I can't look at this cover. Tell you what, for my next record, the whole fucking front cover can be a bar code, but I'd appreciate it if, this time, you'll give me a break."

There was a moment of silence on the other end of the line while he thought about my request. Then he said, "Don't give me that artsy-craftsy shit."

That soulless little fucker. It was the worst possible response he could have made.

"Artsy-craftsy shit? Talk to you later, Walter." I put the phone down, picked it up again, and called my lawyer, Greg Fischbach. "Get me off Columbia," I instructed him. "I don't care where I land. I know this sounds crazy, but I'm not going to record for any label that puts a bar code at the end of my rainbow."

It didn't take long before we got an offer from Capitol Records. They were delighted to get a Graham Nash album that was already finished and ready for release. In addition, they were willing to forgo a bar code. Before making the deal, however, I had one more requirement.

I told Greg, "I'll sign with Capitol if they let me listen to Gene Vincent's original two-track of 'Be-Bop-a-Lula.'"

Now, as a record maker, I would be furious if anyone passed our master tapes over a playback head, because every time you do so, you lose clarity. It may not be evident until the twentieth time, but it breaks down. Take my word for it. In retrospect, I should not have asked Capitol to accommodate me, and they probably should have refused. But there it was, "Be-Bop-a-Lula" in the 1950s tape box, right at my fingertips. I listened to it at the Capitol Towers, in their beautiful studio, with giant speakers turned up *fucking loud.* I wanted to *hear* that song. And it sounded—fantastic! One of the greatest records ever made. Two-track, *live.* Are you kidding me! Brilliant stuff. So I signed with Capitol, put out *Earth & Sky,* and it didn't have a bar code at the end of the rainbow.

Croz was having a more difficult time. He, too, had left his deal at Columbia and found a home, as I had, at Capitol Records. But David wasn't in any condition to record. His voice was too ragged. It was impossible getting him to concentrate in the studio. He was too out of it. The engineers convinced him to sing next to them at the console to avoid the walk from the studio to the control room, otherwise he would detour into the bathroom to hit the pipe. He'd also negotiated a ridiculous deal. David desperately needed money for drugs, so the record company advanced him a large cash sum, using his house as security. In the end, everything fell apart. The band asked to have their names taken off the project, and Capitol eventually refused to put the record out.

I didn't know what to do. Jackson Browne tried to help him with meager results. He literally stood over David at Warren Zevon's piano in Montecito, trying to coax Croz into finishing a new song called "Delta." Jackson wouldn't let him get up or hit the pipe until it was complete. Turns out it was the last song that David wrote— for years.

JACKSON AND I interacted in other meaningful ways. In 1979, he and Bonnie Raitt called, wondering if I'd be interested in assisting with a new cause of theirs. They were working with my old Guacamole Fund friend, Tom Campbell, putting together a coalition of musicians to bring awareness to people about the nuclear industry. The movement was called Musicians United for Safe Energy—MUSE. James Taylor and John Hall were already part of their artistic nucleus. They asked if I would join the board of the new organization and I immediately accepted.

It was time to get more serious about the state of the environment. Everything was deteriorating at such an alarming rate—the atmosphere, our oceans, wildlife, water supply. Everyone is aware of these issues today, but back then people were basically ignorant about the dangers and long-term consequences of nuclear power. Our goal was to bring them to the world's attention. Musicians had clout. Kids would listen to us. Even if they only came out for the music, we knew our message would ultimately get through.

Jackson and I warmed up with our first collaborative effort at the Hollywood Bowl on June 14, 1979. It was called Survival Sunday and raised a ton of cash for grassroots antinuke groups across America. Bruce Springsteen turned out, along with Bonnie, John Sebastian, John Hall, and an appearance by Stephen, who only days before had done a benefit for Greenpeace in San Francisco.

Then, at the end of June, we turned up the heat. There had been a partial nuclear meltdown at Pennsylvania's Three Mile Island power plant in March, which released small amounts of radioactive gasses into the atmosphere. This was catastrophic, a call to arms. A core group of us met in my room at the Chateau Marmont and decided to stage a five-night benefit at Madison Square Garden in New York City. It was an insane event to try to pull off, but we dreamed big. We wanted to make a huge impact. But to fill five nights, we needed some big names. Everyone at MUSE leaned on their pals, and we managed to attract a stellar lineup. By early September, we'd filled four nights with Bruce Springsteen and the E Street Band, the Doobie Brothers, Bonnie Raitt, Tom Petty and the Heartbreakers, Peter Tosh, Chaka Khan, Carly Simon, James Taylor,

Sweet Honey in the Rock, Nicolette Larson, Poco, Gil Scott-Heron, Raydio, Ry Cooder, Jackson Browne, and, of course, me.

A glaring absence was Crosby, Stills & Nash. Jackson asked me to get the group together, but it seemed like folly so I flat-out refused. I didn't feel that we had anything to contribute, and there were plenty of unresolved feelings between us. So much of our music depended on how the three of us were relating, and if the bond wasn't there it was useless to perform.

I went to New York City early in September in an effort to lay down some organizational groundwork. In addition to the five-night concert at the Garden, we planned a rally in Battery Park City for Sunday morning, September 23. A number of us would be on hand to perform, interspersed with speakers to enlighten the crowd. I'd done my own research on the nuclear industry, but Tom Campbell made sure we were all up to speed. None of us wanted to go into something so important without having all the facts at our fingertips.

A few days before the first concert, I stopped in to visit Jackson in his hotel room. "I hate to tell you this," he informed me, "but we're going to have to cancel the fifth night. We just don't have a headline act."

I thought this spelled disaster for MUSE. The first three nights would only cover our expenses. Nights four and five were when we'd raise money for the cause. It would be tragic to let that slip away.

"I know things look a little bleak between you, David, and Stephen," he continued, "but would you reconsider and have CSN take over the fifth night?"

*Damn it!*

I'd been trying to insulate myself from just such a request. Everything in my life had returned to normal. I was happy with my latest solo album. My marriage was wonderful, I loved being a father, and Susan was pregnant again with our second son, Will. I hadn't been in touch with Stephen and David for a while. Did I want to set off that time bomb again?

*Good Lord!*

I thought over what I'd learned in the last few weeks, how the Three Mile Island incident was far worse than what we'd been told. Inevitably, what came out was not the whole truth. The media reported that no one died at Three Mile Island, which is complete bullshit. Independent research revealed horror stories about birth deformities and actual deaths, but they were covered up to avoid panic. The problems we were facing with the nuclear industry were far greater than my differences with Stephen and David.

"Let me give it a try," I told Jackson.

I called Croz first—he agreed right away—and once I had him, Stephen came on board. They were on the next plane to New York. It was that easy. I had no idea what condition they were in, but they sounded good on the phone, very positive. Plus, they understood all of our kids and families were in danger and wanted to do anything they could to help out.

Now we had the fifth night intact. I hadn't performed with David and Stephen in a long time, but it was pretty good—not the best, a little ragged around the edges. We didn't have time to work on recent material, so we stuck with the hits: "Teach Your Children," "Long Time Gone," "You Don't Have to Cry," and the rest. I also did a solo set earlier in the week.

The concerts, promoted by Ron Delsener and Tom Campbell, were incredibly successful. The production team and enormous crew were outstanding. Jackson, Bonnie, James, John, and I did a half dozen press conferences about what we expected, how to spread awareness. Because a benefit of this type was new and unprecedented, we got extraordinary press coverage and turned out the crowds. The rally in Battery Park drew a quarter of a million people. As a result, the nuclear problem became an important social issue. I'd like to say "Mission accomplished," but lately that phrase gives me the creeps.

The No Nukes concerts, as they were called, were all filmed and recorded. But we didn't have the kind of funds it would take to make a movie. Joe Smith convinced Warner Bros. to lend the board of MUSE a half million dollars to make a feature from the footage. Then, at the end of August, Smith cashed in his chit. He said, "You remember that favor I did for you with the money for the movie? Do you think there's any chance you could get the album out for Christmas?"

Now, I know damn well it takes about three months to prepare an album for release. And that's a standard album: one artist with an identifiable sound. This was slated to showcase twenty groups with twenty different identities. The request came in a few days before September. I did the calculations: basically an impossibility. To get it out for Christmas, somebody was going to have to work like a fucking maniac. Jackson and I decided that to repay Joe's kindness we would give it a shot. We brought all the tapes to my studio at Rudy Records and started to produce a three-record set.

Jackson, Stanley Johnston, Don Gooch, and I worked our asses off in an around-the-clock marathon. The last week, in an effort to finish, we stayed at it for the entire seven days. I may have had two short naps; otherwise we never went to sleep. It was unlike any drill I'd ever been through. On the last day, heading back to the studio, I was hallucinating like mad and saw a giant blue flash streak across the road. God bless Jackson Browne. At six thirty every morning, he would go home, shower, and take his kid to school before coming right back to the studio, often without eating. And Stephen dropped by for the last three days to help with the mix.

Somehow, we managed to make the right decisions and get the album finished. We had the album cover designed, and delivered it, got all the names on there—twenty major artists who signed off on the project—and got it out on time for Christmas. Needless to say, our efforts paid off. It gave the rock community—meaning all of us—a sense of how powerful our voices could be. And you'll notice that there hasn't been a nuclear power plant built since. I'm not saying the No Nukes concerts pulled that off, but we certainly made things difficult for the Nuclear Regulatory Commission.

⋙

I'D GOTTEN A taste of that power and liked how it went down. Without wasting time, I got involved with another benefit after No Nukes. A man who worked at the United Nations, Irv Sarnoff, showed up at my studio with a proposal to do something to support people less fortunate than we were. He felt it would be more efficient to funnel money to those in need through local churches, and I agreed. I went away from the meeting committed and enthused, and that night, on the edge of sleep, I mapped out the entire event: who to invite to perform, which people to speak, what organizations to include, the staging, the name. We'd hold it at the Rose Bowl, which held one hundred thousand people, and call it Peace Sunday. I wanted the pope involved, and I plotted to have every church bell in the world go off at a certain time. Most of the religious leaders backed us immediately, although I remember a bizarre conversation with the Reverend Joseph Lowery, head of the Southern Christian Leadership Conference.

Afterward, he pulled me aside and asked, "What's Jesus's cut?"

*What's Jesus's cut?* Did I just hear him right?

I said, "We're going to give as much money as we can to all the local churches. I think *that's* Jesus's cut." End of story.

Everyone we knew was invited. My friend Lisa Law, one of the original Woodstock photographers, put me on the phone with Stevie Wonder, who was the first major artist to sign on to the show. Once Stevie said yes, I used him to seduce the next big act. I called the Eagles and said, "Hey, CSN and Stevie are going to do this. Are you in?" Then I called the next guy and said, "Stevie, the Eagles, and I want to . . ." Before long, the bill was filled with Bob Dylan, Joan Baez, Jackson, Tom Petty, Gary U.S. Bonds, Stevie Nicks, Nicolette Larson, Don Fogelberg, and Jesse Jackson, who brought Mohammad Ali.

I remember driving to the concert not really knowing whether we could pull this off. The Rose Bowl was an enormous place. But when I arrived and saw it packed with a hundred thousand people,

I had to control myself from bursting into tears. It was a spectacular event, an incredible afternoon and evening of nonstop music. And in the process, we raised a ton of money for a damn good cause.

I LOVED THE impact we were making, but at the time I felt as though I were being pulled in twenty directions. My involvement in the No Nukes album and movie was grueling, really exhausting. Rudy Records was taking off as an independent LA studio. And my second son, Will, was born on January 12, 1980, just as *Earth & Sky* was being shipped out to stores. I was really excited about this record. Just before it came out, I was full of optimism. In an interview with a writer, I said, "It's light, it's airy, it's a little ominous in the darker areas. There's hope in it. There are rainbows, good feelings." It seemed like a natural step forward in my musical evolution.

Unfortunately, the press and general public didn't share that outlook. The sales were soft, with no help from the record company's lack of promotion. It just didn't catch fire. The airwaves were humming with exciting music from the Pretenders, the Clash, Bruce Springsteen, the Police, Pink Floyd, and the Wailers, and somehow I got lost in the crowd. My album was softer, more complicated, lyrically abstract. It was very personal—perhaps too personal. And a couple of tracks felt unduly tense, thanks in part to my relationship with David. None of those things were solely responsible, but together they conspired to dampen my prospects.

To make matters worse, *Rolling Stone* sought to pile it on. One of their so-called critics really laid into *Earth & Sky,* arranging certain lyrics out of context in a mock conversation that, on paper, made the songs seem fanciful and inane. As if that weren't bad enough, he ended the review saying, "Even his best friends won't tell him."

The whole thing was sad, incomprehensible to me. The writer seemed intent on slagging off my work without any real understanding or appreciation of what he was listening to. It lacked insight and any kind of value for the reader. A trained monkey might have brought more to the game. That kind of criticism is the worst kind of journalism, cruel, pointless—and it hurt. I'd put my heart into that record.

Stephen came to my defense in the press. "Nobody talks about a friend of mine like that," he said. "It's bullshit journalism. If that writer walked in here right now, I'd deck him." Spoken like a pal.

Despite all of that, I had to get it up to promote the album. There was a two-month tour, mostly small theaters, just a trio, nice and laid-back to complement the songs. Leah Kunkel, Cass's sister, opened for me. The only other participant was Joey the Goldfish, who swam in his bowl onstage throughout all forty-eight shows except the show in Canada, where thanks to immigration I replaced the real fish with a slice of carrot.

It was a very satisfying experience. I learned a lot about myself and about performing solo on that tour. You have to work awful hard to hold an audience's attention, which meant developing an intimacy and a great set of songs. It was easy for me to deliver the new material from *Earth & Sky*. As I said, those songs were close to my heart and, in concert, you can bring something to them that might be missing on record. Plus, I had the trusty CSN catalogue to mix into the set.

After all was said and done, I spent some time in Hawaii, recuperating and planning my next move. Stephen happened to be vacationing nearby at the same time and, as destiny would have it—as destiny *always* has it—we found ourselves sharing the same stage, doing a benefit for JoAnn Yukimura, who was running for political office.

Stills & Nash: We'd never explored that permutation. For one reason or another, I'd always partnered with Croz. But just the two of us onstage made a powerful combo. Our voices combined beautifully. We rocked that place in a way that surprised even us. It was eye-opening, on so many fronts.

Later in the year, we decided to explore that synthesis, jamming together at Rudy Records. We locked into a version of Traffic's "Dear

Mr. Fantasy" that was a killer, just a *killer* of a track. Stephen was in very good shape—rather, he wasn't as messed up as he usually got. We had fun, started looking down the pike. I thought it would be interesting if we tried doing something together. I'm a team member; I like working with others. Solo records are reserved for those times when I have absolutely no other choice. David and I were barely talking at that point. He was completely fucked up and kept me out of his dark loop. He wasn't around, so . . . screw it. We'd just do it ourselves, a Nash/Stills album.

Joel and I actually went to see David perform at the Marin Civic Center. I went in disguise, in a Groucho Marx mask. I didn't want anyone, especially David, to know I was there. And he was horrible; it was heartbreaking to watch. He looked like shit. His voice was shot, he fenced with the audience. This was not the Crosby I knew and loved. His world, and part of my world, was crumbling right in front of my eyes. He needed help. He was losing total control at this point.

Later, David claimed that when I decided to make an album without him he was crushed emotionally. That may be true, but part of him understood why I made that decision. He was totally fucked up, and I couldn't deal with that. Music is supposed to be a joy, it's supposed to have expression. There was *no* expression in David at that time. I couldn't risk that sucking the energy out of our sound. That might sound cold, but not to me. Music is what keeps me going through life. It is a huge part of my essence. I couldn't dilute that.

Through Mac Holbert, I'd also been following the details of a short tour David had been doing so that he and Jan could remain financially solvent. They went out in a van with a mattress in the back, which allowed them to freebase all day, using propane tanks and a torch. According to Mac, it was a horror show from beginning to end. They were going through an ounce of cocaine a day, thousands of dollars. One night, David had a grand mal seizure from the drugs; the next night, the same thing happened to Jan. I didn't want to be around that kind of behavior. The studio had always been a sanctuary for me. I couldn't sacrifice that.

So Stephen and I recorded seven or eight tracks by ourselves, with Mike Finnigan on the extra vocal part. We mixed it at Sea West on the north shore of Oahu and sent it off to Atlantic. A week or so later, Atlantic came back and said, "We're not interested in Stills/Nash. We want a Crosby, Stills & Nash record in time for Christmas." Needless to say, Stephen and I were sadly disappointed. We thought we'd made a good album, but if your record company isn't keen on putting it out, what are you going to do? Instead we cobbled together another greatest-hits package called *Replay,* but if you ask me, *Retread* would have been more like it.

The smart thing would have been to put the Stills/Nash tapes aside until we could figure out a way to redo the project. It might have been a case of just needing better material. We were always writing; a great song lay just over the next rise. But we were forced to do something for financial as well as musical reasons, which wasn't fun. Stephen needed the cash. I've been careful with my money over the years, but Stephen's not as smart with money, never has been. He just spends what he wants, which drives his financial advisors crazy. So it put me in a difficult spot. I didn't need the money, but my friends did.

Atlantic was so insistent on having CSN that I decided to contact David despite the off-putting performance I'd seen in Marin County. I must have called his house forty times from Hawaii. After the first two or three tries, I got the picture. Jan's mother, Harper, would always screen the calls. "David's at the beach." "David's at the grocery." "David's playing tennis." (She should have known I wouldn't buy *that* one.) There was always some excuse that he couldn't come to the phone. We took our tapes back to Rudy Records and called David again. By some quirk, I finally got him on the line and explained the situation, how much we missed his voice on the record and the bind we were in. We arranged for him to come to Los Angeles, but his voice was in incredibly bad shape. He couldn't sing a note. That beautiful mellow Welsh vibrato was completely gone. So we took a couple of his best songs from the album Capitol had rejected—"Delta" and "Might As Well Have a Good Time"—and CSN'ed them, which means that Stephen and I added our voices.

Those early sessions with Stephen had been a joyful experience, but once David came back, the mood turned dark. Everyone was apprehensive. "Can he do this?" "Did we make the right decision?" "Are we torpedoing the positive energy?" The atmosphere was tentative, fragile. The chemistry was different between David and me. On the one hand, both of us realized that he was now a flat-out junkie. He was freebasing without compunction, not even hiding it discreetly. (Although I didn't know at the time that he was also chipping with heroin, which shocks me, even to this day.) On the other hand, David felt triumphant that we had to get him back into the band. He listened to what Stephen and I had done and said it wasn't good enough, that we were kidding ourselves—and, who knows, he may have been right. Maybe we did need David. And that sparked his usual cocky self. "Ah-ha-ha! So you had to come back and get me, didn't you. You have to have me." That vibe wasn't conducive to great music.

I worried about his irrational behavior. I was worried for him physically—he could have dropped dead at any moment. Underneath it all, I knew he was still David, and all I was doing was waiting for him to come back. I had great faith that Crosby would make it through. Whatever makes him an incredible human being was still inside there . . . somewhere. Maybe I was naïve, maybe I was too optimistic, but I never believed that he would die. When you're dealing with a dear friend, you can usually take him by the shoulder and say, "Hey, listen to me for a second." But when that friend is a junkie whose eyes are vacant and whose ears tune you out, you try another approach. I grappled with all these disparate feelings and handled them in my usual way: by examining them in the lyrics of a song. Because David was a sailor and he and I were both familiar with the idea of Valhalla and the Viking funeral of putting a body on a boat and pushing it out to sea, I began to feel there was a way of talking to Crosby that he just might listen to. So I wrote "Into the Darkness," which is brutal and direct.

> *Into the darkness, soon you'll be sinking*
> *What are you doing? What can you be thinking?*
> *All of your friends have been trying to warn you*
> *that some of your demons are trying to drag you*
> *Into the darkness.*

I wrote the song on the north shore of Oahu and recorded it before David came to the session. I was angry. My friend had been taken over by demons. And when I played it for Crosby at Rudy Records, he just glared at me—and from experience, let me tell you, those kinds of looks from Crosby speak volumes. The song had accomplished exactly what I'd hoped, a complete indictment of his behavior. It made him angry and uncomfortable, and he said so. Tough.

In Oahu, I'd also written "Wasted on the Way," which was another song that was critical of our band. We had so many chances to make great music together, but too often we blew it due to ridiculous distractions. Hey, our own fault—but I couldn't resist the opportunity to speak my piece.

> *And there's so much time to make up everywhere you turn*
> *Time we have wasted on the way*
> *So much water moving underneath the bridge*
> *Let the water come and carry us away*

David is not on "Wasted on the Way." It is actually Timothy B. Schmit, who has a great falsetto, standing in for him. And on the album's title track, "Daylight Again," a beautiful song that Stephen wrote instantly onstage one night while thinking about the Civil War, we added Arthur Garfunkel's gorgeous baritone to round out the vocals.

Ahmet Ertegun visited the studio while I was mixing "Wasted on the Way," and at the end of the song, he said, "Hey, man, that's fantastic. CSN never sounded so good." Stanley Johnston, who was producing the session, was about to turn around and say, "Ah, but Ahmet, that's not CSN . . . " when I kicked him *really hard* under the table. Ahmet was too delighted that we had listened to his plea for a CSN album. The last thing I wanted him to know was that David wasn't singing much on that track.

Normally, we have a complete sense of what an album should be, even though we often finish writing some of it in the studio. This one, however, was a pastiche of the Stills/Nash sessions at Rudy Records and Sea West, as well as the best tracks taken from David's Capitol album. Almost two years in the making, from start to finish. One of the most frustrating projects I've ever been involved in. And I thought we did a fabulous job pulling everything together on *Daylight Again,* considering it was bits and pieces.

The cover was also a last-minute slap-together. Tradition has it that a picture works best to sell an album, especially for as identifiable a group as Crosby, Stills & Nash. I would have preferred it that way, with an image of the three of us together, happy and healthy. But David looked dreadful. He was overweight. He looked like Dracula: No amount of makeup could make him presentable. And there were those sores, his famous staph infection. So we approved an illustration by Gilbert Williams called *Celestial Visitation,* three flying saucers hovering above a temple in the canyon of a magical kingdom. Another bit of a smoke screen to mask our ongoing anarchy. Proof, again, that we were wasted on the way.

## chapter 15

C SN DIDN'T TOUR TO SUPPORT *DAYLIGHT AGAIN*, AT least not at first, not when it was released. We were too concerned about David's deteriorating condition, especially from reports that were coming in from the road. His reckless behavior was making his backup band nervous.

I'm not sure whose idea it was to stage an intervention, but once we decided to do it, there was no turning back. The idea of a crisis intervention, as it's called, was an entirely new one for me. Its purpose, ostensibly, was to save someone's life—to assemble a person's family and friends in order to confront a substance abuser and convince them, by telling him or her, gently and with love, exactly how they've hurt them and to voluntarily get help in overcoming the problem. Everything about it was radical and inexact, but it seemed to many of us a logical last resort.

A bunch of us decided to participate: me, Jackson, Paul Kantner, Grace Slick, Joel, Stanley Johnston, Nancy Brown, and Carl Gottlieb, among others. We gathered at David's Mill Valley house on May 11, 1981, when Croz was expected home from the last date of a tour. We were all there, seated in a circle, in his living room, waiting for him to arrive. Gene Schoenfeld, a doctor from the Haight-Ashbury Free Clinic in San Francisco, briefed us on what to do and how to behave: that we had to be strong, to deflect the denial that would come. We were instructed to tell David, calmly and lovingly, how he affected our lives, what it was about his actions that upset us, how it affected us personally. It was just after sunset. We hid our cars. Nothing was evident from outside that would tip Croz off. As darkness fell over the room, we heard David's car pull up in the driveway. A minute later, he slammed the front door, dropped his Halliburton case on the floor, and shouted, "Hey, home—I'm here! Fantastic! This is fabulous!" Then he spotted us sitting there and went: "Oh, fuck!"

I grabbed Jan and gave her a hug, but someone quickly steered her outside, away from the intervention. Since Jan and David were coaddicted, we were told it would be better to separate them and get them into individual treatment centers, but in the end, they went to the same place.

The look on David's face was ghastly. He knew this was a moment of decision, and I wasn't sure if he was up to handling it. I remember Carl Gottlieb looking at David's swollen feet and saying, "Oh, man, you've got edema here." Croz couldn't even put shoes on, with all the swelling in his legs. We sat him down and told him how much we cared about him—his soul, his physical well-being, his music, who he was. Then we began to take turns, each of us going through our personal stories.

Grace, who was a recovering alcoholic, talked about her own substance abuse, as did Paul, who was very frank and confessional. Jackson accused Croz of losing his musical edge, especially his songwriting, which was pretty much shot. When it was my turn, I told him how betrayed I felt. How the drugs had deprived me of our friendship, which I desperately missed, how all the lies and dishonesty sabotaged our partnership, to say nothing of our greatest pleasure, singing together. "Remember how we made a deal not to be victims of this fucking world," I said. It all came pouring out, all of my resentment. I went through a litany of the bullshit that had pissed me off. He was taking all of it in, but I could see him getting fidgety. I figured he wanted to go get high.

The intervention went on for nearly three hours. By the end David was a wreck, he was in tears, unable to function. We

With Jackson Browne, backstage at the No Nukes concert, Madison Square Garden, 1979 *(© 1979 Lynn Goldsmith)*

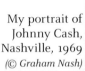

Lunch with Cass at Café Figaro, New York City, 1967 *(© Henry Diltz)*

My portrait of Johnny Cash, Nashville, 1969 *(© Graham Nash)*

With the Everly Brothers, 2005. On the same stage where I did the *Carroll Levis Discovery Show* with the early Beatles in 1959 . . . forty-six years later, almost to the day. *(© Ralph Starkweather)*

Me and Jerry Garcia, Berkeley Community Theater, October 15, 1971 *(© Joel Bernstein)*

Leon Russell and Bob Dylan at the Concert for
Bangladesh, Madison Square Garden, 1971
*(© Graham Nash)*

David Geffen after we threw him in the pool at
Stephen's house, Laurel Canyon, 1969 *(© Graham Nash)*

With Joni, on our way to Big Bear.
She is writing her song "Willie," 1969.
*(© Henry Diltz)*

With Joni, backstage at Carnegie Hall,
February 1, 1969 *(© Joel Bernstein)*

Joni listening to music,
Laurel Canyon, 1969.
I shot this through the
back of a kitchen chair.
*(© Graham Nash)*

Judy Collins kissing
Stephen, Sag Harbor,
1969 *(© Graham Nash)*

Christine Hinton.
Her death in
a car crash
devastated Croz.
*(© Robert A. Foster)*

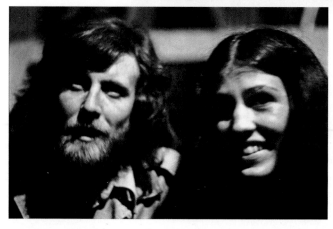

With Rita
Coolidge, 1971
*(© Henry Diltz)*

My portrait of close friend and photographer Joel Bernstein, 1971 *(© Graham Nash)*

My portrait of Susan
*(© Graham Nash)*

Susan, Hawaii, 1983
*(© Graham Nash)*

My son Jackson feeling his brother, Will, 1979 *(© Lynn Goldsmith)*

My two sons, Jackson and Will,
talking about penises, 1984
*(© 1984 Graham Nash)*

My daughter, Nile, Hawaii, 1988
*(© Graham Nash)*

David's wedding and my
"re-wedding," 1987
*(© Henry Diltz)*

Singing "Our House" at my
fiftieth birthday party at the
Continental Trailways Club,
LA, 1992. We're dressed like
old people. *(© Joel Bernstein)*

My beautiful grand-
daughter, Stellar Joy,
Hawaii, 2013
*(© Susan Nash)*

Performing solo, 2010 (© *Buzz Person*)

convinced him that he needed immediate professional help. Jackson and I had arranged for him to go to Scripps in La Jolla, whose drug-detox program was renowned. Jackson paid for a private plane to get him down there the next morning. Since there was no medical insurance, I wrote a personal check for $3,500 to underwrite his treatment.

David went into his bedroom to pack and use the bathroom, which raised my suspicions. I knew this guy well. So I followed him, because I *knew*—I know my friend. Sure enough, he was in there hitting the pipe. I was outraged. Something inside me just exploded. I flipped out. I couldn't help it. We were standing nose to nose, screaming at each other. After all the love that had been directed toward David for three fucking hours, he stole off and got high. I knew he couldn't help himself, but emotionally I was gone. If he wanted to kill himself, that was his business. I threw in the towel. I'd had it.

Jackson volunteered to stay with Croz all night until he could get him and Jan on the plane down to Scripps. It was a bad scene, *another* bad scene. David tried every way to get out of going, delaying, dragging his feet. Jackson even took him to score the next morning so he wouldn't suffer withdrawal once they got in the air. Little did anyone know that David and Jan freebased throughout the entire flight, lighting their pipe with a propane torch they'd smuggled aboard.

Somehow, Jackson got them settled into Scripps without an enormous amount of difficulty, but by the time he flew back to LA that same morning, David and Jan had already checked themselves out. They got into a cab and convinced the driver to take them all the way to Los Angeles while they freebased in the backseat.

Jackson washed his hands of the situation, as did I. We'd done all we could for David Crosby. There was no more left in the tank. I had a family to think of, my kids to protect. It was time for me to get on with my life, even if it meant separating myself once and for all from my friend.

~~~

FUNNY THING HAPPENED while I was minding my own business: The Hollies, of all people, rolled back into my life. In August
1981, a Stars on 45 medley called "Holliedaze" was released in
England and became a smash on British radio. Have to say, I never
saw that coming. It had been about fourteen years since I had anything to do with the Hollies, when I walked out on Clarkie and the
band. Now we were back on the UK charts. Naturally, *Top of the
Pops* wanted the band to appear—the original Hollies, with Eric
Haydock and me. Bobby Elliott called and asked if I was interested
in coming over and doing the show. I said, "Fuck, yeah, let's keep it
all rocking," so Susan and I took off for the UK.

It was a little tentative with Allan at first. It was the first time
I'd seen him since splitting from the band. I definitely felt an edge,
an undercurrent that quickly ebbed away. He looked good; his voice
was great. And even if he was still bitter with the way I'd handled
things, career-wise he had nothing to complain about. The Hollies
had two number one records after I'd left—"He Ain't Heavy, He's
My Brother" and "Long Cool Woman (In a Black Dress)"—the same
kind of success that I had with CSN. If they'd spiraled downward, it
might have been different. But each of us had our respective hits, so
we were even on that score. Time to move on.

We did *Top of the Pops* and the weird thing about it was . . . *nothing* felt weird. The moment we started harmonizing together with
that classic Hollies blend, it was like 1963 all over again. Man, I
slipped right into singing with Allan and the lads. It felt good, as
though I'd never left.

After the TV show, I said, "What are you guys up to?"

"We're heading into Abbey Road to make another record, and
then over to America to tour."

Yeah, well, that was interesting. I had to think, for a moment,
about what I was going to say next. If I suggested teaming up again,
a reunion of sorts—which was so tempting—I'd have to deal with

old fears about moving backward after such a progressive and innovative stretch. I was about to turn forty. Did I want to go back there again? Put myself at a rocky professional crossroad? But, God almighty, was it easier to sing with the Hollies than with CSN! It was certainly more fun, less plagued with personal bullshit. No freebase, no egos, no Neil Young. Unlike my demanding partners in the States, the Hollies didn't give a shit if someone handed them a coffee that was two degrees colder than it should be because they didn't get it right away. I wouldn't have to hear, "Hey, man, my Louis Vuitton bag got scuffed! Who's responsible?" CSN lost several members of the crew because some poor soul didn't take care of the luggage. The Hollies were such easygoing guys. They were all so delighted about making it out of Manchester. Just like that, we were back to being five guys from the pub who had made it.

"I wouldn't mind joining in on the album," I said at last. "Let's see what happens and decide where we go from there."

In the meantime, I went back to LA in time for a benefit on the schedule, a No Nukes rally outside the San Onofre power plant in Orange County on March 28, 1982. We intended to heighten awareness of what was going on at that facility, so we staged a concert outside the gates. In those days, no one interfered with such a demonstration. The owners and the cops generally left us alone. They let us get on with our protest, keeping it out of the press as much as possible, because so many people were making millions of dollars constructing those plants. David was going to perform with Stephen and me, and that was all right: The cause was bigger than our personal problems.

Or so I thought. David was extremely late for the gig. We were waiting, having already rehearsed, unable to contact him, wondering what was up. More of David's bullshit, I figured. Stephen and I quickly adjusted to the circumstances. We can entertain for an hour, just the two of us, no problem. We put our heads together and went, "Okay, 'Southern Cross,' two-part. If Croz shows up, fine, and if he doesn't we'll give the folks what they came for." At the time, none of us knew that David had been arrested en route. But when you're trying to roll a joint and take a hit on a pipe going seventy miles per hour, of course! He drove into a guardrail on the San Diego Freeway. Lucky to be alive. Again.

Things got worse for him when a cop arrived on the scene. He saw Croz's bag on the floor of the car with a .45 pistol sticking out, as well as a lab's worth of drug stuff David used for freebasing. So they busted him and took him to the Orange County Jail, where he was charged with DUI, narcotics possession, and carrying a concealed weapon. Luckily, he faced a sympathetic—or starstruck—judge, who dropped the charges down to reckless driving, hit him with a $750 fine as well as three years' probation, and ordered Croz into a drug rehab program.

I have to believe David wasn't unfamiliar with the consequences. Only a week or two earlier, Jan had blacked out while driving home from the airport, crashed, and lost many of the bottom teeth in her mouth. As I said: lucky to be alive.

But junkies have no judgment. On April 12, 1982, two weeks after the San Onofre incident, Croz was doing solo shows at a funky club in Dallas, which is what you do when you want to make money for drugs. There was a flimsy curtain that divided the main room from his dressing room, which is where he was freebasing, his gun at his side. It didn't take long for a policeman to scope things out. When you live on the edge like that, you've got to expect shit to happen. Well, it did, and David was arrested again. Only, in Texas drug possession and weapons possession were felonies, which ultimately came back to bite him in the ass.

I was in Hawaii when the Texas bust went down. We were toying with a tour to back up *Daylight Again,* and this certainly put a new wrinkle in the plans. If we were going on the road, Crosby had to have his shit together. It wouldn't be like occasional studio work, where we could work around him when he was out of it or worse. He had to be lucid for more than a couple hours each night. Performing, there was no way to cover for him.

David assured us he could handle the road. But during a warm-up on June 6, when we played the Rose Bowl on Peace Sunday, things were pretty bad. First of all, the clergy who were involved didn't want his name on the bill. David could sing, but not well enough, so we had to carefully disguise it by turning down his mike and having Mike Finnigan off in the shadows, singing some of his parts. That really put me on alert. Could we tour? Could we count on Croz to come through? I wasn't so sure, and hedged about going. But by June, "Wasted on the Way" was a top-ten hit and we no longer had any choice. We had to promote a hit album and, frankly, Stephen and David needed the money. And don't get me wrong—I certainly liked the idea of the bread.

We rehearsed on a huge soundstage at Zoetrope, which is Francis Ford Coppola's studio in LA. I was worried from the get-go. David wasn't well at all. He was still wedded to that damn crack pipe, and I was worried that he couldn't survive the road. And old interpersonal issues resurfaced. One afternoon, during rehearsals, we were scheduled to do some much-needed publicity for the tour. Later, a highly rated newsmagazine on CBS called *West 57th* arranged to do a segment on CSN, and a network correspondent was coming to interview us. They set up at Zoetrope around 11:30 in the morning, with taping to begin at 1:00 P.M. An entire TV camera crew was ready to roll on schedule . . . waiting at 1:30 . . . still waiting at 2:00. No sign of Stephen. They were checking their watches, getting more pissed off by the minute. It was unprofessional, really embarrassing. Stephen finally waltzed in around 2:30, and I just attacked him. "You fucking asshole!" I shouted, grabbing him while, I assume, the cameras caught all the action. Fortunately, I never saw the footage, but I'll bet we gave the show a pretty interesting twist.

My partners: priceless.

The night before we left on tour, I had more incentive not to go. Susan gave birth to our third child. Another boy, according to the doctors and the scans. But in our home in Los Feliz, where all of our children were born, all the experts came up short. "Hey, I know a vagina when I see one," I said. A *girl*! We had a baby girl. Susan and I were overjoyed. Nile Ann Mary Sennett Nash. A long time comin', to be sure, but now our family was complete.

CSN started our tour the day after Nile was born, July 29, 1982. God bless Susan for her strength. I took off for the road, leaving her with three young children (including the newborn). Our first show was three days later, in Hartford, Connecticut. We had no expectations about the makeup of our audience, whether they'd be aging hippies, a college crowd newly tuned in to our music, or ghouls waiting to see Crosby collapse onstage. The complexion of the rock crowd was rapidly changing. We, the sixties stoners/radicals, had begun edging into our forties. We'd become classic rockers. *Classic!* Mainstream. *Mainstream!* Relegated to AOR—Adult Oriented Radio—stations. *Adult!* To quote Aristotle: Ain't that a piss! Even Neil, who was on tour in Europe, was shooting off his mouth, comparing us to Perry Como. The next generation, the emissaries of the Video Age, were already claiming their piece of the rock. Rightfully, they followed their own apostles: Talking Heads, Prince, Mötley Crüe, Springsteen, the Clash, Run-DMC, the Police, Michael Jackson. Would they come see us? Impossible to say. But as we rolled out, word drifted in from the network of promoters that we were drawing from across the age spectrum. Still, we had to connect with the kids.

I wasn't worried for a New York minute.

WE TRAVELED ON three individual buses that had been converted into spacious living quarters. In a way, they enabled us to stretch out in privacy, and in another way they enabled David to get high. He could smoke his way from one gig to the next with no interference from Stills or me. He was now traveling with his drug dealer, a pretty shady character named Mort,* who'd taken

---

* A pseudonym.

over most of David's business affairs. They worked out a deal whereby Mort would supply Croz with enough credit for the drugs in exchange for a large chunk of income and royalties. Mort had a piece of everything David did: albums, publishing, tours, concessions, the works. It was sickening to watch it all go up in smoke. Croz kept promising that he would clean up his act, but that part of his act got darker and dirtier. There were plenty of crack addicts who made that sad scene, hangers-on who'd score off him and split. Croz sold one of them the publishing to "The Lee Shore" for dope.

Come showtime, things didn't improve. It actually got so bad, we had to build a room adjacent to the stage so Croz could wander off and freebase between songs. Often, David walked offstage, threw up from the drugs, and was literally dragged back to sing. In Philadelphia, on August 11, he had to leave the stage because he wasn't functioning. On the fly, Stephen and I did a couple of songs together, then Stephen did a solo set—we were creating a show spontaneously, as was needed. When it was my turn to solo, Stephen left the stage while I sang. He found Crosby nearly comatose on a couch in the dressing room, threw a bucket of ice water on him, and when David came back he was completely soaked.

Because of David's arrests, we now became targets. I remember going to a small airport somewhere in the Phoenix area. In those days, you could get counter-to-counter service. Let's say you wanted a lawyer's letter that needed to be signed. You could arrange for someone to go to the United Airlines desk in one city and drop off the letter to be picked up on the other end of the flight. David had arranged to receive some dope that way. We got to the airport and picked up our bags. He went to the airline counter and said, "Is there a package for David Crosby?" The attendant said, "Just a minute, let me go and see." Immediately David's antennae went up, and so did ours. It wasn't "Mr. Crosby? No problem, here it is." "Let me go and see" was weird. Something was wrong. When the guy brought the package out, it had already been opened. David was smart about it.

He said, "No, that's not for me. I'm expecting a letter." And we left—but we all got the message fast.

It was getting hairier and hairier, no doubt about it. And too bad, because the concerts were all sellouts and really well received. It was just as I'd thought; we had no problem connecting with the kids. Our audience actually expanded. Even the press was largely enthusiastic. We weren't *classic* or *mainstream* or *adult*—just *relevant.*

But we continued fighting our own demons. On September 6, at the final gig of the summer portion of the *Daylight Again* tour at Irvine Meadows in California, we hit the end of our last song, "Teach Your Children," put our guitars down, and took bows, which is when the police came for Crosby. They'd been looking for any excuse to bust him again, using an old arrest warrant from 1980. It was a bogus charge and eventually dismissed, but it wasn't going to help that ongoing charge in Dallas. In fact, that case resulted in a formal indictment, which meant Crosby was going to trial.

It made us reconsider continuing the second part of the tour in November. As always, David had promised to clean up and get help, but the reality of it was far from that. Some of my friends thought I was crazy for putting up with this shit. We were always in jeopardy of busts—or worse. In a way, we'd always been walking a tightrope, walking over a chasm with a lake at the bottom, and in the lake were sharks. But it's one of the things that makes us an interesting band to observe. Everybody knew what Crosby was going through. Once again, I chose to see the light, because I knew in my heart that David was worth saving.

Besides, we had to tour because, suddenly, we had another big hit that needed promoting. "Southern Cross" was originally a song called "Seven League Boots" by the Curtis Brothers. Stephen heard it and said, "It's got the essence of something good. Let me try to do something with it." He transformed it, as he'd altered Joni's "Woodstock"—changed it musically, put the chorus in there, souping it up, new title. And it became a smash. We were back on the road, back on the tightrope . . . over the shark pool.

This time out, the cities may have changed, but the offstage scene was painfully familiar. The shows were great, capacity crowds, one encore after another. Great energy, great vibe. A lot of magic—and a lot of pain. For the most part, Crosby was well behaved. The rampant drugs somehow didn't disrupt our performances. But by the time we got to the end of the tour, the onstage facade was beginning to crumble.

On Thanksgiving weekend, CSN played three shows at the Universal Amphitheatre in LA, which we filmed for a two-hour TV special. For some unknown reason, David freaked out. He hit the pipe extra hard before we went on, and the effects of it were all on film. His eyes were completely dead; he wasn't reacting to the music. And his singing wandered off-key. Now, I'm pretty good at the console in the studio. I can fix anything—move vocals from one side to the other, fine-tune voices, and there was a lot of that going on. But with film, combining all three nights into one show, the thing I couldn't fix was how David looked. He looked like death warmed over—barely—so I couldn't show him full-face. It was an engineering and editing nightmare.

By the new year, 1983, I needed a break, something tension-free to take my mind off the CSN upheaval. The Hollies seemed like just the right antidote, so I headed to England to work on their album. Once again, it was a little awkward between Allan and me, and I understood it. I knew how he felt. After fifteen years, I come back into a band that had been his baby since I split. He'd put his whole adult life into it, keeping them in the spotlight. It was a pretty delicate situation at first, but once we got into the studio it was like old times. It was the Hollies, my old mates, and everything just clicked. No one had to explain anything. Singing with Allan and Tony was flat-out fun. We just opened our mouths and all of us were *right there.*

We cut a number of songs just like the old days: fast, no fuss, *bang-bang-bang.* Then I was trapped. I'd done the record, as promised—and now what? "Hey, we're going to have to tour in America." So I agreed to go with them. Part of me felt that it would be a lark, great to hang with Bobby, Tony, and Allan. After what I'd just gone through, it would put the fun back in touring, not having to look over my shoulder for police all the time. And part of me felt absolved of guilt—the guilt of having left the Hollies. Honestly, I wanted to resolve my relationship with Allan Clarke. I still loved that guy and wanted to make things right.

While I was in England, I decided to visit my mother, whose health had been in a steady decline. She was living above the pub in Pendleton with another husband, Alf, a decent man who made her laugh. Only sixty-one, she looked frail, more delicate than I'd expected.

In my family, growing up, we'd never talked about feelings. Everything was on the surface; we never dug down or explored personal issues. A lot of that had to do with the postwar recovery process. You know, that shining English attitude: "Let's just take a deep breath, luv, it'll be better tomorrow." That was the attitude we needed to survive. It was the way I was brought up, and to a certain extent I subscribe to it to this day. One of my survival tools is that it will always be better tomorrow, and working with Stephen and Croz, it's come in pretty handy. But I'd been carrying around a vexing question for twenty-five years that my mother could only answer with some serious reflection.

I wanted to know why all my friends had been forced to get a real job when they turned sixteen, and I'd never gotten that pressure, especially from my mom, who ran the family. "Why was it you encouraged me?" I asked her all these years later. It must have caught her off guard, because she hesitated, glancing away, not sure how to respond.

Finally, she looked at me, sitting at the end of the bar in the pub, and a thin smile creased her lips. "Because, Graham," she said, "you are living the life I wanted for myself."

Man, you could have knocked me over with a feather. She'd never said anything like this before. This was the first I'd ever heard about her ambitions beyond being a housewife and raising a family. I hadn't realized she had her dreams, too.

"What do you mean, 'I'm living your life'?"

She said, "Believe it or not, I thought I had a pretty nice voice and wanted to be on the stage, to be a singer like you. I thought I had something to offer with my talent. But World War II came along, I married your dad, I had three kids—and the dream was over for me. So you are doing what I wanted to do."

This turned me inside out. While I was enjoying my life, getting the girls, living out the fantasy of a young rock 'n' roller, my mom was watching and taking it all in. Inadvertently, I had pulled off my mother's dream.

"Your dad and I were always so proud of you," she said.

Wow! To hear my mother say that was incredible. Of all those teach-your-children moments that I'd been singing about, it took this conversation to put it in perspective. It answered so many questions I'd been grappling with for so long. It dawned on me that my parents were some of the characters I'd written about in "Cold Rain," stuck in their jobs, forced to accept certain circumstances. They sacrificed their dreams for mine. I'm eternally grateful.

A few years later, after my mom passed away, I found myself describing this conversation one night while Crosby and I were playing Carnegie Hall. For some reason, David needed to leave the stage. (No, not *that* reason—he probably just took a bathroom break.) So I began talking to the audience, explaining about my mother's ambitions.

"My mother wanted to be on the stage," I said, "and I thought about how great it would have been if she had made it to Carnegie Hall." As I spoke, I reached into my right-hand jacket pocket, into which I had slipped a few of my mother's ashes, and I started to sprinkle them on the stage. "Mom, you finally made it." It was an incredibly satisfying moment for me. And the audience went nuts.

Incidentally, she also made it to the Greek Theatre, the Hollywood Bowl, and the Royal Albert Hall. She'd helped to fulfill my dreams. I couldn't do much in return, but it was a gesture; it was payback.

## chapter 16

IT WAS TIME TO MAKE SOME HARD DECISIONS.

After the *Daylight Again* TV special was in the can, Stills and I began work immediately on a live CSN album drawn almost entirely from that show. Croz was in no shape to make a new studio record, and lately he'd been making himself scarce. We couldn't count on him for much of anything to do with business. Meanwhile, there was plenty of new, unreleased material to work from, so it wouldn't seem like a cut-and-paste job made up of loose ends.

It was pretty difficult getting it together. Croz's vocals were too lifeless on most of the tracks. We could isolate and soften them, but we needed more of him on a CSN album. So we added a couple of tracks—"Shadow Captain" and a version of Joni's "For Free"—from a gig in Houston that we'd done in '77. The patch job we did was remarkable, if I do say so myself. So with all of that, we had an album we called *Allies*. I chose the cover, a picture of Roosevelt, Stalin, and Churchill with our heads superimposed, but it got scrapped at the last minute for photographs of us performing live.

Yes, we had to tour, and for the life of me I don't know how we managed to pull it off. David was more than a mess. His health had deteriorated, which hardly seemed possible. He was freebasing around the clock. He was filthy, always sickly, irrational, covered in sores. And blisters—he and Jan would nod off while using a torch to light their pipe and were constantly burning their furniture and bodies. He had trouble speaking because his windpipe was coated. David was also broke, heavily in debt to drug dealers of all shapes and stripes. He went through all his cash, including the money set aside to pay for income taxes. And he'd been selling off his prized possessions in order to score. Guitars and collectibles from two decades of rock 'n' roll went for small amounts of cocaine. The *Mayan* lay in disrepair. The Mill Valley place was a ghost house, overrun with drug dealers and hangers-on. I was paying for the schooling of his child, Donovan, named after Debbie. God only knows how he got through these days.

Even so, we were going on the road, touring Europe. Right before we left, David's Texas court case came up on June 3, 1983. I watched it on CNN from my home in Hawaii, with Croz falling asleep and snoring loudly in the courtroom. And, I later learned, freebasing in the bathroom. The judge got pissed because of David's fame, notoriety, and lack of respect for the legal system—and found him guilty, convicting him of two felonies. *Two felonies!* He faced up to thirty years in prison. *In Texas!* Hardball. I was pretty freaked. My heart sank as I watched the reports. For his mug shot, David wore a CSN jacket. Could it get any worse?

Sentencing was postponed when we came back from Europe. I phoned the guy who was chaperoning David and said, "Get out of Dallas, baby!" Simple as that.

We did the entire *Allies* tour on a Viscount jet prop. No wives or girlfriends came along. We didn't need any additional distractions. Jan's appearance was awful and would have attracted attention at passport control. She was pale and frail, with sores and burns—dreadful. So sad. We were nervous about being busted, afraid about being associated with Croz. We had an advance man who had to travel ahead, buying dope for Crosby from local suppliers. If Croz didn't have drugs, he couldn't function. The dope was kept in safe deposit boxes in local banks so no one had to carry. Crosby was too visible, an easy mark. Officials were just looking for him, waiting to pounce.

Somehow, the tour functioned. Music, as usual, wiped out the bad feelings. We did decent shows across Europe. In Germany, we ventured into East Berlin. I was always fascinated with the Berlin Wall, watching home movies of courageous people trying to escape from east to west, getting caught on barbed wire or shot. So I wanted to see Checkpoint Charlie. Man, was it different over there, like going from Hawaii to North Korea: sunny on one side (the west), gray and miserable on the other (the east). Bleak cement buildings, awful architecture.

Even though *Daylight Again* had been a hit, ticket sales at our shows were soft. Many times we booked three nights in a city, but demand was such that we only played one. Venues were too large, prices too high, expectations too great. Who really knows the reason? Shows in France and Spain were canceled at the last minute. Many of the shows in Italy were rained out. Out of the original twenty-five or so dates that were booked, nine were canceled.

That's how we dragged ourselves back to the States, overcast and with restlessness galore.

I WAS DREADING Crosby's sentencing in Dallas. It didn't look good. He'd been arrested too many times to skate, and the judge in the case had run out of patience. The thought of David going to prison scared the shit out of me. I wasn't sure he had the strength to get through it. And it conjured up all the shit that my dad had endured. I couldn't help remembering how much my dad had changed upon his release, the humiliation and loss of self-esteem, and I didn't want to see that happen to Croz.

There was a chance to enter a plea on his behalf, and if anyone was going to speak, who better than me? Who knew more about David and his true worth, apart from all the bullshit that tarnished his image? I viewed him like one of those shiny metallic balls you put in a garden. It gets handprints all over it, then more handprints, and more—obscuring the reflection with each successive touch. But if you cleaned all that shit off, the shine was still there, which was very much how I viewed Crosby. I explained how, at his heart, David was a good man. He'd helped a tremendous amount of people through his music and had done countless benefits for worthy causes. At the moment he might be going through a dark time in his life, but have some faith and trust that his core humanity was still there.

"I truly believe that what David needs at this juncture of his life is help, guidance, and professional supervision," I wrote. "Confinement in prison may make him suicidal or worse. Please don't send him to jail."

Little good it did. Judge Pat McDowell, who heard the case, sentenced David to five years in prison for the drug charge and three years for weapons possession, to run concurrently.

I hadn't expected that severe of a sentence. Five years was a fucking long time, but it was obvious the judge wanted to make an example of him. In a way, I was more worried that David *wouldn't* do time—that he'd either make a run for it, as he'd often claimed he would, or blow himself away. He was terrified of going to jail while still using. David told me that, if convicted and sentenced, he'd had plans to sail away: to stock the *Mayan* with food, take Jan, and head out to sea. But I doubted that he'd be able to pull it off. David needed money—for food, for gasoline for the boat, for repairs, and for drugs—and to get money, you've got to come back into society. He might have been able to escape for a month or so, but I think he concluded it was a foolish and untenable idea.

In the meantime, due to an appeal filed by his lawyers, David was released on $8,000 bond.

Once again, I needed a rest from all the debilitating bullshit and headed to Hawaii, as far off the scene's radar as one could possibly get. Occasionally I'd hear from one of the other guys. David called a few times for money or help. He was trying to clean up, but he wasn't having much success. There were reports from the road that David torched hotel rooms in New York and Connecticut after nodding off while freebasing. Still, intermittently, he attempted to sign in to hospital rehab programs in order to satisfy the terms of his release. At Gladman Memorial in Oakland, California, I wrote a letter at his request so that he wouldn't be confined to a mental unit. David's craziness, I explained, was limited to the drugs. Was he wild? Oh, yeah. Was he impetuous? Yeah and a half. Was he stubborn and argumentative? Double yeah. But he wasn't crazy and didn't belong in that ward. So I assured the authorities at Gladman he would sign in voluntarily and stay put. David swore to me he would do it, too. But he bolted in a matter of hours. He'd broken his solemn promise to me—not for the first time, and not for the last.

I spent my downtime with my family, being a full-time dad and husband. It was heaven for me, exactly what I'd been missing. My kids were growing up and I longed to be more involved. I found out I was pretty good at it, too. There was so much joy to be had from their unassuming routines—making them breakfast, buying them shoes, reading them stories, taking them to the beach, watching them grow. They centered me. They were the innocence I needed so desperately in my life to counterbalance all the decadence dragging me down. As Susan pointed out, "Nobody applauds a good father. They don't give them gold records. But there are other rewards." And I was reaping them in spades.

I also managed to find time to do some sculpting and work on my photography collection. Actually, it was Susan who initially sparked my interest in sculpting. Two days after that tree incident when I first met her, she came over to our bungalow at the Chateau to make dinner for David and me. She brought along a piece of alabaster that she was working on, a bird she was sculpting. I was talking to David about which songs we were going to cut the next day for the *Wind on the Water* album while Susan worked away on the grass right outside the bungalow. Distracted, I looked over at her and realized deep down that, incredibly, I really loved this woman. I was completely enamored of her. She fulfilled all my fantasies of what a perfect woman should be. So I walked slowly over to her, laid my hand gently on her back, and said, "I love you." That gesture so shocked her that she chipped the bloody head off the bird. It was one of those moments you couldn't invent if you tried. So David and I wrote the song "Broken Bird" about that incident, which eventually made it onto *Whistling Down the Wire*.

> *There's a story I'd like you to listen to*
> *About a lady and a broken bird*
> *Broken by the hammer,*
> *She took it so hard she hardly said a word*

I continued to do what I do best: I wrote more songs. I worked on new material, intending to come up with enough stuff to make a new CSN album in the not too distant future. Call it a pipedream, but I truly believed in our ability as musicians, even though the horizon looked pretty damn bleak.

I MANAGED TO stay out of the spotlight until the summer of 1984, when it was imperative that CSN go on tour. We needed to keep the group in the public eye and earn a little money while we were at it. Crosby, in particular, needed the cash. As usual he was broke, up to his eyeballs in debt, and spending whatever money he had on coke and heroin, all while he was out on bail, awaiting appeal.

Just before we left, Mort, David's dealer, talked David into leaving Jan behind in Mill Valley. What David didn't know was that Mort had moved a couple of coked-up bikers into the house to bring her drugs and they beat the crap out of her. They kept Jan prisoner, sometimes at gunpoint, and stole all of her money. When Jan finally broke free and made her way to David, she had two broken ribs, a dislocated jaw, and many missing teeth. Lucky to be alive.

And it got even worse. At one point we took a flight from Kansas City to a gig in Denver. We're all sitting in first class. David and Jan were sitting directly behind me across the aisle, trying to freebase under a blanket, but he'd left his drug paraphernalia and gun in suitcases that were checked. Wouldn't you know it, the plane was delayed and David got agitated, worried he couldn't fix. "I want those bags," he demanded, and ordered one of his guys to recover them and bring them to the cabin. Of course, they X-rayed the bags and found the gun and the stash. When the police came on board, David denied the bags were his. He was out on appeal; another arrest would have revoked his bail and ended the tour then and there. Instead he said, "They're Jan's," and she owned up to them. So the cops arrested Jan for federal air piracy. They took her, David waved good-bye, stared out the window, and didn't say another word.

He was too far gone to have a conversation about the reality of what had happened. The rest of us wondered how a man did that—let them take his girlfriend and not say something or go with her, any of the things that someone in his right mind would have said. But David was *not* in his right mind. The freebase had completely transformed him into something almost inhuman.

I was shocked. Of course, I was equally to blame. I didn't do anything to intervene or defuse the situation. The CSN tour was an enabler for David, and so was I. Absolutely. I enabled David because I wanted him to be able to make music. I tried to confront him, to prohibit the drugs. He'd say, "Want me to sing tonight? Want me to be there, man—awake?" So to appease a junkie, you say nothing while he is getting stoned and happy. And I have to take a certain amount of responsibility. I wanted the music. The music was always the most important thing for me.

Somehow, we soldiered through the tour. It was strangely reassuring. Comforting. There was a lot of good music. And nobody died. On December 9, 1984, at the after-tour party at the Kahala Hilton in Honolulu, we were all looking forward to moving on. Beforehand, in my room, I got loaded, smoking and snorting. The party was in a huge suite, everyone was getting completely whacked. When I came down to it and took in the scene, I realized that everyone there seemed to be faking having a good time. They seemed like marionettes, their faces fixed with superficial smiles, pretending to connect. Then I realized that I was like a marionette, too, the coke pulling my strings. Despite the drugs, it was a moment of extreme clarity. I thought that if this was how it appeared to me, then they must be seeing it in me as well. It made me cringe; it did a number on my head. Plus, David was a walking poster boy for the devastation of coke. He was bloated, some of his teeth were missing, his face was swollen, and he was in serious denial, insisting that he had his shit together. So I decided there and then: no more cocaine for me. It had been a part of my life from 1968 through 1984. I'd done enormous amounts of the stuff—*enormous* amounts. But I didn't want or need it anymore. It wasn't a very difficult decision. I'm a pretty determined man. So I swore off it for good. There has been no cocaine in my life since that night.

DURING THE NEXT YEAR, David hit rock bottom. He was arrested for drug and weapons possession, and after he failed to appear at a court hearing in Dallas to discuss his appeal bond, a warrant was issued for his arrest. It was a few days before Thanksgiving. For nearly a month, from mid-November to mid-December 1985, David Crosby was on the run. He sold his grand piano for $5,000 in getaway money that he immediately blew on dope, and he headed to Florida, a fugitive from justice, which also made him guilty of interstate flight. Ostensibly he was looking for the *Mayan,* which was somewhere in the Bahamas. But the boat proved to be unseaworthy; it was in complete disrepair. Meanwhile, the FBI began a search for Croz and Jan. They were hopscotching around the state, from one drug dealer to the next, one relative to the next, being turned away at every location. Somewhere in this madness, David realized it was over. He ran out of money—and hope. The drugs were killing him and he knew it. There was nothing left but to turn himself in.

On December 12 at around 3:30 in the afternoon, he walked barefoot into FBI headquarters in West Palm Beach, Florida, and surrendered. I watched the news reports from my home in Kauai, heartbroken at seeing my best friend led out of a building in handcuffs, photographers swarming around him, being stuffed into the back of a squad car. At the last moment, before the door closed, he turned to the camera and said, "Wish me luck."

Needless to say, I wished him all of that—and more. In a way, it took guts to turn himself in, but I think it was inevitable once he hit bottom and decided he needed help. That was the point at which he made the decision to live. But I admit, I was secretly hoping to see him go to jail. I thought it was the only way he could stop this downward slide into oblivion. How many of our friends had died in the grip of drugs—Jimi, Brian Jones, Cass, a half dozen crew members? We almost lost Stephen and David any number of times. Those guys must be built like fucking bulls! Like Keith Richards. I didn't want to see anything happen to Croz. I really loved the guy.

DAVID SPENT SEVERAL months at Lew Sterrett County Jail in Dallas before being transferred, on March 6, 1986, to Huntsville, one of the most onerous state prisons in America. He wrote several letters to me from jail, and they were fucking bleak. I know that Jackson and Stephen wrote to him, too. And Neil—he told David that if he cleaned up his act and got straight, then he would gladly come back into the fold. Re-forming CSNY was a powerful incentive. It was all we could do to keep David's spirits high.

While David was in the joint, Stephen kept busy making *Right by You,* one of his less-appreciated albums for Atlantic, with help from Jimmy Page; I was making *Innocent Eyes,* another solo album that I fear was inadequately conceived. I felt as though I had to do something more contemporary and probably pushed that concept too far. The music, much of which was written by other artists, was outside of my comfort zone. I used a drum machine on a lot of the tracks, which threw some longtime fans and reviewers off. In hindsight, there was probably less of me on that record than the music required.

Afterward, I did a string of small shows with Joan Armatrading, mixing a lot of CSN standbys into the set. I also joined Neil in performing at a Vietnam Veterans Benefit at the Forum in LA. We'd been such outspoken forces against the war—all war, in fact—that this gig felt strange and uncomfortable to me. Could I, in all good conscience, support those who had fought? Did I have any business being on that stage? I'd followed the war closely over the years, all the horror stories about the senseless brutality, the napalming of villages, leveling a gorgeous country that had defied America's imperialistic interests, condemning so many thousands of American soldiers to their deaths. Yes, I was opposed to the Vietnam War, as I still oppose it, vehemently, to this day. But I began to realize that many of the soldiers sent into battle were forced to go there over their own personal objections. They were either drafted or felt a duty to serve. And now that they had returned they were treated indiscriminately like dirtbags, which was unfair. Not only weren't they given the standard hero's welcome, they never received even basic assistance in reentering society. Many were regarded suspiciously, forced to deal with the hatred expressed toward them. They sure as hell didn't deserve that kind of disrespect. This forced me to reexamine my position about the men and women who had served. And so I joined Neil onstage to raise money for the veterans, singing spirited versions of "Ohio" and "Teach Your Children." My days as a vocal antiwar activist weren't over, not by any stretch of the imagination, but when it came to veterans there were so many complicated factors. I learned it wasn't all so black-and-white.

One of my greatest thrills as an ardent antiwar activist was singing "Teach Your Children" in Hiroshima, Japan, at exactly 8:15 on the morning of August 6, 1986, forty-one years to the minute after the atomic bomb was dropped on the city. It was a benefit for Children of War, an organization that helps kids who have lost their parents to war. As I stood before that crowd, I said, "I sincerely hope that in some small way this concert represents the hopes and dreams of millions of people throughout the world who struggle to balance the madness of war with the sanity of peace. As individuals, we must never forget that we are not alone. We are not helpless and we *must* work harder together to ensure that the tragedy that occurred here forty-one years ago is never repeated." As I performed the song I'd sung hundreds of times, I was struck anew by its inspirational meaning and the power of the lyric to transcend all cultures. It humbled me, especially when those kids sang along with the chorus. It was incredibly emotional, which I'll never forget.

I rushed home from Japan for another emotional event. Crosby was being released from prison—after eight months. There had been rumblings that he might be paroled early. I'd even written to the Texas Board of Pardons on his behalf. "No one has been affected or more deeply hurt than I by the hold that drugs had on him." Really laying it on thick. "I fully realize that his imprisonment most probably saved his life. I feel that his release at this time would allow him to get back to the more positive side of his life and once again become the creative and sensitive human being I have missed so much throughout this painful ordeal."

It seemed unlikely that he would make his first parole. Usually that first one lays the groundwork for others that follow. They mess with you a little to test your sincerity. But whatever luck had kept David alive through those grisly years continued to serve him at this latest crossroads.

On August 8, 1986, Bill Siddons, our manager, and I collected him from prison. We parked outside Huntsville and waited, just like in the movies. Soon enough, David came strolling through the gate, carrying a little brown paper bag of his possessions. He was wearing shades, his hair was still short, and his mustache had not yet grown out. He looked pale and overweight. But with a huge shit-eating grin on his face. He was out—finally! And there we were, his manager and his best friend. It was an indescribably exciting moment. Immediately we took David to the nearest restaurant and bought him the biggest steak he'd seen in a year.

Naturally I was worried that he might try to score, but everything seemed on the up and up. It wasn't until a few days later that Siddons told me David actually did score freebase after the steak dinner. I was clueless. So Croz wasn't cured. But he was definitely on some kind of upward path.

There was so much positive stuff for us to talk about. Jan, for one thing. She had gone through a rehab program and transformed herself, gaining about twenty pounds and improving her appearance. Her hair was clean and styled, her scars had mostly healed, and her eyes sparkled. Give that girl credit. She looked radiant, alive.

And David was beginning to focus on music again. We made plans to make records and do shows together. He'd been writing inside, a great song called "Compass," along with sheets and sheets of lyrics. And he remembered Neil's promise that if he ever got clean there'd be a reunion of Crosby, Stills, Nash & Young. That was a huge carrot.

Money, or the lack of it, was on his mind. Croz was broke and owed the IRS nearly a million bucks in back taxes; it was clear that he'd have to declare bankruptcy. That was the last thing I wanted David to think about. I assured him that his friends were willing to help get him back on his feet. Susan and I would certainly contribute—anything he needed, just as he'd done for me when I moved to America. Before David went to jail, I knew the IRS would come for every asset he had: his boat, his house, whatever possessions hadn't been sold for dope, and eventually they would come for his publishing. To stem that possibility, Susan suggested that our financial guy Gil Segal and I buy his publishing, with the intention of holding it for the year or so it took to unwind David's debts. Then we'd give it back to him. So he had some income coming in from his songs, which helped, considering the circumstances. I also cosigned a lease on a house for him and Jan around the corner from us in Encino, and fronted them for a couple months' rent. They needed a home, a nest. They needed dentists, clothes, and other essentials—they *needed*. So I was happy to be there for them any way they wanted. Friendship means friendship, no questions asked.

But David's concern always pivoted back to music. Coincidentally, I had a gig booked nearby, at Rockefellers, a club in Houston.

I was beginning a solo tour with three other guys: a ménage-à-tech, Bill Boydston playing patterns on a drum machine and playing keyboards, and Hugh Ferguson on guitar. I asked Crosby, who was turning forty-five that night, if he wanted to come to the show and sit in with me on "Wind on the Water."

Rockefellers was a tiny club, and it was packed that night with maybe three hundred people. Everyone knew that Croz was out of jail, and since I happened to be playing near the prison, the possibility existed that David might show up. So at the appropriate moment, the lights went down and a tape of "Critical Mass," David's a cappella signature intro to "Wind on the Water," came on. Crosby, in the dark, had already crept toward the mike. He had to push a curtain aside to come from the back onto the stage. With the dressing-room lights behind him—it was like seeing the silhouette of Alfred Hitchcock— he was immediately recognizable. And the place erupted, they went crazy, fucking nuts. Crosby had a fantastic grin on his face. He was so happy to be there, to be free, to have paid his debt to society—to have all that shit behind him to some extent. A dark, dark period in his life was ending, and a brighter one was poised to begin.

AT THE END of 1986, Neil kept his promise to sing with us again. However, first he wanted to make sure all four of us could handle it. "We should be physically able to take on the job of setting an example for an entire generation that could be halfway to the fucking grave," he said. "They have to see that we can go through all this shit and come back stronger and sharper than we were before. No matter what has happened to them in their lives, no matter how many good friends have died, how much shit they've piled on themselves, how many losses they've endured—if we can be so strong after everything we've endured, it would be like fresh water running over the entire audience."

So Crosby, Stills, Nash & Young re-formed to do two benefits.

The first was as part of the bill to raise funds for the Bridge School, which Neil and his wife Pegi had recently founded for kids stricken with cerebral palsy, from which both of Neil's sons suffered. Then two acoustic shows—with us headlining—for Greenpeace at the Arlington Theater in Santa Barbara, one of the truly great places to perform. The four of us hadn't played in a long time, and it was exhilarating sharing the stage together again. Especially acoustic, which is when the songs really live.

At the Bridge School concerts, there were two handicapped kids at the back of the stage. Susan noticed that a young boy started to cry, and the little girl next to him slowly put a hand out to reassure him that everything was going to be okay. When Susan described that moment to me, I was so touched that I wrote "Try to Find Me."

> *I'm in here with a lonely light*
> *But maybe you can't see me.*
> *But I'm here with my mind on fire,*
> *Do your best and try to find me.*

Right after that we began working on a new CSNY album, our first studio record together since recording *Déjà Vu* in 1969. All of us had been writing new songs. I brought "Don't Say Goodbye," about a rough patch that most marriages go through and that I'd hit with Susan when I was panicked that she might be leaving me; "Clear Blue Skies," which I'd written earlier in Hawaii; my song "Heartland," and "Shadowland," written with Rick Ryan and Joe Vitale. Neil had "In the Name of Love," "This Old House," "Feel Your Love," and "American Dream," which became the title of the album. Stills brought "That Girl," "Driving Thunder," and "Got It Made," and David contributed "Nighttime for the Generals" and "Compass." We had songs.

We all went up to Neil's ranch, just south of San Francisco, to record. He has a full studio there, along with multiple houses. I'd been with him the first time he saw that property in 1971. We were looking for real estate together and saw about five places, most of which weren't very interesting. But the minute he laid eyes on this spread he was immediately sold, especially after seeing hundreds of red-winged blackbirds on the lake. Utterly beautiful, of course, with giant redwoods, and very isolated, the way Neil liked it. You have to go up Highway 1 to Skyline Drive and then find a little road that gets smaller and smaller until there is only room enough for one car on it. If someone's coming toward you, you've got to pull off into the undergrowth and pray they can squeeze past. It's a couple of miles to the main road—and God forbid you forget the milk! The buildings are ranch style, funky, and there's a large barn in which Neil had recorded some of his *Harvest* album. I remember the day that Neil asked me to listen to the record. No big speakers, but a boat. That's right, he asked me to get into a small boat and he rowed us both out into the middle of the lake. Once there he asked his producer Elliot Mazer to play the record. Neil was using his entire house as the left speaker and his huge barn as the right speaker. What an incredible record it was, and after the music stopped blaring, Elliot came down to the shore of the lake and shouted, "How was that, Neil?" and I swear this is true, Neil shouted back, "More barn!" That's Neil, no doubt about it

All of us settled in at the Red House, as it was called. We were doing great, happy to be alive, David and Stephen in good shape. Neil always takes care of himself, eats well, exercises. We were all getting along like a house on fire. The couple of sessions took only two or three weeks, interspersed between April 24 and September 16. No ego problems other than a lot of strong opinions. Neil wanted to do it, wanted to be there, and that was a big problem out of the way. Besides, we were at *his* house, so he couldn't run away. But, then, neither could we. A pretty clever strategy.

The opportunity to make music with Neil is always enticing. He always was and remains an utterly brilliant musician. When we play with Neil, I expect the unexpected. We make a different kind of music with him than we do with Crosby, Stills & Nash. It's got a harder edge; there is tension and darkness in it. He pushes us into a different direction. And when you write for CSNY, you push back harder, hopefully giving him something to bite into. I never wanted to be in a band that demanded the same solo as the night before, the same one you played on the record and on the last four hundred shows. I'd rather stand there with my mouth wide open, and that's what I got when Neil joined the group. As difficult as our relationship sometimes is, it was hard to argue with what he brought to the mix.

Even though we were getting along, musically I felt we were walking on eggshells. Croz was used to dominating a recording session, he was usually unflappable, and now it seemed, at times, that he was taking a backseat, letting the rest of us call the shots.

Stephen was a little fragile, too. He didn't feel that he had great songs to offer. "Got It Made" was a decent number, but he didn't have a lot of what I considered CSNY songs. I thought Neil indulged Stephen a little too much.

Music was changing a lot at this point. There was still a ton of disco on the airwaves, a lot of Donna Summer and the Bee Gees. New wave and electronica were each attracting their niche. But I have to say that none of it influenced us as we were making *American Dream*. We didn't take any notice of that stuff. We just did what we do, made our music the only way we knew how. We weren't following any trends.

David, if a bit fragile in the sessions, was straightening out his life, to my utter delight. He devoted himself entirely to Jan. It took all of us by surprise when he dropped the big one: that he and Jan were going to get mar . . . mar . . . mar . . . C'mon, Croz, say it! *Married.* Yeah, you heard that right: Crosby getting married, three words I never expected to use in the same sentence. But it was cool. Jan and David had come back from the dead. They were a team, inseparable. They held on to each other for dear life.

Don't get me wrong, we gave him a lot of shit about it. There was a stag party where things got pretty raunchy. The usual shit—guys getting drunk, a couple of scantily clad ladies. Lots of unrepeatable roasts and toasts directed at David. The wedding was the next day, May 16, 1987, at the Church of Religious Science in LA, where Susan and I had gotten married ten years earlier. In fact, Susan and I decided to renew our vows, making the event a double wedding.

When I first married Susan, she gave me ten years. She was perfectly clear about her intentions, saying, "At the end of those ten, if I still like you I'll renew." It wasn't a joke or said lightly. She's an incredibly strong, independent woman. When those ten years were up, if she hadn't been happy, she'd have been gone in a shot—and I knew it. Even though we had three kids together. If I wasn't pulling my weight, she was out of there. And I always worried about it. Was it going to last? Would there be any magic left? I didn't know. So it was a relief when she decided to re-up with me. And Jan and David were generous to share their ceremony with us.

It was a memorable affair, with equally memorable company. Stills and Jackson, of course—even Neil turned up—with guest appearances by Roger McGuinn, Chris Hillman, Paul Kantner, and Warren Zevon. The reception was in the yard of our house in Encino, during which we all jumped into the pool with our clothes on. Silly shit.

We deserved this, and we savored every minute of it. There's no question that we had come through the madness. CSN, not just David, had gone off the rails, and for a while it seemed certain we were headed over the cliff. Smart money was betting we'd self-destruct again, but somewhere in the insanity we turned the mothership around. Don't ask me how. David's going to jail? Possibly that sparked things. My quitting cocaine? It certainly helped. Stephen's coming to terms with his magnificent talent, no longer being intimidated by Neil, as he'd been in the past? All of this figured into the turnaround. Huge relief. From here on out, we stopped trying to live life to the extreme and, at long last, were looking to live life well.

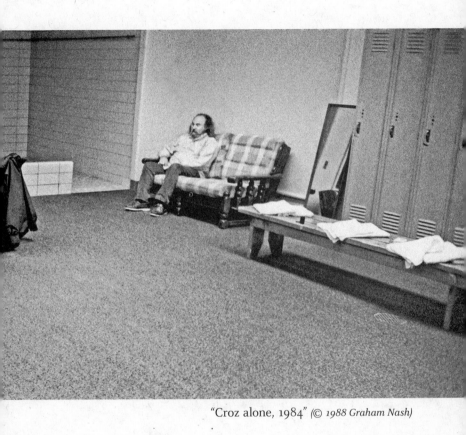

"Croz alone, 1984" *(© 1988 Graham Nash)*

## chapter 17

Whoever thought, at this point in my life, I'd be turning my attention to fine-art photography.

In 1970, when *Déjà Vu* was released, Mac Holbert was a student at the University of California at Santa Cruz and had gone on a field trip to Verde Valley in Sedona, Arizona, living in a tent with a bunch of pals. At the time, Crosby, Stills, Nash & Young were on the cover of *Rolling Stone*. These college kids had a copy of the issue, and, while smokin' it and getting a little drunk, started arguing about whether or not we'd sold out. Mac, who was a devoted fan, defended us, which only aggravated the situation. Things escalated, as those things tend to do, so at some point, he packed up and left and thumbed a ride back to San Francisco. On the way, he got picked up by Steve Cohen, of all people—the guy who handled our stage lighting. Steve was on his way back from Woodstock with my guitars in the van, and Mac came with them and stayed in my life for over forty years.

I liked Mac immediately. He was a bright, artistic kid, funny and self-assured. Great attention to detail, very grounded. Loved photography, played a damn good game of Ping-Pong. I took him under my wing, introduced him to everyone, who felt about him much as I did, and eventually Mac became the tour manager for Crosby, Stills & Nash, as well as one of my best friends.

One evening in 1988, Mac and I were having dinner with David Coons, who worked at Disney (and later got an Oscar for developing the software that created the ballroom scene in *Beauty and the Beast*). A brilliant man who to this day can't find the bathroom in my house. David spotted a green Kodak photographic-paper box sitting on my desk and asked what was in it. My explanation requires a little backstory. CSN's art director, Gary Burden, was doing a book on Joni and wanted to use some of my photographs. He knew I'd lived with Joni and that I'd have some pretty interesting shots of her. Without having the discipline to go through my 35 mm negatives, I simply scooped up everything I had from my first years of shooting images in America—David, Stephen, Neil, Joni, Cass, Woodstock, *everything*—and gave them to him. Of course, I never saw them again. "But I put them on the Greyhound bus," Gary insisted. "You mean you didn't get them?" So this green Kodak box contained all that remained of my work: the proof sheets from those treasured negatives, which were themselves missing.

"Are there any images on them that you really like?" David Coons asked. After I pointed out a favorite shot of Crosby, he said, "Would you lend me the proof sheet?"

*Damn!* I thought: Am I going to lose the proof sheet, too? But he convinced me that he'd take special care of it, so I let him have it, with misgivings.

Ten days later, I got it back along with a twenty-by-thirty-inch print of Croz that knocked me on my ass. It stunned me. It was beautiful: the black-to-white relationship, the texture of the three-hundred-pound cold-press Arches museum-quality paper. I happen to be a great lover of surfaces and of old photographic processes—Bromoils, carboprints, dry plates, daguerreotypes, platinum prints, the works. I wasn't sure which process David had used, but the result just *killed* me.

"I didn't know you had a darkroom that could make prints this big," I told him.

"It's not a photograph," he said.

I got indignant. "Of course it is. I ought to know—I *took* it."

He said, "No, it's an ink-jet print." It was the first time I'd ever heard that term. "At Disney, to make proofs of images of people, we use a 3047 printing machine, developed by Iris Graphics, out of New Bedford, Massachusetts."

I was astounded. "You mean to tell me this image was *printed by a machine*?" It seemed impossible—sacrilege.

Mac and I went to take a look at this . . . machine. It was blue and looked like a low-rise refrigerator but had a slope on one side, with a window so you could see into it. On the other side of the glass was a huge spinning drum. When it slowed and finally stopped, a man removed an image of a bride holding flowers, but it was . . . a *photograph.*

Mac and I looked at each other and said, "Did we just see that?"

I'd been putting off an exhibition of my photographs that Joni helped arrange at the Parco Gallery in Japan because I couldn't supply what the curator needed: fifty images (no problem) in editions of twenty-five each (no problem) blown up to a size of three feet by four feet (big problem). The minute I saw the Iris printer, that problem was solved. It could easily print the show for Tokyo.

I got hold of Al Luchessi, the CEO of Iris Graphics, who happened to be in LA at the time. He explained how his printer was about to revolutionize the way companies advertised. "Say you want a Toyota brochure printed," he said. "You'd normally take the information to a printing house. They'd have several printers half the size of a room, which they'd have to shut down, clean, and re-ink in the process until Toyota was satisfied enough to sign off for a million copies." By scanning the images into a computer and programming the Iris to print them, it took about forty minutes and cost $100 instead of taking three days and costing $7,000. The companies understood the economics very quickly.

Mac and I could barely contain ourselves. We saw the potential immediately. I took Al Luchessi aside and told him that we were sure he could make more money printing fine art than he could printing advertising. I already knew he could get high-grade paper stock through the machine because of the image of Crosby that David Coons had printed.

So I shelled out $126,000 and bought the machine instantly.

Mac and I carted it back to my house in Manhattan Beach, and Mac and Coons voided the warranty within the first ten minutes because we were fucking with the insides, forcing it to do what we wanted it to do. The machine spits out millions of dots of ink; each nozzle on the four print heads—cyan, magenta, yellow, and black—is about one-seventh the width of a human hair. When you put fine-art paper through the machine, it throws off a lot of microscopic lint, each piece of which looks like a tree trunk to the minute printer nozzles. First we cut off the arm that was holding the printer heads close to the print drum, moving them back to allow even thicker paper to go through. Then we borrowed a piece of tubing from the Hoover of Mac's wife, Ruthann, to create a vacuum system that would suck off the lint before it reached the print heads. The last step was having the brilliant David Coons rewrite conversion software from color to black-and-white.

It took no time to print the show for Tokyo, all fifty images, and they were *gorgeous.*

It seemed a shame to let that machine sit idle while CSN was on a tour in Australia, so Mac invited a master serigrapher named Jack Duganne to play with it until we got back. The process for printing serigraphs is tedious and expensive. The artist often has to print the work a hundred times, overlapping layers of ink until the colors and images are right. But the Iris reduced the processing time by 50 percent, which made the job much more profitable. At some point, Jack received an image from a Chinese artist that he scanned and printed the same size as the original and sent it back to the artist as a gift. She was somewhat insulted, thinking that Jack hadn't liked the image, so she tore it up, believing it was the original. But of course it wasn't; Jack still had the original. That's how good our prints were getting.

Charlie Wehrenberg, an artist friend of mine from San Francisco, suggested we turn this into a business, becoming a fine-art press, printing the individual images of artists in many visual media. Steve Boulter, of Iris Graphics, and David Coons helped us realize the dream. *Presto,* Nash Editions was born. It was a hell of an undertaking, necessitating that I pump almost $2 million into the new company. So in 1990, I auctioned off most of my incredible collection of photography at Sotheby's for $2.6 million, the highest ever paid for a private collection, giving Nash Editions the cash infusion it needed.

Convincing artists to utilize the technology was somewhat more difficult. They came to it slowly and with great suspicion, as did collectors, curators, and gallery owners, who initially balked at displaying the prints we made. Once, while I was in San Francisco, I walked into the Vision Gallery. I was about to have an exhibition of my work there and I wanted to show them a couple of my images. The lady who managed the place loved them. "The blacks are like velvet," she said. "You must have a wonderful darkroom." "They're not photographs, they're ink-jet prints," I explained. *Clang!* She immediately hated them. It took me an hour to convince her that it wasn't how you got them on paper—it's what you see, the entire experience. Do you like them? Do they affect you or not?

David Hockney felt the same way as she did—at first. Soon, however, we began printing for him, as well as for great photographers like Douglas Kirkland, Pedro Meyer, Robert Heinecken and his wife, Joyce Neimanas, and painters like William Mathews, Francisco Clemente, and Jamie Wyeth.

Our studio was doing incredible work. Henry Wilhelm, who wrote the definitive book on the degradation of color images, said that the same image printed by another company wasn't as good—that the Nash Editions prints were at least 20 percent more valuable, thanks in no small part to Christine Pan Abbe, our office manager, and John Bilotta, who's been our master printer for the last twenty-odd years. We had our own identifying chop, and we bought more Iris printers, with at least three of those beasts in our studio at one point.

Sad to say, Iris Graphics did not treat me and Mac, two hippies from California, very well. They did not truly believe in what we were doing. They believe in us *now*; perhaps they should have from the beginning because they're out of business *now*. But other people saw the future coming, particularly Epson. In the early days, Epson's images were rather crude. To improve their image quality, they relied heavily on Mac and me to keep the technology moving forward. They've always been receptive, and we've been using Epson printers for the last eighteen years. We've printed images on all kinds of stock—rice paper, white velvet, tin, you name it. We really pushed this technique as far as we could, which is why we are so honored that our original Nash Editions printer is in the Smithsonian Institution's National Museum of American History. They recognized what we accomplished and awarded us the gold medal for technological achievement. We changed the history of photography—just a little. My father would be so proud. From those humble beginning lessons, to this. *Wow.*

In September 1992, I was attending Photokina, a large photography convention in Cologne, Germany, when Susan called. She told me about the devastation caused by Hurricane Iniki, which had struck the Hawaiian islands. She urged me to consider doing a benefit concert. Susan's personal response to the storm was immediate. She flew to the islands, rented a helicopter in Maui, filled it with the necessary provisions—lamps, generators, chain saws, etc.—and flew to Kauai. She was the first civilian to get permission to do so. Stills had put her in touch with one of the commanding officers of the Pacific Fleet and he gave his permission for her to land on the island despite the terrifying conditions. Of course, once the thought of helping was in my head, I expanded the idea. I always want to push a great idea to the absolute limit. I called my friend Tom Campbell, head of the Guacamole Fund in Southern California, and suggested that we rally the troops. I knew how committed Jackson

Browne and Bonnie Raitt were to making the world a better place, so we called them to ask for their help. I also knew that David and Stephen would support the idea of helping out the people affected by the devastating storm. And so, together, we performed an acoustic concert at the Blaisdell Arena in Honolulu and one on Kauai with Jimmy Buffett. We raised over $1 million—giving every dollar to the Hawaiian people. I'm so proud of Susan for spearheading the event. She and our friend Lesley Yardley took great care to make certain that every cent went to help the people in greatest need.

The year after Iniki, the islands had recovered from the devastation and I found myself sitting at a piano and vocal mike that had been set up in the telephone company offices in Lihue, Kauai. I was linked via ISDN, a then-new digital telephone technology, to Joel Bernstein, who was playing along with me live from a stage set up at the Moscone Center in San Francisco, where the audience of AT&T telephone engineers watched me through a video linkup. This was the first instance of a simultaneous live musical performance carried via digital telephone lines.

I've always been fascinated by technology and its global reach. The essence of "Teach Your Children" is about passing along, on a two-way street, knowledge and insight, a mission greatly facilitated by the information superhighway. Any method that enlightens is a move toward greater understanding, making a difference in the world, and new forms of expression—be they interactive multimedia, virtual reality, or digital interface—provide tools that extend our influence to the global village and its children.

But how to take this concept to another, personal dimension? I envisioned a fully interactive computerized stage show, utilizing the latest technology, in which I could talk about my life and all the incredible things that have happened to me. More than anything, however, I wanted it to be thought-provoking and visual, perhaps a new way of teaching our kids.

Our engineer, Stanley Johnston, led me to Rand Wetherwax, the ultimate computer geek, who helped me create a database of my life, from the earliest days—pictures of my granddad, my bedroom in Salford, Clarkie and me at Ordsall Board, that kind of stuff—right up to the present. For the show, however, I wanted to be able to go freely anywhere in my life, not necessarily chronologically. To do that, we needed an interface, a way of accessing the database. So we devised a huge gold watch that moved on a twenty-five-by-thirty-foot screen. It represented the "gold watch theory" of having to do what your dad and grandfather did: working until the owners awarded you a gold watch and replaced you with someone younger and cheaper. I held an infrared remote control that I could click on the watch, causing the hands to spin either forward or backward, landing on a year. This enabled me to go from 1942, the year I was born, all the way through to the early nineties. And once I clicked on a year, other interfaces would appear, and I would talk about, say, listening to Radio Luxembourg. We re-created my bedroom so that young Graham could put his ear to the bedpost, enabling him/me to hear the radio in the kitchen. I made the computer screen image literally move down the bedpost, the Everly Brothers would come up on the radio, and I'd sing "Bye Bye Love" with them in three-part harmony. I then spoke about how important their music was to me.

For another segment, I sent someone to map the interior of Winchester Cathedral so that when I was at the piano, live, banging out "Cathedral," the view on-screen started in the nave, at floor level, rising upward through the church toward the stained-glass windows—which would shatter at the appropriate moment, launching me into space in rhythm with the song. I even had Crosby singing live with me from Los Angeles on my song "Military Madness." No mean feat.

The show was called *LifeSighs,* and we did a week's worth of performances at the Annenberg Center in Philadelphia. I was manipulating images, with the information going over fiber-optic lines to Los Angeles, compiled by computers, and sent back to me in real time (well, almost real time; there was a ten-millisecond delay that I had to deal with). So it was a live interactive computer show. To my knowledge, this was the first time that a live stage performance incorporating this highly complex application of digital technology had ever been attempted.

*LifeSighs* cost me just under one and a half million dollars to mount, and we only performed six shows. CSN was going back out on tour, so the staff and equipment separated, and I didn't have the time or the energy to get it all back together.

Going back to the summer of 1989, CSN headed back East, to upstate New York, for the twentieth anniversary of the Woodstock Music Festival. Talk about déjà vu! It was like an acid flashback. But the first Woodstock was an incredible event. Five hundred thousand people in the rain and mud soaking up all that music, having a great time and perhaps finally realizing that together they were a force to be reckoned with. I believe that Woodstock was the end of something and the beginning of something else, moving from four or five kids playing their hearts out in a garage to corporations realizing that half a million people could become customers. Man, what twenty years can do. I hadn't been expecting much at this "new" Woodstock. It seemed harebrained, trying to recapture the magic of Michael Lang's original festival. That first concert had been so much a part of its time. And the times, as the poet once said, were a-changin'.

There were only about thirty thousand people this time around. But not a bad lineup: Melanie; Buddy Miles; Edgar Winter; Canned Heat; Blood, Sweat & Tears; Humble Pie; the Chambers Brothers— a lot of good music and a pretty good vibe. It had been overcast and rainy throughout most of the show, but right before our set the clouds opened and the sun came shining through. The audience really connected with what we did. It was very much an echo of what had gone on in '69, except that the sound was great, which it wasn't at the original festival.

The twenty-fifth anniversary in 1994 was bullshit, completely overrun by corporate interests. I didn't want to go. It was held on a flat piece of concrete on a boiling-hot day. Water was going for twelve dollars a bottle. An utter rip-off. A lot of people showed their displeasure by burning stuff. I sure couldn't blame them. Some things, no matter how profitable, aren't worth fucking with.

DOING BENEFITS ALWAYS helped us to keep things in perspective. CSN has done so many of them over the years, it's been an ongoing commitment. If the schedule permits, we show up and sing. Very seldom do we say no to doing our share for the worthy causes we support.

On November 18, 1989, we were doing it again—CSN and our friend Michael Hedges appeared at the United Nations General Assembly for a "Children of the Americas" benefit that was connected with UNICEF. (I'd put together an earlier benefit for them in Los Angeles that was able to provide enough money to inoculate three hundred thousand kids against diseases that kill close to a million children a day.) The room we played in was where Khrushchev banged his shoe on the desk and where President Eisenhower had tried to explain to the world about the U2 incident, in which the Soviet Union had succeeded in shooting down the pilot Gary Powers, much to the embarrassment of the United States. At the time of the concert, word drifted in that the Berlin Wall was being torn down. Stephen said, "I know this sounds crazy, but we're already in New York, shouldn't we go?" What insanity that would be on a moment's notice. It's not easy moving the three of us around. There's so much ephemeral stuff that goes on, people handling this and that. "We've got American Express cards. Let's just buy tickets and get on the plane." So away we went, just like that. On our own, with only our friend Stanley Johnston to take care of us. We just went to witness the Wall coming down.

Of course, CSN would never be far from the center of action. Our arrival in Germany was picked up by the media, and we agreed to be interviewed. We were guests on a radio station, talking about the usual shit—music, politics, personal stuff, whatever they threw at us. I'd just released a single, "Chippin' Away," written by Tom Fedora, which James Taylor sang on, about chipping walls down in general: the walls around your heart, your community, around your town, pulling them down. How, slowly but surely, they will eventually fall. So the station played it while we were in the studio.

During the song, I came up with an idea. The next day, we were going to be onstage at the Brandenburg Gate to watch the Wall come down. We had no gear, so we really couldn't play, but there would be microphones. So when we came back on the air, I said to the deejay, "Why don't you play 'Chippin' Away' at exactly 3:40 tomorrow, the time we're supposed to say a few words, and we'll sing along with it?" The host of the show thought it wouldn't work because there wouldn't be speakers to pump out the sound. "That's okay," I said. "Let's just invite everyone listening right now to bring a transistor radio tuned to your station, and they can hold up their radios for everyone to hear."

And that's what we did on November 22. It was a clear, cold day. We had heavy jackets on, trying to keep warm as thousands of people massed outside the Brandenburg Gate. We did "Long Time Gone," inviting everyone to join us and give the song new meaning. Then, at 3:40, right on schedule, everyone held their radios in the air and we sang along with "Chippin' Away." Right after that, we all went to the Wall and started chipping it away, helping to raze it once and for all. Oppression comes in so many guises, but its downfall is always the same: joyous.

That afternoon we went across what remained of Checkpoint Charlie. We had lunch at a restaurant in the East Sector, where a little trio was playing background music. They were pretty good, so during a break, I went over and introduced myself and started telling them how I was in a band in America, but they recognized me, they knew who we were. "Come on over, have a drink with us," I suggested. Oh, *no*, they couldn't do that. "Look," I said, "we're all just musicians—from the east, the west, it doesn't matter." They were adamant, they couldn't do it. Why? "Because you're sitting at a table for four. Here in the east, only four people are allowed to sit at a table for four." I thought they were kidding and said as much. "Oh, *no*," they insisted. "If we joined you at that table we'd get thrown out of here, and we need this gig." They absolutely refused. I could see the manager was already giving us the stink-eye. No wonder they wanted to escape this shit. But that all came down along with the Wall, all the repression, all the crap that went with it. No wall can stop ideas for very long. You can build your blockades, put up your barbed wire, but eventually people *communicate,* and once that happens there's no stopping them.

THERE ARE A lot of perks to being a rock star, and once we all got straightened out, we were able to enjoy them. Yeah, sure, it took long enough—forty-odd years, give or take a couple lives. But what the hell. You've got to try on the clothes before you can wear 'em with confidence.

The biggest perk of all was singing together as CSN. Always was, still is. I'll never get tired of it. That unique sound we make. It's like the pull of gravity to the center of the earth. When I sing with those two, it keeps my world in balance. Call it crazy—and, trust me, some of it is—but musically, I'm happiest in character as Crosby, Stills & Nash.

Through the 1990s, we were humming like a Hemi. I felt better about the three of us than I had in years. We kept busy singing, either together, solo, or in interchangeable pairs, made no difference. Neil came in and out of our lives at intervals. I played on a lot of shows with Jackson Browne and Carole King. Grace Slick and I did a couple of things. And my idols, the Everly Brothers, invited me onstage at a gig of theirs in Toledo, Ohio, in 1992. Singing harmony on "So Sad" fulfilled a lifelong dream.

Before they went onstage, Don said to me, "So . . . what are you going to sing with us?" I was dying inside. Phil said to me, "Okay,

I'll sing underneath Don's melody, you take my part." I asked him why. "Because I've got the top part," he said. *Mmm, think so?* I said, "Don't forget that you're the guy who taught me to sing. You stay where you are. I'll sing on top of *you.*" That kind of threw him, but basically it's what Crosby, Stills & Nash do. The Everlys never sang a three-part that way and I really wanted to impress them, because I'm good at what I do and I've been doing it a long time. Besides, I wanted to pay them back with a blistering three-part, because of how their music had affected me as a kid in Salford. I have a board tape of me singing "So Sad" with the Everly Brothers, a prize possession that thrills me to this day.

In 1986, Paul Gurian produced the movie *Peggy Sue Got Married,* directed by Francis Ford Coppola, and while researching the music for the film, Paul had access to a demo tape that Buddy Holly had made of the title song in his apartment in New York City in 1958. This was just before he was killed in that tragic airplane crash in 1959 that also took the lives of the pilot, Ritchie Valens, and the Big Bopper.

When Paul played it for me, we came up with the idea of adding musicians to the track because it had been recorded by Buddy with only his acoustic guitar. Paul and I wanted to ask Phil Collins to play drums, Paul McCartney to play bass, and George Harrison to play lead guitar. Alas, nothing came of our idea . . . until late 1995. A tribute album to Buddy called *Not Fade Away—Remembering Buddy Holly* was being proposed by MCA Records, and the Hollies were asked to take part. What comes next? You guessed it. The Hollies had a copy of Buddy's original two-track tape transferred to digital, rearranged the song, and added the instruments to make a new track. I then flew to England to record the added vocals, and made my and Clarkie's childhood dream come true by singing (even if posthumously) with our idol Buddy.

Music wasn't the only thing on CSN's agenda. A blur of ongoing benefits sharpened our commitment to the homeless, drug education, victims of earthquakes, the needy, Greenpeace, the antinuke movement, Farm Aid, the Bridge School, the California Environmental Protection Initiative, UNICEF, everything important. And all of those efforts came back to us in spades.

In 1994, CSN received word that the White House had asked if we would sing "Happy Birthday" to President Bill Clinton on the White House lawn when he turned fifty. We'd heard that the Clintons enjoyed our music. And after all, they had named their daughter Chelsea after Joan's song "Chelsea Morning." So we flew down to Washington on David Geffen's beautiful Gulfstream G3. Afterward, Susan and Jan had their photograph taken with the president. There he was with a good-looking woman on either side—instead of saying "cheese" when I took the picture, Susan said, "Hey, it's just like a ménage à trois." I could swear I saw Bill flinch.

Sometimes what goes around comes around. On May 6, 1997, CSN was inducted into the Rock and Roll Hall of Fame, along with Buffalo Springfield, Joni, the Bee Gees, Bill Monroe, the Rascals, the Jacksons, and Parliament-Funkadelic. A hell of a class that year. James Taylor inducted us. And Stephen became the first musician to be inducted twice at the same ceremony. A pretty nifty honor for him and for all of us in the group, even though Neil chose to boycott the event because it had turned into a spectacle, rather than an intimate jam by the inductees.

In 2010, another significant and unexpected honor came my way. I was minding my own business in our Encino house when I took a call that sounded suspicious from "Hello." A lady on the other end of the line introduced herself as Dame Barbara Hay of the British Consulate (really, Dame Barbara!?) and asked me if I was sitting down.

"No, I'm standing in my kitchen," I replied skeptically. "How can I help you?"

She hesitated for a moment before responding. "Her Majesty the Queen of England has bestowed upon you the honor of OBE."

I thought she was messing with me. "Did Crosby put you up to this?" I asked.

"No, no, no, no, *no*. I'm quite serious. Her Majesty the Queen would like you to become an Officer of the Order of the British Empire."

After I picked myself up off the floor, all I could think about was how my parents would have felt. Their kid from Salford, from the slums, just trying to do the best with his life, being honored by the Queen of England. Ridiculous! They'd never have imagined it in a million years.

It took me a while to figure out how this business came about. Turns out Pete Bocking, our original guitar player in the Fourtones, kept petitioning the Palace, saying, "You really should think about honoring Graham Nash." He listed all my accomplishments, the good work that I'd done, the benefit concerts, charitable contributions to worthy causes, the many donations to museums that I'd made. And to think I hadn't been in touch with Pete all these years. I learned much later that he'd come to a CSN show in Manchester, but he never told me he was there. Sadly, Pete died in the midst of his efforts but his friend, Danny Hardman, continued to badger the Palace. Eventually, it must have struck the right chord.

The OBE: I liked the way it sounded. The Beatles were MBE, which is one rank lower, and David Gilmour is CBE (Commander of the British Empire), one above. Would I have to suck up to Sir Paul and Sir Elton? Not in this lifetime. You know me better than that.

I was only allowed to take three people to the ceremony. Obviously, Susan and my sister Elaine were my first choices. I couldn't very well have picked one of my children, because it would mean leaving the other two out. So Susan suggested we ask Danny Hardman to go with us. I'd never met Danny, but he turned out to be the same as me, a real good-hearted north of England lad who never dreamed of entering Buckingham Palace. I'd never been there myself, and I have to admit that it was a phenomenal experience, a total thrill.

There was a forty-five-minute lesson on how to be received by the Queen. I was cautioned not to turn my back to her or touch her or even start a conversation. It was a different story if she talked to me first, but that would have been a rare occurrence. And I knew to look out for a subtle gesture of hers: If she moved her hand slightly to the left after she shook my hand, it was a sign to move away and take my leave. But that didn't happen when we eventually came face-to-face.

"Good morning, Your Majesty," I said, ignoring the conversation rule. "You look stunning this morning."

Don't worry, I wasn't throwing her a line. She looked fantastic: an eighty-four-year-old woman, sharp as a pin, with a great twinkle in her eye, just the way I like them. She had an emerald on her jacket the size of an egg, and I knew damn well it didn't come from Tiffany. After a few pleasantries, I said, "I must tell you, Your Majesty, this is a tremendous honor you're bestowing on me. My mother and father are both dead, but they would have been incredibly proud to find me standing here with you."

She said, "That's very nice. And how are the Hollies?"

*Whoa! Hold on a second.* The Queen of England is asking *me* about the Hollies?

"I'm sure they are all fine, Your Majesty," I said. "But I'm sure you realize that I haven't lived in England for forty-odd years. And quite frankly, Your Majesty, I didn't realize anyone was watching what I was doing to receive this honor."

She looked me right in the eyes, took hold of my hand, and said, "Well, now you know."

Imagine that.

I had taken some of my mother's ashes to Buckingham Palace and sprinkled them in the garden just prior to the ceremony. She would have been thrilled. I'm still astounded that I was honored by the Queen.

I've had two interactions with President Obama. The first one was a fund-raiser Jackson Browne and I did in San Francisco during his initial campaign that raised $7 or $8 million. Obama had delivered a speech at the Fairmont Hotel and came backstage afterward to thank us for singing. He was incredibly charming, sophisticated, and down-to-earth, with a wonderful smile. Before he left, I said, "Would you be interested in knowing what I thought the three most important words of your speech were?"

"I'd be very interested," he said.

"It was at the point when you mentioned something rousing, and the audience began shouting, 'You can do it! You can do it!' You held up your hand and said, 'Wait a second. *Not me—us!*' Those were the three most important words. If you keep that in mind, you'll become president of the United States."

I was reminded of that occasion when I met him again, a couple weeks before the second election, in 2012. My managers got a call from the Obama people saying that the president had personally asked if David and I would sing at a high-tech fund-raiser for him in Silicon Valley. Naturally, we agreed to do it. Both Croz and I are great fans of the president, even though we have our disagreements. But this time it was different—no cell phones or cameras were allowed. The entire event was cloaked in layers of security. Still, Obama was very kind to us. He introduced us by saying, "It's not often you get a couple of Rock and Roll Hall of Famers to come strum their guitars for you, but they are here now tonight." We did "Just a Song Before I Go" and "Teach Your Children" for about fifty people at $38,000 a plate. And they complain that *our* ticket prices are high!

I never performed for George W. Bush, and wouldn't have. I disliked the man intensely. I thought he was a dunderhead, without intellect. And his father made certain that Dick Cheney was chosen as his VP. In my opinion Cheney's one of the most evil men on the planet. Anyone who would vote against every environmental and equal-rights issue, as well as voting to keep Nelson Mandela in prison, is not of this earth and doesn't deserve my support.

〰〰〰

In 1994, considering what we'd been through together, it was gratifying to watch David's rehab trajectory, but physically he seemed to be falling apart. I knew David was under a mountain of stress. The IRS was on his back again, money was tighter than tight, and on top of it all he was battling diabetes and hepatitis C. During one of our sets, Stephen and I couldn't help but notice that David was playing out of rhythm; very unlike him. After we finished the show, he collapsed in excruciating pain and was rushed to Johns Hopkins Hospital in Baltimore, where the diagnosis was dire. "Your liver is shot," they told him. "You're dying—and soon."

Somehow, Croz managed to finish the rest of the tour. And in the middle of everything, Jan learned she was pregnant, a condition they'd been trying to achieve for ten years. Their progeny would carry on the requisite hijinks, but David's future was exceedingly doubtful. He needed a liver transplant. Fast. Except you can't just pick one up at livers.com. He needed a matching donor, hard to come by—and it was a race against time. Every minute counted. Croz was slowly becoming poisoned, fluid was building up in his abdomen, ammonia in his brain. I worried that this time his luck wouldn't hold. How many lives can this cat have? By now, it was way past nine.

Out of the blue, a liver became available, but the chances of Croz surviving the transplant were slim to none. His internal systems were failing. Gary Gitnik, one of the distinguished doctors at the UCLA hospital, lived just around the corner from me, and he called and said, "It's time." He and I rushed to the hospital at four o'clock in the morning to see David just before surgery, to wish him luck, of course, but also to say good-bye. It was one of the most difficult hours I've ever spent, cracking jokes to keep David's spirits high while struggling to hold my own emotions in check the best I could. How do you come to terms with the possibility of losing your best friend? The fear of it scared the hell out of me. As orderlies were about to wheel David into the operating room, I got up close to him, looked him right in the eye, and said, "Hey, if you leave me here with Stills, I'll fucking kill you." Croz went into that operation laughing—and trying not to.

Only a bear like Croz could have come through that ordeal. It was touch and go, but he survived the worst of it. Even so, he wasn't out of the woods and required lots of bed rest in order to recover. News of his transplant had lit up the wire services, and he was deluged with flowers, gift baskets, and get-well wishes from around the world. Hospital attendants carted bulging sacks of mail into his room. The outpouring from fans was heartfelt and touched him greatly. It was impossible for Croz to read all the mail, but one letter he opened from a man named John Raymond pinned him to the wall. It said:

> We've never met, but my wife and I raised a boy that you gave up for adoption thirty-two years ago. We want you to know that he was raised well, in a very loving and caring home, and that he's very, very talented ... I would never intrude upon your privacy except that the news of your health is so ominous that as one dad to another, I could not keep quiet about our son.

*Our son.* The words stunned Croz. He had a grown son he'd never met. That in itself wasn't news to David. He'd always known that a kid existed somewhere out in the ozone, the result of an affair he'd had in 1961, while playing the coffeehouse circuit. He'd behaved badly at the time, just bailed on the mother, who reluctantly gave the child up for adoption at birth.

James Raymond. When Croz finally met him, the elements didn't compute. The guy was ... *normal.* And handsome. Emotionally stable, confident, and multitalented; a professional musician with a gorgeous voice who was making a good living working with bands. He and Croz even shared a love of the same jazz pianist, McCoy Tyner. Talk about genetics. "Here's what you need to know about me," James told him during their initial visit. "I've never been hurt, never been hungry, nobody ever beat me up." His adoptive parents happened to be wonderful people who had raised him with love. Oh, yeah—and just in case this fatherhood business was freaky to David, he had to prepare himself for yet more news: James's wife was giving birth to their first child *that very day*. Croz was a new father and a grandfather, both at once.

Croz loved the news of his just discovered son; it rejuvenated him. He and James hit it off big-time. They bonded in so many different, important ways: over music, certainly, but so much deeper and stronger than that. They became songwriting partners—and *friends*. As did James and I. We've written several songs together, and he's become a full-time member of the CSN band. And when Jan and David's son, Django, was born a few weeks later, the Crosby clan had much to celebrate.

All of these events contributed to David's steady recovery. Discovering a long-lost child, raising a new child, and being a child at heart have served him well. But music, I'm convinced, was his most potent cure-all. When we sang together, I could actually see the mending process. And we sing together as much as humanly possible. In between the big CSN and CSNY tours and the ongoing benefits, we perform as Crosby/Nash every chance we get. It's easier when it's just David and me, because I'm *bonded* to David. We think alike, complement each other, and enjoy a trust that knows no bounds. To put across songs like "Carry Me" or "Cathedral," to stir those quiet pools of emotion that lie within everybody, you have to go there yourself. We can't fake it—and that requires trust. When David gets to the middle of "Guinevere" and talks about Christine being here for such a short day, I'm right there with him. The same with "Carry Me," about his mother's death. It doesn't matter how many times we sing those songs; at some point our emotions take over, and, brother, let me tell you that it generates something sacred. Whatever that might be, Croz and I have it with each other, whether it's intuition, tone of voice, or something much deeper and indefinable.

POLITICS HAS ALWAYS been a staple of any CSN show. We continue to talk to our audiences about the big, important issues, trying to educate people and get them to act on their beliefs. World peace, children, and the environment remain at the top of our list. Recently James and I wrote a song, "Almost Gone," crusading for Private Bradley Manning, the soldier imprisoned for providing classified military documents and diplomatic cables to WikiLeaks. Whether or not you agree with what Manning did, his treatment—some say torture—by his jailers was inhumane. America cannot treat its prisoners with such brutality, and I've been saying so, and singing about it, every chance I get.

When David and I did a tour of Europe in 2011, the only real news that we could get was, strangely enough, through Al Jazeera. They were giving you the straight stuff, nothing slick, which was very different from the American and European reporting. And that's where we first heard about the Occupy movement. Because of who we were, David and I were right there with those guys. We really supported what they were doing, and we talked about it onstage every night in Europe. And every single night, the audience reacted with a round of applause. It kind of shocked us. We never thought the Europeans would be that interested. So we vowed that the moment we got back to the States we'd go down to Occupy Wall Street and lend our support.

Within two days after that tour ended, we went down there with our acoustic guitars and James Raymond. There were no amps, no microphones. It was very much like the Brandenburg Gate show. We didn't care. We did four or five songs and talked to the crowd. Hundreds of people were there, a cross between Woodstock and the benefit shows that we've done throughout the last several decades:

like-minded people who were intent on doing what they could to make the world a better place. We thoroughly understood what they were trying to do, and we wanted to support their endeavors. We did "Long Time Gone" and a song of David's called "They Want It All," about the corporations that want everything, which came from a statement that David Koch, one of the world's truly bad guys, had made when someone asked him why he wanted so much profit. He said, "I want my share, which is *all* of it." And of course we ended with "Teach Your Children." It was very, very heartfelt.

I've also been revisiting "Military Madness" in our recent shows. In the last verse, I'd usually sing something topical, like "I hope George Bush" or "I hope Obama" or whoever is president at the time "figures out what's driving the people wild." But I've taken to substituting Ted Nugent's name instead. To me, he has a very disturbed point of view. Say what you will about his so-called hunter mentality, but when you publicly call Hillary Clinton a bitch and Obama a piece of shit, you've gone too far (and shown your true colors). Ted and I don't agree on a lot of things—especially the NRA and their ridiculous claim that the Second Amendment provides for the right to own a gun. As I read it, I believe that the Second Amendment provides for a militia to be armed. I've never known a hunter who needed an assault rifle with a hundred-round clip. In too many cases, people have a gun on their hip instead of a cell phone. There is a gun for every 2.6 people in America, which is crazy, really scary. When I was growing up, I never saw a policeman with a gun. Or a private citizen. It was unheard of. The English had different ideas about violence than Americans had, but they've become more similar in the last few years, thanks in no small part to the false war on terrorism. It's just a smoke screen, an excuse to militarize the world. Every year, billions of dollars are being made by the worldwide war machine.

I can tell that our political opinions disturb a small fraction of our audience. They either don't want to hear it or don't want to get involved. And some people just flat-out disagree with our positions.

Fair enough. Everyone's entitled to his or her own opinion, even if it occasionally disrupts our shows.

That's what happened in 2006, when CSNY went back on the road. It began with a phone call from Neil to David and me. "Hey, fellas," he said in that all-too-familiar twang, "want to come over to the hotel and listen to my new record?" That's an invitation we'll rarely refuse. He was staying at the Bel-Air hotel in LA, and when we arrived I expected to be ushered into his suite to hear *Living with War* through a set of big-ass speakers. Not this time. Nah, this was Neil. He wanted us to listen to a CD on his car stereo—new songs that he'd just finished recording. So we got into Neil's car, driving up through the canyons, smokin' it, listening to his incredible, heartfelt music. It was political and powerful, no punches pulled. The way I interpreted it, Neil's songs argued that the powers that be in this wonderful country of ours generate an industry for war and profit with companies like Dick Cheney's Halliburton and KBR. At the end of listening to the CD, David and I looked at each other and said, "We're in. We want to help you say this."

Neil, as always, was pretty smart about it. He is an incredibly popular artist with a huge fan base, but he realized that CSNY saying these things would attract a larger, more diverse audience to hear what the songs were saying. He wanted to get his message across to as many people as possible, and our involvement would pump up the volume.

That was the crux of the 2006 tour, and quite frankly I'd never experienced people walking out of a CSNY concert before. At least 10 percent of the audience walked out every night, especially in Atlanta and places across the South. They didn't agree with us that George W. Bush was the worst president ever, or that Bush, Cheney, Wolfowitz, Rumsfeld, Condoleezza Rice, Richard Perle, and all the other neocons had lied us into the Iraqi war. They deplored the way we criticized the Bush administration. What really pissed them off was a song of Neil's called "Let's Impeach the President," which came almost two and a half hours into the show. We'd start to hear catcalls, then see a gradual exodus. But 10 percent is not a majority of the audience. And, for God's sake, if you buy a ticket to a Crosby, Stills, Nash & Young concert, what the fuck do you expect? At least, the way I see it, we were waking people up. The people who left our concerts were expressing their opinions, even if those opinions showed they despised us. No matter what they thought, I agreed with their right to say it. Truthfully, I realized there were still plenty of people in the South trying to figure out why the North won the Civil War.

When it comes to such notions, I just don't have the time. Time is the only true currency we have. Even if Warren Buffett and Bill Gates combined their billions, they couldn't buy an extra second of time. I was reminded of just how precious a commodity time is before we left on the *Living with War* tour with Neil. On the last day of 2005, I got a call from my lawyer, Scott Brisbin, in LA. New Year's Eve—strange time for him to be talking business, I thought. But I could tell by his tone that something was horribly wrong. *God, not Crosby,* I prayed. Nearly as bad: Gerry Tolman, my friend and manager of fifteen years, was dead—he'd crashed his Porsche 911 coming off the Ventura Freeway in a rainstorm. Gerry gone, it was too hard to believe. So young and vital. I was heartbroken. I dealt with the terrible news by writing "In the Blink of an Eye" on New Year's Eve, a song that was only performed once, at Gerry's funeral.

There's no way to turn back time when a tragedy like that happens. The way I see it, you've got to make every minute count, even when it comes to something as fleeting as songwriting. I'm not interested in wasting your time or singing you a song that I don't believe will move you or make you think. I really don't have a minute to waste.

My life has become a battle against time. I have so many pursuits that bring me pleasure that, often, I feel like an air traffic controller, trying to give each its rightful space. I am constantly writing. If CSN or CSNY isn't recording, then I'm working on my own material. Always writing. Because songs drive me crazy. If they are on my mind and unrecorded, I need to get them out of my system. I can't rest while some speck of lyric or melody is rattling around inside my head. It's like a form of foreplay when you just need to come; otherwise the experience is too frustrating. And even in my seventies—*my seventies,* holy shit—I can still get it up for a song. James Raymond and I, with some help from Marcus Eaton, wrote a new song called "Burning for the Buddha," about the 128 Tibetan monks who have immolated themselves as a response to the tensions between China and Tibet. When I saw the first image of a burning monk it was his protest against the Vietnam War and it appeared on the front page of every newspaper in the world. No longer. Those sorts of actions now are ignored. Quite honestly, we've been conditioned to think more about the size of Kim Kardashian's ass. Surprisingly, though, the song goes down rather well.

All of us—David, Stephen, and I—remain extremely prolific writers. So many songs! There's no stanching the flow. Unfortunately, we don't have the time or wherewithal to record even half of our new material. It's not logistically or economically feasible. And today's recording contracts aren't what they used to be. Back in the seventies and eighties, we basically had carte blanche in the studio. Atlantic gave us fantastic advance money, underwrote the sessions, and turned us loose to create. That doesn't happen much anymore.

In the summer of 2003, Joel Bernstein and I began production on a series of eleven major CSN-related archival projects, beginning with a three-CD box set retrospective of David Crosby's life in music. Over the next ten years, Joel and I completed seven of these projects, including similar retrospectives for me and Stephen.

In between the business with CSN, writing, recording, and performing, my art and photography have taken center stage. If I'm not making music, I'm painting; if I'm not painting, I'm sculpting; if I'm not sculpting, I'm drawing or taking pictures. I direct my energy in whichever direction I want. If I can create a fine song, why can't

I make a fine painting or take a good photograph or sculpt a good piece? I keep trying to touch the flame any way I can—without getting too burned.

Since the time Joni first encouraged me to express myself in photography and painting, I've been working feverishly in all forms of media: acrylics, stone, linoleum cuts, lithography, collage, a variety of printmaking, and, of course, ink-jet art. Painting released some skill I never knew was there. During the early tours, CSN didn't stay in particularly great hotels. We were still rock 'n' roll dogs. The scene in those days was a lot of Holiday Inns, places that had strange wall-size drawings of, say, a Roman ruin or the depiction of a lady in crinolines, that kind of generic stuff. Because I was doing a tremendous amount of cocaine at the time, after our shows I would paint those drawings. Just took out my brushes and went to work. I painted at least seventeen walls in motels around the country so that an untrained eye wouldn't notice they'd been altered. Looking at them, it would never occur to you: "Hmm, that should be black-and-white." They were delicately colored. I even signed them. I can turn a sow's ear into a silk purse in a second.

Those hotel and motel walls served as my apprenticeship in art. I've gotten better since then: I've graduated to bona fide galleries, with exhibitions of my work shown all over the world. Mostly painting and prints mixed harmoniously with my photography. To this day, a camera is never far from my reach. I get such a unique perspective looking at the world through a lens, an outlook that has captivated me all of my life. My dad knew what he was doing when he put that Agfa camera in my hands. He was giving me an enormous gift—the ability to look at things in a different way, simply, imaginatively, magically, with open eyes. He unleashed my curiosity. Learning how to see that way has been a lifelong education. It has taught me to become more aware of my surroundings, to see the beauty that exists around us all the time, to appreciate all forms of imagery. I'm amazed anew every time I look through a lens.

≈≈≈

SOMETIMES MY LIFE seems to take place in the air. I'm constantly traveling, either with the band or to an event that benefits a cause or for my art or some session I'm producing. But in between all the madness, my refuge is Hawaii. It's always been my idea of paradise. A sanctuary in the middle of the Pacific Ocean, miles from anywhere, stunning scenery, and all that rainfall—*water*, precious water. Guests are always amazed at all the rainbows, but where I live they're an everyday occurrence. Even double rainbows (up yours, Walter Yetnikoff).

When Susan and I moved there in 1979, our land was almost third-world primitive. Just a tiny shack with no glass on the windows surrounded by lots of lush, untamable growth. Kind of like a Gauguin landscape without the wild beasts and bare-breasted women (too bad). I'm surrounded by acres of unspoiled mountain scenery, with countless waterfalls sluicing down the banks. Over the years, Susan, with our friend Bill Long, has turned our property into an extraordinary Balinese-style compound, with four houses—ours and one for each of our children—a studio for my ongoing musical and artistic experiments, a studio for Susan, and a heated pool. What a great craftsman Bill is, and what a fine road manager. With all that pristine beach just minutes from the house, you'd think it would satisfy our recreational urge, but the beach is anathema to this pasty English lad. Susan practically has to put a gun to my head to lure me onto those stretches of white sand, and since you already know my feelings about firearms, you can imagine how seldom a beach outing occurs. No, I'm content to sit on our patio and watch nature conspire right before my eyes. I'll leave walking in the sand well enough alone—or to the Shangri-Las.

My son Jackson, an artist, an activist, and a world traveler, and his lovely soulmate, Melissa, both have an infectious, positive spirit. They live on a five-acre piece of land just up the road; they live humbly and quietly in a repurposed shipping container with our first grandchild, an extraordinary baby girl called Stellar Joy. They're conducting an experiment in permaculture, a form of ecological engineering that emphasizes natural and sustainable ecosystems. Some of my environmental proselytizing must have rubbed off, because Jackson and Melissa seem to do their best to strike a balance between focusing on their family's well-being and concentrating on the well-being of the planet.

Will, his younger brother, is an equally brilliant young man, so grounded, so levelheaded. He's a whiz at math, golf, and chess and for a while went to MIT. Years ago, when Will was twenty, he accompanied Susan and me on a visit to a friend's office on Wall Street, where we got a firsthand look at the chaotic trading scene. In one room, where forty computers lined the walls, Will happened to glance at a machine and said, "Ah, the Fibonacci formula." One of the traders sitting there spun around, openmouthed. "No one has ever noticed what our software is producing and understood it on sight," he said. "Give me this kid for two weeks and I'll change his life." So Will wound up working for a very successful Wall Street firm in Los Angeles, one of the youngest stockbrokers in the country, but eventually bailed when the economy turned sour. I always wanted him involved in the family business, so these days he works alongside me, managing the details of my affairs, which I guarantee you are more complicated than that Fibonacci formula. A few years ago, Will met a beautiful young woman from Omaha named Shannon, and they got married in 2012 year in a joyous ceremony at our home in Kauai.

Nile's life is more serenely composed. When my daughter was seven, Susan took her along to visit a friend who was in the throes of having a baby, and Nile watched the process from beginning to end with wide-eyed interest. None of the gory bits seemed to have an impact on her. While everyone else was distracted, Nile talked soothingly with the mother in an adult, compassionate way. After graduating summa cum laude with honors from UCLA, all she wanted from life was to bring babies safely into the world. In addition to being a nurse practitioner of women's health, she is also a registered nurse and a certified nurse-midwife. Her services are in great demand. And every time I check in with my managers, Buddha and Cree Miller, I have the distinct pleasure of knowing that Nile chaperoned their daughter Marta's birth. On my birthday. Now that's what I call managers. Did I say pleasure? Make that pride. That's my kid facilitating childbirth. What could be more meaningful than that?

I was really touched when, in 2010, Nile and Britt Govea coproduced an album of my music called *Be Yourself*. All the songs on my first solo album, *Songs for Beginners,* were performed in sequence by an astounding variety of younger musicians. What CSN always believed—that the music is far more important than ourselves—is borne out by this project. To think that much younger musicians are eager to play our songs today is very moving to me.

I am grateful that my family allows me to be who I am. Still. At my age—seventy-one—making music the way I want to, on my own terms. I'm an authentic mutt: part Hollies, part CSN, part CSNY, part Englishman, part American, part inveterate hippie, part gadabout, all heart. What a luxury. Hard to believe. I often look in the mirror and wonder who that is staring back at me with the snowy white hair and timeworn face. Inside, I'm still the same fifteen-year-old boy who sat next to Clarkie in the balcony at the Bill Haley concert all those many years ago. Same enthusiasm, same spirit.

Speaking of Clarkie, he came through it pretty well. Years and years as the face of the Hollies is a pretty amazing legacy any way you look at it. In 2010, my agent phoned and said, "You're going to have to make arrangements to go to New York. The Hollies have been elected to the Rock and Roll Hall of Fame." I was thrilled—for Allan and me, for all of us. I thought the Hollies should have been in the Hall a long time ago. I don't know why we didn't make it sooner. Maybe we weren't cool enough. It didn't matter. It was a great honor, even though by that time Allan had left the group due to a problem with his voice. So I called the rest of the Hollies and said, "Cancel all your plans and come to New York for the ceremony." I should have known better. They said, in their peculiar north of England way, "Oh, sorry, but we've got a gig that night. We won't be able to make it." *Are you fucking kidding me!* "You're not going to come?" No, they insisted on playing their show. "You know, you can *cancel* a gig," I said, "and you can rebook it. It's done all the time." Nope, nothing doing, they weren't coming.

So I called Allan and asked him to come with me. I explained how it was an incredible circle that was being closed in our personal relationship. "And we're going to have to sing two or three songs. So—what about your voice?" He wanted to talk it over with his vocal coach to see if it was feasible. He got back to me a couple days later. "My coach said I really can't sing," he explained. So I suggested we get a couple of my kids' friends from Maroon 5—Adam Levine and Jesse Carmichael—to do the Hollies' parts. My son Will knew them from school when they were called Kara's Flowers, and they'd opened for CSN at two benefits we did for the Brentwood School. I'd asked Will one day what had happened to the band. "Ah," he said, "they are packing it in. They can't make it in this crazy scene. Instead they'll be dentists and doctors." This didn't sound right to me because I thought they were talented, so I lent them money to make more demos. A year later they were on top of the charts as Maroon 5. Go figure. Got to keep it all moving forward.

"You just have to be present," I told Allan on the phone. After all, he and I *were* the Hollies, which we'd started in 1962. So Allan finally agreed. I knew they'd want us to sing "Long Cool Woman," even though that was made after I'd left the band. Allan thought we should get Pat Monahan from Train to sing the lead, which we did. A good idea.

Everything was on track. Allan came to New York. I met him at the Waldorf Astoria, got a suite for his wife, Jeni, and him and their son Toby with flowers, water, the works. A couple days before the ceremony, we rehearsed with Paul Shaffer and his band. They wanted us to do "Carrie Anne," "Bus Stop," and "Long Cool Woman." Perfect. Allan watched a lot of the rehearsal from the fringe of the stage, looking and listening . . . and fidgeting. I could tell he wanted to get into it. When we got to the choruses, Adam, Jesse, and Pat were right there. Everything was fine. But I could see Allan start edging toward us. Eventually he sang a line here . . . a line there . . . Now, Allan wrote "Long Cool Woman," with Roger Greenaway and Roger Cook, and that's him on guitar on the record. It's *his* song. Pat was doing a great job on the vocal, but now Allan, unable to contain himself any longer, took over. And he ended up singing all three songs in *great* voice. He *kicked ass* that night. The two of us, in the Rock and Roll Hall of Fame. For me, it was a dream come true. Many dreams come true, in fact, because with the Hollies' induction, every member of CSNY was in the Rock Hall *twice*, the only band to ever hold that distinction.

In 2011, when Crosby and I played the Royal Albert Hall, we worked up a version of "Bus Stop" just for fun. All these years later, we'd done Byrds and Springfield songs, but hardly ever a Hollies song, so this was a unique moment for me. Before the show, I found Croz backstage and said, "Just bear with me here. Do me a favor." I knew Allan was going to be at the show that night, so I introduced him and got him up singing it with us. Man, some voices are just meant for each other.

After the show, I had another little surprise. The Buddy Holly Foundation decided to make nineteen exact replicas of Buddy's acoustic guitar—the number being significant because there were nineteen frets on his guitar neck, and each replica contained a fret from one of Buddy's old guitars. Incredibly, they gave one to me, but I felt a little weird that Allan didn't get one. After all, we'd started the Hollies together. So I called Peter Bradley, the head of the foundation. I knew all nineteen guitars were spoken for but wondered if there was anything they could do to include Allan. There weren't any frets left, but they made an extra guitar and I gave it to Allan that night at Albert Hall.

Those are the moments, baby, the ones you never forget. And all these years later, the moments keep on coming. In the summer of 2012, with David and Stephen, I played eighty-seven sold-out shows in gorgeous little theaters and festivals. Still out there, slinging the hash. We hit the road in our fully decked-out tour buses with a teenager's resolve. Every night, the minute the lights go down and the band kicks up, it feels like the first time. I always get a rush. There's nothing better than singing with my mates. All that energy coming from every direction—from the band behind us and the audience out front, Stephen and David on either side. And suddenly I'm twenty-five again, bouncing like a kid. I can't control it, it just happens. It's inside me, an incredible feeling, and I feed off it greedily. City after city, night after night.

I still enjoy touring. It's a part of my life, a great experience. I get to go to a different location every few days. I stash my shit in the hotel room, grab my camera, and I start walking. Beforehand, I hit the computer and check out what's at local museums, if there are flea markets, galleries, places of interest. I want to learn everything I can because I'm running out of time and the world is large. I would *never* believe I'd be doing this in my seventies, never in a million years. You know how fast that went? *Insanely* fast. And the rest seems to be coming at warp speed.

At the beginning of May 2013, CSN played two concerts in the beautiful Lincoln Center in New York City. Wynton Marsalis and his entire jazz orchestra had made arrangements of twelve of our most well known songs, and we performed along with them. What brilliant musicians they are; it was an incredible experience for all of us. So much respect, so much joy, so many smiles on so many faces. Especially ours.

I am a complete slave to the muse of music. I will do anything for good music—*anything*. That's my one enduring addiction. With Crosby, Stills & Nash, I have realized that no matter what we do to each other, no matter how many great or sad times we have, we know that the music is far more important than any of our individual lives. I have learned so much from David and Stephen—so much of how to live my life, and so much of how I won't live my life. They encompass all the best and worst in people, and I'm sure I'm the same way.

The jury is still out on my long, strange trip with Neil Young. Neil has a big heart with two faucets on it: the hot and the cold. You never know which you're going to get, and that's one of the traits that makes him so interesting. But often Neil steps over a line that you cannot cross with me without expecting to hear me roar. A while ago, I poured my heart out to him in an e-mail about several things that had come between him and CSN. It was one of those confessionals, and I held nothing back. That's the way it has to be between mates.

He answered me in few words, the crucial five of which were: "What a load of shit." Quite the poet.

That hurt like hell. But several days later, he apologized for his hasty reply—he'd been devastated by the loss of one of his very closest friends, Ben Keith. I understood completely. Nevertheless, the ups and downs between us are not just emotionally draining; they can also be so disheartening that I feel my soul is being drained. On the other hand, I know I could always pick up the phone and hear that familiar voice say, "Hey, Willy—want to hear four new songs?"

*Aw fuck!* Here we go again.

It all comes down to the music.

—*Graham Nash, 2013*
*Kauai, HI, and Manhattan Beach, CA*

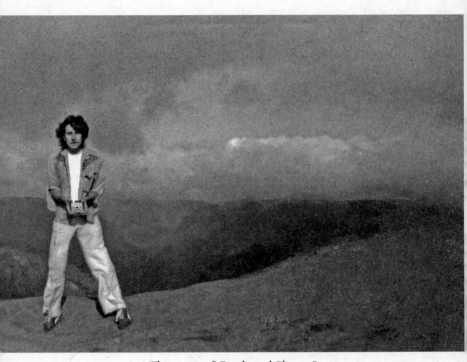

The cover of *Earth and Sky,* 1980 *(© Joel Bernstein)*

# acknowledgments

I have had much help from many, many people on this long road and I'd like to take a moment to acknowledge and thank them.

First of all, my partner in my early life, Allan Clarke. We started this musical journey together and remain friends to this day.

Don and Phil Everly, whose music changed my life.

Tony Hicks and Bobby Elliott, the lead guitarist and drummer in the Hollies, and our producer Ron Richards. I learned much from them, as I did from one of my oldest friends, Ron Stratton.

Rodney Bingenheimer, who helped this story to unfold.

Cass Elliot, my muse, great friend, and mentor, who knew what I was going to do before I did and is largely responsible for one of the best decisions I ever made in my life.

David Crosby, my partner and great friend, and his wife, Jan. I may have been brutally honest in my descriptions of them in their past, but I'm delighted to tell you that they both came out of the darkness and into the light in a big, big way.

Stephen Stills, one of the finest musicians in the world; my compadre who has a great heart and soul.

Neil Young, the strangest of my friends. He remains true to himself, his family, and his music.

Joni Mitchell, my unforgettable inspirational mentor and girlfriend.

David Geffen, whose absolute brilliance guided the career of CSNY with love, cunning, and amazing skill. His business partner, Elliot Roberts, is one of the funniest men I've ever met. He's the one man who really kept our spirits high.

Ahmet Ertegun, one of the classiest men I've ever met, who believed in us from the start.

I'd like to thank all my musician friends. I have made a great deal of music in my life and I am honored to have played and sung with all of them.

Jackson Browne and Bonnie Raitt: The world is a much better place because of you. I'm proud to be your friend.

I can say exactly the same thing for Tom Campbell and Margaret Holmes, and everyone at the Guacamole Fund.

Mike "Coach" Sexton, surely one of the great tour managers.

Jimmy Deluca who safely drives all our equipment to this day. Stanley Tajima Johnston, my producer and engineer for all these years.

Mrs. Sumiko "Baba" Masuda, my housekeeper and teacher.

Leslie Morris, my business associate and great friend for all those many years.

The lovely and soulful Rita Coolidge.

The calming, steadfast, and striking Calli Cerami.

My great friend Bill Long, Vietnam veteran, master builder, and road manager.

Rance Caldwell, John Gonzales, Mason Wilkinson, Jimmy Hatten, Kevin Madigan, Noel Casler, and Crook Stewart, crew extraordinaire.

John Bilotta, my master printer, and Christine Pan Abbe, who keeps Nash Editions running smoothly. Charles Wehrenberg, who first suggested the idea of starting Nash Editions.

Jane Tani, Jerry Rubinstein, and Gil Segel, my longtime business managers. And Todd Gelfand and Tyson Beem, my current business managers.

Barry Ollman, friend and trusted advisor.

Pete Long, for his mathematical memory.

Michael Jensen, my dear friend and publicist for the last twenty-five years.

I give special mention to R. Mac Holbert who has been my trusted companion and advisor since 1969.

My longtime friend and manager Gerry Tolman. He was taken much too soon and is missed to this day.

My present managers and friends, Donald "Buddha" and Cree Miller. They are so together, so wise. Ask anyone who has ever dealt with them.

Thanks to David Zimmer, longtime friend and chronicler, whose excellent CSN biography helped jog my memory of stories and comments from the past.

I'm writing this on the forty-fourth anniversary of meeting Joel Bernstein, archivist, teacher, historian, and great photographer, on February 1, 1969, the night Joni played Carnegie Hall. My life is all the richer because of him. He is my confidant and partner in music, photography, and life.

I owe a great deal of gratitude to Jillian Manus, my book agent. She was the first person to seriously suggest that I write this book and had the great wisdom to put me together with Bob Spitz, who faithfully took my words and made sense of them. Thanks to you, Bob, and to our editor, Peter Gethers.

Thanks also to jacket designer Michael Nagin, production editor Tricia Wygal, interior designer Lauren Dong, production manager Linnea Knollmueller, and everyone at Crown Publishers for their delightful interest and hard work.

Finally: to the Great Spirit of the Universe, for letting me live this life.

This is how I remember it.

*I have tried to write Paradise*

*Do not move*
*Let the wind speak*
*That is paradise.*

*Let the Gods forgive what I have made*
*Let those I love try to forgive what I have made.*

—Ezra Pound

Unless otherwise specified, entries in *italics* indicate albums. Those in quotes indicate song titles.